Stevar
11/22/95

FAIR GAME

What Biographers Don't Tell You

DENIS BRIAN

 **Prometheus Books**

59 John Glenn Drive
Amherst, New York 14228-2197

Published 1994 by Prometheus Books

98 97 96 95 94   5 4 3 2 1

Library of Congress Cataloging-in-Publication Data

Brian, Denis.
      Fair game : what biographers don't tell you / Denis Brian.
            p.   cm.
      Includes bibliographical references and index.
      ISBN 0-87975-899-6 (cloth : acid-free)
      1. Biography as a literary form. 2. Biographers—United States.
I. Title.
CT21.B65   1994
808′.06692—dc20   94-5401
                                                          CIP

Printed in the United States of America on acid-free paper.

Dedicated
with Love to

Martine, Danielle, and Alex

Contents

Acknowledgments 9

Preface 11

Introduction 17

1. Truman Capote's Answered Nightmares 43

2. Kitty Kelley Takes on Frank Sinatra,
Jacqueline Onassis, Liz Taylor, and Nancy Reagan 115

3. Charles Higham's Victims: Errol Flynn, Rita Hayworth,
Cary Grant, and the Duchess of Windsor 185

4. Bob Woodward, "Deep Throat,"
and CIA Chief Bill Casey 231

5. Joe McGinniss and His Enemies: From Murderer
MacDonald to Ted Kennedy and William Manchester 293

6. Murder by Other Means: Leonardo da Vinci,
Woodrow Wilson, Adolf Hitler, Winston Churchill,
and Lawrence of Arabia 325

Index 359

The journalist-biographer is "a kind of confidence man, preying on people's vanity, ignorance, or loneliness, gaining their trust and betraying them without remorse."

—Janet Malcolm, author of
The Journalist and the Murderer

Acknowledgments

Many thanks to my wife, Martine, for her unfailing encouragement and invaluable help.

To editor Steven L. Mitchell, for buying the idea and for his challenging questions.

To assistant editor Mary A. Read, for her understanding.

Preface

The greatest enemy of the truth is very often not the lie—deliberate, contrived, and dishonest—but the myth—persistent, persuasive, and unrealistic.

—John F. Kennedy[1]

For example: "The (President Calvin) Coolidge myth of oral reticence is one of the inventions of American journalism. Coolidge was a garrulous man. He started the legend about the time he turned the first spade of dirt at an excavation for a public building in Washington, looked into the hole, and—as all the reporters waited—said, 'Nice worm.' "

—Leo Rosten[2]

In her will, Jacqueline Kennedy Onassis asked for her privacy to be protected. Wasn't she too late? Hadn't biographer Kitty Kelley told *everything* about her in *Jackie Oh!,* including her trip to a hospital for a secret session of electro-shock therapy?

Years ago Truman Capote gave me a plausible explanation of why Mrs. Onassis was reluctant to expose herself to journalists and would-be biographers: her fear of what Janet

Malcolm calls "the writer's unholy power over another person."[3]

"Jackie was always a shy, sensitive, and withdrawn person," Capote said, "and through various circumstances and accidents of fate she feels she's been turned into a freak of some kind."[4]

Kitty Kelley, who believes everyone in the public arena is fair game, also went after Frank Sinatra, and refused to let his lawyers scare her off. She produced a no-holds-barred biography documenting his Mafia connections and brutal way with women; even reporting that his mother had been an abortionist. Kelley hardly mentioned the fact that he sang for a living. Her portraits of Elizabeth Taylor and Nancy Reagan were shocking enough to have sent weaker women into cardiac arrest, though both survived the Kelley treatment. But can these books stand the truth test, or does she print sensational gossip and innuendo as fact, to cater to the huge, insatiable appetite for "dirt"?

As Kelley and several other biographers covered in this book are now themselves in the public arena, I thought it fair game to go after them. So the hunters become the hunted. By knowing about their lives, their motives, and methods, readers can decide if they are to be trusted.

After all, their views, often converted to the TV or movie screen, give tens of millions of people an enduring impression of what public figures are "really" like. So the biographer's attitude and integrity—or lack of it—is critically important in judging the validity of the work. If you knew, for example, that a biography of George Bush had been written by Saddam Hussein, wouldn't you be a little wary?

I focused on five contemporary biographers: Truman Capote, Kitty Kelley, Charles Higham, Bob Woodward, and Joe McGinniss, and four from the recent past who wrote controversial biographies of Woodrow Wilson, Adolf Hitler, Winston Churchill, and Lawrence of Arabia.

In an effort to clarify one controversial aspect of the

Watergate era, I recently (1994) questioned Bob Woodward, G. Gordon Liddy, Jack Anderson (the columnist Liddy offered to kill), and former CIA chief Richard Helms.

Capote's *In Cold Blood* is regarded as a classic; Kelley is the leading exponent of "tell-all" biographies; Higham uses massive documentation to "prove" his shocking revelations about celebrities; Woodward is regarded by many as the greatest investigative reporter of all time; McGinniss was pilloried by Janet Malcolm in her book, *The Journalist and the Murderer,* in which he is treated with more contempt than the convicted murderer whose biography he wrote.

Critics raved over Truman Capote's *In Cold Blood,* virtually the biographies of two murderers, as a meticulously accurate portrait of the men and their victims. Capote, himself, swore that every word of it was true. Was it? And how about his *New Yorker* profile of Marlon Brando, his "true" account of a serial killer in *Handcarved Coffins,* and his poisonous portraits of high-society friends in his final *Answered Prayers*?

Can Charles Higham successfully defend attacks on his exposés of Errol Flynn, the Duke and Duchess of Windsor, and Cary Grant? Was Flynn, as Higham claims, a Nazi spy; Grant a bisexual gigolo; the Duchess a drug pusher; and the Duke an effete, anti-Semitic wimp as well as a traitor?

Is Bob Woodward a great reporter or a faker? Who is "Deep Throat"? Did Woodward really get a death-bed interview with CIA Chief William Casey?

The beleaguered biographer Joe McGinniss has been condemned for deception by almost all critics, including his subject, a murderer. Are they justified? And how accurate is his much maligned recent biography of Ted Kennedy, *The Last Brother*?

Did Sigmund Freud allow personal animosity to warp his judgment when he coauthored a biography of President Woodrow Wilson? And what drove him to write it when he said biography was an impossible task?

Was the outcry justified when Churchill's doctor, Lord Moran, published his own private, secretly kept diary, exposing the statesman's mental and physical frailties?

The OSS (forerunner of the CIA) commissioned a biography of Hitler by a psychiatrist during World War II hoping to know what kind of enemy they faced. The psychiatrist even speculated on Hitler's future actions based on patients with similar character traits. How insightful was it? And how does it compare with the works of more conventional Hitler biographers who had access to expert witnesses and massive documentation?

The enigmatic Lawrence of Arabia: what do we know for sure about the five-foot-five-inch T. E. Lawrence portrayed in the movie about him by the six-foot-two-inch Peter O'Toole? Thought by Churchill to be "one of the greatest beings alive in our time,"[5] was Lawrence, as several biographers said, a fraud?

During the past quarter of a century I have been seeking answers to these questions, starting when I first interviewed Truman Capote in 1970 and ending—for this book—with a brief conversation with Bob Woodward on June 8, 1994.

Meanwhile, I have produced my own biographies of Tallulah Bankhead;[6] Professor J. B. Rhine, the parapsychologist;[7] and Ernest Hemingway;[8] as well as a book on the art of interviewing,[9] and one on capital punishment.[10]

Among those I interviewed or with whom I corresponded for the Truman Capote chapter were Capote himself; prosecuting attorney for the *In Cold Blood* case, Duane West; Gore Vidal; James Michener; Arthur Schlesinger, Jr.; Capote's aunt, Marie Rudisill; Alice Lee; Harper Lee; John Kenneth Galbraith; and Capote's biographer, Gerald Clarke.

For the Kitty Kelley chapter I interviewed Kelley; her fans; her critics; people she interviewed for her books; Gerri Hirshey; Ben Bradlee; Philip Geyelin; Barbara Howar; E. J. Kahn, Jr.; Justin Kaplan; Kelley's biographer, George Carpozi, Jr.; Ronald Reagan's authorized biographer, Edmund Morris; Jack Anderson; Fred Barnes of the *New Republic*; Jack Nelson of the *Los Angeles Times*; and David Heymann.

In investigating Charles Higham, I questioned him; David Niven; William Donati; Helen Rich; C. Z. Guest and her son, Alexander, who were friends of the Windsors; Leicester Hemingway; Stewart Granger; and Melvin Belli.

For informed views of Bob Woodward I spoke with Sophia Casey, widow of CIA Director William Casey; Arnaud de Borchgrave, roving editor of the *Washington Times*; Richard Cohen of the *Washington Post*; former CIA operative Dr. George Carver; Constantine Menges; Casey's personal physician, Dr. Alfred Luessenhop; Fred Barnes of the *New Republic*; Seymour Hersh; Joseph Persico; William Colby; Bobby Ray Inman; Melvin Laird; Thomas Moorer; Bob Woodward; and others.

Joe McGinniss was the only biographer who declined to be interviewed for this book. So I contacted those who knew him: Anne Bernays, Justin Kaplan, John Katzenbach, Liz Smith, and Robert F. Keeler of *Newsday*. I also interviewed two who challenged his work, Theodore Sorensen and Arthur Schlesinger, Jr.

My thanks to all who willingly cooperated in this investigation of biographers and their work. Unless otherwise indicated, quotations from these sources are excerpts of tape-recorded conversations, the dates of which are cited on the appropriate pages.

Notes

1. From President John F. Kennedy's Yale commencement address, June 11, 1962.

2. Elizabeth Janeway, ed., *The Writer's World* (New York: McGraw-Hill, 1969), p. 24. John Mason Brown responded to Leo Rosten's comment by saying, "I remember once hearing Mr. Coolidge speak unstoppably up in Plymouth for one hour."

3. Janet Malcolm, *The Journalist and the Murderer* (New York: Knopf, 1990), p. 161. Malcolm also says of her contact with a lawyer she interviewed, "He was completely at my mercy. I held all the cards."

4. Interview with Truman Capote, September 25, 1970.

5. A. W. Lawrence, ed., *T. E. Lawrence by His Friends* (New York: McGraw-Hill, 1963), p. 161.

6. Denis Brian, *Tallulah, Darling: A Biography of Tallulah Bankhead* (New York: Macmillan, 1980).

7. Denis Brian, *The Enchanted Voyager: The Life of J. B. Rhine* (New Jersey: Prentice-Hall, 1982).

8. Denis Brian, *The True Gen: An Intimate Portrait of Hemingway by Those Who Knew Him* (New York: Grove, 1988).

9. Denis Brian, *Murderers and Other Friendly People: The Public and Private Worlds of Interviewers* (New York: McGraw-Hill, 1973).

10. Denis Brian, *Murderers Die* (New York: St. Martin's Press, 1986).

Introduction

William Manchester was appalled when told fellow biographer Joe McGinniss had invented dialogue for his biography of Ted Kennedy titled *The Last Brother,* and described such a hybrid of fact and fantasy as "a nightmare." But McGinniss is simply part of a trend, producing the print equivalent of television docudrama. Truman Capote, for example, won universal acclaim for his *In Cold Blood,* a group biography of two killers and their victims, partly on the strength of his assurances that it was meticulously accurate. It wasn't, as I discovered by questioning his sources. It was laced with lies. Prolific biographer Charles Higham resorted to using a doctored FBI document to back his sensational charge that Errol Flynn was a Nazi spy. Bob Woodward claimed to have interviewed William Casey on his deathbed. Did he invent the episode to hype his biography of the CIA chief? Casey's widow and daughter, who kept an around-the-clock vigil at the hospital, his Secret Service guard, his surgeon, and Arnaud de Borchgrave (editor at large of the *Washington Times*) all insist that the interview was impossible. Woodward steadfastly refuses to tell how he got it. Although Kitty Kelley does not promote herself as a spirit medium, according to *her* biographer, she claims to have interviewed people for her biography of Frank Sinatra on dates when they were dead.

Were their predecessors more reliable? Take James Anthony Froude, noted nineteenth-century biographer of Julius Caesar, Thomas Carlyle, and Cicero. One critic panned him for his inability "to represent the exact sense of a document which lay before him, or even to copy from it correctly." Though ridiculed by scholars for his glaring mistakes, he was widely read because he was entertaining. This incensed rival biographer Edward Freeman, a fierce advocate of accuracy and primary sources, whose own portraits of William the Conqueror and Frederick II were judged to be dull but accurate. Froude's frailties exasperated Freeman into homicidal hyperbole, calling him "the vilest beast that ever wrote a book," and expressing the wish to live long enough "to disembowel James Anthony Froude." No blood was shed but, ironically, on Freeman's death in 1892, Froude succeeded him as professor of modern history at Oxford University.

Many of today's biographer's are less engaged in such internecine warfare than in disemboweling their subjects, confident they can always find sources to supply the weapons. I got the first hint of this killer instinct in 1971 while discussing the late novelist John O'Hara with a reporter who had worked with him on a Manhattan newspaper. "What was he like?" I asked.

"He was a first-class prick," he said. "A sour, arrogant bastard. He came to the *Mirror* from the *Tribune* as a rewrite man."

"Do you know anyone who liked him?"

"Nobody liked him. He had a negative personality."

"What were his good qualities?"

"I don't know of one."

One man's creep, of course, is another's crony. But to counter the few cronies and love-blinded relatives there are scores of people willing to savage him, overwhelming by weight of numbers any positive testimony. If, in addition, the biographer fakes the record, then any approximation to a fair portrait is in double jeopardy from tainted sources and slanted writing.

The father of this school is Lytton Strachey. From the end of World War I until his death in 1932 he was arguably the world's most admired and emulated biographer, and maybe still is, gleefully following in a path mostly abandoned during Queen Victoria's long reign. Victorian biographers usually embalmed even living subjects in stilted, stuffy, and sanctimonious prose, then entombed them in multi-volume mausoleums. Grave robber Strachey revived and freed the corpses to dance, drink, and generally raise Cain, especially in his brief, flawed biographical masterpiece *Eminent Victorians*.

He obviously chose that title intending to bring the "eminent" down to earth, and began writing after dipping his pen into an effervescent mixture of gall and laughing gas. Yet he advocated in *Eminent Victorians* that a biographer should "lay bare the facts of the case as he understands them, dispassionately, impartially, and without ulterior intentions."[1]

However, Strachey blithely ignored his own advice and ridiculed others. This may have been a form of self-defense, a pre-emptory first strike, because he was such an obvious target for satirists with his fuddy-duddy beard, thick-lensed glasses, and skinny body resembling a wilting asparagus. At first glance a woman took him for a bum, recognizing him at a second for what he was: "A gentleman, but a queer one." Fellow-writer William Plomer looked beyond his appearance and languid gestures to note Strachey's formidable equipment as a biographer, including a mind that moved "as swiftly as a bat, with something of the radar-like sensitivity of a bat."

Strachey revolted some but captivated others with his offbeat looks, falsetto squeak when aroused, and chameleon-like personality. At times shy, at others coldly sarcastic, he was kind, thoughtful, and malicious, with a penchant—though not in print—for ribald jokes and corny puns. Among the repelled was writer-politician Harold Nicolson who dismissed Strachey as "a bearded and bitchy woman." It was the bitch in Strachey that caused Bertrand Russell, while reading *Eminent Victorians* in his jail cell, to burst out laughing, bringing an anxious guard at the double to warn him he was not supposed to enjoy himself in prison.* To arouse such spontaneous laughter through his sardonic firecrackers, Strachey let the fabulist in him swamp the fact finder.

Out of prison and able to check on Strachey, Russell concluded that the acclaimed biographer was "indifferent to historical truth and will always touch up the picture to make the lights and shades more glaring and the folly or wickedness of famous people more obvious. These are grave charges, but I make them in all seriousness."[2]

A frustrated novelist, Strachey did more than touch up the picture: he faked it. He ridiculed the British military hero General Gordon of Khartoum, insinuating that he was a chronic drunk and a coward. Despite credible evidence to the contrary from friends and servants, Strachey quoted only the denigrating opinions of Colonel Chaille-Long, an American formerly on Gordon's staff. Strachey failed to mention that this was a highly suspect witness who had been fired by the general as incompetent, and was known to have written several books containing distortions.[3] In 1988 John Waller, a former CIA inspector general, debunked the debunker. In *Gordon of Khartoum: The Saga of a Victorian Hero,* Waller redeemed Gordon as a courageous—though slightly cracked—charismatic leader.[4]

Strachey also mocked Henry Edward Manning, a Church of England archdeacon turned Roman Catholic cardinal, by

---

*In 1918, during World War I, Russell was sentenced to six months' imprisonment in Brixton Jail for publicly advocating acceptance of a German peace offer.

suppressing evidence in his favor. And, to jell with his own romantic speculations about Queen Elizabeth I, Strachey blithely manufactured the material.⁵

This is not to belittle the gifts that imaginative, intuitive writers like Strachey can bring to biography, enhancing its shape, tempo, and vitality. But he misused these talents to twist the record and follow his fancies. Had Strachey been challenged in his heyday, he could have cited the much-admired Greeks who were just as partial to fabrications.

Aristoxenus, a fourth-century disciple of Aristotle, scorned biographical accuracy in favor of anything likely to beguile and astonish his readers. The same, of course, might be said of those who wrote the Bible.

At least Strachey made no claims to being divinely inspired. His present-day heirs have been characterized as anything but: "literary ghouls," and "purveyors of biographical schlock," according to critic Alyn Brodsky, eagerly engaged in lurid acts "of forensic medicine or necrophilia."

Mockery as a modus operandi is encouraged by a *Kirkus Reviews* critic who praised Giles St. Aubyn's biography *Edward VII: Prince and King* as "clear, witty and refreshingly snide," and by John Updike, who begins his 1987 *New York Times* report on Colin Simpson's book, *Artful Partners,* about art experts Bernard Berenson and Joseph Duveen, with: "It is always a pleasure to see a reverenced reputation besmirched." Critic Charles Krauthammer (also a non-practicing psychiatrist) assured those who might hesitate to hunt for the dark and disreputable that "it's a venerable tradition for adolescents to stand on the shoulders of giants and pee down their trousers." And that "anyone who achieves celebrityhood, should expect the slings and arrows of outraged unfortunates."⁵

Does that include pulling down the subject's pants and giving us a urologist's report? Apparently so. A young woman sitting next to the new husband of Erica Jong at dinner some years ago suddenly realized to her embarrassment that, having read a Jong *roman à clef,* she knew the exact size of the man's penis.

To produce her often moving and affectionate biography of her husband, English drama critic Kenneth Tynan's widow admits she "excavated and plundered" his life, one that's recalled by the British as reaching its apogee when he was the first to say "fuck" on television. In an urge to suppress nothing, Kathleen Tynan seems also to have taken a widow's revenge by providing intimate details of his infected urinogenital system.

President Nixon, for one, deplored and dreaded such scrutiny, saying he could tolerate the microscope, "but, oh boy, when they use a proctoscope, that's going too far!" His worst and understandable fears were realized when a writer reported the contents of Nixon's White House medicine cabinet, including Ex-Lax and Preparation H, which might account for his language on the White House tapes.

Kill the Widows!

With notable exceptions, such as Tynan's, biographies produced or okayed by widows suffer from what A. E. Hotchner deplores as "widowfication." This is a partial view in which the surviving spouse becomes the star and the subject is seen mainly through her eyes. Hotchner may be somewhat jaundiced, having been taken to court by Ernest Hemingway's widow, who claimed to have suffered "traumatic shock" when she read the galleys in which Hotchner had vividly, if not always accurately, described Hemingway's mental breakdown and suicide.

I asked Hotchner,* "Did you think Mary Hemingway's objection to your publishing the book *Papa Hemingway*—that

---

*Interview with A. E. Hotchner in 1972.

there were things about a man that should be kept from the public—was justified?"

"Who would determine just what things should and should not be kept from the public?" Hotchner replied. "This omnipotent censor of good taste, who would it be? The author's wife? Well, Mary had the opportunity to set an example for all of us. Ernest had left a collection of chapters about his life in Paris in the twenties. One of those chapters recounted how F. Scott Fitzgerald had one day come to Ernest and confided to him his anxiety over the size of his penis. The chapter then spelled out how Ernest assured Scott, after inspecting his penis, that it was 'normal' by taking him to a museum and showing him the penis on a statue. I was helping Mary with this manuscript at the time, so I can tell you firsthand that the publisher suggested that in the interest of good taste this particular chapter should be eliminated. It was pointed out that this material would be particularly offensive to Fitzgerald's daughter, Scotty, and that it was not integral to the book. Mary was not to be deterred. It was her decision and her decision alone to print this chapter."

"You're saying that she had a different standard of what should and should not be published in regard to Hemingway."

"I'm saying it's the widow syndrome, a process I call widowfication. When Ernest was alive, Mary felt very differently. She once wrote an article, 'My Husband, Ernest Hemingway,' for a publication called *Today's Woman,* in which she confided such delicate intimacies as her fondness for kissing the soft places on the back of his ear. But now Mary wants to control everything that's written about Ernest. I think her basic objection to *Papa Hemingway* is that I wouldn't let her see my manuscript, and I told about the last tragic years before the authorized biography [by Carlos Baker] was published. Mary also maintained in her lawsuit that Ernest had no idea I'd ever write about him— an act which she brands as a stab in the back. Mary doesn't know much about writers' innards . . . that a writer is an undisciplined animal who will write about anything that touches his life."

Losing the lawsuit didn't stop her. She persisted in complaining that Hotchner had invaded her privacy and appropriated her literary property, saying to me* that his book "cheated all the way, and was full of exaggerations for the sake of sensationalism and royalties. . . . I don't know if you understand, but at no time ever did Hotchner give the slightest hint to Ernest or to me that he was making notes with the idea of producing a book about Ernest."

"No, I didn't know that," I said. "But I suppose, as he was a practicing writer, it might have been expected."

"No, he always professed himself to like Ernest, you know, just for the fun of it, and all that. He wrote this book and made a great deal of money on it, as a totally traitorous thing to Ernest. If Ernest had known that he intended writing a book he [Ernest] would never have seen him again, *ever*. This was a knife-in-the-back job. I'm sure Ernest would kill him, would have disposed of him."

James Thurber's widow was also disturbed when she read about him in Brendan Gill's *Here at the New Yorker* in which, according to Arthur Cooper, Thurber came across as "Almost mean enough to drop napalm on the Westminster dog show." Even admirers conceded that Thurber had a mean streak. But, wanting to perpetuate a more favorable image of him, Mrs. Thurber chose Burton Bernstein (Leonard's older brother) for the task of restoration, promising him complete cooperation and no interference. "She hated the result," said Bernstein. "I was after the truth. And when Helen saw it she really blew her stack. She felt the tone was too negative. We haven't spoken since."[7]

Before Bernstein wrote the Thurber biography, and when the cartoonist was alive, Justin Kaplan had been approached

---

*Interview with Mary Hemingway, November 18, 1970.

to do it. "I spent a couple of evenings with Helen and Thurber," Kaplan recalled.* "And decided that was the last thing in the world I wanted to do, because she was obviously rather an obstructive person."

Kaplan had his own problem with widow Ella Winters after he'd written a biography of her late husband, the great muckraking journalist Lincoln Steffens. "She was cooperative up to a point," Kaplan told me. "But she got pissed off at me when she read the American edition of my Steffens biography, and she made some noises about getting an injunction against publishing it in England, and she wrote threatening letters to my English publisher. Her main gripe had to do with a few rather indiscreet witticisms I made at her expense. I told Simon and Schuster and Jonathan Cape to pay no attention. I think she was pissed off because I had described her ideological process as more resembling a lurch then a walk [which is also the way he described how she moved]; and she wrote someone a letter saying what really pissed her off is that I had described her as spinsterly looking as a young girl."[8]

Edward Gibbon, author of *The History of the Decline and Fall of the Roman Empire,* had nothing to fear from his long-dead subjects or their widows, so it is no surprise that he thought *nothing* should be suppressed in recording the lives of others. Samuel Johnson agreed, then changed his mind to recommend the near impossible: that a writer should avoid hurting the feelings of "a widow, a daughter, a brother, a friend"—advice that Boswell obviously ignored. Sinclair Lewis's biographer, Mark Schorer, took Gibbon's tell-all view with one cautious proviso: he approved of writing anything "that is true and relevant to one's theme—anything that is, that will not bring us into court."[9]

Lady Bird Johnson seemed to go along with this attitude in cooperating with Robert A. Caro for his biography of the

---

*Interview with Justin Kaplan, October 13, 1974.

late Lyndon Johnson. In the first of a projected three volumes, Caro convincingly demonstrated that the man he had expected to love was a greedy opportunist and a liar who cheated on his wife and betrayed his friends. The widow's response to these discoveries was to pull out and clam up, except to say she had not read the 1,246-page first volume, but that it would make a good doorstop.

Caro might have anticipated her behavior had he read biographer Edmund Gosse (1849–1928), a Cambridge University lecturer in English literature and later the House of Lords librarian. He derided widows as "the worst of all the diseases of biography. . . . She paints her husband quite smooth and plump with a highlight on his forehead and a sanctimonious droop of his eyelid."[10]

What was Caro to do? He could hardly disavow his first volume and promise to go easy in volumes two and three. Biographer William Allen White had suggested drastic action when foiled in his biographical efforts by the widows of both Woodrow Wilson and Calvin Coolidge. They urged all their friends not to talk to him. White advised fellow writers in the same spot to kill the widows![11]

Biography in Disguise

There is a less deadly way of dealing with widows bent on sabotage: subterfuge. It is specially popular in Britain where state secrets are still too carefully protected and where, in the "best circles," it's bad form to be mentioned in print except briefly when you are born, marry, or die. So, many British authors, constrained as well by punishing libel laws, resort to biography in disguise.

Maybe it's a hangover from the military tradition and the empire's glory days to regard strangers as the enemy entitled only to name, rank, number, and a snooty stare—nothing more. Or, perhaps the British stiff upper lip is Nature's way of scrambling talk and precluding sharing sensitive information without an interpreter. In such a secretive—Anglophobes might say constipated—atmosphere, writers who otherwise attempt probing biographies turn out *romans à clef* with the hollow pretense that "all characters in this book are entirely fictitious."

Attempts to deny the obvious, that his book is based on real characters, can turn an author into his own worst critic, as it did Lawrence Durrell. He wrote of his *Justine*: "The characters in this novel are all inventions together with the personality of the narrator, and bear no resemblance to living persons."

Hugh Walpole appears large as life and just as sycophantic in Somerset Maugham's novel *Cakes and Ale*. Maugham denied that Walpole was his model for the pathetic Alroy Kear, but Walpole knew better. To sue for libel would only have alerted a wider public to the character's model, so he simply complained to Maugham and a few close friends. Walpole once admitted to P. G. Wodehouse that after a bad review he cried for hours. He must have cried for days over Maugham's callous though convincing portrait of him, an echo of his humiliating youth when jeering schoolmates had tormented him, stripping him and pricking him with pins.

Not long after *Cakes and Ale,* a novel titled *Gin and Bitters* appeared, in which Maugham was unmistakably described as Leverson Hurle, "a small dark man, proud of his smallness, rather sallow; showing, even then, yellow pouches under his dark eyes: eyes as sad and disillusioned as those of a sick monkey." Most who read *Gin and Bitters,* especially Maugham, must have suspected that Walpole had taken bitter revenge, using fiction as his weapon and "A. Riposte" as his pen name.

The truth was as strange as some fiction. The author of the vicious portrait of Maugham was a woman novelist, and her real name Elinor Mordaunt. (It is interesting that "mordant"—close enough—means "biting," "cutting," "caustic," or "sarcastic.") Incredibly, Walpole sympathized with Maugham and urged him to sue for libel, because "the book is *foul* and you ought to stop it." Maugham chose not to sue, justifiably afraid it would only boost sales. He waited until 1950, nine years after Walpole died and thirty years after publishing *Cakes and Ale,* before publicly admitting "the ridiculous creature" Walpole had been the model for Alroy Kear.

Like Walpole, Lady Ottoline Morrell had no trouble penetrating her fiction-character disguise, and it revolted her. Its author, D. H. Lawrence, even had the nerve to send her the manuscript before publication, in which she appears as Hermione Roddice. She thought her friend's view of her so loathsome that "one cannot get clean after it." Graham Greene and Aldous Huxley, among a gaggle of others, couldn't resist portraying the same woman in their fiction, but none hit harder or hurt more than Lawrence. "For many months," she said, "the ghastly portrait of myself written by someone I trusted and liked haunted my thoughts and horrified me."

It may have consoled her to see D. H. Lawrence himself derided in Richard Aldington's novel *Death of a Hero.* (That would have been a more appropriate title for Aldington's warped biography of T. E. Lawrence [of Arabia].) Aldington showed D. H. Lawrence the manuscript in which he was clearly described as "a sandy-haired, narrow-chested little man with spiteful blue eyes and a malevolent class hatred." Furious, Lawrence warned: "If you publish this you'll lose what reputation you have—you're plainly on the way to an insane asylum." Not so. It enhanced Aldington's reputation, and he protected himself from a lawsuit by calling the book fiction and renaming the Lawrence character "Comrade Bobbe."

Aimee Semple McPherson, an amorous California evangelist, ran off with a lover and staged a fake kidnapping to cover her tracks. Barely disguised by a grotesque pseudonym, "Mrs. Melrose Ape," and Evelyn Waugh's satirical touches, she reappears in his novel *Vile Bodies* as the woman evangelist whose favorite hymn is "There Ain't No Flies on the Lamb of God."

In *Gone with the Wind,* Margaret Mitchell, news reporter turned novelist, based the feisty fictional heroine Scarlett O'Hara on herself, and Rhett Butler on her ex-husband, Berrian Upshaw. She also modeled Belle Watling on a famous still-living madam, and Archie on a real murderer. Mitchell could not immediately relish the almost unprecedented success of her book because she was in hiding from the real-life models she feared would recognize themselves and seek revenge or sue for libel.[12] Though no one sued her successfully, the dread that someone might made her sick with worry for months. She was most wary of her ex-husband, a former Georgia University football player with a murky past. He had been expelled from Annapolis Military Academy, and after working as a merchant seaman became a bootlegger. Mitchell's novel was in part a blueprint and a celebration of their lives together, though she shifted time from the 1930s to Civil War days. As Rhett walked out on Scarlett with his "Frankly, my dear, I don't give a damn," so Upshaw abandoned Mitchell. Although she remarried, Upshaw continued to intrigue her. But she was also scared of him and they never reconciled. Upshaw was convinced Rhett was himself in superficial disguise and phoned her to say, "After reading your book, I figure you still love me." Their lives ended as dramatically as anything in fiction. He fell to his death from a fifth-floor flophouse window. A few months later, in 1949, Mitchell was fatally hit by a car, fulfilling her own premonition that she would die in a traffic accident.

Simone de Beauvoir also wrote of a former lover under the guise of fiction, publicizing her affair with Nelson Algren in her novel *The Mandarins,* where he appears as Lewis Brogan. Because he seethed in silence, she was encouraged to use his real name when printing highlights from his love letters to her in a subsequent work of nonfiction. Outraged, Algren complained bitterly to *London Times* reporter W. J. Weatherby: "I've been in whorehouses all over the world and the women there always close the door, whether it's in Korea or India. But this woman flung the door open and called in the public and the press."[13]

Biography has been called murder by other means. In Nelson Algren's case it was closer to manslaughter. Three days after his angry outburst to Weatherby, Algren had a fatal heart attack. Kiss-and-tell biographers are sometimes called whores. Algren gives them an even lower rating. And he's sure to find agreement from fellow victims.

Resistance by Sigmund Freud and Carroll O'Connor

In resisting and squashing Arnold Zweig's plan to put him on paper, Sigmund Freud responded:

> Anyone who writes a biography is committed to lies, concealment, flattery, and even to hiding his own lack of understanding, for biographical truth does not exist and if it did we could not use it.[14]

Freud, of course, had to protect the Victorian sensibilities and confidences of patients. But his valid objections also partly explain why fame and money aside, some biographers work with such zest and perseverance—to expose lies and reveal what is hidden.

The dead have no recourse, but the living often treat their potential biographers as the enemy and immediately take evasive action. When suspecting biographers were on his tail, reclusive and secretive billionaire Howard Hughes even appealed to the U.S. Supreme Court in 1966 to make it a federal crime for anyone to pen a Hughes biography without his say-so. Not inclined to repeal the First Amendment, the justices turned him down. His apparent paranoia was justified, however. Two writers were plotting an even more provocative assault on his privacy than mere biography: an autobiographical smash-and-grab. When Clifford Irving and pal Richard Suskind concocted such a work, going to hilarious lengths to delude the publisher into believing it was genuine, it was eagerly accepted. The two conmen gambled that Hughes, who had shut himself away from the world, would be loath to brave the limelight, and so would not make a move to discredit them. They lost the bet, in 1972, and went to prison.[15] They could easily have published their book and have avoided punishment by simply calling it what it was, an unauthorized biography.

To escape from a biographer's clutches, actor Carroll O'Connor took more effective action than Hughes; he stifled his biography at birth. Incensed when he heard author Arthur Marx, Groucho's son, was on his track, O'Connor went public, protesting in full-page ads in Hollywood trade papers. His *cri de coeur* reads:

From Carroll O'Connor to His Friends and Colleagues of the Bizness [sic] 1951–1977 in Dublin, London, Paris, Rome, New York and mostly Hollywood:
Dollings All,
A furtive fellow may come among you hunting bits of information for a biography of me. I do not approve. I have seen his other unauthorized biographies and they are wretched; they have provoked some unwilling subjects, his father included, to furious legal reprisals. He does not invite collaboration—like an "as told to" joint authorship—because that would require sharing the proceeds from the book, and the mind of the poacher runneth not to the even split. He knows I would not work with him anyway. If he approaches you, show him your backs, my loves! Show him not, I beg you, the way

to my property! The still-forming vines of my life are hardly
burgeoning, God knows. What fruit may come, let mine own
hand offer when I judge it worthy, but expose not my pale
buds to the ignorant teeth of the fox. Or to put it more
succinctly, I am writing my own book, so tell the bum nothing.

Your imperiled pal, Carroll.[16]

O'Connor dropped his Old Testament prose parody when
questioned by Aljean Harmetz for the *New York Times,* to
say he felt endangered by

a shabby hack writer who said he was going to write my
biography and hoped for my cooperation "if possible." How
dare these people come in and take your life without permission? They couldn't come in and take your furniture.

He is only half right. The law protects his furniture, but not
his life story. Fame has made his biography public property.

Marx, biographer of several Hollywood celebrities including Samuel Goldwyn and his own father (Groucho), said to
Harmetz that the actor's attempt to stop the book "makes
O'Connor look like an ass. A fellow who claims to be liberal
should not be trying censorship."[17]

O'Connor's opposition worked: many years later, neither
his autobiography nor Marx's version of his life has appeared.

Hidden Treasure

The prospect of biography adds to death a new terror.

—Oscar Wilde

When should a biographer with scruples reveal the disreputable
or sordid in a subject's life? The enemy can expect no quarter.

Western biographers do not hesitate to expose Hitler and Stalin to remorseless scrutiny. But would they or should they treat Winston Churchill or John F. Kennedy without fear or favor?

"I think it's a matter of time," Arthur Schlesinger, Jr., told me.* "So long as what happens in the private life of a public man does not affect his attitude on public issues, or some decision, there's no urgent need that that be disclosed. It's a matter of time. There are things about, say, the relationship between Abraham Lincoln and his wife which there was absolutely no point in writing about or disclosing in the 1860s. But Carl Sandburg could write about these things with no problem a century later. There is no point in gratuitously wounding people, so long as it doesn't bear on questions of public policy. But, in time, I think, historians should write about everything."[18]

That's not always possible. Over three-hundred-and-fifty years after the death of Galileo, the Vatican still keeps under wraps the records of the Roman Inquisition that condemned him; obviously more concerned with the Church's reputation than with Galileo's. As for Abraham Lincoln, his records were hidden from the public for eighty-two years after his 1865 assassination. His son Robert made exceptions for Lincoln's secretaries, John Hay and John Nicolay, who were coauthoring a reverential biography. Even they were given only partial access to the Lincoln papers, and Robert heavily blue-penciled their work before publication. All other would-be Lincoln biographers were refused even a glimpse of the archives.

This veto incited U.S. Senator Albert Beveridge, one of the frustrated would-be biographers, to a frenzy in which he threatened to obtain the papers by using "dynamite, or chloroform, soothing syrup, quinine, cocaine, or TNT."[19] But neither his threats nor the pleas of others weakened Robert Lincoln's resolve. Some believe Robert had been disturbed by a biography

---

*Interview with Arthur Schlesinger, Jr., March 26, 1994.

in which his father was described as having been born out of wedlock. The author of this slur—which it was in those days— was Lincoln's former law partner, William Herndon, who had based the assertion on flimsy evidence.[20] It's just as likely, though, that Robert despised the whole enterprise, and shared a contemporary congressman's view that a biographer of the recently dead was "a cur that enters a graveyard and wantonly digs up the bones." One contemporary writer, Elizabeth Hardwick, epitomizes and disdainfully dismisses the breed as "the quick in pursuit of the dead. It's become a scrofulous enterprise."[21]

Lincoln had been a scrupulous truth teller, describing himself, for example, as "nearly" six-feet-four-inches, after taking off his socks before measuring to make absolutely sure. By releasing the papers Robert would have followed in his father's footsteps and ensured that the truth prevailed: by hiding them he allowed scandalous rumors to flourish.

Senator Beveridge continued agitating for the Lincoln material. To deprive him of it permanently, Robert is suspected of having asked actuaries to work out Beveridge's life expectancy, before leaving the Lincoln papers to the Library of Congress with instructions to keep them sealed until twenty-two years after his own death and, presumably, long after Beveridge's. Robert got what he wanted. When in 1947 the papers of "the greatest character since Christ"—in the eyes of Lincoln's secretary, John Hay—were available to writers and scholars, Beveridge had been twenty years in his grave.

It may seem that after hundreds of JFK biographies, we know everything there is to know about him.[22] But we must wait until 2014 to read sensitive Warren Commission testimony about his assassination. Lyndon Johnson embargoed two hundred other relevant documents for a further quarter-century. A report of the Senate select committee investigation of intelligence activities will remain secret until 2025, and testimony before the House Select Committee on Assassinations will not be public until 2029. So there's a good chance that when it's all released, everyone concerned will be dead and so unable to answer tricky follow-up questions. Which, of course, may be the whole idea.

FBI reports on Martin Luther King are also locked away for years to come, consequently all biographies of both King and Kennedy to date, and those being written during the next half-century, will lack vital information.

Freedom of Information

Despite these obstacles, this is the biographers' golden age in the United States. They can use tape recorders as impartial witnesses with flawless memories; television cameras to catch the gestures and body language of their subjects; computers to identify myriad sources in a flash; the Freedom of Information Act to provide access to declassified top secret documents from the White House, the FBI, the CIA, the National Security Council, the National Security Agency, the Justice Department, the State Department, and the Pentagon. Through these channels they can even get at British MI5 and MI6 material that's still forbidden to the British in their own country.

With all this information available, and in the present atmosphere in which the urge to confess or condemn seems contagious—just look at television talk shows—and when almost nothing is taboo, the temptation is to indulge in overkill. Consequently, the evil that men (and women) are rumored to have done lives after them, and the good is eliminated as dull or buried in the footnotes. Knowing the public's insatiable appetite for the shocking and salacious, publishers lure them with such lines as:

"Full of scandalous gossip, gripping and hard to put down" (a book about Richard Burton by his brother).

"A shocker. . . . Absolutely hypnotic" (a biography of the Duchess of Windsor by Charles Higham).

"Ripe with juicy gossip and luscious anecdotes" (*Lilly: Reminiscences of Lillian Hellman* by Peter Feibelman).

"A major jaw-dropper. Hypnotically lurid, gossip-rich portrait of the late actor" (a memoir of Peter Lawford by his widow and Ted Schwartz).

Through the eyes of biographer Arianna Stassinoulos Huffington, as reviewer Ryan P. Murphy sees it, Picasso shrinks to just another wife-beating, repressed homosexual mediocrity. Former Columbia University English professor Albert Goldman gives us an Elvis Presley who masturbated in front of his monkeys, and a drug-doped John Lennon whose power-mad, no-talent wife, Yoko Ono, amused herself by placing cat droppings under his bare feet as he stumbled around in a daze.[23]

Maybe these biographers are graduates of what Arthur Schlesinger, Jr., calls the "heads-I-win-tails-you-lose school of psychohistory," whose members are out "to get" their subjects. Schlesinger cites the Kennedy clan as victims of this school: "If a Kennedy went up in a balloon, he would be an exhibitionist; if he refused to go up, he would be a coward."[24]

Are they, in the spirit of our times, practicing character assassination, euphemistically touted as "setting the record straight"? Or are they even-handed seekers of the truth? I see them as, on one extreme, the Holy Crossers, and on the other, the Double-Crossers. Whether or not they admit it, the Holy Crossers follow the tenets of Saint Ignatius, founder of the Jesuits, who believed that no matter how worthy the cause, the end does not justify the means.

Holy Crossers are usually authorized biographers. Their subject is offered to them on a plate, personal diaries and letters supplied, friends and relatives softened up and made available for interviews. In this benign atmosphere biographers are constantly fed or exposed to the party line and discouraged from contacting the opposition.[25] In a sense, they are hired hands and in constant danger of being muzzled or kicked out if they make unwelcome discoveries. Yet this is not always the case: Michael Holroyd's authorized biography of Lytton Strachey is one magnificent exception.

As their name suggests, the Double-Crossers do almost anything to get information: lie; steal; betray confidences; make false promises; quote "off the record" remarks; expose their confidential sources; use anonymous and questionable witnesses, some of whom will say anything for spite or money, ferret through garbage; masquerade as doctors, policemen, friends, relatives; threaten, intimidate, blackmail, or trick people into spilling the beans. It takes a certain daring. They risk shotgun pellets, spit, guard dogs, and libel suits, as well as book reviewers searching the thesaurus for variants of "sleazebag."

The most admirable, even heroic, among these Double-Crossers are those operating in enemy territory where truth is held hostage. Ian Gibson, for one, gathering material for a biography of the democratic Spanish poet Federico García Lorca, "practiced the art of sleuthing, lying and bribing people," masquerading "as the grandson of an Irish fascist general . . . researching the Irish contribution to the Spanish Civil War."[26]

If the biographer knows his quarry personally, another Oscar Wilde dictum may apply: "Every great man nowadays has his disciples, and it is always Judas who writes the biography." Instead of Judas, I propose Peter as the ideal biographer's patron. Standing at the gates of heaven, eyes wide open, research notes in hand, head crammed with questions, he seeks to know all: the good, the bad, and the debatable.

In Justin Kaplan's more down-to-earth terms,

> There's an entire range of biographers: some are interested
> in dirt and sensation, and others on the other end may be
> terribly timid and overly respectful. But in between there's
> a lot of room for an honest writer who comes at the subject
> with goodwill and sincere curiosity.[27]

This last approach was Schlesinger's intention in his *Robert
Kennedy and His Times*:

> I have tried to tell that story as accurately as I can, strengthened
> by the conviction that the last thing Robert Kennedy would
> have wished was hagiography. He was not a hard man, but
> he was a tough man. He valued bluntness, precision, and
> truth. I have not hesitated to portray him in his frailty as
> well as in his valor.[28]

Even so, a biography by a friend or admirer is bound to
be suspect. Theodore Sorensen, John F. Kennedy's friend and
special counsel, admitted that his biography of the president
is seen through the eyes of "an impassioned participant" who
omitted certain facts for reasons of security or propriety.[29] It
will be a valuable source for future biographers unrestrained
by the demands of security or propriety.

Retrospective Raspberries

Restraint is hardly practiced by many of Sorensen's fellow
writers, nor is it appreciated by a significant number of readers
who seem to regard full disclosure as a biographical imperative.
This explains the current reigning school.[30] Its members purport
to be on a moral quest to strip away the phony public-relations

camouflage that protects and promotes the famous, and to expose them to the harsh light of truth. They fail to mention that light, biographers, and their sources can play tricks. As writer John Garraty points out, even

> the average person is so complicated and contradictory that by selection of "facts" a biographer can prove almost anything about anyone, and can interpret the same events in a negative or positive light.[31]

Millions read celebrity exposés that have the awesome power to drastically redefine, often for the worst, the public's view of those who strut or once strutted the world's stage. Such books damage or advance the reputations and careers of the living, while the lives of the dead are subjected to radical and invariably negative reassessments, what might be called "retrospective raspberries."

Most biographies are lives filtered through one pair of eyes— the author's. In a sense, all writers are liars, especially novelists and poets who mix fact and fancy. Biographers, too, whether intentionally or not, fall short of the truth. No subject can fully explain his or her subconsciously motivated behavior. And there is no such animal as a perfect witness. Even the most scrupulous writer, when working with a living subject or those close to the recently dead, must suppress some facts to get at others, and is sometimes sworn to secrecy, handling material supplied anonymously or with only one informant to confirm it. Rarely can a biographer reveal all. If the writer is not scared of libel, then the publisher is. And at times the biographer is misled by the fantasies or faulty memories of others.

Perhaps, like judges, which they are, too, biographers should be sworn in. I suggest this oath: I promise to record the facts; seek pro and con opinions with equal fervor; not to twist or exclude material to fit my preconceptions or prejudices; to brave widows' and widowers' threats; to resist the looming lawyers; to endure and, if possible, relish the battle, especially if my subject is alive and kicking.

Notes

1. Lytton Strachey, *Eminent Victorians* (New York: Harcourt, Brace, 1918), p. ix.

2. *The Autobiography of Bertrand Russell* (Boston: Atlantic-Little Brown, 1967), p. 99.

3. Anthony Nutting, *Gordon of Khartoum, Martyr and Misfit* (New York: Clarkson Potter, 1966).

4. John Waller, *Gordon of Khartoum: The Saga of a Victorian Hero* (New York: Atheneum, 1988).

5. John A. Garraty, *The Nature of Biography* (New York: Knopf, 1957), p. 124.

6. Charles Krauthammer, *New Republic* (April 22, 1985): 43.

7. Arthur Cooper, "His Life and Hard Times," *Newsweek* (March 24, 1975): 83.

8. Interview with Justin Kaplan, October 13, 1974.

9. Mark Schorer, *Sinclair Lewis: An American Life* (New York: McGraw-Hill, 1961).

10. Garraty, *The Nature of Biography,* p. 156.

11. Ibid., p. 171.

12. Her only book won Margaret Mitchell the 1937 Pulitzer Prize for fiction and has sold over eleven million copies worldwide.

13. Deidre Bair, *Simone de Beauvoir* (New York: Simon & Schuster, 1990), p. 502.

14. Ernest Freud, ed., *The Letters of Sigmund Freud and Arnold Zweig* (New York: Harcourt, Brace & World, 1970), p. 127.

15. Clifford Irving with Richard Suskind, *What Really Happened* (New York: Grove Press, 1972).

16. Aljean Harmetz, "Carroll O'Connor Fights with a Biographer," *New York Times,* March 10, 1977, p. 47.

17. Ibid.

18. Interview with Arthur Schlesinger, Jr., March 26, 1994.

19. John S. Goff, *Robert Todd Lincoln: A Man in His Own Right* (University of Oklahoma Press, 1969). Lincoln's biographer, William Herndon, wrote to a correspondent: " 'Bob' [Lincoln] religiously hates me for telling naked truths about his noble father." Also, widowfication must be added to the equation. Lincoln's widow, Mary, and Herndon hated each other.

20. Ibid.

21. Interview with Elizabeth Hardwick, June 6, 1994.

22. In the fall of 1993, the Library of Congress computer listed 686 JFK books and related material.

23. Ryan P. Murphy, *Miami Herald,* December 28, 1988, p. 4D.

24. Interview with Arthur Schlesinger, Jr., March 26, 1994.

25. Stephen B. Oates, ed., *Biography as High Adventure* (University of Massachusetts Press, 1986), p. 101, in which he quotes Barbara W. Tuchman, saying of her biography of General George Stilwell, "Friendly relations, I have to acknowledge, inevitably exerted a certain unspoken restraint on writing anything nasty about the deceased general, had I been inclined." *Stilwell and the American Experience in China* (New York: Macmillan, 1970).

26. Joseph A. Cincotti, "The Grandson of an Irish Fascist?" *New York Times Book Review,* October 8, 1989, p. 41.

27. Interview with Justin Kaplan, December 30, 1988.

28. Arthur Schlesinger, Jr., *Robert Kennedy and His Times* (Boston: Houghton Mifflin, 1978).

29. Theodore Sorensen, *Kennedy* (New York: Bantam, 1966), p. 7.

30. Oates, *Biography as a High Adventure,* p. 103: "Do we really have to know of some famous person that he wet his pants at age six and practiced oral sex at sixty? No doubt many would unhesitatingly answer yes to that question"—Barbara Tuchman.

31. Garraty, *The Nature of Biography,* p. 12.

1

Truman Capote's Answered Nightmares

Bamboozling Brando

Film director Joshua Logan sounded unusually agitated when he warned Marlon Brando: "He's after you! Don't let him get you alone!" The threat to the burly superstar seemed wildly overstated: Truman Capote had merely focused on Brando as a possible subject for a *New Yorker* profile. True, some saw Lillian Ross's recent *New Yorker* profiles of Ernest Hemingway and of John Huston on location as high-toned hatchet jobs; but if they were, the scalping was exceptional and largely unintentional. William Shawn, the man at the helm of the magazine, was scrupulously fulfilling the pledge of founding editor Harold Ross to publish nothing that would make a twelve-year-old girl blush.

Why then should Brando fear this undersized *New Yorker* writer—five-feet-three at a stretch—who spoke in a baby voice as if a bee sting had swollen his tongue? He had already revealed his sensitivities in published tales of his childhood fears and fancies. And his recent slightly satirical account of his trip with an American opera company in Soviet Union brought fan mail from Jacqueline Kennedy and Britain's Queen Mother. Surely this little fellow was harmless.

Reading the same material, Logan glimpsed savagery behind the satire and saw Capote as a mischief-making misanthrope who wrote about people as if they were bugs. Alarm bells went off when Logan heard that the party-going Capote had been boasting of his plan to squash Brando's enigmatic superstar image by ridicule. About to direct a film of James Michener's novel *Sayonara* on location in Japan with Brando as its star, Logan knew that the actor was vulnerable to Capote's ingratiating approach, and that once Brando's suspicions were overcome and his interest aroused he would be revealed for what he was: a compulsive, uncensored, and sometimes zany talker with whimsical weaknesses and eccentricities. So Logan banned Capote from the film set and warned Brando to be on guard: "I had a sickening feeling that what little Truman wanted, little Truman would get. . . . Truman is dogged, ruthless, devious, and driven when he smells something sensational he can write about. And Marlon was his perfect pigeon."[1]

With that on his mind, when Logan saw Capote checking in at a Japanese hotel occupied by the *Sayonara* film crew he went berserk. Grabbing Capote as if to perform the Heimlich maneuver, Logan carried him from the reception desk to the entrance, where he dumped him like a load of garbage. Capote couldn't help but get the hint, but didn't take it. Unfortunately for Logan, he had a stolid Maginot-Line mentality while Capote was an exponent of biographical blitzkrieg: if you can't make a direct attack, try a pincer movement. He landed his prize catch off the forbidden film set, recording in his diary:

Had dinner with M. Brando in his Japanese-style room at Hotel Mikado. What an egocentric; and how he loves to talk— and *such* a vocabulary; he sounds like an "educated negro" very anxious to display all the long words he's learned. He talked non-stop from 7:15 until 2:30 in the morning, was interested in the story of his alcoholic mother who "began to break apart in front of my eyes like a piece of porcelain," until "one day I could step right over her lying on the floor, and not feel a thing, not give a damn." How well I understand that.[2]

Despite Logan's precautions, Capote netted and gutted Brando. How was he able to accomplish this?

"It is rather a tricky thing to do," Capote admitted to me.* "But, nevertheless, it always works. If you're having a difficult time with a subject then you, in effect, change roles. You begin by making little confidences of your own that are rather similar to things you think you will draw out of them. And suddenly they'll be saying: 'Ah, yes, my mother ran away with five repairmen, too.' See what I mean? [Capote himself had an affair with an air-conditioning repairman.] Or, 'Ah, yes, my father robbed a bank and was sent to prison for ten years, too [not great exaggerations of the activities of Capote's father and stepfather]. Isn't it extraordinary we should have the same things happen in our lives?' And then you find you're off to the races."[3]

Brando fell for it, returning confidence for confidence, telling Capote traumatic tales of his own crippled, emotionally deprived childhood, as well as saying whatever came into his head. The mix of drinks and Capote's casual manner lulled Brando into a false sense of security, especially as Capote was neither taking notes nor tape-recording their free-and-easy exchange. According to Capote, he waited until he reached his own hotel room before typing a detailed account of their seven-hour conversation, liberally sprinkled with verbatim Brandoisms. Quite a feat!

Logan thought the subsequent *New Yorker* profile, "The Duke in His Domain," to be "as bitchy as I had feared: it

---

*Interview with Truman Capote, September 18, 1970.

made us all idiots." Especially Brando who, in a frantic phone call to Logan, yelled: "That little bastard told me he wouldn't say any of the things I asked him not to, and he printed them all. I'll kill him."[4] Their outcries bounced off Capote, now basking in the approval of his normally reticent editor, William Shawn, who called the Brando profile a masterpiece. Recalling the occasion,* Capote chuckled and said: "It was a hatchet-job," quickly adding, "When I said it was a hatchet-job, I didn't mean that at all. I was just making a joke." It wasn't funny to Brando who felt sure he'd been scalped, and Capote's later comment that he'd "trapped" Brando makes it likely that no eulogy was intended. In retrospect, it looks like a dummy run for his final devastating exposé of his intimate friends, *Answered Prayers,* the last, unfinished book before his death.

"There were reports," I pointed out, "that Brando didn't realize you were interviewing him."

"That's not true. Of course he knew it. He knew perfectly well he was being interviewed."

"Then what was his complaint?"

"I think they think you're going to edit this whole thing somehow, for them. Then they're shocked when you, according to their lights, didn't have the good taste to leave this or that out."[5]

Idolized by millions as a cinematic demigod, Brando did not challenge the article's accuracy, but Capote's right to reveal him so nakedly: as naive, self-centered, oversensitive, under-educated, troubled, and slightly paranoid. In his own exotic words, Brando resented having "the network of one's innards guywired and festooned with harlequin streamers for public musing."[6]

---

*Interview with Truman Capote, September 18, 1970.

In Hot Pursuit of *In Cold Blood*

The storm over the mini Brando biography was followed by several years of silence during which Capote all but disappeared in Kansas farmlands in hot pursuit of two murderers. He was living up to Joshua Logan's view of him as someone driven to seek out the sensational. Though Capote had briefly contemplated dogging the steps of and climbing the stairs with a New York City cleaning woman, he abandoned the project in favor of two murderers, Perry Smith and Richard Hickock, after reading a sketchy news report of their crime. Misled into believing a fortune was hidden in a farmhouse, they slaughtered the entire Clutter family there: father, Herbert, 48; mother, Bonnie; son, Kenyon, 15; and daughter, Nancy, 16.

I wondered how, considering the gruesome, depressing nature of the crime, Capote had persuaded the victims' friends and neighbors to discuss it with him, a stranger with weird East Coast ways.

"It wasn't a matter of just going in there, bang, bang, bang, like some ordinary reporter," Capote explained.* "I went to the town and I moved into that town. And I began to cultivate the people. On a very friendly basis they'd introduce me to another person, who introduced me to another person. When I first lived there the case had just happened. It was a couple of months before it was solved. Nobody had ever heard of Perry or Dick. I didn't know whether I'd have a book or not. I was just sort of experimenting with the whole thing. So I cultivated people. I even went to Sunday School. I don't ordinarily do that. [He laughed.] It was the first time I went to Sunday School classes and I didn't much enjoy them. But I came to respect all those people. And when the case broke I was on such friendly terms with Alvin Dewey, the detective in charge, that I was the first person he told."[7]

---

*Interview with Truman Capote, September 18, 1970.

To induce the two caged killers to confide in him, Capote used his breakdown-Brando technique, as well as giving them cash—fifty dollars each for a start—and then supplied them with magazines and writing paper

> and all the little things nobody else would think of doing. And they became dependent on me. There they were the first year I knew them, and I knew them almost six years in this little town in Kansas; nobody had heard of them, nobody had even heard of the case, you know. There was nothing. I was this person who was there doing this thing, and I was very attentive to them. I was drawing them out, out of boredom and out of loneliness, if nothing else. And they were grateful to me.[8]

But how could animal-lover Capote, who cried at the thought of cruelty to animals, feel warmly toward Richard Hickock, who boasted of killing stray dogs by deliberately hitting them with his car?

"It isn't a question of feeling warmly," Capote said, "but when you get to know somebody as well as I got to know those two boys—I knew them better than they knew themselves—feelings don't enter of like or dislike. It's like some kind of extraordinary condition of knowledge takes place. I found that [killing dogs] appalling and repulsive, of course. But there it is. It was part of his insensitivity and indifference to life in general."[9]

Capote watched them hang, then returned from Kansas with material destined to establish him as creator of a new art form: the facts and nothing but the facts subjected to all the magic of a talented illusionist. Several critics refuted his cocky claim to have pioneered this new genre, among them Malcolm Cowley, who said:

The nonfiction novel has been around a long, long time: *Romany Rye* and *Lavengro,* for example. It's often best in autobiographies: *The Autobiography of Henry Adams* is a nonfiction novel. It's done by selection, you see, instead of invention.[10]

Under a gathering onslaught, Capote shifted his ground to stress that unlike other claimants to the title, *In Cold Blood* was unadulterated facts, transmuted by his wizardry, and he had living witnesses and piles of documents to prove it. It was this every-word-a-fact claim, he said, that distinguished his work from any possible rivals, past or present.

One critic reported seeing Capote at work on the book with a stash of *True Detective* magazines nearby, implying that in style and content *In Cold Blood* was merely an imitation of crime stories printed in that magazine. But the charge failed to stick.

The most ferocious attack came from Capote's onetime buddy, Kenneth Tynan, who implied that a third murderer was involved in producing the book—Capote himself. By failing to use his considerable clout to save Smith and Hickock from the rope, said Tynan, Capote had virtually been their hangman. And his motive to have them killed? Simply to give his book a blockbuster ending. This is an implausible accusation, at odds with Capote's widely reported behavior: after watching the subjects of his book executed, he was emotionally distraught, crying uncontrollably. Even discussing it with me a decade later* he was so choked up he could hardly talk, especially when I asked, "Could you say anything that was extraordinary or moving in the one-hundred-page farewell letter Perry Smith wrote to you?"

"It was about. . . . It was about. . . . Oh, my God, I really

---

*Interview with Truman Capote, September 25, 1970.

shouldn't go into this. It just upsets me so much, anyway. [He sighed.] All the time they had been in prison, all those years, they were only allowed to have a certain amount of money, and I always gave them each whatever it was they were allowed to have. Anyway, the thing was in the letter [from Perry Smith] there was a check for the money. Perry had never spent a penny of it and he was, you know, giving it back to me. I don't know why, but that one thing upset me more than any other thing. It just tore me up. Because, I mean. . . . Oh, God. . . . It was touching, as though all along. . . . I can't go into it."[11]

Counterfeit grief, sneered Tynan. He maintained that Capote could have saved the lives of both men by hiring psychiatrists to declare them insane but, instead, being a greedy, heartless opportunist, he welcomed their violent end on the gallows. After all, it provided the climax needed to make the book the best seller and movie it became and its author a feted multimillionaire.

Capote called Tynan's charges sneaky and cowardly, and his accusations those "even a man with the morals of a baboon and the guts of a butterfly" would shrink from making. He said he had done all he could to help them—had even paid for their gravestones—and denied that having the murderers declared insane would have saved them. Kansas law being what it was at the time, he was right, which was true.

Even so, Capote's conscience was not entirely clear. Despite his distress over the hangings, he admitted to his friend Cecil Beaton that for one frustrated moment, at least, his book meant more to him than the killers' fate: "I'm finishing the last pages of my book," he wrote. "I *must* be rid of it regardless of what happens. I hardly give a fuck anymore *what* happens."[12]

Tynan also joined the chorus mocking Capote's claim to have given birth to the nonfiction novel, and ridiculed his baboon-and-butterfly outburst as "the semidocumentary tantrum."[13] Calling Capote a bitter and twisted man who strongly identified with Perry Smith—both being the stunted, neglected offspring of alcoholic mothers (while Tynan was the illegitimate offspring of a titled Englishman)—Tynan suggested that Capote had the same urge as Perry to express his homicidal rage but lacked the courage. However, said Tynan, Capote's role as "confessor" to both pitiless killers allowed him to indulge his own murderous tendencies vicariously, and to wallow in their bloodthirsty deeds without fear of punishment.

Capote's childhood friend Harper Lee, who had joined him in Kansas as an assistant, partly agreed with Tynan's analysis, saying: "Perry was a killer, but there was something touching about him. I think every time Truman looked at Perry he saw his own childhood."[14]

What triggered Tynan's contempt for Capote never came to light, but his attack unleashed Capote's murderous temper. "Tynan is absolutely evil," he told me,* "because he's the ultimate in hypocrisy and duplicity. There he was pretending to be such a good friend of mine, and living in my house, and I was so generous to him in every way. And all the time, months before the book came out, he was plotting this attack on me. For no reason except what he was going to make out of it. [Though peanuts compared with Capote's *In Cold Blood*.] To me that's really evil. And all because of greed and jealousy. If ever I see him again I'm going to kill him. He'd better stay out of my path."[15]

I told Capote I'd record that he laughed when he made that death threat, and he replied, "But I usually laugh when I mean it most."[16]

Still, his detractors—and none was more devastating than Tynan—were vastly outnumbered by his ardent admirers.

Before its book publication, *In Cold Blood* appeared in the *New Yorker* where it went through the literary equivalent of the third degree. The magazine's fact-checker, Sandy

---

*Interview with Truman Capote, September 18, 1970.

Campbell, gave it the ultimate accolade as the most accurate nonfiction feature he had ever vetted.

Capote then promoted it with the flair and fervor of his showman father, Arch Persons (To his father's chagrin, Truman had adopted his stepfather's name, Capote.) In his checkered, check-bouncing past, Persons had shilled for a carnival "wonder man," whose act was to imitate Christ by being crucified and Harry Houdini by enduring hours in an airtight coffin. He survived both death-defying "miracles" until the fatal day when, through miscalculation, he ran out of oxygen in the coffin.

In resurrecting the recent past in such compelling detail, Truman spoke as if he, too, had worked a miracle—a literary miracle. He insisted that despite his skillful use of novelistic sleight-of-hand, his account of the lives and crimes of the killers was meticulously accurate. Even their most intimate thoughts, he stressed, were never guesses or even informed speculations, but precisely what they told him they had been thinking at various critical moments. They, of course, weren't around to confirm or deny, and most of the critics took his word for it.

"Superb" to the *New York Times*; a "spellbinding masterpiece" to a *Life* magazine reviewer, *In Cold Blood* was an even more dazzling performance to the sophisticated *New York Review of Books,* which raised Capote to the top of the heap as author of "the best documentary account of an American crime ever written."[17]

Who then would suspect Capote of creating anything but an authentic though artful piece of work? After all, he had testified in the book's preface that: "All the material in this book not derived from my own observation is either taken from official records or is the result of interviews with the persons directly involved." Anyone daring to suggest otherwise he quickly squashed as envious, uninformed, or "my enemy."

He frequently mentioned his state-of-the-art memory, trained and perfected for such an enterprise. He claimed that it was so reliable that when interviewing, and even during the trial, he took no notes. He relied instead, as with Brando, on memory alone, committing the talk to paper when he reached his room, sometimes hours after the events.

Nelle Harper Lee had worked with Capote in Kansas for several weeks. "She and Truman took very little notes when Truman was interviewing people," said her sister, Alice.* "They would jot down basically key words that would help them recall. Truman had a theory that people they were talking with would be intimidated by someone writing [in their presence]. That was before the days of recorders being in use [generally]. When she went back to the hotel at night she would write what she thought she heard people say. He would do the same thing and then they would compare to see who had heard what. And that was the way it was done. Actually, neither one of them took anything but the barest notes."[18]

However, there is evidence that Capote sometimes took more detailed notes. In a green-covered spiral notebook now in the Library of Congress, writing in his small, round, backward-sloping longhand, Capote listed twelve questions for Perry Smith and his replies.

Question number 7 is "What is your feeling about marriage? Have you ever wished to be married? Would you say that you had a father complex—a combination of love and dislike and longing and fear?"

And he records Smith's reply as:

Yes, very much, I expected too much out of a girl. I consider myself the rugged life (sic), like the outdoors, marriage has entered my mind for the last few years. I wanted to be settled before I got. I didn't want any hardships. Afraid of money troubles. What kind of girl would want to marry a guy who

---

*Interview with Nelle Harper Lee's sister, Alice, August 23, 1993.

always wanted to travel, ride on a motorcycle. I've gravitated towards the more intellectual type of person—and that type of person wouldn't want my kind of life. Travel—I don't like to be in any one place any length of time, always a wanderer. Wanted to spend the rest of my life in Japan. They are the nicest [can't decipher Capote's next word] people I've ever met. Went to Kyoto. Like seaports. Yokohama: liked the sounds of birds and the water sport. Always liked watersports. Never liked the planes (sic)—like forests. I've always loved my father very dearly. We were so different in our ways. Always liked older people. I've always preferred "elderly" person.[19]

Capote's notebook also shows he paid $314.68 for the court records, which indicates that even if he didn't take full notes at the trial, he had an accurate record available when he wrote the book. Capote also told his friend Donald Windham that he spent over $8,000 on research for *In Cold Blood,* but records in his notebook—a final figure of $6,343.69.

The killers were tried for premeditated murder and Capote wrote in his book that they had agreed in advance to kill all witnesses. Which, of course, justifies the title *In Cold Blood.* But when Hickock learned that was to be the book's title he was extremely disturbed, because, as he wrote Capote, "I have repeatedly informed you, there was *no* discussion at *any* time to harm the Clutters."[20]

And this revives the question: Could Capote have saved the lives of these two men by testifying to that effect, or by hiring a psychiatrist to persuade the jury that the pair were mad, thus saving them from the death penalty? I will return to this point later, to establish whether or not Capote was the monster Tynan made him out to be.

White House Wag

Murderers continued to occupy Capote's mind and he began to prepare a television documentary about them. But he spent less time on death rows, at his typewriter, or testifying as a murder expert before a U.S. Senate subcommittee—or so it seemed—than flaunting his quick wit in a slow drawl on television talk shows. There he was treated as a hybrid of Socrates, Suzy the gossip columnist, and J. Edgar Hoover, the man with the secrets.

Much of his gossip came from his daily dalliance in cafe society, and with the jet-set wives and mistresses of the powerful. Warned that this was hurting his literary output and reputation, Capote confided that these people were his passport to immortality as the unsuspecting source for a book that would raise him to the ranks of Boswell, Proust, Henry James, and Maupassant.

As previously mentioned, both Jacqueline Kennedy and Britain's Queen Mother had sent him fan letters, but Mrs. Kennedy went a step further, taking him home to dinner to meet her husband. Capote recalled a later occasion when he sat on her bed chatting as Mrs. Kennedy dressed (a claim almost anyone can make without fear of contradiction, because the late Mrs. Onassis never commented on such reports).

Capote's account to me* of how he catered to President Kennedy's ready ear for gossip was a foretaste of what he intended to include in his future masterpiece:

"I liked him [Kennedy] very much. He was straightforward, had a nice offbeat smile and an offbeat sense of humor. He was unshockable. You could tell him absolutely anything. He loved gossip. I used to tell him all kinds of things about other people or myself. I can tell you something I told him in front of about fifteen people at a state dinner. It's a true story.

"The previous week I had gone to a party also attended

---

*Interview with Truman Capote, September 25, 1970.

by Cecil Beaton. He was with Greta Garbo and they were sitting on a couch in front of me. And I was having a drink and idly listening to this conversation they were having, or over-listening to it. And the designer was saying: 'You know, my dear, the older I become I find this extraordinary thing, the most depressing thing is happening. My private parts are shrinking!' There was a long pause and then the actress said, 'Uh, if *only* I could say the same!'

"So, anyway, at this state dinner there were all these people being very quiet upstairs in the Kennedys' living room. And I suddenly began telling this anecdote [about Beaton and Garbo], and after a minute he [Kennedy] roared with laughter. But the whole room was completely still until he laughed. They were really shocked that I would have the gall to tell something like that in front of all those people."[21]

Through the Kennedys Capote met Jacqueline's sister, Lee Radziwill, whom he thought even more stunning and simpatico than the First Lady, who topped the polls as the world's most admired and discussed woman. He soon became Radziwill's adoring, lovestruck instrument and advisor, persuading her to step out of her sister's shadow and into the international spotlight. Though a mother and married to a former Polish prince, Radziwill longed to do her own thing, without knowing what that was, despite or because of her jealous husband's resistance. As her Svengali-like promoter, Capote often extolled her charm, intelligence, taste, and talents, as if others had only to meet this paragon to share his infatuation. He encouraged her urge to act and helped her land the starring role in Philip Barry's *The Philadelphia Story* at a Chicago dinner theater. It was a disaster. One of the more compassionate reviewers commended her for knowing her lines.

Besotted and bedazzled, Capote saw something in Radziwill that was invisible to others, and scouted around for another stage to display her. Throwing himself in as bait, he promised to write the script for a television version of the movie *Laura* if David Susskind produced it and Radziwill starred. Susskind fell for it. This was another fiasco, underscored by *Time* magazine, which ridiculed Radziwill for being "only slightly less animated than the portrait of herself that hung over the mantel." Capote was still enthralled by this woman, whom many of his friends thought self-centered and superficial. She in turn cherished him as her "closest friend."

> More than with anyone else, I can discuss the most serious things about life and emotional questions. I miss him *terribly* when I'm away from him. I trust him implicitly. He's the most loyal friend I've ever had and the best company I've ever known. We've always been so close that it's like an echo. We never have to finish sentences. We just know what the other one means or wants to say. I feel as if he's my brother, except that brothers and sisters are rarely as close as we are.[22]

Their empathetic communication was doomed to fail, and Gore Vidal was the unwitting cause of the breakdown. Vidal was at a White House dance in honor of Radziwill, which Capote had been unable to attend. During the evening, Vidal and Robert Kennedy had an angry quarrel over Jacqueline Kennedy. Years after, during a 1975 interview with *Playgirl* magazine, Capote gave his version of the incident. (He told me that he heard of the fracas, not from Radziwill, but from Jacqueline Kennedy herself, who had witnessed the fight.) Reading the interview, which made him look like a jerk, Vidal sued Capote for libel, putting the damage to his reputation at $1 million. (The case was settled out of court in 1983 when Capote wrote a letter of apology to Vidal.)

Capote once dismissed an unsympathetic reporter as "a little, wretched, lying bitch." Now, Vidal was more or less saying the same thing about Capote, and during his deposition for the case couldn't resist another plunge of the needle. Vidal recalled that at the start of their last meeting, he mistook the diminutive writer for a stool and almost sat on him.

Aware of this sitdown putdown, I was surprised when Capote welcomed my proposal to question Vidal about Capote's credibility as a biographer, almost as if he expected Vidal to be a favorable character witness. I should have guessed that Capote had anticipated Vidal's reply, and wanted to put him on the spot. "Go ahead," Capote said to me, with a slightly diabolical chuckle. "Whatever Gore tells you he thinks of me, that's what I think of him."

I then quoted to Vidal* part of my interview with Capote as follows:

Brian: Did you ever know why Gore Vidal was anti-Robert Kennedy?

Capote: Sure, don't you know? Jacqueline Kennedy was wearing a Japanese dress with an obi. And I think it was the only time they'd ever invited Gore there [to the White House], and he spent the whole time whispering in her ear. And as he was walking out of the room he put his hand on her bottom, of this obi dress. So Bobby Kennedy walked over to him and grabbed hold of his hand and said, "Cut it out, Gore. That stuff doesn't go around here." The exact quote. And Gore turned to him and told him to take his damned hands off him. And said to him: "You Kennedys really think you have it made, don't you?" And he began this crazy sort of tirade. . . .[23]

At this point, Vidal interrupted me to say that if I published the rest of Capote's version of what occurred I, too, might face a libel suit. But he okayed my using what I had already quoted of Capote's account as "surrogate for the truth."

"But," I said to Vidal, "Capote told me he got the story from an unimpeachable source."

---

*Interview with Gore Vidal, September 30, 1970.

"Who could that be?" Vidal asked. "There were only two people present, Robert Kennedy and me."

"He [Capote] said Arthur Schlesinger was there."

"He wasn't. He was at the party [for Lee Radziwill], but he wasn't present [at the quarrel]."

"There was also Mrs. Kennedy."

"Ah, yes. I suggest you ask Arthur Schlesinger: 'Were you indeed there?' And he will say, 'No.' Mrs. Kennedy isn't going to say anything."[24]

Vidal proved half right. Mrs. Kennedy, as predicted, was mum. But, Arthur Schlesinger said:* "As I recall I observed part of it. Truman's version was secondhand and was the cause of Gore Vidal's litigation. I made a deposition in which I recalled seeing Gore's hand around Mrs. Kennedy's shoulder. After that, Gore was very drunk and got into a fight with Lem Billings, and Jackie asked me to get Gore out of there."[25] Schlesinger gives more details in contemporary notes he made:

On November 11, 1961, the Kennedys gave a dance at the White House for Lee Radziwill. Vidal was there. As the evening passed, he gave the strong impression of having drunk far too much. Someone, I forget who, perhaps Jacqueline Kennedy, asked me whether I would get him out of there. I enlisted Kenneth Galbraith and George Plimpton. We took Vidal back to the hotel. The next day Vidal came to see me. He often did in those days, but he later told someone that, assuming I was the White House chronicler (not in fact my job or expectation), he wanted in this case to explain particularly what had happened the night before. I noted in my journal, "Gore Vidal got into a violent fight, first with Lem Billings, then with Bobby." According to Gore, Bobby found him crouching by Jackie and steadying himself by putting his arm over her shoulder. Bobby stepped up and quietly moved the

---

*Interview with Arthur Schlesinger, Jr., March 26, 1994.

arm. Gore then went over to Bobby and said, "Never do anything like that to me again." Bobby started to step away when Gore added, "I have always thought that you were a god-damned impertinent son-of-a-bitch." At this, according to Gore, Bobby said, "If that is your level of dialogue, I can only respond by saying, 'Drop dead!' " At this, Bobby turned his back and walked away.[26]

Vidal's enemies preferred Capote's version in which Vidal was humiliated, but Schlesinger later testified that Gore

was not forcibly ejected, nor cast bodily into Pennsylvania Avenue, nor was there any hint of major scene. Jacqueline Kennedy, however, was irritated by his behavior and resolved not to have him in the White House again.[27]

By contrast with other accounts, John Kenneth Galbraith's memory of Vidal's exit from the White House is almost idyllic: "I remember leaving the party with Gore in a relaxed and friendly way."

Assuming the Schlesinger-Vidal-Galbraith accounts—alcohol intake aside—to be reasonably accurate, it is worth mentioning how close Capote stuck to the facts. Apart from lowering Gore Vidal's hand from the First Lady's shoulder to below her waist, and having Vidal heaved rather than helped from the White House, he was near the mark. Still, as Schlesinger concluded, "Truman liked to embellish stories and in this one he did."

Capote treated Vidal's lawsuit with amused contempt, confident, he told me, that he would be exonerated by his unimpeachable sources, Jacqueline Kennedy and Lee Radziwill. Instead, the woman he had cheered and championed denied her Deep Throat role with a frosty "I do not recall ever discussing with Truman Capote the incident of the evening which I understand is the subject of the lawsuit."[28] For someone who claimed to admire loyalty above all else, Radziwill's "betrayal" hurt and disillusioned him. Why had she done it? She refused to take his calls, and he learned of her insulting and evasive explanation: "I'm tired of Truman riding on my coattails to fame. And, Liz, what difference does it make? They're just a couple of fags."[29]

Capote believed Radziwill to be largely to blame for his losing the libel suit, and that her motive was fear of Vidal. It can be imagined with what muttered obscenities the by now critically ill Capote—drugs and booze having all but destroyed him—threw in the towel and wrote an apologetic letter to the triumphant Vidal. But apart from occasional irrational outbursts he still spoke sympathetically of JFK's widow, now an Onassis through marrying the Greek tycoon. Years before Capote had told me,* "Her father was an alcoholic. She adored him. His alcoholism was not part of her unhappiness. It was just that her mother and father separated. Jackie was always a shy, sensitive, and withdrawn person, and through various circumstances and accidents of fate she feels she's been turned into a freak of some kind."[30]

He no longer spoke of Lee Radziwill with anything but contempt. Before the libel suit he described her to me as if he had a crush on her: "There are very few people in the world who are as extraordinary as that girl. She gets no credit for it, of course. She might as well be completely in oblivion. But she's really a brilliant girl, extremely intelligent and sensitive, and she's got tremendous style and kindness and heart and brains and energy and courage and she's really somebody."[31]

After the "betrayal" she was "a little cunt."[32] It's a safe bet that had he written a Radziwill biography in the 1970s it would have been hagiography. In the 1980s the halo would have been shredded and around her ankles.

---

*Interview with Truman Capote, September 18, 1970.

If he wasn't in any condition to write an *In Cold Blood,* he could still go public, and he phoned artist Andy Warhol to discuss his plans. Shaken, Warhol noted in his diary for June 2, 1970:

> Truman called and he was so mad at Lee Radziwill for giving the deposition against him in the Gore Vidal lawsuit. It was so scary. He said she'd be "shitting razor blades" after he goes on the "Stanley Siegel Show" on [television] Tuesday to "really let her have it." . . . It was really horrible. He said, "She's going to wake up and hate herself. Don't you agree?" and I said, "Well, Truman, she's so weak now she might commit *suicide.*" And he said, "Too bad." He said, "If I told you all the things she said about you." . . . It was scary how vicious he could get over someone he was best friends with. When Truman turns, he really turns.[33]

After watching Capote more than live up to his threats, Warhol again confided to his diary:

> Truman went into a "Southern Fag" character and began telling all the embarrassing things that Lee had told him over the years about people—that Peter Tufo looked like a ferret and was publicity-crazy riding on her coattails, and that Newton Cope who she's engaged to marry, still—even after calling off the wedding a few weeks ago—was "no great catch," except maybe he would be, in a "provincial town." And he told how she tried to seduce William F. Buckley, Jr., by asking him for spiritual advice and when he didn't respond she accused him of being a queer. If Lee was drinking *before* this feud with Truman, can you imagine *now*? Oh, Truman's making such a fool of himself. He should at least be drunk. . . . Halston said he was all for Truman, that Lee deserved what she got.[34]

The next day Capote called Warhol again to say his television appearance had been well reported in all the Washington and California papers, but the New York press had played it down. The following day he told Warhol of receiving a telegram from a fan congratulating him for being "the best thing on TV since Ruby shot Oswald."[35]

Fruits of Fame

"Much of my mail," Capote told me* with a sigh, "would make most people climb the walls. I have the extra burden of receiving an enormous amount from the prison population of the world. They all want me to tell their stories. 'If only you could write my story, I know that the world would listen.' Or, you know, making a deal. If they aren't doing it, their lawyers are. I get tons of letters from lawyers asking me don't I want to write the story of their clients, to have exclusive rights? Now, for instance, this boy who committed all the Manson murders, Watson. His lawyer from a little town wrote me this long letter right after they were all caught and in prison, and asked would I be willing to buy the story of this boy's life, exclusive rights for $50,000. [He laughed.] Can you imagine?"

Capote was now scared of all hitchhikers. "I don't think I used to be scared of anything I automatically saw, but after doing all that research for *In Cold Blood* and all the hundreds of murderers I interviewed [for a television project] the very sight of a hitchhiker gives me the shivers. [Smith and Hickock had planned to hitchhike across the United States, robbing and killing all who gave them lifts.] I've driven back and forth across the country several times, and the idea of running out of gas in one of those lonely Midwestern places creates a tremendous

---

*Interview with Truman Capote, September 18, 1970.

sense of anxiety in me. And I have a real, true dread of being on some isolated road, depending on the kindness of strangers. [He chuckled.] As Blanche Dubois would say."

Nowhere was safe. He was alone at his Long Island house when a stranger appeared, "a psychopath out of the mental institution fairly recently; a rather good-looking young man, but so sinister. He just walked in through the lane and through the fields and up to the house. And the next thing I knew he was knocking at the door. And I went there, and there he was. He was an instantly recognizable psychopath. He began talking to me in what seemed a normal way, and was in the house before I knew what I could do, and it took forever to get him out of here. Then I had to drive him to the railroad station. All the way he kept hammering his hand against his fist. He had found out where I was. He had taken a great deal of time and research and located this house out here in the country. I mean, how he found me here was really frightening, extraordinary. Afterwards he appeared several times in a building I live in in New York, but I was never there. Finally, the doorman there called the police about it. But there's nothing you can do about that."

An ex-con Capote had interviewed for *In Cold Blood* also appeared uninvited at his home, stayed all day, and got away with some money. "It was quite frightening," Capote said. "A bit like 'The Desperate Hours' " (a television drama based on a real event, when an armed and dangerous escaped convict held a family hostage in their own home).

As well as uninvited guests, *In Cold Blood* brought him riches, fame, repeated emotional breakdowns, and a growing compulsion to treat frequent bouts of depression—"I slide in and out of them"—with heavier doses of drugs washed down with alcohol.

He had no faith to sustain him at such times.

"I don't even believe Christ ever existed," he said, to emphasize his skepticism.

"Have you heard John Allegro's theory that Christ was a mushroom?" I asked.

"No." He laughed. "Whose theory is this?"

"Allegro's. One of the translators of the Dead Sea Scrolls, and an expert on philology. He says that early Christianity was a drug-taking cult and that Jesus was a mushroom."

Capote laughed again. "I think that's quite good. I like it."

"And the early Christians used the word 'Jesus' as a code for mushrooms."

Capote (still laughing): "I think that's pretty good."[36]

He thought there was a God of some vague sort, but not the deity of either Testament, and not one of any consolation to him. If reincarnation was true, and he hoped it might be, he'd like to be a buzzard next time around.

To his about to be bitterly disillusioned friends, his wish had already been granted: this *was* the next time around.

"May All Your Wishes Come True"

It had been in the works for some twenty years, his "greatest *memento mori,*" a book that he exuberantly predicted "will rattle teeth like *The Origin of the Species.*"[37] Like a one-man FBI, he collected dirt on his high-profile friends, cajoled their sordid secrets from them, noted their inanities and the most repulsive aspects of their lives—and filed it for special treatment. After all, it was to be his claim to literary immortality.

The theme of Capote's *Answered Prayers* illustrates an irony also expressed by the Chinese curse: "May all your wishes come true." In this book—itself an answered prayer, an irony Capote seems not to have anticipated—he did to others what he damned Tynan for trying to do to him: exposed them as self-absorbed monsters. Consider this, one of his notebook entries: "Doris

Duke [tobacco heiress]. . . . Her eyes are somewhat sinister, lizard-grey, slightly dead, slightly slanted. She has beautiful skin (courtesy of Dr. Lazlo [skin expert]). . . . Doris talking about her Indian religious beliefs ('But is it getting you anywhere, dear?' her mother asked,"[38] and his comment about Alice Toklas [companion of Gertrude Stein]: "She's really a dear. If only she'd shave off that Fu Manchu moustache."[39] These were Valentines compared with his disclosures in *Answered Prayers*.

He wrote it as a *roman à clef* with an easily turned clef, and sometimes used real names. Though the still-incomplete book was not published until 1987, three years after his death, *Esquire* printed four of its chapters while he was alive and able to relish the reaction. It was an almost uniform shriek of outrage. If answered, the angry prayers of those he had humiliated must surely have hastened his imminent death. They certainly haunted his last years.

Through sharing with the world the sick or silly secrets of his circle, he deserved their blighted view of him as a disloyal son-of-a-bitch—their Judas.

James Michener Attacks

A sharp, unexpected rebuke came from author James Michener, who had been an admirer of Capote's talent and eccentricities, comparing him favorably to Lord Byron. (It was while Michener's novel *Sayonara* was being filmed in Japan that Capote did the sneak-attack interview of Brando.)

Michener now knew, from the pages of *Answered Prayers*, what he hadn't known at the time, that in their younger days he and Capote not only shared the same publisher, Random House, but the same woman friend, the tall, spectacular offspring of a Montana miner. It seems that when one wasn't available to escort her around Manhattan's hot spots, she called on the other. But the two men were never, in any sense, rivals. Michener delighted in Capote's professional triumphs and followed his progress up the social ladder with amused interest, noting his graduation from the miner's daughter to Marilyn Monroe, then to Barbara Paley (daughter of a famous doctor, Harvey Cushing, and wife of CBS chairman William Paley), and finally, his conquest of sisters Jacqueline Kennedy and Princess Lee Radziwill.

Michener accepted Capote at his own evaluation—"an alcoholic, drug addict and homosexual"—but not his claim to genius. Tennessee Williams and chess champion Bobby Fischer were the only ones Michener rated among his acquaintances as worthy of the title "genius."

Capote had been in a fix over one of his books some twenty years before and Michener came to his rescue, trying to save Capote from the fury of Bonnie Golightly. She had accused him of using her as the model for his Holly Golightly in *Breakfast at Tiffany's*. In the novel, Capote has his heroine arrested as a suspected international drug smuggler, and the publisher blurbed her as "a bad little good girl adrift in New York." Besides their almost identical comic-opera names, Bonnie said she and the "fictitious" Golightly had too much in common to be coincidental. Each was single, about the same age, had a Southern background, and lived alone in an East Side Manhattan apartment with a cat for company.

"Why did he have to name the horrid creature Holly Golightly in that horrid book?" she complained.

Holly was loose and vapid and totally illiterate. . . . Capote is not a creative writer. He's a biographical writer. He takes somebody he'd heard about and just BUILDS. I'm convinced that somebody who knows both of us "dished me"—that's a "Beat" expression for "gossiped."[40]

But Michener was sure another woman, the one they had both squired around town, had inspired the character, the "stunning would-be starlet-singer-actress-raconteur from the mines of Montana" with

> a minimum talent, a maximum beauty, and a rowdy sense of humor. Also, she was six feet, two inches tall, half a head taller than I. A head and a half taller than Truman.[41]

In a letter to Random House publisher Bennett Cerf, Michener said he didn't want to see Truman "crucified" by the lawsuit and could testify "without question" that Capote patterned Holly Golightly on their shared girlfriend from Montana. The publisher responded with an urgent call to Michener advising him to burn any copies he might have of the "crazy letter," and saying that when Capote heard of Michener's offer to testify he had wailed, "I've been afraid she was going to sue, too."[42] But to his delight, the miner's daughter reveled in being the "real" Holly, and didn't take him to court. And, in the end, neither did Bonnie Golightly.

Capote told friends that Holly Golightly was a mixture of Doris Lilly, Carol Marcus, Oona Chaplin, and himself. But in a 1968 *Playboy* interview, as if still fearful of libel suits, he said the inspiration for Holly was a teenage German refugee who landed in Manhattan at the start of World War II and after the war left for Portugese East Africa where she had (conveniently!) disappeared. He insisted that everything he wrote about her personality and lifestyle was "literally true."

He remembered Michener's well-intentioned offer to save him from the fury and financial demands of Bonnie Golightly, and repaid him with an invitation to the social event of the decade, his spectacular masked ball at the Plaza Hotel. Michener was otherwise engaged.

Despite his fondness for Capote, when Michener read the early chapters of *Answered Prayers* and accounts of the outraged protests of the victims, he did not come to his defense. Instead, he challenged Capote's integrity and truthfulness, deploring the "shocking betrayal of confidences, an eating at the table and gossiping in the lavatory. I am familiar with four of the people T.C. lacerates," he said,

> and I can categorically deny the allegations he makes. A masterly study in pure bitchiness which will close many doors previously opened. Why did he do it? Has he no sense of responsibility or noblesse oblige? A proctologist's view of American society. But I am sure that if he can bring off the whole, *Answered Prayers* will be the *roman à clef* of my decade, an American Proust-like work which will be judged to have summarized an epoch. . . . But only if he can finish his work in high style, only if he incorporates enough leading or relevant figures, only if he masters his subject rather than allowing it to overwhelm him, I hear he's drinking so much and into drugs so heavily that the chances of his making it are slim.[43]

Michener had blunted his attack by praising Capote as a potential Proust and by neglecting to name any of the four people he claimed he could personally exonerate from Capote's smears. Who was telling the truth, Capote or Michener?

I wrote to Michener, quoting his comments and asking if he would identify the four maligned individuals. He replied on September 29, 1989:

> Your letter on 15 August really staggered me. I don't know who "quoted me as deploring" various aspects of Truman Capote's life. He and I were casual friends. I helped him in one crisis, and he invited me to his major bash. The words sound like nothing I would say. I never use the words *lavatory* or *bitchiness*. The quote is much cleverer than I ever come up with, and seemed to be completely fabricated. I disown

it. As a matter of fact, in Larry Grobel's book about Capote and in certain of my own writing I applaud the little fellow, deplore some of his exhibitionism, and place him high on my list of contemporaries. Among his papers will be found two letters I wrote to him late in his life when things were going poorly, letters of support [one was: "Hang in there, Kiddo. We need you."], and in one I told him what I've said publicly: "If you ever get *Answered Prayers* finished the book will be the subject of Ph.D. theses a century from now at Harvard." I hope your work goes well. You have an incredible subject for your pen.

To jog Michener's memory and to establish that I had not misquoted him, I sent him a copy of his foreword to Grobel's book, and again asked if he would give the names of the four he knew for sure Capote had lied about. He didn't respond.

I wrote him again in August 1993 and he replied:

I think your quote from my earlier letter says all I'd care to say on the subject. I still think Capote might have copped the Nobel had he ever finished his *chef d'oeuvre*. Good luck in your work on an important book, *vide* the McGinniss horror.[44]

The *Washington Post*'s Charles Trueheart believed Capote had hurt himself more than his targets with a sketchy account, by turns "sly, coy, bilious, demoniac," as well as "indiscreet and salacious," and by providing "a coldly accurate memorial to the writer's worst days," with "isolated examples of Capote at his keen-eared best, and of Capote at his pickle-brained, gossip-mongering worst."[45] Trueheart's review appeared after Capote's death, but others made similar charges while he was alive, to which he responded:* "My book isn't gossip except in the sense

---

*Interview with Truman Capote, September 25, 1970.

that all literature is gossip. If a certain kind of writer like Proust or James was living in America today, this is what they would write about. Everything in Proust was true."[46]

If he thought that, and knew of Proust's devious method, it explains Capote's Alice-in-Wonderland view of the truth as whatever you chose it to be. It took biographers years to trace the model for "Albertine," the woman with whom Proust said he had been desperately in love. Albertine turned out to be Proust's chauffeur, Alfred Agostinelli. He further disguised "Albertine's" identity by adding some characteristics of several male and female acquaintances. At the same time, Proust was meticulous in establishing some facts: going to the Ritz Hotel to question the headwaiter, and asking to see a hat worn twenty years before in trying to make *Remembrance of Things Past* accurate. Still, all the characters were composites, whereas in *Answered Prayers* some characters were so lightly camouflaged that Capote seemed eager for instant identification. When warned that they might counterattack, Capote said they were too dumb to recognize themselves. These included Tennessee Williams and Katherine Ann Porter. With others he made no effort at disguise, using the real names of "big-bellied show-off" Gertrude Stein; Jacqueline Onassis and sister, Lee Radziwill; Gloria Vanderbilt; Cole Porter; Ned Rorem; J. D. Salinger; Joshua Logan and wife, Nedda; and "rapist" Joseph Kennedy, Sr. Capote defended as absolutely true his account of JFK's father raping a woman of sixteen, and denied to interviewer Charles Ruas that he was giving currency to gossip. It was hard to confirm or deny, and as the old man was dead and the woman anonymous, Capote was safe from libel action.

Some who were named had been among the five hundred guests at his 1966 Plaza Hotel masked ball to celebrate and publicize the triumphant completion of *In Cold Blood*. "How many of those at the party were your friends?" I asked. "Forty-five," Capote said, after a moment's calculation. *Answered*

Prayers shrank that forty-five to a precious few, mostly women, all of whom escaped mention in the book. Among them was Nancy Reagan (the second and last First Lady in his life); Joanne Carson, the TV celebrity's ex-wife and Capote's good friend; and C. Z. Guest, whom he had encouraged to lead a life of her own.

He expected friends he'd savaged in *Answered Prayers* to forgive him once they saw things his way: that they were privileged to appear in a work of art. But none saw it his way. Slim Keith (his Lady Coolbirth) thought him loathsome and the book "junk"; Tennessee Williams drawled that he was "a loony liar"; Nedda Logan called him "a dirty toad." CBS chairman William Paley claimed to have fallen asleep while reading the pages exposing him as a crude philanderer, but read enough to characterize Capote as "a little shit." No one threatened bodily harm, but Gloria Vanderbilt promised to spit on him on sight.

"The reason why these people are so upset," Capote told a reporter,

> is that almost without exception they struggled like galley slaves to get where they are, which is nowhere. Then somebody who was absolutely at the center of all this comes along and says, "Oh, well, I think this is a lot of bullshit, the emperor has no clothes."[47]

The shock of their response shook Capote's immune system. He suffered from bursitis and his left eye began to hemorrhage from an infection. He no longer convulsed admiring galley slaves at the White House, nor held them entranced in chic restaurants or on yachts skirting the Greek islands. Instead, he holed up in his Manhattan apartment, leaving phone messages for former loving friends who never called back.

Slumped in a chair near his constant companion now—a stuffed rattlesnake posed to strike—and facing the occasional interviewer, Capote tried to justify his role as the jet-set's Judas. Hadn't the "betrayed" heard of Bernard Shaw's quip that a writer after material will even sacrifice his mother? "Well, then, they knew I was a writer. What did they expect?" A surprising question for a man who told me he prized loyalty above all. More to the point, what did he expect?

Perhaps fame, booze, and hard drugs had bloated his ego along with his body, deluding him into thinking he could squeal on friends with impunity. A few of them had another explanation: over the years he had expressed a fear of going mad; it had happened.

A more detached observer, Tina Brown, then editor-in-chief of *Vanity Fair,* acknowledged that Capote was not the only pariah on the block and pointed out that he was following in a "time-honored literary tradition for a writer to bite the hand that feeds him." Still, she conceded he had outbitten the competition and raised "ingratitude to an art form," in producing "a rubbishy *roman à clef*" and socio-pornography "rife with the cackle of camp." Yet, "between the cloudbursts of malice," she rooted for the "flashes of prose that bring the aching reminder of a more whole writer, prose that makes the heart sing and the narrative fly."[48] Had he been alive to read it, Capote might have cackled over the singing heart and flying narrative, and even tried to bite the hand that typed it—but this was to be about as kind as his critics were going to be. Most put thumbs down, or up, to hold their noses.

Molly Haskell, a *Vogue* film reviewer, resurrected the charge made by Kenneth Tynan that Capote was a killer. She thought he had become a killer even though he had triumphed "over the sort of background that turns people into ax murderers. The killers that Capote encountered when he went to Holcomb, Kan., to write about the murder of the Clutter family and met Perry Smith and Dick Hickock. The killer that Capote himself became—far more efficiently than Perry and Dick—when, in poisonous prose and on talk-shows, he laid waste his friends and skewered his competitors with malice as pure as the air in an oxygen tent."[49]

Norman Mailer was all for the book and to hell with the friends to whom it laid waste. As early as 1959, he wrote: "I would suspect he [Capote] hesitates between the attraction of society which enjoys and repays him for his unique gifts, and the novel he could write of the gossip column's real life, a major work but it would banish him forever from his favorite world. Since I have nothing to lose I hope Truman fries a few of the fancier fish."[50]

Tina Brown agreed, except she believed Capote "had the raw material for a best-selling nonfiction book and should have written it as just that. It could have been the definitive portrayal of the witches of the East Side, gleaned from his 20 years as their walker-in-chief. Capote knew he had that material but he also felt it was unpublishable. Even if he managed a path through the libel laws, his revelations would kiss goodbye to the ladies who lunch."[51]

By intermingling fact and fiction, he weakened both. The ladies who lunch would have given him the heave-ho, anyway, even those in the flimsy guise of false names and slightly altered body parts. The possibly major work became a minor and malicious potpourri.

Biographer's Biographer

The first time I asked Capote what he most admired in others, he said, "loyalty." The second time, he said, "truthfulness." Note that that was a quality he liked in *others*. Capote scorned the reporter's maxim, "when in doubt leave it out," preferring to tune in his imagination.

It seemed that no situation, no matter how baffling, proved

beyond Capote's understanding and ability to analyze, except for his own weird relationship with John O'Shea, a Catholic who left his wife and four children to live with Capote. O'Shea became a disturbing central figure in his troubled life almost to the end: an episode as bizarre as anything Capote had dreamed up.

Thanksgiving Day 1975 saw the unlikely pair living in a rented Beverly Hills house, while Capote made his film debut as an eccentric who planned a murder in Neil Simon's *Murder by Death*. And why not? He'd been putting on a performance for years. According to Gerald Clarke's biography of Capote most of the violent action in Capote's life was offscreen. During a boozy, no-holds-barred fight, O'Shea smashed everything breakable within reach, which almost included Capote, who ran for his life, barefoot and bleeding, to the sanctuary of the Beverly Hills Hotel. There, Joanne Carson picked him up and sheltered him in her home until O'Shea simmered down.

Looking for love, companionship, and unusual sexual experiences, Capote thought he'd found them all in O'Shea, an overweight bank vice president whom others called crude, obscene, and a phony. Several times Capote broke up with O'Shea, until O'Shea turned the tables and ran off with a young woman.

Bent on revenge, Capote admitted to his biographer (Clarke) that he hired a barroom buddy to sprinkle sugar in O'Shea's gas tank. Fearing, as was the case, that Capote had hired a hit man to work him over, O'Shea went into hiding, Capote then told his pal to hunt him down and demolish his car. The hit man found his quarry, attached a bullet and a threatening note to a brick, and threw it onto the terrace of O'Shea's apartment. Hidden in shadow, the hit man watched O'Shea get the message, then went into the building's underground garage and set his target's car ablaze. The fire shot up through the building sending residents, O'Shea among them, scurrying for safety. O'Shea kept moving, hiding out for the next few months in different towns and under various names. The fire could have killed him! Is that what Capote wanted?

Capote admitted to being dominated throughout his life by an intense, uncontrollable jealousy. He called his almost deadly relationship with O'Shea "the greatest love affair of my life."

Was there a more vivid example of his seeing things as he *wanted* them to be? His knowing friend, Harper Lee, said: "If it's not the way he likes it, he'll arrange it so it is."[52]

Surprisingly, Capote chose as his Boswell Gerald Clarke, someone unlike himself, not tempted to fabricate but to ferret out the facts. Capote also gave him a note to display inviting anyone with sensitive information to tell all. Armed with this, Clarke found that few could resist the offer. Although convinced others were spooked by tape recorders, it didn't bother Capote. So Clarke was able to record hundreds of hours of their conversations over almost ten years.

Clarke does not name himself in the finished work, but appears as "the friend"—not otherwise defined—who became a confidant with access to Capote's secrets, personal letters, and private diaries. At times, he was painfully involved in Capote's increasingly agitated life.

Trying to explain his inexplicable relationship with John O'Shea, Capote told Clarke:

> What happened between us was too complicated, too idiotic. I could write it as a comedy, but it wouldn't be true, because there was nothing funny about it. But if I wrote it as something serious it would be ridiculous. People would say that if the person O'Shea is really as dreadful as that, then Capote must be a complete moron for having become involved with him.[53]

Having the unlikely cooperation not only of O'Shea but also of the wife and children he had deserted to live with Capote, Clarke could produce an evenhanded account of the odd situation. If anyone understood the tragicomedy, it was Clarke, who had appeared on the scene when Capote's "long decline had begun. . . . He was a very, very unhappy man, and especially toward the end he had an insatiable need for attention, love, and recognition that just couldn't be filled by anybody. It was clear that he wanted to die for a long time."[54]

Capote was in such a mood when he met Clarke for lunch at Manhattan's Quo Vadis restaurant shortly before Christmas 1976. A wraith had replaced the former pudgy figure, the result of shedding forty pounds. He had hoped that losing weight and finally deciding to end his lunatic life with O'Shea—a mutual torment—would bring relief. It hadn't. For hour after hour he held Clarke with a monologue of misery, confession of failure, and a cry for who knows what—help, sympathy, a miracle? His answered prayers were killing him, he told Clarke. He was rich, famous, and desperate: his waking hours were nothing but anxious moments interrupted by sudden, inexplicable stabs of terror, and his sleep was plagued with nightmares.

Nowhere was safe, not even his home in the country. Recently, an autograph fanatic had smashed a car through the gates of Capote's Long Island home, breaking his pet bulldog's jaw and ripping open her stomach. Maggie had survived, though the injuries had paralyzed her legs. Was it any wonder he dreaded autograph hunters and never refused them for fear of being beaten up? He loved the dog and naturally grieved over her pain, but he also wept uncontrollably for no apparent reason. He would wake and moments later be crying. Two psychoanalysts could neither explain nor stop his tears.

He knew that his terror of being abandoned was a legacy of his emotionally deprived childhood, when his mother locked him in hotel rooms while she pursued her various affairs, and that the rejecting reactions of friends to their appearance in *Answered Prayers* had revived and increased that fear. They had no idea of the pain they were inflicting, nor understood why he wrote the book.[55]

With all he'd endured, not the least of which was a fear of going mad, he went on, was it surprising that for fifteen years now he had been an alcoholic? He could still go on the wagon for months, until the awful moment when he *knew* that if he didn't drink he would die. So, then, of course, he started again. Time and again he tried to dry out, going to AA meetings, to clinics—Silver Hill, Riggs, Hazelden, Smithers, to name some—and to two psychoanalysts. What good had it done?

Though, as he spoke, Capote was steadily drinking, he never became loud or obnoxious as he gave a tearful, rambling account of his life. Clarke kept his tape recorder running, but he was no longer a detached observer. "I tried to be very sympathetic and I was sympathetic," Clarke recalled.* "With someone like Truman you could very rationally go down a list of things and say, 'Look, Truman, you've broken up with someone and you may not have everything you want, but look at the things you *do* have.' But it's not enough. If you've ever been with someone like that, you can see it's not enough. I talked to an analyst who said if he'd had help when he was young it might have done some good. But when I knew him he seemed beyond ordinary help. He was a manic-depressive. And once he was on lithium and drinking at the same time, which is a terrible thing to do. When he went in for something it often helped for a time. I think the psychoanalysts may even have helped— for a time."[56]

The restaurant closed, but Capote wasn't through. He persuaded Clarke not to leave, but to join him in a bar across the street.

"Sometimes he would say he had something dramatic to tell me and it would turn out not to be dramatic at all, at

---

*Interview with Gerald Clarke, January 6, 1990.

least by my standards," Clarke said. "At other times, I'd meet him quite unsuspectingly and discover it was something quite dramatic."[57] This was such an occasion: Capote threatened to kill himself. He had saved enough pills to do the trick, or he might use the gun Alvin Dewey had given him during the glory days of *In Cold Blood*. It was in a drawer at his home, ever ready.

Fame had come too soon. That was part of the trouble, Capote said, and part of the reason why, at age fifty-two, he wanted to die.

At around midnight, to Clarke's relief, Capote's most enduring friend, Jack Dunphy, who had been searching for him, arrived at the bar and they left together.

Though he didn't shoot himself, Capote's last years were a prolonged suicide attempt. Carried into Southampton [Long Island] Hospital in a straitjacket, he later escaped from the room pursued by two giant nurses who found him hiding outside behind a bush. They took him back and strapped him to a bed. He was beginning to live a macabre Thurber cartoon.

He suffered worse and more frequent convulsive seizures and sudden inexplicable terror attacks. In response to these, he upped his already huge intake of vodka, cocaine, valium, codeine, and barbiturates. He swallowed "uppers," and sniffed cocaine to fight fatigue, and took "downers" to sleep free from nightmares and daytime demons. That didn't work. "All my dreams are anxiety dreams," he told me. He began to hallucinate. Once, being confronted by the ghost of his stepfather, Joe Capote, he thought of taking an overdose to join him. He made futile attempts to master his addictions and pathetic efforts to recover his youth with a face lift, hair transplant, and major dental surgery. The result was ghoulish.

Whatever his excesses and degradations—being found drunk in bed or lying in his own dried excrement—Capote was never totally abandoned by friends willing to come to his aid. After convincing him it might work, fellow alcoholic Winston Guest and his wife, C. Z., flew with Capote to an addiction-rehabilitation hospital. Capote emerged after a month convinced he had licked his addictions. A few weeks later he was drunk again.

Handcarved Coffins Revisited

A brief, fragile renewal of energy and ambition led Capote to emulate his biographer and take a tape recorder with him on his rounds. He produced several lively features for Andy Warhol's *Interview* magazine: an encounter with Marilyn Monroe, his memories of childhood, and an abortive book idea about the life of a cleaning woman. Capote's most ambitious undertaking was his account of a serial killer in a Midwest town in the 1970s—the sinister subject of his *Handcarved Coffins: A Nonfiction Account of an American Crime*. Capote began investigating this diabolically inventive murderer in 1975, just a year before his pursuit with intent to kill of John O'Shea. So it is possible that Capote had been inspired to emulate the terror tactics of the serial killer he was studying, though on a more modest scale.

Capote said that the detective in charge of the case, Jake Pepper, put him on to this true story of a killer who first surreptitiously took photographs of his victims and then warned them of his intent by mailing them the photos, gift-wrapped, so to speak, in miniature handcarved coffins. He had killed nine so far, dispatching them in increasingly gruesome ways. He stretched a wire across a road to decapitate a man driving an open car without a windshield, incinerated others, and eliminated a lawyer and his wife by adding to the car's optional equipment several frenzied rattlesnakes.

Astonishingly, Capote met the killer and found him charming. He was ambitious and owned a large ranch. His apparent motive for the bizarre, elaborate murders was that each victim (except for two unfortunates he accidentally burned alive) had voted to divert water from a river running through his ranch. The police, said Capote, were sure he was the killer but because he was so socially and politically powerful, they hesitated to bring him in, short of a smoking gun or talkative rattlesnake. Detective Pepper even introduced Capote to the next intended victim, who had recently received the usual death threat—a miniature coffin with her photo enclosed. She was a first-grade teacher. Pepper was in love with her, they planned to marry, and Capote had promised to attend their wedding. Because the young woman packed a gun and practiced karate, Pepper believed she was safe. But Capote didn't and felt "weak, feeble, and disgusted" when he realized her detective-lover was using her as "a goat waiting for the tiger to strike."

Capote was right. Neither gun nor karate saved her. She was found drowned, and no witnesses came forward who had seen her die.

Because Capote described these vengeance killings in such raw detail, they haunted *Newsweek* reviewer Walter Clemons and disturbed his sleep. However, Clemons had one reservation that cast doubt on the truth of the "nonfiction" story. Using rattlesnakes as murder weapons seemed to him too wild and unpredictable a modus operandi to have succeeded so perfectly. According to Capote, these murders of a husband and wife occurred on a sizzling hot day, when the couple entered their car and were attacked by nine deadly rattlesnakes injected with drugs to keep them in a fighting frenzy. Clemons wondered:

Wouldn't the amphetamine-crazed rattlers be swarming visibly inside the car before the victims opened its doors? And if you find your windows rolled up on a very hot day don't you pause to roll one down before you take your seat? In which case, the snakes might get you, but wouldn't the snakes have slithered away? [According to Capote, the snakes were found after the killings in the closed car.] Would both victims, entering the car from opposite sides, close themselves in at the same moment? Wouldn't one [snake] have escaped?[58]

And how was it that until Capote brought these serial killings to light—all crying out for newspaper headlines—they had not been reported in the press? *Handcarved Coffins* first appeared in *Interview* magazine and then *Music for Chameleons,* which was published by Random House in 1980. Questioned by Joel Swerdlow for *Writers Bloc* that same year, Capote said he had done something perhaps unique in crime writing: he had not only named Robert Hawley Quinn as the bizarre serial killer before the police had charged him with the crimes, but had risked getting a miniature coffin himself by showing the manuscript to Quinn before publication.

Quinn's response, according to Capote, was, "This is just a joke. Ha. Ha. What a joke."

It soon became clear why the killer had laughed. "Quinn" was not his name. Capote had protected him and everyone concerned—except himself—by using pseudonyms, and he had not even named the state in which the serial killings occurred. But he claimed to be an expert on serial killers, having amassed twenty-two files about American criminals with details of their crimes. He also said he had had a recent conversation with the still-at-large killer, continuing to guard his identity by referring to him as "Quinn."[59]

Andy Warhol gave Capote six thousand dollars to investigate the bizarre Midwestern murders. But there the trail fades because, shortly after getting the cash, Capote was spotted in his birthplace, New Orleans, and soon after that, he moved for a time to Miami. Was he trying to put anyone who might be following off *his* track? Did Quinn exist or had Capote fooled everyone? I determined to find out.

Capote's End

Capote was still in Miami when O'Shea reappeared, after eighteen months "on the run." Their reconciliation was brief and uneasy. Capote now feared the tables had turned and that O'Shea meant to kill him, while O'Shea was concerned that this time Capote would do the walking out and leave him in the lurch. An argument led to a fierce drunken brawl. Capote was outmatched and emerged with a broken nose, a fractured rib, and other injuries that kept him in the hospital for twelve days. He returned, weak and scared, to the comparative safety of his Manhattan apartment twenty-two stories above the East River. At night he could see Wall Street as a honeycomb of lights and bridges festooned with green lights as if celebrating their existence.

Warhol thought Capote had suffered brain damage, as he recorded in his diary for September 15, 1981:

> Truman called on Monday and his voice—I didn't even know it was him on the phone. He was saying cuckoo things, like that his brain had stopped for thirty-two seconds so that's what he was going to call his next book—*Thirty-Two Seconds.* The next day at 6:30 he collapsed and all the newspapers and TV reporters rushed over to the UN Plaza. He was taken to the hospital and it was front-page news, he got the cover of the *Post* and everything.[60]

He survived, but only just. Rarely leaving home during the day, at night he haunted the discos, appropriately looking like a cadaver, satisfied to just watch the action.

In August 1983 Capote was staying at Joanne Carson's Palm Springs home, sitting at poolside and tinkering with his biographical sketch of Willa Cather. One morning he was too tired to get out of bed but asked Carson not to call an ambulance. She sat at his bedside and he told her that when he recovered, he hoped to get away from it all, perhaps to China. Not long before in New York he had suffered frightening hallucinations: menacing ghosts were lurking in his apartment and he rushed from the place in terror, pleading with neighbors to let him in. Now he seemed to be hallucinating again, but pleasantly, taking a trip not to China, but back to his childhood in Alabama. "Mama! Mama!" he called out. Then, as if greeting the also long-dead Sook Faulk, he said, "It's me. It's Buddy." Sook had given him that nickname and her loving care when he was a child. She had been his simple, shy, much older cousin. "A saint," he called her if pressed to name anyone he had known worthy of the title.

Although Capote had told me he did not believe in God and doubted if there ever had been a Jesus, later, in a self-interview he said he had begun to believe again in the God of his childhood, "and understand that Sook was right, that everything was His design."[61] When he seemed to have fallen asleep, Carson left him, returning at midday with towels should he decide for a swim in the pool. "The room was too still," she recalled. She touched his forehead. It was cool. He had no pulse. He had died just short of his sixtieth birthday from "liver disease, complicated by phlebitis and drug intoxication," though, apparently, not from an overdose.[62]

Other Voices, Other Views

Four years later Gerald Clarke's account of Capote's life was welcomed by reviewer Molly Haskell as an "enthralling, novel-like biography,"[63] while Capote's Aunt Rudisill damned it as "a scandal, a disgrace, and a pack of lies from beginning to end."[64] They might both be right, of course, though Marie Rudisill's objectivity is suspect, judging by her own often implausible account of Capote's early years in *Truman Capote: The Story of His Bizarre and Exotic Boyhood*.

Haskell continued, in her approval of Clarke's biography, to say,

> How Capote went from an enchanter, the startling fresh voice in his first novel, *Other Voices, Other Rooms,* to someone you wanted to hold away from you with a pair of tongs is an amazing story. In this work of prodigious research gracefully presented, Mr. Clarke, who had his subject's confidence during the last years, gives Capote what the writer himself, in a last grand, gutsy gesture, declared he wanted: a book in which nothing, nothing at all was left out.[65]

But was Capote's grand gesture inherited from his showman father, Arch Persons? Perhaps Capote had the last mocking laugh after all, gleefully lying his way to the end and conning all of us. Capote's aunt Mary Ida Carter supports this view, saying, "Truman is a marvel with words, but he can't stick to the truth."[66] His aunt Marie Rudisill vehemently agreed.

Marie Rudisill

Rudisill herself had a chance to steer Clarke right, but, "I told him straight up and down I wouldn't help him. What he was trying to do was write an *Answered Prayers* himself."[67] She told me she was correcting all the mistakes and outright lies in Clarke's biography and giving the annotated copy to the New York Public Library. But Rudisill herself is a shaky source. In describing Capote's early years, she claims to remember verbatim long conversations that occurred fifty years before and precisely what she had for lunch twenty years before. So I questioned her about it.*

---

*Interview with Marie Rudisill, January 17, 1988.

"In your account of Truman's boyhood you remembered exactly what you had for lunch on the day of your sister's—Truman's mother's—funeral. And detailed conversations with your black servants. Did you keep notes, or a diary?"

"I don't see any problem to remembering things like that."

"This is from your account: 'Lillie Mae [Capote's mother, Rudisill's sister] took no interest whatsoever in Truman. She hardly noticed him when he was around. One day Truman went back to the kitchen to find Sook [his beloved older cousin]. Instead he overheard his mother talking to Little Bit [a black maid] about him—"I know it's contemptible of me, Little Bit, but I can't stand the sight of my son, not because he is my child but because he is not my child." Truman stood outside the door listening. "That boy is so strange, so utterly strange," she went on. "He does not look or act like a normal boy. He's just like his father sometimes—little Miss Mouse Fart." ' "68

Marie conceded she had written that and, I asked: "How did you know that?"

"Because I was there, that's how I knew it. I was always there. I overheard the conversation."

"How do you remember the detailed dialogue between Arch Persons [then Capote's father-to-be] and your sister, when he was courting her in the 1920s?"

"Well, my lord, I have a very good mind. I mean, a very good mind. I remember anything I want to remember. I have a picture memory of everything in my life and I have a very keen memory."

"You say his mother was revolted when she discovered Truman was a homosexual."

"Well, naturally, I think any mother would be. But some get reconciled. She was never reconciled to that."69

Driving him one morning for what Capote thought was a trip to Manhattan (New York City), his mother admitted they were headed for a doctor's office for him to be "cured" of homosexuality through male-hormone injections. Incensed, Capote accused her of sleeping with the doctor. She pulled up at the side of the road and slapped his face. He then threatened to break her nose if she ever did that again or tried to change him. They turned around and drove back home. At least, that's what Capote told his biographer, Gerald Clarke, some fifty years after the event and with the only other witness dead. But Clarke had evidence from other sources that Lillie Mae disliked and feared Capote's homosexuality. Joe Capote, Truman's stepfather, confirmed that she had taken Truman to some doctors for such treatment. So Clarke printed Capote's version, without comment, and let readers judge its authenticity.

Clarke also quoted Capote as saying about the mother of his neighbor and friend, Harper Lee:

> her mind was not altogether right. . . . She wandered up and down the street saying strange things to neighbors and passers-by, and twice she tried to drown Harper in the bathtub. Both times Nelle [Harper Lee's first name] was saved by one of her older sisters.[70]

Marie Rudisill had already disputed this story in an interview before I questioned her. "You know good and well she never tried to drown Harper Lee in the bathtub," Rudisill had scoffed. "Mrs. Lee was the most delicate of all people, a very accomplished musician and an elegant lady."[71]

Alice Lee

Rudisill was hardly an authority on what happened in the Lee family's bathroom. The supposed victim, Harper Lee, wasn't willing to talk. [She later wrote me.] So I asked her sister Alice, an attorney in Monroeville, Alabama, if the story was accurate.*

"Clarke wrote that your mother twice tried to drown your sister Harper."

"I know it, but that is a lie."

"What about Clarke writing about your mother: 'Her mind was not altogether right. She wandered up and down the street saying strange things to neighbors and passersby'?"

"Pure fantasy."

"Capote told me that as a child he briefly ran away from home with a girl named Martha Beck, who was visiting your area. She grew up to be one of the two 'Lonely Heart' killers and was electrocuted in Sing Sing."

"They ran away and got over to a little town about thirty miles from here and then came back. That was when he was a little fellow, very small."

"Then Capote's account about that is essentially true. Did he then make up the story about your mother?"

"It is not true, so I would have to assume he made it up."

"How truthful was the book about Truman by his aunt, Marie Rudisill?"

(Long pause.) "I'd rather not say."

"Is it possible that when they were children, Harper's response to Truman's tall stories was to impress or shock him in return by making up the story of her mother twice trying to drown her in the bathtub?"

"Not at all. Truman's whole life has been spent in a world of fantasy, and he had great difficulties in sorting out, within his own mind, fact from fiction. And that was the story of his life."

"In Marie Rudisill's account of Capote's life what did you think of her picture of her sister, his mother, as a woman who drank heavily and had many affairs?"

---

*Interviews with Alice Lee, September 15, 1989, and June 6, 1994.

(She chuckled.) "All of that business about her and her Indian lover was just absolutely existing in somebody's imagination."

"Couldn't it have happened without you knowing?"

"Well, when Lillie Mae was here she was right next door. I was quite aware of her comings and goings, sir."

"According to Rudisill, Lillie Mae used to go out secretly to meet him in the woods."

"Well, Mr. Brian, the names Mrs. Rudisill used in that book were not exactly names in many instances of people here, but a very crude take-off on the names of actual people. You remember the Indian lover was supposed to be named Waterford? Well, we had a very prominent family in this county, who were eminently Indian in their background, named Weatherford. But there was nobody in the family who would have even fallen into the category of Lillie Mae's Indian lover. There's a great deal of fiction in that book."

"Does Mrs. Rudisill have the same facility for fiction as her nephew Truman."

"We'll say it runs in the family."

"Some explain his behavior by pointing to his tragic childhood."

"That is fantasy, too."

"Didn't his mother hate his homosexuality?"

"She probably deplored it. But the picture that's been given of Truman's childhood, of this poor, abandoned little boy who was left to sink or swim with the elderly people, isn't so. Truman was a very beloved child in the family circle and a very indulged child, overindulged. Anything he wanted could be his, that sort of childhood."

"Didn't his father desert him?"

"I wouldn't say his father deserted him. Have you ever known anybody that maybe should not have been a father or mother? A man who was not particularly paternal, or a mother who was not particularly maternal? Truman's father was the kind of man, one step ahead of the law, that I don't think would ever know what to do with a child. As long as I knew Joe Capote, Truman's stepfather, he was very devoted to his stepson and extremely helpful to him. Joe was a fine person."

"What did your sister, Harper, think of Truman?"

"They had been friends from early childhood and she would never have done or said anything to offend him in any way."

"And you?"

"I thought a great deal of him. His mother was a very dear friend of mine and I've been friends of the whole family for years and years and years."[72]

Clarke's Rebuttal

"I don't think Truman's account of Mrs. Lee trying to drown Harper is a fabrication," Gerald Clarke told me.* "People in Monroeville will tell you about it, if they remember, or if they are honest. She was a very strange woman. They will basically confirm what I said. Truman was the source of her trying to drown Harper. The rest about her being strange came from other people. I don't think it's too hard to see why Alice and Harper Lee would want their memories of their mother to be of a different nature."[73]

If Marie Rudisill thought Clarke's picture of Capote was scandalous and riddled with lies, I wondered what he thought of hers.

"Even Harper Lee says it's fictional," he replied. "And it is. I have a galley of her book. She took out some of the mistakes, but she sure didn't take out all of them. I'm sorry the Lee sisters don't like certain things I wrote. Mrs. Rudisill I don't

---

*Interview with Gerald Clarke, October 26, 1989.

care about. I feel sorry for the Lees and I'm sorry if I gave them pain. All this happened sixty years or more ago, but people still feel things very strongly, and I can understand that. I felt I had to put in the bit about the mother because of Harper Lee. She said to other people as well as to me that her childhood was an anguished one, just as Truman's was. That's one of the things that drew them together, besides living so close. If Harper Lee had come from an apple-pie, all-American family there would not have been much sense why there had been all that anguish."[74]

Alice Lee Responds

Alice Lee welcomed my additional questions,* saying, "I wished that somewhere down the line somebody would be interested enough to write the truth about Truman's childhood. I'm sure Capote's mother was loving to him as a child. I never saw any indication in his childhood that she rejected him in any way. And my sister [Harper] was very interested that you wanted to check that story about my mother."

When I read Gerald Clarke's response to her, she said: "He's entitled to his opinion, but I can't in my wildest dreams imagine who in Monroeville said those things about my family."

"Did Harper have an anguished childhood?"

"No."

"Clarke said she told him she did."

I laughed. She laughed.

"Did she have a blissfully happy childhood?"

"As far as I know, and I only lived in the house with her."

"I think as you do that Capote was a great storyteller with a terrific imagination, but I also think Clarke is honest. I don't

*Interview with Alice Lee, November 10, 1989.

think he would have said your sister told him she had an anguished childhood if she hadn't said so."

"Well, I'll be glad to enquire of my sister if she ever said anything like that, but I'd be very surprised if she did."

"As I have the feeling she'll agree with you, that she didn't talk of an anguished childhood, could you ask her to speculate? Why does she think he got that misimpression, why might he have misunderstood?"

"All right."

"Was your mother slightly eccentric, as Clarke says?"

"I never thought of her as being eccentric, sir. I don't think any of my mother's friends, or any of her generation, thought she was any different from anybody else as far as eccentricities were concerned."[75]

I again spoke with Alice Lee on August 23, 1993. She said: "My sister can recall vividly what transpired. You probably know she does not like publicity. Well, her friend Truman Capote asked her to lunch when he'd gotten in hot water over his high-society friends, the *Answered Prayers* episode. When she met him for lunch, she was horrified to find he had photographers and reporters there. The first thing that Truman opened up to tell her was that Babe Paley would not speak to him. Then she and Truman discussed the loneliness of childhood, because there were no other small children in the neighborhood. We lived in a neighborhood of elderly people whose families had long since left home. And she spoke of the anguish of loneliness. And Mr. Clarke applied the anguish to her whole childhood. This is typical of why she doesn't like to talk to reporters: they always take what is said like they want to take it, not like it is said. I would like to know who, other than Truman or one of his demented relatives, ever made that statement about my mother. Truman lived in a world of fantasy and apparently Clarke made no attempt to distinguish fantasy from fact."

"He had a hard job because his main source was Truman

himself. As a lawyer you must know how witnesses tell very different stories."

"My sister finds this statement that our mother tried to drown her very abhorrent. None of us ever heard the story until we read it in Clarke's book, so it was something of a shock. I can't find where he would have gotten any confirmation from people in Monroeville to such a thing."

"He doesn't name them."

"Of course he doesn't. He hasn't got any."[76]

Novelist Harper Lee

Finally, Harper Lee wrote to me: "One of Truman's sickest lies was my gentle mother's reward for having loved him. Mr. Clarke's account of Truman's early childhood in Monroeville is the weakest part of the biography. He relied far too much on the word of one of Truman's aunts, Mary Ida Carter, for information that he obviously did not check. Mrs. Carter and other members of her family were never notorious for truth-telling. They were/are capable of telling the truth when it serves their purpose, but preferred/prefer to deal in fantasy, which, I suppose, served/serves to bolster their sense of self-importance and bring color to their feckless lives. Truman was one of those rare examples of heredity over environment; he got it from both sides hot and heavy: from his father, who may best be described as an unsuccessful entrepreneur, and from his mother's people, some of whose works of fiction (they call them "memoirs") are available on remainder discount bookshops. The difference between Truman and his relatives is that Truman was gifted and did not need the help of collaborators to write a clear English sentence. "Anguish": You see how a poor choice of one word can result in a whole childhood of anguish (especially when a biographer is straining to prove a point). I don't recall having discussed "anguish" with Mr. Clarke. I remember that I was quoted in a *People* magazine interview years ago in which I said something to the effect that Truman and I shared a common anguish. What I was thinking of was that we were simply lonely. In our early childhood, we were the only children in the neighborhood. Truman was a year and six months older than I, which made him much closer in age to me than I was to my brother, who was five years and six months older. (In childhood, that's a great difference in age!) I was lonely when Truman was away, because there was nobody else to play with. What my sister says about us, and about everything else, is absolutely on target. My sister, by the way, does not lie and does not seek shelter from painful facts. (Mr. Clarke would probably have discovered this had he wished to, by asking her to verify Truman's story.) As to my-mother-tried-to-drown-me nonsense, I'd like to know who will "basically confirm" my mother's trying to drown me! Mr. Clarke missed something that should have been a dead giveaway (if you'll pardon the expression in these circumstances!) if he had known Truman as I did. You will note that my mother was supposed to have tried twice to drown me; much later, on page 287 of the Simon & Schuster hardcover version of *CAPOTE,* we find Truman saying, "Twice I saved her when she tried to kill herself. . . ." This is in reference to Babe Paley (and which I don't believe for an instant. For what it's worth, I was acquainted with Babe Paley, and was closely acquainted with two members of her family, and I think I'd have heard at least some echoes of it along the way.) *Once* wasn't good enough for a Truman story: my mother had to try twice, and poor Babe had to try twice. Truman was ever the one to embellish his own lies!"[77]

Columnist Liz Smith*

"He was a real poet and a real artist. And tormented, the way a lot of great artists have been, from Rimbaud to Oscar Wilde and Proust. A desperately unhappy, insecure person and this manifested itself in this intense braggadocio and his acceptance by a certain social group—who lived to regret it. And then, he began at the end of his life to say absolutely anything, whether it was true or not. I think when he sat with me and told me stories of Jackie Onassis and Lee Radziwill or Babe Paley he would always be in a fantasy. The greatest manifestation of this was when he was very anti–Jackie Onassis and very pro–Lee. And my impression was he somehow wanted to be Lee. He wanted to be a beautiful woman. He wanted to be Mrs. Paley. He adored the ground Mrs. Paley walked on. And he got himself all mixed up. Society punished him when he published his thinly disguised stories about them. I had a lot to do with Truman after that because he was really shunned by everybody. But not by me, because I didn't care. I wasn't social. And I was interested in him, and he was a fabulous source of information. But you had to be real careful. He would just get the germ of something, but you could never take his word for it. And, in the end, he had his heart thoroughly broken by Lee Radziwill who turned on him and refused to give a deposition for him in this lawsuit by Gore Vidal. He entreated me to call her to give the deposition. Now he was a man who had given her her greatest acting chance by writing *Laura* [television version] for her and forcing David Susskind to take her. She wasn't even an actress, but Truman was determined to make her a star. He would have done anything for her. He was absolutely in love with her in this kind of insane transference. And she said, 'I don't really care, Liz. I'm not going

---

*Interview with Liz Smith, March 1, 1994.

to testify. After all, they're just a couple of fags.' I wasn't going to repeat that to him but Truman wouldn't rest. He forced me to say why she wouldn't do it. I told him finally. I thought there's no point in him going on thinking this woman is his friend. Boy, I lived to regret that. He went crazy. He behaved so badly he almost self-destructed. And then he began to go on the air and be drunk and take drugs and nobody knew what he was talking about. Meanwhile he was falling in love with a plumber or someone. All just very sad. I was once in a room with several people and he came and said, 'Do you ever do cocaine?' And we all said, 'No.' And he came back with this mound of white powder and looked at us and said, 'Oh, no. It would be wasted on you.' Which was true. Then he took it away."[78]

Taping Truman

Clarke had a better chance than most to set the record straight with his tell-it-like-it-was note from Capote. But how about when Capote was the only living witness?

"When you write a biography," Clarke said,* "in my opinion you're required to adhere to a law of probability. It struck me, for example, that Truman's supposed affair with Errol Flynn was inherently *improbable*. When Truman told me about it in the mid 1970s, I thought of Flynn as a man I had seen on the screen, a great swashbuckling movie hero famous for womanizing. But subsequently there were two biographies, one of Flynn and one of Tyrone Power, which pretty conclusively showed that they had an affair, and that Flynn had affairs with other fellows. Now that doesn't prove that Truman had an affair with Flynn, but it certainly gives it more probability. When

---

*Interview with Gerald Clarke, October 26, 1989.

certain people who had known Flynn hooted about this when I suggested it before I finished the biography, they were thinking of Truman at that time when he was middle-aged, rather unappealing and fat. But if you put him back in 1947 when he would have been twenty-two, it seems much more plausible, which isn't proof beyond a shadow of doubt. Though it's not something I'd hoot at now; whereas I did hoot at the time."

"How did you know Capote was telling you the truth?"

"His reputation for lying was somewhat exaggerated. I've interviewed an awful lot of writers and they do tend to exaggerate and to make things up. That's really part of their job."

"Even biographers?"

"I'm not sure Truman was a whole lot worse than a lot of other people. He had a remarkable memory and would tell me stories that were so amazing I couldn't believe them. And they would turn out to be *absolutely true,* as I later discovered from talking to others who were at the place, or from reading diaries or memoirs that subsequently came out. Truman had told me the *exact* truth and he'd even got the color of the flowers in the room right. On the other hand, he could make up things and sometimes stories that were not extraordinary, that you wouldn't even begin to question because they sounded so ordinary. So I checked everything as best I could by interviewing an awful lot of people and by triangulation [to get information from at least three sources]."

"Did you ever challenge him when you found him out?"

"I did confront him several times. It took me so long to do the book I would index everything. So he would tell me one story, for instance, and I would write it down, and a few months or even years later he'd tell me the same story in a different way. Then I had the advantage of knowing him and having him there. I'd say, 'Look, Truman, you've told me these two stories. Which one is right?' Sometimes it was quite innocent—people misremember. And this would jog his memory and he'd tell me what I was pretty sure was the right story. Other times he would make something up. For instance, not long before he died—we lived about two miles from each other on Long Island—and he would stop by and we'd have lunch. Sometimes every day for a week, or four or five days. And sometimes when he had lunch with others, he would stop by my house afterwards. One time he came by my house after he'd been interviewed by Lawrence Grobel for *Playboy,* and he told me a story he had just told Grobel. And I said, 'Truman, that sounds very interesting. Why didn't you tell *me* that?' I became rather jealous. And he said, 'Well, you always look at me as if you don't believe me.' And I said, 'Well, I don't always believe you because you don't always tell me the truth.' I then reminded him of the two stories he had told me about how he met Babe Paley (a great figure in his life, the wife of Bill Paley, the head of CBS) and asked, 'Which one is right?' And he said, 'The second one.' I said, 'That's right.' After hearing the first story, I spoke to someone quite reliable who had been at the meeting and they told me the second version was right. The true account which I have in the book is a wonderful story. [Capote was with the Selznicks of Hollywood fame when the Paleys phoned to invite the Selznicks to be their guests, and to bring Truman with them—it would be an honor—under the misapprehension that Truman was President Truman.] The untrue story was rather humdrum: that he had met her in the ordinary course of events in New York."

"In your book [John] O'Shea reveals himself in a very poor light. Any idea why he was so frank with you?"

"Yes, to a degree. He told me that he'd had a heart attack in the early '80s and he'd rethought his life, and believed he might as well tell the truth. Also, he was annoyed that the rest of his family had talked to me and got their sides of the story out, and he might as well do the same. Although he didn't come out terribly well in the book, I feel some sympathy for him and think most readers would. He's not altogether bad. You have to feel some sympathy for this guy who's lower-middle-class and has been yanked out of that life to another life entirely, and then left kind of stranded."

"I was thinking of how he broke Capote's nose and rib."

"Of course I don't sympathize with O'Shea about that. And, of course, Truman was probably drunk at the time."

"Did you give Capote any advice after O'Shea beat him up? Like 'Get the hell out of there!'?"

"Sure. I'm not sure when he was beaten up. But all the time he would come to me, and I'm in the book as the friend to whom he showed letters. He showed me letters, for instance, after one of their breakups, that seemed quite transparent. It would have to, to you or to anyone else who saw it. O'Shea was broke and he wanted to get back together with Truman because he was broke. I told Truman that, and I told him many times that this was a bad relationship for both of them. Capote wanted to believe that O'Shea's motive was not money, but love or at least affection. So that's how he misread the letter. He once told me he was aware of his tendency for self-deception in personal relationships."

"Why did Capote hire people to harass and intimidate O'Shea? To get rid of him or for revenge?"

"It's extraordinarily complicated. I think it was to get O'Shea back, not to break up with him. A bit of both. He did it several times over a period of years. Truman's motives may have been different one time from another. A couple of times, I think, it was to scare him into returning."

"Why did Capote turn against Jacqueline Kennedy and vice versa?"

"Because she resented his indiscretions, I guess. She was a very discreet woman and didn't want Truman chatting about her private life. He really fell in love with Lee Radziwill, and the two sisters had a famous friendly-nonfriendly relationship.

A great rivalry. And Truman took Lee's side very strongly. From what I gather Lee was obsessed with her sister. I don't think Jackie was as obsessed with Lee. After all, she had come out on top."

"What was Capote's evidence for Joseph Kennedy, Sr., raping a young woman?"

"It was a reliable source. I don't think it was an absolute rape, though. She could have screamed and shouted, and didn't."

"Why did he expect his friends to understand his motives for writing *Answered Prayers*?"

"He thought they should have understood. He was a writer. He was just doing what Proust had done. His reasons were contradictory. He said they were too dumb to recognize themselves, but he obviously knew a woman like Slim Keith and a man like Bill Paley were not stupid people; otherwise he wouldn't have been with them all those years. Clearly he knew they'd recognize themselves and he wanted them to."

"Do you think his rewriting Flaubert's *The Legend of Saint Julien* was because he took it as a metaphor for his own life and an attempt to make amends to those he had loved and then, in a sense, destroyed?"

"No. He knew that he was coming close to the end and he probably wanted there to be a God, and that there would be a happy ending. I don't think he did destroy anybody's life, first of all."[79]

Despite Clarke's disclaimer, *Answered Prayers* may have killed Ann Woodward, who had once called Capote "a fag." In his biography of Capote, Clarke wrote that in 1955 Ann Woodward, a showgirl, fatally shot her wealthy husband and persuaded a jury she had mistaken him for a prowler. In Capote's *Answered Prayers,* in which she is transparently "Ann Hopkins," she murdered him. After reading it, the already depressed Ann Woodward took a fatal dose of Seconal. It was the same drug Capote's mother used to kill herself.

"Capote certainly made Barbara Paley miserable."

"He made her unhappy for a while. It wasn't the happiest event in her life, but it certainly did not destroy her life. I think he knew he had destroyed himself. I don't think he thought he had destroyed anybody else. He never thought he had turned against Babe Paley, for instance. He thought he was helping her."

"By revealing she had a rotten husband who should have treated her better?"

"Yes."

"But Capote was intelligent and knew how she had reacted to that revelation."

"But he didn't know how she *would* react. People of intelligence can sometimes do extremely unintelligent things. Truman was extraordinarily intelligent, intuitive, and feeling, and yet he could do quite unintelligent things, as the publication of 'La Cote Basque' demonstrated. ["La Cote Basque, 1965," the first installment of *Answered Prayers,* was published in *Esquire* magazine in November 1975.] I among others told him they would be very upset about it."[80]

In Cold Blood Revisited

Capote told Haskell Frankel in 1966:

> I traveled all over the country and to all of the places that appear in the book, all those motels where the boys [the killers] stayed, all those sordid motels and hotels in Acapulco and Miami. And I wrote 6,000 pages of notes before I ever sat down to write the book. . . . It took me two years of constantly writing to Dr. Johnson [the killers' psychiatrist] before he finally gave me these things they [Smith and Hickock] had written [their autobiographies].[81]

He had a chance to tell the truth when George Plimpton said to him, "with the nonfiction novel I suppose the temptation to fictionalize events, or a line of dialogue, for example, must be overwhelming." Then he asked: "With *In Cold Blood,* was there any invention of this sort?" To which Capote answered, "No. . . . One doesn't spend almost six years on a book and then give way to minor distortions."[82] Then he made a strange admission, telling Plimpton he had enough source material to fill a room to the ceiling, which he intended to burn, because "I don't want people poking around the material of six years of work and research."[83] Why not? Four years later, in 1976, he told Beverly Gary Kempton, "*In Cold Blood* was pure journalism; every word of it was true."[84] And in case there was any doubt, in 1980 he informed Charles Ruas, "I didn't do [*In Cold Blood*] as fiction at all, I did it as pure factual writing."[85]

But it wasn't true.

Biographer Clarke learned that the book's ending in which detective Dewey and Nancy Kidwell meet and chat in the cemetery was not a small blunder, but an episode that never took place—except in Capote's imagination. Capote wrote it to provide a touching, sunspeckled, springtime finish, rather than end with dangling murderers. Life rather than death. The two pages are simple, direct, moving—and fabricated.

What else was fiction? Little of consequence, said Clarke, who checked with several people in the Holcomb and Garden City area. However, Clarke did not question prosecuting attorney Duane West, who complained to me:* "Capote took license with the facts of the trial, taking my closing remarks and attributing them to some other counsel. So when he does something like that and attempts to make a hero of Mr. Dewey, who was not a hero of the piece at all, why should I doubt that he'd misquote someone else or several others? I don't think

---

*Interview with Duane West, December 10, 1989.

Mr. Capote had any scruples." West also scoffed at Capote's proclaimed modus operandi, relying on a phenomenal memory rather than note-taking on the spot: "Of course, this reportage [Capote's claim to have a phenomenal memory] . . . that's a laugh. Capote didn't take notes, but Harper Lee was right along with him and she took notes. She was out there every time he was. I call his reportage 'garbage.'

"Capote made Dewey the hero of the book and he wasn't even in town when the murders occurred. Mr. Rohleder [Garden City's police chief] did the initial investigation on which the conviction was based. He took photographs with the flashlight shining across the surface which brought out the footprints on the mattress-box cover, and they were the basis for our convictions. A book can be misleading by what it leaves out as by what it puts in. But Rohleder didn't complain about Truman's account [in which Rohleder is quickly dismissed as 'a police photographer' and given one brief paragraph, while Dewey plays a leading role and gets scores of pages]. He chuckled about it, and that's the way it was with me. Rohleder's photographs of the bloody footprints proved those guys did the killings.

"The funny thing was, when we got this report out of the pen that this guy [convict Floyd Wells] claimed to know something about the murders, Dewey said, 'Ah, those guys are always making claims like that. I don't believe it's so.' So, instead of sending Dewey up to talk to Wells, Logan Sanford, the chief of the Kansas Bureau of Investigation [KBI], sent Clarence Duntz. He came back and said, 'Hey, I think this guy [Wells] has got the straight skinny. This is the story he told and I think it's true. We'd better check it out.' Dewey just poopoohed the whole thing. So Harold Nye and Roy Church, KBI agents, were sent to investigate and when they went back east they found that Hickock and Smith had spread all these rubber checks around, and that they had been here. So we got a warrant to search Hickock's parents' home, and came up with a shotgun and a knife. I handled all the evidence and sent it to the FBI. I have seven or eight letters in my file from J. Edgar Hoover. The knife had blood on it that matched Mr. Clutter's blood, and shells we recovered up on the county line had been fired from that shotgun. So there was no question that was the murder weapon, and that's what brought the convictions.

"Floyd Wells was the convict who testified that he had told Hickock and Smith [who were then in prison with him] that Clutter had money in the house. And Wells said he had heard the two planning the robbery and the murders. That was the tragic, ironic thing: Because Clutter never did have cash. He'd write you a fifty-cent check for a fifty-cent item."

"You remember it well."

"Well, my friend, when you go through that kind of a meatgrinder you don't forget. It's just like it was yesterday to me."

When I asked West why I should believe him rather than Capote, he said, "My word, as far as I am concerned, is a lot better than Capote's. I'm not an alcoholic, drug-addicted degenerate." But he did exonerate Capote from Tynan's charge that Truman betrayed the murderers by withholding the letter Hickock wrote him claiming that the killings had not been premeditated.

It wouldn't have helped, said West. "Under Kansas law [then] if a murder is committed in commission of a felony then it's first-degree murder, and the penalty can only be death. Now [December 1989], unfortunately, we don't have a death penalty."[87] The death penalty was restored in Kansas in 1994.

Two others disputed Capote's accuracy: the undersheriff at the Finney County Jail, Wendle Meier, and his wife, Josephine. Mrs. Meier denied she had ever said of Perry Smith that "he wasn't the worst young man I ever saw," denied she had ever seen him cry, or that he ever held her hand and said, "I'm embraced by shame," all of which Capote had published as facts in *In Cold Blood*. Wendle Meier confirmed that his wife had been misquoted, so I asked him how he could explain it.*

He said: "He made up a hell of a lot of stuff that's not true."

"Did he misquote you?"

"Yes. We got so misquoted we don't even care to talk to anybody about it."[88]

Confronted with this criticism, Capote told me:† "What I wrote in the book was true. It was absolutely accurate. Mrs. Meier turned against me, and Duane West is one of my bitterest enemies. And they were sort of working tooth and tong."[89]

To which Duane West responded:** "I didn't know he was such a paranoid little fellow. It makes me truly sad. I don't really like for anybody to think I'm a terrible enemy. I don't really harbor hate in my heart towards anybody."[90]

Handcarved Coffins: An Autopsy

Capote told Clarke he had changed all the names except his own in *Handcarved Coffins* because he "had been burned by libel problems with Vidal and others." Clarke told me,†† "Truman wouldn't mention the state where the murders occurred although I found out it was Nebraska. He wouldn't give me the real names of the people. But much of it was true: I found that out independently. At least, the kernel was true."[91]

If so, it's a hard nut to crack.

"It's strange," I suggested to Clarke, "that no crime reporter got on to the case. Surely it would rank as one of the crimes of the century."

---

*Interview with Wendle Meier, September 10, 1970.

†Interview with Truman Capote, September 25, 1970.

**Interview with Duane West, October 25, 1970.

††Interview with Gerald Clarke, November 2, 1989.

My guess is that the story is a mix of accounts of crimes Capote heard from the scores of murderers he interviewed. His own traumatic experience as a child of being bitten by a snake may have sparked that horrific rattlesnakes episode, colored by details of a 1935 murder in Los Angeles. (Didn't someone notice Capote had a collection of *True Crime* magazines?) In that murder the killer had been five-time married barber Robert James, who had insured the life of his fifth wife. He persuaded her to have an abortion for which she would need to be tied up and gagged. When she was immobilized he poisoned her with a rattlesnake. She survived the bite, so he drowned her. A previous wife had also died suspiciously, from drowning. This time he was found guilty of murder and executed.

Fiddling with the Facts?

His mother often accused him of lying, and she worried that he might have inherited Arch's inability to distinguish truth from falsehood. . . . It is impossible to know which of those tellers of tall tales, father or son, told more lies during their hours together, but the honor probably belongs to Truman.
—Gerald Clarke in *Capote*

He was always at heart his father's son, though instead of promoting an illusionist he promoted himself with zest and to spectacular effect. His writings usually spring from first- or secondhand experiences, which he then twists, as if handling a kaleidoscope, to stop at the most scintillating scenes, and then plays around with it in his mind. Or, like a play doctor, he juggles lines to get the best response. But isn't that how most writers of both fiction and nonfiction work? Aiming for the most arresting effect? Adding a little spice here, and a little salt there? Shaping the narrative and sharpening the dialogue?

Except that, when a writer of fiction moves to fact, he is expected to turn in his poetic license—his license to lie. Capote clung to his. Starting his professional career sorting cartoons for the *New Yorker* and soon becoming famous through his fiction, Capote had no academic or on-the-job training as reporter, historian, or scientist that might have imbued him with the biographer's imperative not to deceive readers or fiddle with the facts.

Discussing his Brando interview, one of his last comments about it was

> I let Brando go on and on, talking and talking himself into the grave for eight solid hours. No notes, nothing. I went back and I typed the entire thing verbatim. Then I spent two months cutting it, shaping it into what it was, into what he could never forgive.[92]

This was probably the first and only eight-hour interview in which not a word was recorded on the spot.

Before the early chapters of *Answered Prayers* were published in *Esquire,* Capote told me, "I personally don't care what anyone writes about me, so I'd just as soon that whole right was given to me."

I missed the chance to ask him to elaborate and am left wondering: Did he want to lie about others with impunity? Was he expressing approval of some Italians, for example, who enthusiastically greet an anecdote with *Se non e vero e ben trovato!* ("It may not be true but it's a great story!")? Or was he after a free hand to tell what he believed to be true, without the likes of Gore Vidal suing him for libel? He made a good point when he said,* "All art is artificial. Any artist distorts what he touches. You can't take actual life and make it into art. It's

---

*Interview with Truman Capote, September 18, 1970.

impossible. Even given the most careful documentary kind of writing or filming, it's impossible, because by the very nature of what you're doing, framing something, it turns into art."[93]

Impossible, yes, but doesn't biography attempt the impossible? Capote failed to distinguish between a frame and a frame-up, or consciously flouted the facts in favor of artifice. His natural heirs are the creators of television's oxymoronic docudramas, in which the scenery, situations, and even some words may be authentic or fair copies, yet much is deliberately distorted, disguised, or invented. Fact and fiction intermingle and only the writers know for sure which is which. It is impossible to tell how much of *In Cold Blood* is docudrama, because most of the players are dead.

At times, Capote doubtless deceived himself. For instance, when I asked how he had been able to report the murderers' thoughts, he said,* "Because that is what they told me they had been thinking at the time." And he discounted my suggestion that they might not have told him the truth, or had imperfect memories. He claimed to have a way of detecting liars. "I've often noticed you can tell a liar by looking him or her in the eye," he said. "When you get right down to the hard ground with them, their eyes will start shifting. Shifty eyes. [He chuckled.] It's an old phrase."[94]

Or an old wives' tale, but on the other hand, he admitted,† "I'm very gullible personally, in a purely social way. I really and truly believe what people tell me. If they say something to me, I just take it automatically and believe it. Then, when it's something important [and he'd been deceived] I get a real sinking feeling."[95] He stressed that this occurred only in his personal life, never in his work when he carefully examined what he was told. But he did not explain how he "carefully"

---

*Interview with Truman Capote, September 25, 1970.
†Interview with Truman Capote, September 18, 1970.

examined what the murderers told him they had been thinking. I regret I didn't ask. He might have said, I suppose, you occasionally have to accept some things on faith—or that they weren't shifty-eyed.

A large part of his claim to have brought off a great and unique coup in *In Cold Blood* was that in it he had put into practice his theory "that a factual piece of work could explore whole new dimensions of writing that would have a double effect fiction does not have—the very fact of its being true, every word of it true, would add a double contribution of strength and impact."[96] He had been leading up to this experiment in authenticity, he said, with *Porgy and Bess,* his account, in *The Muses Are Heard,* of an American opera company in Russia, and his profile of Brando. But *In Cold Blood* was the ultimate achievement: the perfect, pristine prototype. And he stuck doggedly to that proud boast.

For the Record

This brings me back to the time when Capote said to me with a laugh,* "Ask Gore Vidal what he thinks of me and that's exactly what I think of him."[97]

I asked Vidal,† who said: "Truman Capote is a pathological liar. You can't believe a word he says. Not even when he tells you what he had for breakfast."[98]

Capote made no death-bed confession, but once he said he wanted the private journals he had written since 1943 kept secret for 150 years. Who was he protecting? If they exist, maybe he tells all in the journals. Will they confound or confirm Vidal's view of him as a pathological liar, or Clarke's more benign

---

*Interview with Truman Capote, September 18, 1970.
†Interview with Gore Vidal, September 30, 1970.

view that he wasn't much worse than other writers? I'd put him hovering somewhere between these two views, swooping at times, happily, from fact to fancy, like the buzzard he hoped to be if reincarnation was in the works.

I thought of him recently while browsing in Brentano's, when I was approached by a white yuppie couple, and a few days later in a local library, by an eight-year-old black girl. Both times I was asked the same question: "Does nonfiction mean it's true?" Soon after these two encounters I returned to the bookstore and noticed *In Cold Blood* was still going strong after a quarter of a century, but had been reprinted as "Signet *FICTION*," and stacked in the *fiction* section. Had they finally figured him out or were they, like me, "guilty of scavenging great works for small blunders"?

Telling it the way he *wanted* things to be was a temptation Truman Capote, at times, found irresistible. He was, above all, a creative artist. But there had been no need for him to have faked anything in his *In Cold Blood*. If he had lived up to what might be the biographer's equivalent of the Hippocratic oath—"I promise not to do intentional damage to the truth"—the book would still have been a triumph. Flawed as it is, *In Cold Blood* remains an enduring minor masterwork, his real *memento mori*.[99]

Notes

1. Joshua Logan, *Movie Stars, Real People, and Me* (New York: Delacorte, 1978), p. 106.

2. Truman Capote Collection, Library of Congress.

3. Interview with Truman Capote, September 18, 1970.

4. Logan, *Movie Stars, Real People, and Me,* p. 120.

5. Interview with Truman Capote, September 18, 1970.

6. Gerald Clarke, *Capote: A Biography* (New York: Simon & Schuster, 1988), p. 303. From Brando's letter to Capote.

7. Interview with Truman Capote, September 18, 1970.

8. Ibid.

9. Ibid.

10. Interview with Malcolm Cowley, June 29, 1980.

11. Interview with Truman Capote, September 25, 1970.

12. Clarke, *Capote: A Biography,* p. 352.

13. For Kenneth Tynan's attack, Capote's response, and Tynan's counterattack, see *New York Herald Tribune,* April 3, 1966, pp. 20–21.

14. Mary Connelly, "The Truman Capote You Ought to Know," *New York Journal-American,* February 28, 1966, p. 4. Harper Lee, an attorney's daughter, wrote the novel *To Kill a Mockingbird.*

15. Interview with Truman Capote, September 18, 1970.

16. Ibid. Capote remarked that the scores of murderers he interviewed on Death Row invariably laughed when discussing their crimes.

17. It was translated into twenty-five languages, including Hebrew, Afrikaans, and Icelandic. It earned him three million dollars, half a million of which came from the movie rights.

18. Interview with Alice Lee, August 23, 1993.

19. Truman Capote Collection, Library of Congress.

20. Clarke, *Capote: A Biography,* p. 346.

21. Interview with Truman Capote, September 25, 1970.

22. From Lee Radziwill's February 6, 1976, letter to Gerald Clarke, *Capote: A Biography,* p. 382.

23. Interview with Gore Vidal, September 30, 1970.

24. Ibid.

25. Interview with Arthur Schlesinger, Jr., March 26, 1994.

26. Arthur Schlesinger, Jr., *Robert Kennedy and His Times* (New York: Ballantine, 1978), pp. 641–42.

27. Interview with Arthur Schlesinger, Jr., March 26, 1994.

28. Clarke, *Capote: A Biography,* p. 517.

29. Interview with Liz Smith, March 26, 1994.

30. Interview with Truman Capote, September 18, 1970.

31. Ibid.

32. Clarke, *Capote: A Biography,* p. 519.

33. Pat Hackett, ed., *The Andy Warhol Diaries* (New York: Warner, 1989), p. 222.

34. Ibid., p. 223.

35. Ibid., p. 224.

36. Interview with Truman Capote, September 18, 1970.

37. John Malcolm Brinnin, *Truman Capote: Dear Heart, Old Buddy* (New York: Delacorte, 1981), p. 119.

38. Truman Capote Collection, Library of Congress.

39. Ibid.

40. From Sally Hammond's interview with Bonnie Golightly, "A Word from the Girl Who Says Capote Took Her Name in Vain," *New York Post,* January 28, 1959, p. 58.

41. James Michener's foreword to Lawrence Grobel, *Conversations with Capote* (New York: New American Library, 1985), p. 4.

42. Ibid., p. 6.

43. Ibid., p. 11.

44. James A. Michener's letter to author, August 25, 1993, referring to the Joe McGinniss biography of Senator Edward Kennedy, *The Last Brother.* McGinniss is tackled in chapter 5 of this book.

45. Charles Trueheart, "Truman Capote's Table Talk," *Washington Post Book World,* September 20, 1987, pp. 1, 8.

46. Interview with Truman Capote, September 25, 1970.

47. Patricia Burstein, "Tiny yes, but a terror. Do not be fooled by Truman Capote in repose," *People* (May 10, 1976): 13, 14.

48. Tina Brown, "Goodbye to the Ladies Who Lunch," *New York Times Book Review,* September 13, 1987, p. 13.

49. Molly Haskell, "Unmourned Losses, Unsettled Claims," *New York Times Book Review,* June 12, 1988, p. 1.

50. Norman Mailer, *Advertisement for Myself* (New York: Putnam's, 1959), p. 427.

51. Brown, "Goodbye to the Ladies Who Lunch."

52. "*In Cold Blood* . . . An American Tragedy," *Newsweek* (January 24, 1966): 63.

53. Clarke, *Capote: A Biography,* p. 522.

54. Leslie Bennetts, quoting Gerald Clarke, *New York Times Book Review,* June 12, 1988, p. 30.

55. Burstein, "Tiny yes, but a terror." Capote said of *Answered Prayers*: "I was born to write that particular book. It is the only true thing I know about a certain level of American society. Nobody else could have written it—not one of them would have had the pure guts. I lived through it, backwards and forwards. The book means a lot to me. It means everything."

56. Interview with Gerald Clarke, January 6, 1990.

57. Ibid.

58. Walter Clemons, "Handcarved Capote," *Newsweek* (August 11, 1980): 70.

59. Charles Ruas, *Conversations with American Writers* (New York: Knopf, 1985), pp. 54–55.

60. *Andy Warhol Diaries,* p. 407.

61. Truman Capote, *Music for Chameleons* (New York: Random House, 1980), p. 261.

62. Julie Baumgold, "Capote: The Final Years—His Losing Battle with Drug Addiction," *Chicago Sun-Times,* November 25, 1984, p. 14 (excerpted from *New York Magazine*). The autopsy report is from Department of Chief Medical Examiner-Coroner, County of Los Angeles, September 13, 1984.

63. Haskell, "Unmourned Losses, Unsettled Claims."

64. Dannye Romine's interview with Marie Rudisill, "Capote's Aunt: New Biography 'Pack of Lies,' " *Charlotte Observer,* July 31, 1988, p. 9F.

65. Haskell, "Unmourned Losses, Unsettled Claims."

66. Dannye Romine's "Truth, Fiction in a Small Town," *Charlotte Observer,* July 31, 1977, p. 1F.

67. Ibid., p. 9F.

68. Interview with Marie Rudisill, January 17, 1988.

69. Ibid.

70. Clarke, *Capote: A Biography,* pp. 21, 22.

71. Romine, "Capote's Aunt."

72. Interviews with Alice Lee, September 15, 1989, and June 6, 1994.

73. Interview with Gerald Clarke, October 26, 1989.

74. Ibid.

75. Interview with Alice Lee, November 10, 1989.

76. Ibid., August 23, 1993.

77. Harper Lee, letter to author, March 9, 1994.

78. Interview with Liz Smith, March 1, 1994.

79. Interview with Gerald Clarke, October 26, 1989.

80. Ibid.

81. Haskell Frankel, *Saturday Review* (January 22, 1966): 36, 37.

82. George Plimpton, "The Story Behind a Nonfiction Novel," *New York Times Book Review,* January 16, 1966, p. 41.

83. Ibid., p. 43.

84. Beverly Gary Kempton, "A Candid Conversation with the Outspoken, Orchidaceous Author of *In Cold Blood; Breakfast at Tiffany's; Other Voices, Other Rooms,*" *Playboy* (March 1968), p. 51.

85. Ruas, *Conversations with American Writers,* p. 43.

86. Interview with Duane West, December 10, 1989.

87. Ibid.

88. Interview with Wendle Meier, September 10, 1970.

89. Interview with Truman Capote, September 25, 1970.

90. Interview with Duane West, October 25, 1970.

91. Interview with Gerald Clarke, November 2, 1989.

92. Ruas, *Conversations with American Writers,* p. 52.

93. Interview with Truman Capote, September 18, 1970.

94. Interview with Truman Capote, September 25, 1970.

95. Interview with Truman Capote, September 18, 1970.

96. Roy Newquist, *Counterpoint,* 1964.

97. Interview with Truman Capote, September 18, 1970.

98. Interview with Gore Vidal, September 30, 1970.

99. The concluding pages of *Answered Prayers* have not been found and may have been destroyed, mislaid, or, more likely, were never written.

2

Kitty Kelley Takes on Frank Sinatra, Jacqueline Onassis, Liz Taylor, and Nancy Reagan

Fans

Ovid Demaris: "I think she's a very thorough researcher and interviewer."

Joyce Haber: "This Kitty has the tenaciousness of a panther stalking its prey."

Foes

Nancy Sinatra: "I hope she gets hit by a truck."

Barbara Howar: "Somebody said to me, 'Do you want to do a piece on Kitty Kelley?' And I said, 'Not unless it's her obituary.' "

As a fledgling author Kitty Kelley was urged by her agent to go for the gold by writing what sells: sex, fat, and violence.

She had already done fat, squeezing all she could out of the subject in a book about the tricky ways of fat farms and their pudgy, gossip-gorging patrons. To do so Kelley had gone "undercover" as a client at a series of such establishments euphemistically called "glamour" rather than "blubber" spas. At one she shared a room with the divorced wife of U.S. Senator George Smathers, a buddy of John F. Kennedy. She emerged with a load of dirt about JFK, a disdainful view of other "jiggling pink blimps," and the knowledge that when Liza Minnelli, Barbra Streisand, Joan Kennedy, and Luci and Lynda Bird Johnson lose weight, they also shed their inhibitions.

Her spicy inside stories about the fat-farm follies first appeared in the *Washington Star-News*. Kelley then expanded it into a book titled *Glamour Spas*.

What next? She took her agent's advice and contemplated sex and violence. Kelley set her sights higher than the gruesome lives and dastardly deeds of anonymous freaks. Provide both sex and violence in a biography of a super-celebrity and you can guarantee almost an eternity on the best-seller lists. But what could she offer that had not already been explored in countless dissections of the reigning celebrities who aroused such insatiable curiosity that writers repeatedly tackled them? They were "revealed," "exposed, "brought vividly to life," and done to death, only to be resurrected a few months later.

How could she top these previous biographers? She would tread where others feared to tiptoe, turn over fresh ground and the subject's garbage, rifle FBI files, hire a private eye for muscular support, cajole and intimidate those in the know into "telling all," and when in doubt, lean on the First Amendment or its moral equivalent with something like "Isn't it important that truth be told?" On the track of "the truth" Kelley can make it almost un-American not to spill the beans.

And that's how she came to floodlight the lives of Jacqueline Onassis, Elizabeth Taylor, Frank Sinatra, and Nancy Reagan.

As Kelley's version of their lives and loves shot to the top of the charts, the subjects seen through Kelley's narrowed eyes tumbled from their pedestals like so many clay pigeons.

Now a semi-celebrity herself with a minipack of hyper fans, Kelley is lauded by some as a resourceful, probing, and entertaining equal of leading reporters and biographers, admired for her guts in taking on the powerful and not buckling under to threats. Even when critics taunted her as "the pit bull of unauthorized biography," and "the doyenne of dirt," she responded with breezy quips.[1] But being called a piranha stung her into denying she had a killer instinct: "I think it's a cheap shot for writers to go for the negative, but by the same token if there's something there, there is no way I would keep it out."[2] This is the creed, perhaps, of every responsible reporter, biographer, and historian in the Western world, but from Kelley it smacks of the disingenuous. With the subjects she chooses she knows there is always "something" there, attested to by previous researchers.

For someone probing so eagerly the mysteries and machinations of others, Kelley is strangely evasive about herself. Why, for example, did she suddenly quit the University of Arizona in 1962? She won't say. And why did she refuse to answer *any* questions repeatedly posed by her biographer, George Carpozi, Jr.?

What is known is that her father was a leading Spokane, Washington, attorney, and her mother a demanding, autocratic housewife who ended her days—as writer Gerri Hirshey discovered—as an alcoholic.

Kelley, the eldest of seven children (six girls and a boy), graduated at age twenty-three from the University of Washington, with a Bachelor of Arts degree in English and a teaching certificate. She turned her back on schoolrooms, however, to work as a hostess at the General Electric Progressland, an exhibit at the 1965 New York World's Fair.

This brought her face to face with Julie Andrews, Margaret Truman, and Jacqueline Kennedy. As she escorted these celebrities around the exhibition, Kelley noted little flaws that humanized them, or brought them down to earth, such as the run in Mrs. Kennedy's stocking.

After the fair closed, Kelley moved to Washington, D.C., where she worked the photocopying machine in Senator Eugene McCarthy's office and distributed his press releases. In 1969, after four years with McCarthy the *Washington Post* hired her as an editorial-page researcher, with Philip Geyelin as her immediate boss. She is remembered as being energetic, sparky, and outgoing. She was literally outgoing after two years. Kelley says she quit to freelance. Others say she was forced to leave.

Did she jump or was she pushed? And if pushed, why?

When I asked *Washington Post* editor Ben Bradlee, he advised me to "call Philip Geyelin. He's at S.A.I.S. [School of Advanced International Studies], the Johns Hopkins place."

Geyelin said Kelley was fired.* I told him she said she resigned.

"Oh well," he replied, "you can play with semantics all you want. I told her to resign."

"Because she was taking notes not related to her duties during editorial meetings?"

"That's right."

"As if she was collecting material for a biography?"

"It was self-evident that she was. I saw some of the notes. And some she said she had at her house. I asked her to bring them into the office. When she didn't, I asked her why not; and she said she had destroyed them. So my suspicions were redoubled."

"Was it your impression that she was going to write a biography of your publisher [Katharine Graham]?"

---

*Interview with Philip Geyelin, March 2, 1990.

"It seemed quite possible. A good many of the notes had to do with the things Mrs. Graham was saying at an editorial meeting. At a meeting of that kind you can't get people to argue unless the whole proceedings are confidential. Everybody understood that. There isn't any point in having one if you can't say what you think. And Mrs. Graham is somebody who generally says what she thinks. I couldn't detect this [what Kitty Kelley was doing during the editorial meeting] from where I sat, but somebody sitting next to Kitty Kelley noticed it. The purpose of her being there at all—she started as a secretary and was overqualified—was to do research and it seemed to me she could do it a lot more effectively if the designated writer could say to her, 'Could you pull the files on such-and-such?' And it would be more helpful if she was inside than out. But she was taking notes totally unrelated to that."

"You say she was overqualified to be a secretary. Wasn't she talented enough to be forgiven for the note taking?"

"No. Because it was obvious she was betraying confidences."

"So she *was* fired?"

"Ben Bradlee put it more scatalogically than that. I told her, 'I would like your resignation.' The option to stay was not left open. But not wishing to blight her career, I said: 'Just resign and that's the end of it.' "

"You must have sympathy for biographers, though. Aren't you writing a biography?"

"Yes. About King Hussein of Jordan. I told him: 'This is not going to be a Kitty Kelley book.' I don't know if he got it."[3]

Betrayal or Revelation?

Kelley was fired for betraying confidences, although, in fact, she hadn't at the time "betrayed" anyone. She was merely caught with the goods, and might have considered herself dedicated to a higher goal; the goal of most biographers, to gather inside information.

Her forestalled attempt could be described by a friendly witness as research on the inner workings of a great and influential newspaper and its female owner. Commendable, or reprehensible? It depends which side you are on. If she had been on Hitler's staff, for example, we would probably commend her as a recorder of historical fact.

Kelley's daring or sneaky approach—take your pick—and propensity for getting the lowdown on the haughty, naughty, and the high and mighty was welcomed eagerly at the *Washingtonian,* an irreverent magazine that feeds on the failings and foibles of the famous.

Though Barbara Howar was neither high nor mighty, she had been in their orbit. As an ambitious journalist about town and Henry Kissinger's occasional date, she was soon to be stung by a Kelley caper.

Howar, in the throes of rewriting her autobiography, *Laughing All the Way,* in 1973, kept her only copy in the third-floor study of her Georgetown home. She was also holding a garage sale on the ground floor.

At that sale a woman bought a small table, opened a drawer, and found Howar's manuscript. How it got there still mystifies Howar, who insists she kept it in her off-limits study during the sale.

Whatever its mode of transportation, Kelley got it, buying the manuscript from the woman who found it for two dollars, then gleefully taking it to the *Washingtonian.*

Howar failed to live up to the title of her book, *Laughing All the Way,* when someone from the magazine phoned to say they had her manuscript and intended, without her permission, to publish highlights from it.

To Howar it looked like robbery and she made the appropriate "Stop, thief!" cries of dismay. But Kelley and the *Washingtonian* stood firm, as if possession was all points of the law. Howar was incensed. Wasn't it hers? She hadn't given or sold it to anyone. If it had been inadvertently put into the wrong table drawer, hadn't she the right to prevent its piracy? Besides there was much of a personal and sensitive nature that on second thought she'd probably eliminate.

She eventually found out that as her property she could prevent the *Washingtonian* from printing any of the manuscript, but it cost her sixteen thousand dollars in legal fees.

Kelley took the furor lightly, with a wisecrack: "You'd think I'd purchased a copy of Dr. Teller's atomic bomb secrets."

The fallout was still lethal after several years when Howar told me:* "They were going to print just enough excerpts in the *Washingtonian* to kill a deal I had with the *Ladies Home Journal* to print it. My feelings all along were that she was out to make mischief. That's certainly her prerogative. What was pointed out to me was, that whether she had purchased the manuscript in a piece of furniture for twenty-five cents, the moral fact is it wasn't hers to do with. And she had no moral right to do it. That didn't bother her. She thinks everything is her prerogative. And that was the problem for me."[4]

Some believe, I told Ms. Howar, that almost all is fair in getting biographical material from secretive people or organizations—if the aim is to tell the truth.

Barbara Howar is not among them: "I do TV unauthorized biographies myself, but browbeating people into giving their personal secrets would not be my style. I'm very chagrined that the First Amendment extends to cover her. I would assume that anybody who knows anything about Kitty Kelley, unless they have an axe to grind, would close their sources to her on any subject, including a fire in a theater."

---

*Interview with Barbara Howar, November 12, 1988.

I asked Ms. Howar if I could use her comments.
"You can use anything you like."[5]

Slandering Joe Biden

One sour note was sounded during Kelley's *Washingtonian* days. In a you-are-there profile of Senator Joe Biden of Delaware, she followed him around and reported: "Biden tells him [Senator Thomas Eagleton] a joke with an anti-Semitic punch line and asks that it be off the record."

Not only did Kelley put it on the record, but she got it wrong. Both Eagleton and Wes Barthelmes, Biden's administrative aide, called Kelley's quote a misleading distortion, explaining that Biden had told the joke to illustrate and deplore the anti-Semitism he had encountered in Delaware County. Kelley apologized in a later issue of the magazine for having misinterpreted Biden's remark.

Every reporter makes mistakes. These days the *New York Times* prints a daily list of corrections. And not a few reporters will break a confidence by identifying and quoting sources who have spoken on condition that their remarks are kept off the record.

But if Kelley was to make such a mistake about Biden when she had been in his presence, how carefully would she record second- and third-hand information for her future biographies? Is she to be trusted? I tried to find out.

From Fat Farm to First Lady

Having had moderate success in writing about "spoiled piggies" who crowded the fat farms and "gossip like bilge pumps," Kelley was searching for an even more arresting subject for her next book project.

Her maverick publisher, Lyle Stuart, proposed a biography of Jacqueline Onassis. Kelley balked. There were at least forty look-alike Jackie books—a glut on the market.

"Garbage!" said Stuart, or words to that effect, according to her biographer George Carpozi, Jr. The truth about Jackie, Stuart insisted, has yet to be written, and Kelley was just the woman to do it.

Kelley recalled their brief encounter at the New York World's Fair, the humanizing run in Jackie's stocking, her surprising whisper of a voice as if fearful of being overheard. The widow of both JFK and Onassis, she was known to be acutely secretive or, as friends would say, discreet.

Jacqueline Bouvier married John F. Kennedy when she was twenty-five, buried him when she was thirty-four, married Aristotle Onassis when she was thirty-nine. She was widowed for a second time at age fifty-five. At the time of her death in 1994, she was sixty-four years old. Her most recent biographer, David Heymann, and his researchers interviewed 825 people, after she had tried and failed to stop them from trying to discover what she was really like. Heymann admits defeat, concluding that she is a mystery.

Though Kelley suspected no one close to Jacqueline Onassis would respond, let alone share intimate information, she decided to go for it. Her gloomy expectations proved right. Neither Mrs. Onassis nor anyone in her immediate circle would talk. There seemed an impenetrable, protective wall around her composed of those who, from fear or affection, wouldn't let Kelley through.

As a last resort, Kelley went to her friend, gossip-columnist Liz Smith, who was willing to share her thick files. Some of the material was hearsay, or speculation. But armed with this material Kelley discovered she was able to get all except the most cagey individuals to talk. Normally reticent people are often willing, even eager, to confirm or deny or interpret—and often to expand—what had already been printed or broadcast about them.

"Can You Spot a Married Man?"

As a reporter-photographer for the now defunct *Washington Times-Herald* in the early 1950s, Jacqueline Bouvier had asked strangers such innocuous questions as: "Are men braver than women in the dentist's chair?" and stopped shoppers in the street with, "Can you spot a married man?"

Now the widow of a U.S. president, she was the unwilling subject of Kelley's much more personal questions.

Gossip gathered from her fat-farms book helped Kelley. By assuring Senator Smathers that while sharing a room at a fat farm with his ex-wife she had already heard of JFK's freewheeling sex life, she cajoled Smathers into confirming the story.

JFK admirers damned Smathers for squealing on a pal, causing the ex-senator to groan: "Kelley is just a pain in the ass as well as a substantial provocateur."[6]

In this case, maybe the penalty fitted the crime, although he was only one of the first of many. But as an attorney and former politician he must have known Kelley would make the most of it. All he had to do was keep his mouth shut.

If Kelley had any qualms about the price some paid for confiding in her, she has never expressed them publicly. Like most writers, her allegiance was to her book. And with so many other biographers covering the same ground, her antennas were aquiver for a new angle: new, provocative material to distinguish her book from the opposition.

She thought she was on to it, thanks to a tip from a doctor friend, something everyone else had missed. And this is how it appears in *Jackie Oh!*

The strains imposed on her [Jacqueline Kennedy] by her husband's political career and the demands of his family tortured her. Tormented by her own wild extremes and deepening depression, she finally sought help at Valleyhead, a private psychiatric clinic in Carlisle, Massachusetts, which specialized in electro-shock therapy. . . . About the time she was in Valleyhead clinic, a young St. Louis lawyer by the name of Thomas Eagleton was hospitalized for electro-shock treatment at the Mayo Clinic in Rochester, Minnesota. "At that time it was part of the prescribed treatment for one who was suffering from nervous exhaustion and the manifestation of depression," he said. Eagleton, too, kept his therapy a secret. Many years later, when he was a United States Senator and had been selected by George McGovern for the Vice Presidential spot on the Democratic ticket, the secret became public.

The startling revelations of Eagleton's need for such drastic treatment sent tremors through the Democratic party, which began to wonder about his stability and stamina. Confronted with the facts, he finally admitted them, saying that with the electro-therapy he also received psychiatric counseling. . . . In anticipation of just such a scandal, which might politically embarrass John Kennedy, his wife's electro-shock therapy was kept a secret and rarely referred to even within the family. For many years celebrities and socialites went to Valleyhead. The confidential files of the famous patients who visited the facility—which closed in 1977—are now safely buried in a vault in Springfield, Massachusetts, and cannot be unearthed without written permission of the patient.

Few would have known of Mrs. John F. Kennedy's trip to Valleyhead if it had not occurred on a weekend when the staff anesthesiologist was on vacation. Substituting that day was an anesthetist employed by Carney Hospital in Boston, who worked on a regular freelance basis at Valleyhead, anesthetizing patients for electro-shock treatments, The man, still employed at Carney, later told his wife that one of his patients that weekend was the wife of John F. Kennedy. Years later, when the office manager, Mrs. Josephine Delfino, was asked about Jackie's visit to Valleyhead, she said, "I wasn't there at the time, but I remember people more famous than her who came here for electro-shock treatments." . . . Few of Jackie's friends ever knew about her visit to Valleyhead for electro-shock therapy, but none would be too surprised.[7]

Though Kelley doesn't say in the book how she got this "scoop," she does in a *Washingtonian* article. There she revealed that a doctor friend told her his cousin was married to a man who had anesthetized Jacqueline Kennedy for shock treatment.

Anxious to confirm the story, but unsure of herself, she enlisted the aid of Don Uffinger, a former Washington, D.C., policeman, and now a private detective. He and Kelley had become friends after she had interviewed him for an article.

Kelley put herself into his hands for this delicate and difficult mission. How do you get a doctor to skirt his Hippocratic oath by giving to two strangers medical information about a living and now-famous patient?

Though not exactly a dizzy blonde, Kelley could be mistaken for one. Uffinger saw her appearance as a handicap to the enterprise. So he suggested a makeover and she agreed. Kelley put her curly hair up into a businesslike bun, quit chain-smoking, and changed her name for the visit from Kitty to the less frisky Katherine. Not convinced that even these transformations would do the trick, Uffinger told her that if the ice got too thin, to leave the talking to him. She agreed. Uffinger has a quiet, steady manner of speaking that would tend to defuse any potentially explosive situation.

Reaching the anesthesiologist's Massachusetts home they found him out but confronted his wife. Then they pulled the "we already have the information" approach. Furthermore, they pressed on, they knew she was the one who had leaked the "secret" to her cousin. If she wouldn't admit it, then they would go to her husband—part of the shock-treatment team—for his confirmation.

That worked. The woman appeared to be afraid her husband would discover she had been the source of the leak if they spoke with him; she admitted that such therapy had occurred at Valleyhead, a private clinic in Carlisle. Then she ordered them from the house.

When I questioned Uffinger,* he modified Kelley's account, saying the doctor's wife had given the information willingly and he denied any suggestion that she had been intimidated.

"But why," I asked, "did Kelley need you on the interview?"

"She didn't know how the doctor was going to react. She asked me if I would go along to assist her getting the information."

"But how would you assist her? You're an ex-policeman and she's a journalist and interviewer. Why would she need an ex-policeman?"

"I think she felt she needed someone that had a lot of experience in interrogating, interviewing."

"In Kelley's own account she indicates that the woman was frightened and you really put the screws to her."

"There was no real pressure. No 'screws to her.' She might have been concerned about who we were."

"Who did you say you were?"

"Katherine Kelley and Don Uffinger."

"Did she ask why you would be interested in this information?"

"She didn't."

"But you're a private detective. When you go as a private detective, don't you tell people you're a detective?"

"Sometimes. I don't always."

"And this woman made no effort to find out who you represented or why you wanted this information?"

*Interview with Don Uffinger, March 27, 1989.

"That's right. I believe we told her we were writing an article or a book. I'm not sure."

"So it appeared that you were journalists?"

"That's right."[8]

I asked *Washington Post* editor Ben Bradlee* his view of Kelley using a detective and apparently intimidating a woman into confirming the account of Mrs. Kennedy's shock treatment.

"I don't know the facts of it," Bradlee replied. "I really don't. And I can get into enough trouble by myself, without other people's facts. But, obviously, if that were true it doesn't sound right to me at all."[9]

John Sansing, editor of the *Washingtonian,* which printed Kelley's own story of the encounter, admitted "the interview turned into an interrogation," but defends her tactics. "Knowing Kitty Kelley I don't think it would have been intimidation," he said, when I interviewed him on March 27, 1989. "It would have been persuasion. She's a very persuasive person."

"Then why," I asked, "did she take a private eye with her?"

"She sometimes needed moral support."

"How far do you think a writer should go in interviewing sources?"

"I think you should be up front. You can use all your arts of persuasion but not deceive, mislead, or intimidate."[10]

Jackie Oh!

Critic Jonathan Yardley characterized Kelley's writing style as "deadpan," which might be a jazzy synonym for "dull." But the sales of *Jackie Oh!* were anything but. Such scoops as the electro-shock therapy and confirmation from a friend of JFK's overactive sex life ensured bestsellerdom, and it held

---

*Interview with Ben Bradlee, March 27, 1989.

the lead for three months as the nonfiction paperback most in demand.

Still, had Kelley discovered "the truth" about Mrs. Kennedy's shock treatment, or was the scoop a bust? There was no danger of Jacqueline Kennedy denying it. So much fiction has been written about her that she simply hadn't the time to set the record straight.

But two well-informed people are positive Kelley was misinformed and that Jacqueline Kennedy never had shock treatment.

The first, C. David Heymann, may be suspect as a rival who has published a recent biography, *A Woman Named Jackie,* and is continuing to cover the same territory, with a biography in progress of Elizabeth Taylor. However, Heymann has evidence to refute Kelley.

Heymann, a former university lecturer and author of books on Ezra Pound and the Lowells of Boston, turned to less literary lights to feed his family, going after Barbara Hutton for *Poor Little Rich Girl,* and Jacqueline Onassis for *A Woman Named Jackie.* He calls Kitty Kelley "a third-rate biographer. She writes biographies that aren't biographies, taking advantage of the fact that these people can't sue her. [Sinatra tried!] The scandal is untrue that she puts in her books. Her biographies are so bad and such hatchet jobs and so unreliable. She's a boldfaced liar."[11]

One Heymann "revelation" in his Jackie book was that she had offered to divorce JFK if Marilyn Monroe would marry him and move into the White House. True or not, the source for that tidbit was Peter Lawford, then a drug and alcohol addict—not the most believable of witnesses.

Despite his disdain for Kelley, Heymann's own credibility is shaky. In 1984 Random House recalled fifty-eight thousand copies of his Hutton biography when Dr. Edward A. Kantor threatened to sue. Heymann's goof had been to report that Kantor had been overmedicating the drug-addicted heiress at a time when the doctor was a fourteen-year-old schoolboy! But we all make mistakes. That said, here are Heymann's reasons for believing Jacqueline Kennedy never had shock treatment.*

"It's hard to have the evidence of a nonexisting something. But there is no evidence whatsoever that she did. I went through the Massachusetts Health records for that hospital which had moved to Boston. And Jacqueline Kennedy's name never came up. And people I spoke to, relatives such as John Davis [her cousin on his mother's side and author of *The Kennedys: Dynasty and Disaster 1848-1984,* and *The Bouviers*] who said it was absolutely untrue. If you think about it, you'll realize it is impossible. Anyone who spends four years studying Jackie [as Heymann did for his biography of her] realizes that that's the farthest thing from her character and personality—to surrender control over her memory. That's what shock treatment does. If you read Kelley's book carefully, you'll see it says Jackie went one weekend to this hospital. First of all, she wasn't in psychiatric treatment at that point.

"To get into a bonafide mental hospital for shock treatment, a bonafide psychiatric person would have to recommend it. She wasn't in therapy of any kind at that point. So it's impossible. And shock treatment is given as a series, it's not given as a single instance, as Kitty Kelley claimed in her book."

"Isn't it possible Jacqueline Kennedy could have gone under a pseudonym [as Ernest Hemingway did]?"

"No, it's not possible because, as I just told you, she wasn't in therapy at the time."

"Why would Kelley make up this story, which Uffinger supports?"

"She may not have made it up. In her book she doesn't name her doctor friend. A person may well have said they [sic] recalled somebody who *looked like* Jacqueline Kennedy having been there. But it's absolutely untrue [that is was her]."[12]

---

*Interview with David Heymann, January 27, 1990.

Kelley noted that she had made several futile attempts to get Mrs. Onassis to respond to letters and phone calls. She did contact Nancy Tuckerman, then Mrs. Onassis's secretary, who declined to cooperate in any way.

Rather than retrace Kelley's route, I first questioned a close and longtime friend of Jacqueline Kennedy Onassis—William Walton. An artist and writer, Walton had been chairman of the U.S. Commission of Fine Arts from 1963 to 1971. Although a layman, he happens to be an expert on electro-shock treatment.

"I'm as positive as one can be that she didn't have shock treatment," Walton said.*

"Her attitude is not to respond to anything in that line, is that right?"

"That's absolutely correct. And it saves lots of trouble and misunderstanding and misquotations."

"How sure are you?"

"I'd certainly stake my claim to fame on it. I can always be wrong but I doubt it very much. Our friendship has been so long. After all, I've known her since she was about eighteen, so I've known her all the way. I don't believe there was any period when she was subject to depression—a subject about which I have a great deal of information. Someone very close to me was a deep manic-depressive and we went to every institution, every hospital. I know that world."

"But how about in later years? Wouldn't it have been understandable that after the president's assassination she would have been very depressed?"

"Yes, but I don't think shock is used in that kind of depression. I think technically it's very wrong, and it has been terribly discredited, anyway. The technique is very seldom used any more."

"Can I quote you saying you think it very unlikely?"

---

*Interview with William Walton, February 7, 1990.

"Certainly."

"You stake your reputation on it?"

"Certainly."[13]

His reputation is safe—but Kelley's isn't. Nancy Tuckerman, Jacqueline Kennedy's longtime confidante, friend, and her social secretary at the White House (they worked at the publisher Doubleday), categorically denies Kelley's shock treatment story.

"I've got the information for you," said Ms. Tuckerman, in response to my letter followed up by a phone call.* "She did not have electric-shock treatment."

"Did you get that from Mrs. Onassis?" I asked.

"No, but I was around then and I would have known."

"May I quote you?"

"Yes."

"Do you get many biographers asking for information?"

"You mean asking for information about Mrs. Onassis?"

"Or asking for information she could give about other things?"

"Sometimes, if it's a biography on somebody that was in the administration or something like that, we do."

"Do you help in those cases?"

"Not usually. Because she's asked quite frequently, so if you did it for one you'd want to do it for others. And it would take too much of her time."[14]

Kelley versus Bradlee

In Kelley's *Washingtonian* account of her biographical triumphs, she claimed:

---

*Interview with Nancy Tuckerman, March 5, 1990.

Jackie apparently does read everything written about her, and if she doesn't like it that's the end of the relationship. Ben Bradlee found this out several years ago when he cashed in on his JFK friendship to write a gossipy memoir titled *Conversations With Kennedy*. The *Washington Post*'s executive editor had maintained a friendship with Jackie since the days the Bradlees and Kennedys were neighbors in Georgetown.

Shortly after publication Bradlee was in New York with Sally Quinn and saw Jackie walking down the street with Peter and Cheray Duchin. He ran up and threw open his arms for a big bear hug. Jackie glared at him and without breaking stride she continued walking, nearly knocking him down. She then told the Duchins how much she despised him for writing the book.[15]

When I read this out to Bradlee,* he took a deep breath and said, "It did occur about three or four weeks after the funeral [of JFK]. I put out my hand—there was no attempt at a bear hug—and she didn't take it. I don't know why. I don't remember the Duchins being there. I sent her [Jacqueline Kennedy] the manuscript of my book [*Conversations With Kennedy*], and she called me and said she thought it was more about me than about him. I haven't had any contact with her since."[16]

Kelley also accused Bradlee of treating a woman shabbily, writing in the same piece:

I called the woman who had researched Ben Bradlee's *Conversations With Kennedy*. . . . Formerly the top researcher for the *Washington Post,* this woman had spent months organizing Bradlee's notes and writing much of the material he used as his own. He promised her credit, possibly on the cover of the book, plus a percentage of the profits, but all she ever received was a check for $400. "He never even thanked me," she wailed.[17]

---

*Interview with Ben Bradlee, March 27, 1989.

When I read this also to Bradlee he responded with, "Jesus Christ! That woman! She wasn't the chief researcher. She was a librarian. And of course I didn't promise her a percentage of the profits or her name on the book. They were notes I'd written, 40,000 words, and all she did was check facts."[18]

Near the end of her article, Kelley quotes political journalist Theodore White:

Now, older and wiser, and having been tugged too often by friendship and affection for men I have reported, I am as wary of friendship for the great as a reformed drunkard of the taste of alcohol.[19]

White lists three

great men [Kennedy, Chou En-Lai, and General George Stilwell] in whose presence I had near total suspension of disbelief or questioning judgment. . . . In all three cases, I would now behave otherwise.[20]

Kelley adds,

Ben Bradlee was tugged by the same friendship and affection for John F. Kennedy. Yet he had no reservations or apologies. "If I was had, so be it," he said.[21]

"That last quote [by Kelley] is accurate," Bradlee conceded. "I have a terrible time convincing people I knew nothing about his womanizing. Since my meetings with him were usually with my wife and his wife—naturally the subject of his womanizing didn't come up."[22]

Forced to rely on unfriendly or second-rate sources, Kelley sums up Mrs. Onassis in gloomy negatives, as "erratic, neurotic, lonely and unfulfilled." Had they been willing to talk, close friends such as William Walton and Nancy Tuckerman, for example, would have given a brighter picture by at least mentioning her lively sense of humor.

Monkeying with Liz Taylor

Next came Kelley's *Elizabeth Taylor: The Last Star,* the sedate title belying its salty contents. The last star of what? *The Planet of the Apes?* You might assume so from Kelley's vivid description of Taylor as having "hair all over" and looking like "a monkey."

There's more animal talk in the book, especially of Taylor's pets, which caused an exasperated French maid to exclaim: *Les chiens pissaient partout!* ("The dogs pissed all over!") which prompts Kelley's disapproving comment: "Elizabeth Taylor and her incontinent animals became well-known to the finest hotels in Europe."

Taking the first dictionary definition, "not restraining the passions or appetites," this biography might be read as a treatise on incontinence; of a woman unable to resist booze, fattening foods, furs, jewels, and husbands.

Kelley's own husband, Mike Edgley, joined her on the star quest. She eulogized him as a sort of Herculean flight instructor, writing: "His solid support lifts the wings I fly on." And helps her lay the golden eggs.

When Kelley was hunting for the inside dope on her George-town neighbor—Taylor was then married to U.S. Senator John Warner—husband Mike was sent out on dawn patrol. Ostensibly jogging, his main purpose was to get the dirt on Taylor from, appropriately, her garbage. Some may admire this as enterprising and providing insight into the actress's lifestyle and appetite.

To those who sneer that Kelley crawls rather than flies, she might respond that garbage collection is a vital information source probably used by every intelligence agency in the world, and by respected reporters.

New York Times critic Cathleen Schine thought the resulting biography "delightful." But David Heymann, treading much the same ground for his account of Taylor's life, scorns all of Kelley's work: "People assume when Kitty Kelley writes a book it's a kind of comic-strip version. Hers are such hatchet jobs. Mine will be as different from hers as my Jackie book was from hers. Night and day. It's going to be the story of Elizabeth Taylor, rather than some figment of Kitty Kelley's imagination. I know Elizabeth Taylor now because I'm doing the same biography Kelley did. She wrote that Liz Taylor had numerous treatments by Dr. Max Jacobson, then known as Dr. Feelgood. Categorically untrue. She had *one* treatment. I have all Jacobson's records: I got them from his widow. There are numerous inaccuracies like that throughout all Kelley's biographies."[23]

Journalist Max Lerner agreed, denying "everything and anything Kitty Kelley said I told her [about Liz Taylor]. She [Kelley] is a journalistic debaucher."

Sinatra Jumps the Gun

When Frank Sinatra realized that Kelley was on his track and wouldn't quit, he tried to scare her away. At first he ignored her several letters inviting his cooperation, as if his silence would paralyze her plans. But he didn't know Kelley.

Several years before he had tried to discourage Earl Wilson from publishing his *Sinatra: An Unauthorized Biography* with a three-million-dollar lawsuit. Wilson, an established columnist, had a powerful newspaper behind him, and Sinatra's opposition failed to stifle the book, which appeared in 1976.

Wilson's book depicted a power-drunk, paranoid Sinatra. But Wilson strained to be evenhanded, balancing almost every punch with a pat, and clearing Sinatra of serious mob connections, despite those who had hinted for years about the singer's ties to the Mafia.

Sinatra's much publicized persona is of a generous, caring man who often helped friends and strangers in distress, championed the underdog, and enjoyed close contact with almost every heterosexual female in Hollywood and stops en route.

In his maturing years he punctured that persona by snarling at the press, who snarled back in calling him a paunchy, loud-mouthed bully with a short fuse, protected by an entourage of sycophants and muscle men.

New Yorker writer E. J. Kahn, Jr., who claims the daffy distinction of dancing with the Duke and Duchess of Windsor at the same time—because the duke refused to give her up— also achieved a rare but unsatisfactory conversation with Sinatra a year after Wilson's biography appeared.

"It was not the ideal setting in which to conduct an interview," Kahn recalled. "The sidewalk outside was littered with squealing bobby-soxers, and inside [the restaurant] was Sinatra, surrounded by his usual retinue of flunkeys: press agents, gofers, and the omnipresent Mafia-type sidekick who functioned more or less as a bodyguard, On top of everything else—almost literally on top of Sinatra—was the fat, ugly Shor [Toots Shor, owner of the restaurant], hopping around that single glittering patron like a toad hoping to be changed into a prince."[24]

I asked Kahn to sum up his impression of Sinatra and he said: "He was surrounded by a lot of people; agents and all that kind of crap. I think he was a pretty hardboiled and terribly conceited person." Kahn was lucky to exchange a few words with Sinatra. Normally, as Kitty Kelley would find, he recoiled from would-be interviewers as if they had communicable diseases.

Before Kelley began her Sinatra siege, Gay Talese had made a major effort to bring him back alive. A respected former *New York Times* reporter with Sicilian forbears, Talese had written about Mafia chief Joseph Bonanno as a warm, sympathetic character. With that alchemic talent Talese seemed capable of producing a sanitized, even saintly, portrait of Sinatra. It's not magic, just a different point of view.

Sinatra agreed to the interview, but when Talese arrived on the scene, Sinatra repeatedly and inexplicably rebuffed him. Talese was reduced to writing a comic piece about how the big fish got away.

There's no doubt Sinatra is a valuable property. Agent Irving Lazar, who knew almost everyone's price, estimated that if Sinatra penned his own life story he'd get a $6 million advance. Kelley might not match that but was assured that her account would make her a millionairess—but not if Sinatra could help it. In 1981, his silence having failed to stop—though it did interrupt—her working on the project, Sinatra took action. Charging that Kelley focused on sensational, scandalous, and deprecating events in the personal lives of her subjects, he sued her for damages of two million dollars. This seemed like scare tactics. How could he claim he had been damaged? Kelley hadn't yet published one word about him.

His lawyers then tried to damage Kelley. They had evidence, they said, that Kelley had practiced deception to get information for her book by masquerading as Sinatra's authorized biographer. The tape of a phone conversation was played, in which a female voice said: "I'm the official biographer and I'd like to talk to you." Who was misrepresenting what became a moot point: the voice sounded less like Kitty Kelley than a woman doing a feeble imitation of comedienne Joan Rivers.

The David-and-Goliath battle became more balanced when groups representing thousands of writers came to Kelley's support. Their representatives applauded unauthorized biographies as "the essence of free and open critical commentary on public figures' lives and work." If the court sided with Sinatra's "novel" interpretation of the law, they pointed out,

Henry Kissinger could have silenced Seymour Hersh, the Kennedy family could have silenced William Manchester, "The Brethren" on the Supreme Court could have quashed Armstrong and Woodward, and the late [Chicago] Mayor Daley could have paralyzed Mike Royko.[25]

The thought of a muffled Hersh and Manchester, a quashed Armstrong and Woodward, and a paralyzed Mike Royko moved the editorial writer for the *Baltimore Sun* to explain that although many Americans supported Sinatra, they were on the losing side:

"Whose life is it, anyway, his or hers?" The very easy answer to that is neither, it's yours. . . . The "life" of a public figure belongs to the average American citizen. If all the public can learn of the person is what the person himself wants [the public] to learn, then ours will become a very closed and ignorant society, unable to correct ills, quite unlike what the drafters and subsequent generations of the free speech Amendment had in mind.

If Frank Sinatra's friendship with presidents or criminals affected his own career or theirs, and therefore your society and your life, you have a right to know whatever an objective biographer can find out about that. . . . No biographer has the right to damage someone with malicious falsehoods. There are ways for damaged subjects to get their due after publication of such reporting. But prior restraint of the sort Mr. Sinatra is seeking is censorship, no matter how you dress it up.[26]

Advised by friends and family to give it up or risk being badly hurt, Kelley plowed on, stuffing anonymous threats in a file marked "Frank Sinatra—Broken Legs." Although not scared, she was wary and cautious, especially when meeting informants in strange places. Her limbs remained intact.

Probably overwhelmed by the press onslaught, Sinatra dropped the suit and *Sinatra: His Way* was published in 1986.

Bantam went bonkers and printed almost a million hardcover copies. But the publicity paid off and it shot straight to the head of the *New York Times* best-seller list.

William Safire acclaimed it as "the most eye-opening celebrity biography of our time," and the *Los Angeles-Examiner* thought it had made "all future Frank Sinatra biographies virtually redundant."

Rival biographer David Heymann disagreed: "I think of all the books she's done it's the best. But then slowly it began to crumble apart for me. For example, I, too, in pursuing the Kennedy thing [for his biography, *A Woman Named Jackie*] began to get some of the same documents she did about Sinatra. I noticed that in quotes from the FBI documents, she quotes one sentence taken completely out of context. She leaves out the whole germane aspect. She not only makes him look worse, but it's not truthful. It's an aberration.

"And in the book she claims to have met Peter Lawford twice. Once when he was dead! [On the date Kelley gives for one interview with Lawford, he had been dead several days.] I know for a fact that Peter Lawford never gave her an interview about Sinatra.

"The woman who was present on the occasion when Kelley interviewed Lawford, Lawford's fourth wife [Patricia Seaton Lawford], states categorically that there was no talk whatsoever about Frank Sinatra. Kelley's photographer friend, Stanley Tretick of *Life* magazine, accompanied her and said he was doing an article on Kennedy's anniversary. They spent a few minutes talking about the Kennedys. And they never got past talking about the Kennedys. [A later account in this chapter gives a different version.]

". . . Kelley wrote about Frank Sinatra in five hundred pages; not devoting one paragraph to his craft, his singing, which is absurd. No one can deny that he is the best singer of his type this country has ever had. She doesn't deal with that at all. It's like writing about Picasso and not talking about his art."[27]

In her book Kelley established Sinatra's mob connections, noted his wild tantrums and violence to women, told how he introduced JFK to a woman the president then shared with a Chicago mobster, and characterized several of Sinatra's relatives as hoods and his mother as an abortionist. It was not a pretty picture.

Sinatra fans remained uncustomarily silent. One exception, Joey Bishop, appeared on Phil Donahue's television show with Kitty Kelley. He was there to defend Sinatra's reputation as a good guy, but muffed it, supporting rather than discrediting Kelley.

Justin Kaplan, National Book Award and Pulitzer Prize-winning biographer of Mark Twain, Lincoln Steffens, and Walt Whitman, supports Kelley with reservations, saying:* "She was obviously out to get him and she had every reason to be pissed off, because he'd threatened to sue her before she wrote the book. In many ways, in being so assertive and hostile to Kitty Kelley he did himself a disservice, because it meant that many of her sources were FBI reports and Freedom of Information material. I can tell you from my own experience with reading through FBI files on Charlie Chaplin [a biographical project Kaplan has abandoned], a lot of it is terrible garbage, often gossip in the most dunderheaded way. I think the rule is that the FBI opens a file on someone it wants to get the dirt on."[28]

Did Kelley want to get the dirt on Sinatra?

"No," says her detective friend Uffinger. "It's ridiculous to say that. Her attitude is to get the facts and print the facts, good and bad; printing whatever she can establish to be the truth."

I decided to find out if he was right, by questioning Kelley herself as well as some of her sources.

---

*Interview with Justin Kaplan, December 30, 1988.

Recovered from an exhausting publicity tour for the Sinatra book on both sides of the Atlantic, an ebullient and energized Kelley agreed to a taped phone interview,* which went as follows.

Kelley Talks

After Sinatra threatened to sue you, did you ever contemplate giving up?

"No."

Do you use any special technique or approach to break down the resistance of those reluctant to talk?

"No, I don't. I wish I did."

A straightforward approach? Saying what you're going to do and asking for their cooperation?

"Very straightforward."

And when they said, "I'd rather not talk about Frank," did you drop the subject?

"It depended on who it was. In Hoboken, Sinatra had an Irish Catholic godfather, Frank Garrick, which was a phenomenal thing for an Italian child. I knew that both the Sinatra parents and Frank had grown up with Frank Garrick. I needed him very much, and he wouldn't give me an interview. I asked a nun to ask him, and he wouldn't say yes to her. A librarian called on him on my behalf and he said no. Finally, a photographer friend, a man to whom I dedicated the book [Stanley Tretick], said, 'You've just got to go over and knock on his door.' I said, 'I can't. I'm not a paparazzi.' He said, 'You've got to do it. Do you want to write the book, or do you want to be a member of the Junior League?' 'I want to write the book.' So I went over and knocked on his door and two and a half hours later I walked out with a wonderful interview."

---

*Interview with Kitty Kelley, February 14, 1987.

Are you a Catholic?

"I was raised one."

You knew the nun personally?

"Yes."

Of those close to Sinatra, who were the most daring to talk frankly to you?

"Every one of them."

His godfather, Frank Garrick, who gave you that long interview, his career did not depend on not offending Sinatra.

"He was terrorized to give that interview. He's now fallen out of favor with Sinatra, and I think he's very angry with me."

But his career wasn't at stake. He wasn't an actor or director.

"It doesn't make any difference. It was just as important to him. He had had a personal relationship with Sinatra. Sinatra told him never to talk to the press. I think it's just as important as a career when you are eighty-six years of age and you live in a twelve-square-block town of Hoboken, and you're suddenly cut off of the free trips to Atlantic City and the tickets to the concerts."

What broke his resistance to being interviewed?

"I don't know."

Apparently it was just your being there.

"Yes."

Who among actors and directors was most daring in talking to you about Sinatra?

"Everybody was. The hardest thing in writing the book was dealing in the fear people had about Frank Sinatra. They were afraid they were going to suffer some kind of reprisal; going to be hurt in some way. Their careers would be harmed. Their children would be harmed. So nobody spoke willingly and easily. Not everybody told me one hundred percent of the story, which is why I had to interview eight hundred and fifty-seven people to write my book."

Isn't it remarkable then that they did speak with you?

"Yes. And there were many that did not."

What do you think motivated those who did talk?

"I think most people's motives were to tell the truth. There'd be times when I might call someone and they wouldn't talk to me, and I'd have to call back and say: 'It's very important. It's a matter of accuracy. I know you don't want to talk but I was told this and this and I was told you said this, and I really need to know.' "

Because so many of Sinatra's relatives and friends refused to cooperate, didn't that almost force you to write a negative picture of him?

"No, not at all. No. I don't want you even to continue with the assumption. Just because someone doesn't give you an interview does not mean you're forced to write a negative book. Most public figures who have press agents on retainers have made sure that Americans know every positive thing about them. You're assuming that because Frank Sinatra didn't give me an interview that I went only to his enemies and that's not true."

What are your principles in writing an unauthorized biography? Does everything go if it's confirmed as accurate? Do at least two reputable sources have to confirm a controversial incident? For example, do you know Jim Bacon the columnist?

"Oh, god, yes!"

He told me that he wouldn't have done what columnist Joyce Haber apparently did: to write that Betty Grable was in a hospital dying of cancer. Bacon said that Grable didn't know it was fatal until she read it in Haber's column, and that it destroyed her.

"I don't want to be in the position of making judgment on Jim Bacon, but I certainly wouldn't write the kind of crap that Bacon writes. So, for him to pass judgment on Miss Haber is out of my territory."

Do you believe the public has the absolute right to know *everything* about a public figure?

"Probably."

Has anyone been able to refute what seems to be your watertight FBI reports about Sinatra's mob connections?

"No."

Do you assume your revelations of the mob connections were what most enraged Sinatra?

"I don't assume anything. I know that a lot of things enraged him: the fact of his mother being an abortionist and having an abortion business, and the way she died. The fact that I went into such detail bothered him. The fact that I reported he ate bacon and eggs off the chest of a prostitute, that he threw a plate of spaghetti into his black valet's face, that he threw a woman through a plate-glass window and nearly severed her arm."

So he read the book.

"Of course."

Does he in any way emerge as a different man from the one you thought of when you began the book?

"I started out having a great deal of respect for Frank Sinatra, because I thought he was somebody who said he would never perform before a segregated audience. And I thought this demonstrated quite a bit of integrity and principle, to put your career alongside of your personal beliefs."

He does that, doesn't he?

"Well, I don't know. I think anybody that performs in Sun City sort of obviates the other. I started out with a great deal of respect for the man."

Do you think Sinatra was justified in being alarmed when he learned you were working on his biography, if he knew of your Liz Taylor and Jackie Onassis books?

"I don't know."

Did either of them try to prevent you from writing their biographies?

"Liz Taylor tried to get people not to talk to me."

In your biography of Liz Taylor you quote an anonymous man on shipboard who says of her, "she had hair all over and looked like a monkey." Why do you think it's okay to print such a comment, when celebrity haters could be persuaded to say the most atrocious but inaccurate things about a person if assured they would remain anonymous?

"The man's name was St. Clair Pugh. Does that do anything for you?" [He is an aide to gossip columnist Liz Smith.]

Was he willing to be named?

"Yes, and I probably should have: which is why I made a vow when I did the Frank Sinatra book that I was going to have no blind quotes. I don't like blind quotes and I don't think they're fair."

Who is Pugh?

"He's a man."

You implied I should have known him.

"No, I was trying to make a subtle point, Mr. Brian; you don't know him when I give you his name."

No, but to readers a name makes them feel confident of the information.

"I agree it should be done. I don't like blind quotes. It's not fair to the reader. The only time I did it in the Sinatra book was when people demanded absolute confidentiality, or were law enforcement officers. And I can't jeopardize the jobs or pensions of those people who came forward to help me."

The point about giving the name, of course, even if it meant nothing to me, is that somebody else could say on a talk show or in a review that your informant was a psychopath or a compulsive liar—if that were the case. What were the most provocative questions or revelations you had on your book promotion tour?

"The most interesting statement was made by William Safire in the *New York Times*. He said that the worst thing that President Reagan had done in his administration was to award the Medal of Freedom to Frank Sinatra, who stood alongside Mother Teresa. The most interesting observation probably came from the European journalists when I went to England and Ireland. They felt it was an indictment of the American political system. I was a bit jolted by that. And they explained that upon reading it they saw that politicans in America, Republicans and Democrats, were totally amoral; that they would deal with a man so closely tied to organized crime just for the money he could raise, knowing full well what he was about in his other life."

Were the Los Angeles area interviewers wary of you?

"Oh, yes. Many of them wouldn't go near me. Michael Jackson [a Californian interviewer] wouldn't have me on the air."

And didn't some late-night TV interviewers refuse you?

"Johnny Carson and Joan Rivers."

Because they're Sinatra's friends?

"I don't know. Carson isn't a friend of his."

The *New York Times* reviewer of your book wrote that you pen unauthorized biographies of people "she has little affection and no empathy for, precisely those people who wish least to be written about and who have the power to exact silence from those who know and love—or fear—them best."[29] But I take it that you did have affection for Sinatra.

"Uh huh, and quite a bit of empathy."

And how about Liz Taylor and Jackie Onassis?

"Yes. You have to when you're doing these books. I could never spend four years—as I did with Frank Sinatra—on someone I disliked."

Here's more of Barbara Harrison's review: "A good reporter, unless she is capable of an imaginative leap into someone else's consciousness, does not have access to the human heart. . . . Can the Freedom of Information Act, which Miss Kelley employed extensively, tell me why Mr. Sinatra is given on one hand to vicious King Kong tantrums and on the other to sweet family feeling and acts of fabulous generosity? It cannot."

"Miss Barbara Grizzuti Harrison let her Italian background get in the way when she did that review. Also, Miss Harrison is very naive. I did not write a psychohistory. I didn't write a book that said, 'He felt this way, he thought that way,' unless I knew for a firm, unshakable certainty that he felt or thought that way. The only way I would know that is if he gave an interview and it was in print and he said: 'I felt this way.' That's the real drawback of docudrama. Nobody has the right to go inside somebody's heart and mind."

Still more of Barbara Harrison's complaints about your book on Sinatra: "She never tells why [if they were so cozy] none of these wiseguys, so powerful, [the Mob] could or did come to Mr. Sinatra's aid when his career was on the skids in the early '40s and '50s. Ms. Kelley can't in fact tell me why Mr. Sinatra did anything."

"She shows how naive she is. There's no sentimentality involved with the Mafia. Their main thrust in life is money. And they did come to his aid. They gave him nightclub gigs."

Just before Sinatra got his part in *From Here to Eternity,* I believe he was broke.

"He was living off Ava Gardner. And they were still giving him nightclub gigs."

Finally, Mrs. Harrison says that you are ignorant of Italian immigrant life.

"I don't know how to respond to this poor woman's review. She's an Italian. She's in love with Frank Sinatra. What can I say? Really? Remember, I wrote this book that was quite an exposé. This man had been in the public eye for fifty years and there are a lot of things in the book that nobody knew. That is rather an indictment against the press, is it not? Why didn't they have it?"

I suppose you mean your accounts of Sinatra introducing Judith Exner to JFK, who then shared her with a Mafia chief. But in those days the press had a gentleman's agreement not to reveal intimate details in the lives of presidents. Isn't at the answer?

"Yes, to that one."

And also in those days the movie studios had such power and influence they could control information unless it had reached the law courts.

"That's a generalization that doesn't apply to Frank Sinatra. He was fired from MGM."

Have you had any hate mail as a result of the book?

"Yes, but the majority of the mail has been truly phenomenal. Ninety-six percent has been truly phenomenal. Believe it or not, a lot of Sinatra fans like the book. Most of the hate mail was unsigned."

What are the most enlightening things you've learned from your mail and from interviews you've given since your Sinatra biography was published?

"Mia Farrow issued a statement saying things in the book regarding her weren't true, that Frank really hadn't beaten her up, as David Susskind [TV producer] said he had. And a man called me when I was on the road promoting the book and said, 'I used to be the owner of this particular disco in Beverly Hills and Mia came in one night and told me how Frank had beat the shit out of her and thrown his wedding ring out the window.' That was a very nice thing for that man to do. He stepped forward and gave me even additional confirmation."

Did he give you his name?

"Of course. But you see, if I had been really wrong in my book Miss Farrow would have sued me into oblivion. And if I had been a different person than I am, I would have written Miss Farrow and said, 'Listen, Joe Johns has just contacted me giving me an interview on tape saying this is what you told him in in 1966. Do you want to confirm or deny?' "

I don't agree that if it was a lie, she would have sued you.

Many celebrities are afraid to go to court for fear other things will be brought out which they don't want made public.

"That's a generalization you don't want to apply to most people. You have to go on the individual. There was a time when it was reported in the press that Mia Farrow couldn't stand Robert Redford when they were making *The Great Gatsby*. She brought suit. So you have to know who you are talking about to say that."

I see. She even went to court over a fairly innocuous comment.

"Exactly."

How do you respond to Nancy Sinatra's complaint: "Sinatra's troubles with the press are most often with columnists who care less for the truth than for the dirt. Seeing him hurt is devastating to me because he suffers as violently as he loves.

"Almost any daughter in her position would say that."

Sinatra's friend, Joey Bishop, appeared with you on Donahue's TV show.

"And didn't he do a stunning job!"

He confirmed much of what you'd written, but said it was exaggerated. Is he now out of Sinatra's good graces?

"Sinatra hasn't spoken to him in five years. Joey Bishop was going to write a book about Sinatra and Sinatra's lawyers got in touch with him and Bishop dropped the project right at the time I was starting mine."

Did your publisher's attorneys persuade you to omit anything you'd still like to have in the biography?

"One thing, a financial matter. Under-the-table payments."

Anything else?

"I'd put in the Mia Farrow business I mentioned to you."

How would you feel about someone writing your unauthorized biography?

"It would be pretty boring."

Would you be upset?

"Depends who writes it."

Would you warn friends not to talk to the biographer?

"No."[30]

I phoned Frank Garrick on April 12, 1988, to find out how Kitty Kelley had persuaded him to talk despite, according to Kelley, Sinatra's warning him not to. Garrick's widow answered: he had been dead for a year.

I asked her* if Sinatra had ever asked her husband not to talk to the press.

"Oh no," she replied. "What could he say about Frank? Only nice things. He knew him since he was a boy, and his boyish pranks. What could he say bad about him? He couldn't say anything bad."

Why wouldn't your husband speak to Kitty Kelley originally when she sent a nun and then a librarian over on her behalf?

"Because there was so much talk about her writing books about Elizabeth Taylor and Jacqueline Onassis, and saying things that she shouldn't say. And my husband didn't want to get involved."

So, how did she break his resistance?

"In the morning she had called and my husband told her he didn't want to get involved nohow. Anyhow, at night, around six o'clock, there was a knock at the door and I opened it and there was Kitty Kelley. I'd never met her before, but I figured that was she. What was I going to do? I invited her in. I didn't know what to say. So she stood here for about two hours and she was very nice. But she wrote a lot that we didn't say."

What for instance?

"I just couldn't tell you, because there was so much in the book and I just can't recall. I was right here when we were

---

*Interview with Frank Garrick's widow, April 12, 1988.

talking to her. There were a lot of things that he didn't say at all. But that makes a book, let's face it."

According to Kelley's book, Sinatra and your husband quarreled and then didn't speak to each other for fifty years.

"There was a little trouble there. My husband was circulation manager for a newspaper in Hoboken and Frank wanted to work there as a copy boy. I guess there wasn't a vacancy and Frank felt hurt because he didn't get the job."

This is Kitty Kelley quoting your husband: "Oh the temper and the words and the filthy names he called me! You have no idea what his temper was like in those days. Murderous, like he was going to kill me. He flared up something terrible, cursing and swearing and so vulgar. The words he used were hateful, awful. He called me every terrible name in the book and then he stormed out. He never said a word to me until fifty years later, after his mother died. She wrote me off, too, and even though we lived in the same town she never said another word to me for the rest of her life."[31] Is that all accurate? Dolly never spoke to your husband again?

"They spoke. They were always friends."

Kelley quotes your husband as saying, "Marty [Sinatra's father] still came around but it was never the same, I wasn't invited to Frankie's wedding to Nancy Barbarto."[32]

"We were invited to the wedding but we weren't able to go at that time. She got that wrong, too."

What accounted for fifty years silence between the two men?

"Frank was on the go all the time, you just couldn't keep in touch. Hoboken is only a mile square and you do meet people. And every time my husband and Dolly met they were friendly. Dolly's husband, Marty, Frank's father, was a wonderful person. He and my husband were great friends."

Despite their early quarrel, your husband and Frank were eventually reconciled?

"Yes, finally Frank came to his senses and he came to see

his godfather, and it was a very special meeting. They both started to cry. They put their arms around one another and it was very touching. After that, Frank was very good to us. He took us all over and couldn't treat us any nicer. Before my husband died he [Frank] came over here with his wife and invited us down the shore when he was entertaining there. And he said he was sending his chauffeur to pick us up, take us down. And he treated us royally. Coming back—I never flew before; I was always afraid to fly—so he said: 'Come on, Minnie, don't be a sissy! You can drive back if you want, but you'll be back in New York in an hour's time, flying.' So I looked at him and I thought, 'Why not?' So I got on the plane like a professional and I didn't mind it one bit. But it was lovely; I mean the way he did things. So I could never say things about Frank, only the best. About five years ago he sent us a picture that he'd painted. It's a modern oil painting on canvas, blended into different colors. It's up on the wall now. A beautiful thing to look at, and my husband was so thrilled when he got it."

You know, of course, that Kelley revealed Sinatra's mother was an abortionist?

"That I couldn't say. The woman is dead now. I wouldn't even talk about these things."

What was your husband's reaction?

"I guess he knew everything. Talk goes around fast in Hoboken. But I don't believe those things, because Dolly didn't seem to be that sort of a person. It seems when you're in the limelight like her son was, they bring things out that are not true."

Did Kelley's biography of Sinatra shock you, or change your view of him?

"Oh, no. We love him. My husband loved him. After all, he was his godfather, he saw him as a baby; and it's only natural he would feel that way about him."

Was Sinatra mad at your husband for speaking to Kitty Kelley?

"No, he never mentioned it. But my husband spoke to him and said, 'Frank, you can believe me if you want, but there's a lot of stuff in that book that I never even said.' Frank said, 'I understand; I know what goes on.' My husband loved Frank dearly, he loved that boy."

So you didn't feel sorry you'd spoken to Kitty Kelley, because you thought most of what she reported was true?

"To be honest, if I knew she was at the door I certainly would have never opened the door. But after I opened it, you can't be ignorant. I'm not fresh. And I invited her in. But I was sorry that Kitty ever came up to the house, because we could never say anything bad about Frank. . . . He was very nice. Still it hurt me to think that that happened."

How did he react to your husband's death?

"He really felt bad about it. We had no idea he was going so fast. His son took him to the doctor. I was getting supper ready for him to have when he got back, but instead they took him to the hospital, and in a week he was gone. He was ninety and I'm eighty-seven, and I miss him more and more each day. Because we were together for sixty-three years. The night of the wake the phone rang and it was Sinatra's wife, and she told me how sorry she felt, and if there was anything they could do they'd be only too happy to do it. Frank also called a couple of times, and his secretary, Dorothy. He sent a beautiful floral piece and on a card he wrote: 'You gave me your name. Now I give you my arms with love.' I thought that was the most beautiful thing. He couldn't have been nicer through everything."

Then the Kelley biography didn't cause a breakup between the two men?

"Oh, no. My husband loved Frank dearly. He could never say anything against him. He was an Irishman, you know, and he wouldn't let anyone say anything against Frank."

What is your general feeling about Sinatra?

"I think he's the greatest person living."[33]

Sinatra's High School Girlfriend

Following in Kelley's footsteps, I questioned Marion Brush
Schrieber,* described in the biography as a pretty, red-haired
neighbor who became Sinatra's girlfriend when she was in high
school. Mrs. Schreiber confirmed Kelley's account that Sinatra's
mother was an abortionist who was sentenced to five years
probation after a girl almost died from an illegal operation.
I asked her: Was Kelley's book a fair portrait of Sinatra?

"I was with him at an age when he was very nice, let's
put it that way. I didn't know him later on in California or
anywhere like that."

Kelley wrote that when Sinatra failed to get a job on the
Jersey Observer, he blamed his godfather and was furious with
him.

"Frank never showed it. And he never told me he was
disappointed. His mother would say that, but he wouldn't."

Kelley quotes Frank Garrick as saying that Sinatra went
into the paper's editorial office, sat in the seat of a man who
had recently died, and told the editor—though it wasn't true—
that he'd been given the job by Garrick.

"I don't think Frank would have had that much guts at
the time, to be honest with you. He was never forward, not
when I knew him, anyway."

Did his mother say "son-of-a-bitch bastard!" as Kelley
reports?

"I knew Dolly very well. She had quite a vocabulary. [She
chuckled.] I'm telling you, on Saturday night she and her best
friend, Rose Vaughn, would get dressed up to high heaven and
go to various beer parlors where people sang. And Dolly would
get up and sing, and if anyone said anything to her she'd let
them know it, okay?"

---

*Interview with Marion Brush Schreiber, December 11, 1988.

Did she have a good voice?

"Yes, I'd say so. For the time. Loud."

Was Frank's father henpecked?

"For all the years I knew them I never saw Mr. Sinatra in the house with Dolly. He was generally not there."

So Dolly was a presence in Hoboken.

"Oh, yes. Listen, she was loud-mouthed, let's face it."

Was she liked?

"I wouldn't say so. She was a showman and she was pushy."

Any regrets that you didn't marry Frank?

"Oh, no. We were very good friends and that was it. And we remained so."

What was he like as a young man?

"Very sensitive and extremely moody. When I knew him he would be very sullen and quiet. We went together for about two years, and I was three or four years younger. But he was also a very generous and thoughtful person. When I was going to college I went through a window and had to have twenty-two stitches in my arm. Frank came to the house with a bouquet that filled about four pots. I'm certainly sure his mother stimulated him to do it, let's put it that way. His mother had a great influence on him."

She was ambitious for him?

"And how! I was his friend and everything else under the sun while I was with him, and I tried to promote his ambitions, too. I was forward enough to get a group together to go over to the Witch Barn in New York City and all yell 'Frankie! Get up and sing!' because we figured that maybe he'd make a contact there. We were all for him. The only ones that disliked him in Hoboken were the Irish Catholics. They thought abortion was worse than murder, and still do, and they took it out on him. I thought that was very unfair. Then I went to New Jersey State Teachers College and then to Fordham [University] for a while, and when I graduated I taught school for eleven days, and hated it. So I went to work in the steamship business in New York City. Whenever I met Frank after he was famous he was very friendly. He was never a snob. He treated me like family."

Was there ever any talk of his mob connections?

"His uncles, not him. Babe Garavante, Dolly's brother, was in prison, I think. And his Uncle Dominic was charged with malicious mischief, but it was nothing. Babe was the real thing. His Uncle Gus had a run-in with the law for running numbers, but that wasn't too bad. Gus was a nice guy; I knew him really well. But Babe was the one. He was a pretty tough animal. He was shot in the leg here in Hoboken. They never said anything about that."

Kelley reported that Babe Garavante took part in a murder, driving the getaway car.

"I wouldn't be surprised. Garavante was a tough character."

What did Sinatra think of that uncle?

"I never saw him be friendly with any of them. And I never saw Marty, Frank's father, in the house. And I knew Dolly for a good four or five years. I'll never forget one year—my father was in the clothing business and I gave Marty a tie for his birthday. He never forgot it. He'd be on Washington Street, here, and I'd be coming home from New York City. He'd stop the car in the middle of the street and come over and kiss me. And he was just ever so friendly. He liked me."

He was more likeable than Dolly?

"Oh, definitely."

What were her good qualities?

"She was generous."

And, presumably, she idolized Frank.

"Of course. That was the whole thing."

Was he a mother's boy?

"I never saw him eat a meal in the house. That's the god's honest truth."

Did Kitty Kelley accurately quote you in her Sinatra biography?

"I would say so."[34]

When I asked Steve Capiello* if he'd been accurately quoted by Kelley, he said, "Not altogether."

Kelley writes as follows: " 'The mouth on that woman [Dolly Sinatra] would make a longshoreman blush,' said Steve Capiello, a former mayor of Hoboken, who knew Dolly when he was growing up. 'Her favorite expression was "son-of-a-bitch bastard." She'd curse your mother to hell without even blinking.' " Did you say that?

"No, I never said any of that."

She also has you saying of Frank's father: "He was a weak man. Not physically weak but weak in the sense that he could never stand up to Dolly. Never." Your words?

"No. I think Kitty Kelley took a lot of freedom with her words."

What did you tell her about Dolly Sinatra and her language?

"I never used the quotes she used. Dolly was a woman who knew the streets, was wise to the ways of the streets, and nobody was going to pull the wool over her eyes. And she was something of a suffragette before her time."

Did you like her?

"Yes. She was a friend. She even supported me when I ran for mayor."

What did you say that might have given Kelley the idea she could use "son-of-a-bitch bastard"?

"In a lot of the conversations with Kitty Kelley there were more than one person around. I think she took liberties."

So someone else, not you, might have attributed "son-of-a-bitch bastard" to Dolly Sinatra.

"Yes."[35]

---

*Interview with Steve Capiello, December 10, 1988.

Kelley says she interviewed most of the 857 people questioned for the Sinatra book, and studied FBI and Justice Department files and grand jury testimony about her subject, as well as wire taps. Even with some help, it was a massive enterprise.

She failed to persuade eight important women in his life to talk: wife, Barbara; former wives Nancy Sinatra, Ava Gardner, and Mia Farrow; his two daughters; and Elizabeth Taylor. And, of course, Sinatra himself.

After interviewing Kelley for the *Baltimore Sun,* Alice Steinbach got this response from Mia Farrow through the actress's publicist: "The references to how Frank Sinatra treated me are absolutely untrue."[36]

There's persuasive evidence that Sinatra's son, Frank, Jr., gave Kelley an interview—a photo of them together, with Kelley's notebook on her knees and a smile on her face. But he disputes what Kelley wrote about him, as well as quotes from the interview, saying, according to Steinbach: "All lies. Any facts are coincidental."

Did he have second thoughts, and was he now trying to appease his irate father, as Kelley suggests?

Elizabeth Taylor chose this reply, through gossip columnist Liz Smith, to Kelley's claim that Taylor had aborted Sinatra's baby: "Kitty Kelley is no lady. She is not even a writer but a fabricator."

Kelley also reported that Ava Gardner had aborted Sinatra's baby because "I hated Frank so much, I wanted that baby not to be born." When pressed by Steinbach for the source of the story and the quote, Kelley conceded she took the word of one woman for it, the wife of cameraman Robert Surtees.

Kelley's Capers

With success Kelley took on some of the trappings of the man she had pilloried, acquiring a red Mercedes, a hilltop Georgetown mansion, and an entourage. Sinatra's entourage is beefy, audible, and visible; Kelley's is elusive and eccentric. But their message is identical, with the same warning undertones: Watch Your Step, Buster!!!

In summing up Sinatra, Kelley echoed Tommy Dorsey: "Frank is the most fascinating man on earth—but don't put your hand in the cage." Kelley, too, leaves no doubt of her displeasure and is swift to strike back, though her ways are more devious.

Washington Post reviewer Jonathan Yardley* discovered his offense was rank when, after panning Kelley's Elizabeth Taylor biography, several anonymous "friends of Kitty Kelley" sent him a box of fish heads.

Writer Gerri Hirshey got the message in a more disturbing and protracted form. She began gathering material for a three-part profile of Kelley, who had named Nancy Reagan as her next project. But all of Hirshey's many efforts to interview Kelley failed: instead of Kelley returning her calls, "Kelley fans" were on the line, or letters arrived eulogizing Kelley and hinting that nothing less than a rave report on their idol would fit the case.

At first mildly amused, as calls and letters escalated Hirshey found them upsetting, even sinister. It was as if, having reached celebrity status, Kelley had attracted a loyal and wacky gaggle of groupies determined to discourage those not equally spellbound. Their messages ranged from mildly obscene to the impassioned.

---

*Yardley is also the biographer of Ring Lardner.

Kitty Litter

Finally, when writing her portrait of Kelley for the *Washington Post,* Hirshey tried to defuse the odd communications by reproducing some in the article and calling them "Kitty Litter."

Hirshey had hired expert David Crown to examine the "Kitty Litter," much of it anonymous or from people who could not be found at their given addresses. Crown concluded that one unsigned letter had been typed on the same machine that typed some of Kelley's business correspondence.

I asked Crown* how he could be sure and he replied: "I've been doing this for over thirty years and as you might have guessed I used to run the CIA laboratory. It's absolutely accurate. If there was doubt, I would have expressed it. It's totally unethical to make a definite identification if you're not certain. So if I say it is, you can count on it, it is."[37]

Dan Moldea, Kelley's former friend who has published three books on the Mafia, was briefly quoted in Hirshey's piece, praising Kelley for getting an interview with the dying Peter Lawford. "But," he told me,† "I wouldn't trust her as far as I could throw her. The *Post* was having difficulty getting people on the record on this [Hirshey] story, because Kelley had been known to seek revenge on those who crossed her. Kelley had really double-crossed me for no reason, really unprovoked. And I was furious. So when the *Post* asked me to go on the record, I agreed. And when Hirshey came to do the interview—and I would die for one of my sources to do this for me—I gave her a five-page, single-spaced typed statement detailing my relationship with Kelley. She and I had never been close friends, but there was a lot of professional respect and good feelings and good faith. My father was sick, for example, and she called

---

*Interview with David Crown, March 27, 1989.
†Interview with Dan Moldea, March 27, 1989.

a couple of times to say hello. You know how you appreciate things like that when you have a family crisis. And I had detailed all this in the five-page statement I gave to the *Post*.

"When the series came out I was appalled by it, because I had been very critical of Kelley in this statement; and in the story, basically, I came across as one of her biggest fans. Now, I said two nice things about her in the piece to balance off everything else. But the *Post* decided to make me one of her fans and I was infuriated by it.

"Our little group [of fellow writers] had talked at first and had decided not to cooperate for the *Post* series because, number one, we didn't want to think about Kitty Kelley for two minutes in our lives because she wasn't worth the trouble. All of us were friends of hers at one time, whom she had double-crossed without provocation.

"The second reason: we didn't want to look like we were going after her. We didn't want to look like we were vindictive; that we were trying to do the same thing she was doing to us.

"As far as me helping with the Mafia stuff for the Sinatra book, that's all true. And I respect the Sinatra book. As for the Lawford interview, that's one of the nicest things I said about her Sinatra book in my five-page statement."

That Kelley got Peter Lawford to talk as he was dying?

"I thought that was very important."

Do you think it's difficult to get to a dying man? [Bob Woodward said he got an interview with dying CIA Chief William Casey, even though he was heavily guarded.]

"I think it is a very interesting proposition. It's important to get to someone and say, 'This is your moment, and this may be one of your last moments to get things off your chest,' to get that person to decide not to die with their secrets. That, I think, in itself is an important contribution to the body of literature there is about Sinatra and his connections. I couldn't care less about Sinatra: what I care about are his connections."

Despite your experience with her, do you think Kelley is a fair, balanced biographer?

"I had a big problem with her *Jackie Oh!* book. I thought it was unfair because I'm tired of Kennedy bashing and, secondly, when you consider the Kennedy bashing you consider the sources doing the bashing. In Kitty Kelley's case it was George Smathers. Now Smathers may have pretended to be a friend of the Kennedys, but I don't believe he ever was. He was a big stockholder in a company which was run basically by [Meyer] Lansky's people."

Is that in print?

"I printed it in my Hoffa book.[38] And I felt that by exploiting the Smathers interview it did not present a balanced view of Jackie Onassis or the Kennedys. Kitty's story about Judith Exner in *People* magazine—JFK and the Mob—I thought that was the worst damn thing I'd ever seen."

Fabricated?

"No. It was a matter of mutilating the facts."

How did Kitty Kelley double-cross you?

"I helped her considerably on the Sinatra book. And another person was writing a book similar to mine. I did not know that they were friends, and apparently closer friends than she and I were. I was in the midst of my work when I found out this relationship was going on. So my tactic was to feed her disinformation. When she asked me when my book was coming out I'd give her a date like 1988, when in fact it was coming out much earlier."

She was passing on to your rival material you had given her?

"Yes, basically and presumably saying, 'Don't worry about Dan, he's not coming out until 1988.' So the other guy relaxed—and my book came out in 1986. And that was my *Dark Victory: Ronald Reagan, MCA and the Mob* (Viking)."[39]

Kitty Kelley bristles at the suggestion that she is not a fair or balanced biographer. But just look at how she launched her Sinatra book.

On page one, paragraph one, she tells us he was arrested in 1938 on a morals charge. And talk about guilt by association! She gives us a picture of the family early in the book that makes the Ma Barker crowd seem like your friendly next-door neighbors.

Uncle Dominic was charged with malicious mischief, and Sinatra's dad, with receiving stolen goods. Uncle Gus was constantly in trouble with the cops as a numbers runner. And those were the respectable members of the family! Uncle Babe was an ex-con who had been charged with taking part in a murder. And Frank's mother, Dolly, was often in court accused of performing abortions.

After that Kelley gives us the bad stuff.

It's the out-for-blood prosecuting attorney approach. To beat the rap Sinatra would have had to have been a monk, eunuch, or orphan. And with Kelley as recording angel, preferably all three.

Inevitably, a counter-puncher, aroused by Kelley's notoriety, determined to uncover the secret, unflattering aspects of *her* life. This was a tough task because Kelley became as elusive as Howard Hughes during his neurotic heyday.

George Carpozi, Jr., was well-equipped for the job. A former U.S. Marine, he had published two books about Jacqueline Onassis and a book about Frank Sinatra years before Kelley's appeared. As a reporter he had exposed insurance rackets, phony medical clinics, and police shakedowns. He had even helped capture New York's "Mad Bomber," who terrorized the city in the 1940s. This is not to equate Kelley with insurance racketeers or a "Mad Bomber." But what they all had in common was the urge to run for cover.

When Carpozi told me* his book would be titled *Bimbo: The Kitty Kelley Story* (finally *Poison Pen: The Unauthorized Biography of Kitty Kelley*), I said the title alone cried out "hatchet job!" "Not so," he replied. "That came about this way. Kelley had written a piece for *People* magazine on the so-called ties between John Kennedy, Sam Giancana [chief of Chicago's Mafia], and Judith Exner. Kelley went on the 'Larry King' TV show to discuss it. And they took calls from viewers and one said, 'Miss Kelley, suppose someone were to go and look into your closet, would he find any skeletons?' She suddenly looked stunned, but she recouped quickly: 'No, I don't think they'd find anything there. I have nothing to hide.' And that made me bolt out of bed, thinking: 'What an idea!' So I immediately worked out a title for the book: 'An unauthorized biography: *Down and Dirty on Kitty Kelley! All the terrible truth you never knew about the wicked word slinger!*' And I called up Allan Wilson, editor-in-chief of Citadel Press, which is another company in the Lyle Stuart family. He said, 'I love the idea.' So I saw Lyle and as we were discussing the book, he said, 'I have plenty of stuff about Kitty Kelley and I know people who'll give you more.' Then he said, 'I'm going to change the title to *Bimbo: The Kitty Kelley Story.*' "

So you *are* going to do a hatchet job.

"No, I'm going to be fair," he replied. "But I'm sure I can find enough people who hate her guts who will spill their guts about her. For example, I know a biographer who is researching a book similar to what Kelley has written; and he has found thirty people so far that said they never spoke with her though she had quoted them in her book. I've checked about twenty-four and all told me they never talked to Kelley, and they are mentioned in her book as having been interviewed. That includes Peter Lawford, who I didn't speak to because I have no way

---

*Interview with George Carpozi, Jr., May 21, 1988.

of interviewing him where he is. Kelley claimed she interviewed Lawford twice: once on his deathbed [when he was an alcoholic and cross-addicted to drugs] and again on January 5, 1985, when he had been dead twelve days.

"There's absolutely no connection between what Kelley said in her Sinatra book and what Peter Lawford's wife told me. She's the daughter of George Seaton, who did *Miracle on Thirty-Fourth Street*. She said Kelley came to the house with Stanley Tretick, a *Life* magazine photographer, under the ruse that he was doing a twentieth-anniversary piece on the death of JFK. When Patricia Seaton Lawford came back from the beach five or six minutes after the interview started, she found Kelley in her house. She didn't know who she was except that she did recognize her because she had seen her on TV. But she couldn't imagine why she was there with Tretick.

"When Patricia saw this broad sitting on the couch talking to her husband and asking him questions about Sinatra, when this was supposed to be an interview about JFK, she went in the bedroom and called *Life* in New York. They said, 'We have no Kitty Kelley working for us.' Then she came and threw Kelley out of the house. Tretick was using his *Life* credentials to get Kelley interviews with people she couldn't otherwise get to."[40]

Kelley protested to Norma Langely of *Star* magazine, saying: "They claim Peter Lawford, whom I interviewed, was deceived in some way. If he was deceived, why did he talk for eight hours running his mouth about Frank Sinatra?"

"The truth is," countered Carpozi, "that she didn't speak to Lawford for more than ten minutes and even that was done through deception."

I asked Carpozi, "You think it's terrible to mislead in order to reach a difficult subject?"

"I think it's a horrible, outrageous thing to do. You should always be upfront."

Do you also believe Kelley makes up quotes?

"Absolutely. She takes them from anybody who has ever written about him and she also makes them up. She twists them and turns them until she has them figured into what she wants them to say."

You mean the Lawford quotes may be accurate but somebody else, not Kelley, got him to say them?

"But then she twists them so she makes them come out of somebody else's mouth as she wants them to be."

Does that distort the meaning?

"Of course. She's a journalistic whore and you can quote me on that." (Journalist Pete Hamill agrees, also calling Kelley "a journalistic whore." And to fellow journalist Max Lerner she's a "journalistic debaucher." Lerner denies "everything and anything Kitty Kelley said I told her" about his relationship with Elizabeth Taylor.)

I suggested to Carpozi that, "It's still possible, though, that Kelley interviewed Lawford twice. Perhaps she just goofed on the date."

"No way. No way. She's a big liar."

How do you think she was able to quote people without interviewing them?

"By going through the clippings."

That's what you do for your books.

"But I don't say that these people spoke to me. I just say that's what they said. Kelley has a spot in the back of the Sinatra book which she called 'Author's Chapter Notes.' In it she claimed to have interviewed 857 people on certain dates, and one of them [Lawford] was very dead on the day she claimed to have talked to him. That was one person. And a whole bunch of others denied she had interviewed them. All she did was to pull clips, which she always does. I would say she might have talked to ninety or a hundred people.

"She's totally unscrupulous in a thousand ways. She stole a manuscript from Barbara Howar and sold it to the *Wash-*

ingtonian magazine. [Kelley denies she stole it.] Her first book, about fat farms, was a big fraud, too. She freeloaded on every one of the thirteen famous fat farms she visited, mainly because she was looking to lose weight at the time and figured she could get a story out of it."

She gave the fat farms publicity. How is that so bad?

"She did a number on a lot of the farms that won't ever allow her to come back again. One of them was La Costa Hotel and Spa in California."

In other words, she gave a negative report.

"Oh, terrible. She said the Mafia had invested money to open the farm."

Why didn't they sue her?

"Probably, because it's true."

Well then, what was wrong with that?

"She bit the hand that fed her. They gave her carte blanche entre. And what she said was not any secret. It was the Teamsters that supported this fat farm."

If you went to a fat farm as an investigative reporter and found it was Mafia supported, wouldn't you say so?

"But when she went there she knew that ahead of time. It was no secret. It had been widely, widely publicized."

I can't see how she did anything wrong in that case. Do you see my point?

"I do. But she was totally unscrupulous in other ways. I've found a lot of interesting information about Kelley from her friends who are not really friends and she's got a whole bunch of enemies."

Where's her elusive husband, Mike Edgely?

"She sent him off to the South Seas to get rid of him, so he wouldn't be able to talk to me."

Did you check on Kelley's report that Ava Gardner had aborted Sinatra's baby?

"Ava Gardner wrote me and said she didn't want to be

interviewed, that she doesn't read the 'lady's' rubbish, and it's not worth responding to. I checked with the MGM records where Kelley said she saw an account of Ava Gardner having had an abortion. There's no such record. When Ava Gardner was ill at the time it was from drinking poisoned water in Africa."

How do you feel about doing an exposé of a fellow biographer?

"I feel I'm doing the world a service. I don't think, for example, that what she wrote about Elizabeth Taylor was kosher. Taylor had all those marriages, but there were no great scandals except for the scandalous affair with Eddie Fisher. All the others seem pretty clean. She's been a drinker, and she's taken drugs. And she's not exactly the kind of woman you'd want to be among nuns. But still, she hasn't done anything to draw the kind of attack Kelley went after her with."

In your own book, *Sinatra: Is This Man Mafia?*, what did you conclude?

"Very definitely he has ties to the Mafia. So there was no hesitation on my part to say that."

That was also Kitty Kelley's conclusion.

"And in his book on Sinatra, Earl Wilson laid a good foundation for her. Bad as the guy may be, and as bad as his connections with the mob are, I don't think I'd ever write that his mother was an abortionist. This is an outrage. The woman is dead. Why dig her out of the grave and brand her an abortionist?"

Most biographers, I think, would disagree with you. One aim of a biographer is to resurrect the dead, and if your subject's mother was an abortionist and especially if it had an effect on him—perhaps humiliated him—then you say so.

"In the old days among the Italians, if a woman was a midwife, she took care of this stuff. It was done so many times in those days. To call her an abortionist is ridiculous. This is why I'm going after Kitty Kelley."

Are you telling me you'll deliberately bias the book against her?

"I'm going to do the story right down the middle. I'm going to do it totally honestly. And so far I haven't found one person who likes her. I call her every day and leave a message on her recorder. Every day I ask her, 'Why does Barbara Howar say you are a woman with no honor at all?' Howar says she's the worst woman she's met in her whole life. I've got terrific quotes in the book. It's going to be dynamite. My publisher loves it. He's eating it up. What I'm going to do to Kelley is going to be the biggest number. She did three books, *Jackie Oh!*, *Elizabeth Taylor: The Last Star*, and *His Way*, about Sinatra. I'm going to do *her* so much, she's going to have to jump off the Washington Monument."[41]

Promoting her Sinatra biography on Larry King's TV show, Kelley was asked how she would feel if someone pulled a skeleton out of her closet. "Awful," she replied. "I'd feel just terrible." She was also asked if she would like someone to write a book about her. "Yes, I would," she answered. "If a Kitty Kelley does it."

If that meant concentrating on the dirt and the degradation, she got her wish in Carpozi. "Answered Prayers," as Capote would have put it with a diabolical chuckle.

Nancy the Terrible

Hugh Sidey, a Washington-based editor for *Time* magazine, read only parts of Kelley's book *Nancy Reagan: The Unauthorized Biography,* but thought it "Outrageous. I had the sense of it that every rumor unconfirmed was picked up and put in that book," he told me.* "Nancy Reagan was a strong figure

---

*Interview with Hugh Sidey, December 14, 1993.

in the White House but about half of what was attributed to
her never happened. In our world of openness there isn't anything
wrong with printing all the rumors—as long as they're so
branded. But in Kelley's case there's a lot of confusion about
what she presented as facts and what was kind of a fancy of
some people."

"But," I pointed out to Sidey, "even when Kelley prints
a rumor and the denials of the principals, many of her readers
will think: 'Of course they'd deny it. But there must be something
to it.' "

"That's right. That's an old dodge in the business. The same
thing was done about Kennedy by virtually everybody up till
Richard Reeves [a recent JFK biographer].[42] If you just dwell
on the scurrilous tales and pick them up from every place and
pack them into a book, then it gives a gravely distorted view
of this person. Though I think Reeves is a little too condescend-
ing. We people in the business have gotten so arrogant and
so self-centered and self-righteous about things. I think Reeves's
is quite an accurate book but I get the sense that Reeves likes
him better than the book reads."

"Were you amused by Kelley's implication that Nancy
Reagan and Sinatra were having an affair in the White House?"

"Yes. I don't think Nancy Reagan's passions ran to sex
at that point."[43]

Kelley stuck to her guns but, when asked for hard evidence
to confirm the Nancy-Frank affair, lamely cited the legal definition of adultery "which just calls for time, place, and opportunity."
This moved Edmund Morris to write to the *Washington Post*:

> Readers shocked by Kitty Kelley's recent revelations of private
> tête-à-têtes upstairs in the White House don't know the half
> of it. As Ronald Reagan's authorized biographer, I can now
> report that every Thursday noon for eight years, Mr. Reagan
> and George Bush retired to a small chamber adjoining the

Oval Office for intimate "lunches" or "luncheons." Staff were under strict orders not to disturb the couple as long as they stayed there. . . . And here's the really kinky detail—on at least one occasion the two men were joined by photographers. . . . I think the above flagrant facts speak for themselves.[44]

Sophia Casey, the widow of CIA Director William Casey, took Kelley's book more seriously. It was there that she learned for the first time of Nancy Reagan agitating to replace Casey as CIA director while he was hospitalized after brain surgery. She wrote a letter to Mrs. Reagan asking "Is it true?" but got no reply.

I asked Sidey if he believed the Kelley charge. "I would have to hear from Nancy Reagan precisely what it was she wanted," Sidey replied. "The idea of having Casey fired I question. The idea of somehow bypassing him or moving him aside until events took their course—that I could understand."

"In his memoirs Don Regan said she wanted him fired."

"There's a character who had his own axes to sharpen. It's possible, but it was a tough situation. You needed to keep things running and at the same time Casey was incapable."[45]

Mrs. Reagan's personal friend, columnist and political pundit George Will despises Kelley as

a professional retailer of falsehoods. Her work in the sewers of journalism exploits the fact that public figures can be recklessly written about with impunity. . . . For the record, I, unlike Ms. Kelley, know Mrs. Reagan. Many people, who admire her as I do, refused to cooperate with Ms. Kelley, knowing her to be the journalistic sociopath that her book shows her to be. So most of the "sources," if they exist, are hostile to her subject. . . . Much of the book reeks of fabrication.

Even Ms. Kelley's acknowledgments are absurd. In a list of "editors, writers, and reporters" who "took the time to answer questions and share their stories," there appears the name of the man who runs the mail room in *Time* magazine's Washington Bureau.[46]

She also lists Jack Nelson, Washington bureau chief of the *Los Angeles Times,* and Fred Barnes of the *New Republic.* Both deny they were her sources.

Nelson said,* "She mentioned me with a thousand other people who had helped her and I had nothing to do with the book. I read enough to know what is in it. There is no reason to read the whole book. She took a lot of things on faith which she didn't substantiate. Some was probably accurate and some of it she wrote on assumptions. The publishing industry has lowered its standards tremendously. It's almost unbelievable the kinds of books they publish."

I asked Nelson, "How do you know that one of her researchers didn't contact you and chat about Nancy Reagan without telling you it was for Kelley?"

"Nobody ever contacted me about the book."

"Suppose they didn't mention the book but simply wanted to discuss Mrs. Reagan?"

"I would know about that. Nobody ever talked to me about anything that had to do with Nancy Reagan."

"Do you recall how Kelley writes of a woman who claimed Ronald Reagan had date-raped her, but then says it wasn't exactly date rape?"

"Yes. She throws it in there even though there's no proof."[47]

Fred Barnes did get a phone call from Kitty Kelley and agreed to meet her for lunch to discuss Nancy Reagan. "She told me she was writing a book about Mrs. Reagan," says Barnes,† "and although I knew of her reputation for hatchet

*Interview with Jack Nelson, November 30, 1993.

†Interview with Fred Barnes, November 30, 1993.

jobs, I still agreed to meet her. But it never happened, because she didn't call me again. I'd written several pieces about Nancy Reagan including a cover story about her constructing her new image as the antidrug Czarina, which she did very well. She's a very smart woman. Brittle but very smart. I also wrote a very critical piece saying that although she claimed she wasn't involved in public policy and personnel roles, she was actively involved, particularly in firing Don Regan.

"I've always thought there is a role in journalism for rumors, innuendos, and outlandish statements and tips. But then you are supposed to verify them. If you can verify them, you can use them. If you can't, you ought to forget them. Unfortunately, that's becoming sort of a quaint idea. But Kelley isn't the only one writing these tawdry books.

"As for listing me as a source, I think she fudged it. A very big fudge."[48]

Criticized for publicizing Kelley's book as front-page news, the *New York Times* somewhat redeemed itself by handing the reviewing assignment to Joe Queenan, who called it,

> one of the most encyclopedically vicious books in the history of encyclopedic viciousness . . . one of the least balanced biographies in recent times. Joseph Stalin has received more affectionate treatment than Ms. Kelley affords the Reagans. On the other hand, families that make a habit of laying wreaths in cemeteries filled with the remains of Nazi storm troopers deserve everything they get.[49]

Does Kelley deserve everything she gets? Is she the sloppy reporter some imply, who juggles with the truth and treats rumor as holy writ? I asked Edmund Morris, now at work on an authorized Ronald Reagan biography. Morris had a unique insider's view of the Reagans. He had met Kelley socially and found her charming, but politely declined her request for an interview.

Morris, the acclaimed biographer of Theodore Roosevelt, considered Kelley's biography of Frank Sinatra to be "excellent—courageous, carefully researched, and convincing. For that reason I was interested in what she might tell me in *Nancy Reagan.* But to tell the truth, I never read more than about six or seven pages of the latter book. Its style was so vulgar, and its hostility so uncontrolled, that reading it made me feel slightly queasy. This may make me sound like an apologist for Mrs. Reagan, but really what I resented, as a reader, was the feeling that the author was trying to manipulate me. Her opening sentence, for example, states: 'Two entries on Nancy Reagan's birth certificate are accurate—her sex and her color.' The implication is that all the other facts on the certificate [reproduced in facsimile] are inaccurate—or to quote Ms. Kelley's second sentence, 'Almost every other item has been invented.' There are, by my count, forty facts on the certificate, only four of which Ms. Kelley plausibly cites as untrue. All the rest look pretty accurate to me. What we have here, therefore, is a book starting with two 'weasel' statements. The first is technically true: there indeed are 'two' accurate facts on that certificate—along with about three dozen others. The second puts a severe strain on its qualifying adjective. If four out of forty is 'almost' then I'm almost Arnold Schwarzenegger. I think Ms. Kelley's problem with the Nancy Reagan book was that she allowed the weight of her own negativism to flatten her."[50]

Kelley also describes a party Morris and his wife gave for the Reagans and a group of friends on November 15, 1987, concluding with,

> Reagan went upstairs and looked at the dome that divided both houses of Congress. "Oh, boy," he said, rubbing his hands with glee. "I could finish those guys off with a .22 from up here." Relishing the prospect, he stared out of the big glass windows until the Secret Service agents moved him back.[51]

Without disputing Kelley's version of that incident, Morris maintains, "there are no fewer than thirteen small errors of fact in Ms. Kelley's account of our dinner party for the Reagans."

Stephen Birmingham, also a Jacqueline Onassis biographer, is even more critical: "I know Kitty Kelley," he said, "and I don't believe a word she says. She makes things up. She tricks people, and I don't think she is to be trusted."[52]

Ronald Reagan himself, stopped on his way to church in Bel-Air, replied to a reporter's question: "While I am accustomed to reports that stray from the truth, the flagrant and absurd falsehoods cited in a recently published book clearly exceed the bounds of decency. They are patently untrue—everything from the allegation of marijuana use to marital infidelity to my failure to be present at the birth of my daughter Patti. Many of my friends have urged me to issue a point-by-point denial of the book's many outrages. To do so would, I feel, provide legitimacy to a book that has no basis in fact and serves no decent purpose. I have an abiding faith that the American people will judge this book for what it really is: sensationalism whose sole purpose is enriching its author and publisher. Neither I, nor Nancy, intend to have further comment on this matter."[53]

He doesn't have to. His authorized biographer, Edmund Morris, surely will, believing as he does that a biographer should "tell all he knows of significance, good and bad." So we can expect him to tackle some of Kelley's wildest charges.

The comments of incensed reviewers [who could, of course, have ignored the book] sent the public racing to the bookstores and justified the multimillion-dollar advance Kelley reportedly received to "expose" Nancy Reagan.

Not all reviewers found the book repulsive. Biographer Peter Collier praised Kelley for her "admirable amount of research," and suggested that some critics were simply motivated by envy.[54]

White House correspondent Maureen Dowd gave both

women the back of her hand, slamming the book as "tawdry
. . . loosely sourced and over the top . . . pie-in-the-face journalism," yet acknowledged Kelley's extraordinary achievement
in providing

> a reason for sympathy with Nancy Reagan. She has taken
> one of the shrewdest, coldest, most manipulative women in
> American politics . . . and transformed her into a victim. Kelley
> is a mean and greedy writer, so drunk on sensationalism that
> she lacks compassion and understanding. Her subject was a
> mean and greedy First Lady, so drunk on power that she lacked
> compassion and understanding. . . . Both are soap opera vixens
> who accrue so many enemies in their climb to respectability
> and riches that the air around them is rancid with revenge.[55]

Kitty Kelley giggled all the way to the bank, then took
a vacation, while her biography by Carpozi was about to hit
the bookstores. Carpozi had unearthed other lurid details about
Kelley's past every bit as degrading as what she dredged up
about the President and First Lady.

Former White House staffers couldn't let Carpozi go un-
rewarded. Still smarting from Kelley's poisonous portraits of
the Reagans, they gave him a victory party—at the Watergate,
of course. "Led by Elaine Crispen, Mrs. Reagan's press secretary,
about 350 overcrowded the place," said Carpozi.* "I signed 130
books and it was one of the most brilliant and most beautiful
book parties I ever had. Everybody covered it and it was on
TV and radio. And I had a book party in New York, where
Mayor Koch showed up and a whole bunch of people."[56]

Flushed with pride, Carpozi turned his sights on the new
White House occupants. He would do a combined biography
of the Clintons.

---

*Interview with George Carpozi, Jr., January 10, 1994.

I asked him: "How would you respond to those who say you are like Kitty Kelley in that you go for the negative and don't attempt a balanced portrait?"

"I do look for a balanced portrait, but I haven't found one," he said.

Meanwhile, the Brits should be warned: Kelley is at work on her next demolition project—reportedly Prince Philip and his wife, Queen Elizabeth. If she should find them too tame, there's enough dirt around about the rest of the royals to bury the lot of them.

Could Kitty Kelley's poison pen and doubtful sources bring about the fall of the monarchy? Has she really such power? Harold Brooks-Baker, publishing director of *Burke's Peerage,* raises this awesome prospect when he speculates: "Had a Kelley approach to describing the monarch's life existed when James I bestowed favors on homosexual lovers, there would be no [British] monarchy to love or hate."[57]

Kelley the Fearless

Newspaper columnist Liz Smith is something of a Kelley expert and a former friend. She says:* "Kelley is a good reporter and fearless in a lot of ways, although she always claims she's frightened to death. Loyalty and honesty are not her strong suits. In the end she's intensely mean-spirited. Let's take the issue of Nancy Reagan's lesbianism: one of the most ridiculous things I've ever heard, in which Kelley indicts the entire Smith College. That alone made me feel sympathy for Mrs. Reagan that I just would never have known I felt. Kelley jumps to conclusions, such as Mrs. Reagan's love affair with Frank Sinatra, which I don't think ever happened. Then there's the

---

*Interview with Liz Smith, March 1, 1994.

classic story about Kitty Kelley where she's led on by someone who tells her something and then they say, 'I was just pulling your leg, it didn't really happen.' And she says, 'Gee, I wonder if there's some way I could use it, anyway?' "

"How definite is that?" I asked Smith.

"I think it's in Carpozi's book. It's a famous anecdote, though I wouldn't give him too much more credibility than I would now give her.

"Judith Exner wrote a book in which she didn't tell the truth, because she was terrified of being killed. She thought she would be assassinated by the Kennedy people or the Mob. She decided to set the record straight and wanted me to write it. I said I didn't have the time and why not let Kitty Kelley do this? Well, Kelley wanted to distort the story. Exner had had a child out of wedlock that she gave away for adoption and Kitty wanted to write this as though it may be Jack Kennedy's child, because it made it more interesting. Well, the time frame was not even accurate. Also I knew who the father of this child was, a fairly well-known movie executive. So poor Judith Exner had to wrestle all the way down the line with Kitty Kelley for which Kitty Kelley was going to get about $150,000. Here was Judith Exner trying to pay society back and tell the truth and Kitty Kelley wanted to sensationalize everything. *People* magazine finally rewrote the story. They realized it had been an enormous mistake to let Kitty Kelley do it.

"She thought I had taken Judith Exner's side—and I had. And she never forgave me for it.

"When she wrote her book on Jackie Onassis, I gave her all my files. I never saw them again. I tried to help her on her Sinatra book, introduced her to a lot of people. This didn't cut any ice. She just laid me to filth in her Nancy Reagan book. She tells the story about Barbara Walters giving a luncheon for Nancy Reagan and she paints me as this ass kisser. Mrs. Reagan was no longer First Lady. We were all journalists there to celebrate her book. And the room fell silent and she said something about the press criticizing her. And I said, as a sort of a joke, 'Well, Mrs. Reagan, you've got to be philosophical. Now you belong to the ages.' Just to fill a vacuum, a sort of nicety that didn't mean anything. And Kelley prints this as evidence I was Mrs. Reagan's stooge.

"I was totally done up by her. It was one thing for her to be sloppy, and to write sensational books. That still doesn't take away my admiration for her diligence and her ambition. She isn't a person of any real discernible talent. She can't write. But she does things that are quite amazing. She gets help from Stanley Tretick, who's well respected as a photographer. He goes with her on many of these interviews and takes pictures of her with the person. If the person says 'I never gave an interview to Kitty Kelley,' she's got the picture. She wormed her way into a Mafia guy's home, had dinner there, she and Stanley, and got reams of things that are true.

"I used to really help her because she used to be a really good source for me and most of the things she ever suggested I do panned out. But she wrote me stupid, anonymous letters. That was just too low. So I gave up on her. Now I would not believe anything of hers I read.

"When I protested to Simon & Schuster about things Kitty Kelley had written about me, they were taken out of the paperback. Kelley is writing about Mrs. Reagan and all she could to say was that I was her great defender. And the implication is that I'm gay and Mrs. Reagan went to Smith College and she's a lesbian, too, while at the same time fucking Frank Sinatra in the White House. I found this the most outrageous leap of judgment I'd ever heard and so gratuitous since I really was the most minor player in Mrs. Reagan's life. My theory is that her [Kelley's] editors don't read anything in these books: they're too trashy."[58]

Notes

1. Gerri Hirshey, "Oh Kitty!" *Washington Post Magazine,* October 30, 1988, p. 22.
2. Gerri Hirshey, *Washington Post,* November 1, 1988, p. E2.
3. Interview with Philip Geyelin, March 2, 1990.
4. Interview with Barbara Howar, November 12, 1988.
5. Ibid.
6. George Carpozi, Jr., *Poison Pen: The Unauthorized Biography of Kitty Kelley* (New Jersey: Barricade Books, 1991), p. 115.
7. Kitty Kelley, *Jackie Oh!* (New York: Lyle Stuart, 1978), pp. 75–78.
8. Interview with Don Uffinger, March 27, 1989.
9. Interview with Ben Bradlee, March 27, 1989.
10. Interview with John Sansing, March 27, 1989.
11. Interview with David Heymann, January 27, 1990.
12. Ibid.
13. Interview with William Walton, February 7, 1990.
14. Interview with Nancy Tuckerman, March 5, 1990.
15. Kitty Kelley, "What It Was Like to Write *Jackie Oh!*" *Washingtonian,* October 1978, p. 74.
16. Interview with Ben Bradlee, March 27, 1989.
17. Kelley, "What It Was Like to Write *Jackie Oh!*" p. 76.
18. Interview with Ben Bradlee, March 27, 1989.
19. Kelley, "What It Was Like to Write *Jackie Oh!*" p. 85.
20. Ibid.
21. Ibid.
22. Interview with Ben Bradlee, March 27, 1989.
23. Interview with David Heymann, January 27, 1990. Dr. Max Jacobson got his nickname by giving his celebrity patients amphetamines which made them feel good.
24. E. J. Kahn, Jr., *About the New Yorker and Me* (New York: Putnam's, 1979), p. 65.
25. American Society of Journalists and Authors: Professional Rights Committee, October 7, 1983.
26. *Baltimore Sun,* December 4, 1983.

27. Interview with David Heymann, January 27, 1990.

28. Interview with Justin Kaplan, December 30, 1988.

29. Barbara Grizzuti Harrison, "Terrified and Fascinated by His Own Life," *New York Times Book Review,* November 2, 1986, p. 13.

30. Interview with Kitty Kelley, February 14, 1987.

31. Kitty Kelley, *His Way: The Unauthorized Biography of Frank Sinatra* (New York: Bantam, 1986), p. 28.

32. Ibid., p. 500.

33. Interview with Frank Garrick's widow, April 12, 1988.

34. Interview with Marion Brush Schreiber, December 11, 1988.

35. Interview with Steve Capiello, December 10, 1988.

36. Alice Steinbach, "Is Kelley's Sinatra for Real?" *Baltimore Sun,* October 5, 1986, pp. 1G, 6–7G.

37. Interview with David Crown, March 27, 1989.

38. Dan Moldea, *The Hoffa Wars* (New York: Paddington Press, 1978).

39. Interview with Dan Moldea, March 27, 1989.

40. This contradicts Heymann's previous comment—quoting Lawford's wife—that "there was no talk whatsoever about Frank Sinatra." If Kelley asked questions about Sinatra, presumably Lawford answered some of them.

41. Interview with George Carpozi, Jr., May 21, 1988.

42. Richard Reeves, *President Kennedy: Profile of Power* (New York: Simon & Schuster, 1993).

43. Interview with Hugh Sidey, December 14, 1993.

44. Edmund Morris, *Washington Post,* April 11, 1991.

45. Interview with Hugh Sidey, December 14, 1993.

46. George Will, "Only Envious Read Garbage Like This," *Palm Beach Post,* April 14, 1991.

47. Interview with Jack Nelson, November 30, 1993.

48. Interview with Fred Barnes, November 30, 1993.

49. Joe Queenan, "No Stone Unthrown," *New York Times Book Review,* May 5, 1991, p. 3.

50. Letter to author from Edmund Morris, December 26, 1993.

51. Kitty Kelley, *Nancy Reagan: The Unauthorized Biography* (New York: Simon & Schuster, 1991), pp. 572–73.

52. Brian E. Crowley, *Palm Beach Post,* April 21, 1991, p. 2B.

53. *New York Times,* "Reagan Calls New Book About Wife 'Untrue,' " April 9, 1991, p. 18.

54. Roger Cohen, "Reagan Biography: In Quest of What?" *New York Times,* April 10, 1991, p. A16. It should be noted, though, that much of Kelley's research is done by hired guns. She named ten researchers who helped for her Sinatra biography and twelve for her Nancy Reagan biography.

55. Maureen Dowd, "Ol' Blue Lips," *New Republic* (May 13, 1991): 28–34.

56. Interview with George Carpozi, Jr., January 10, 1994.

57. Harold Brooks-Baker, "Kitty Kelley Could Rock the Royals," *New York Times,* April 25, 1991, p. A15. The working title is *The House of Windsor.*

58. Interview with Liz Smith, March 1, 1994.

3

Charles Higham's Victims:
Errol Flynn, Rita Hayworth, Cary Grant,
and the Duchess of Windsor

The son of a six-time-married British advertising tycoon who became a conservative member of Parliament, Charles Higham emigrated to Australia in 1954, at age twenty-three, and fifteen years later emigrated to the United States. He preceded Rex Reed at the *New York Times,* quizzing celebrities and penning personality profiles. He also wrote poetry, published by Hand and Flower Press, and biographies that ranged from Arthur Conan Doyle to Orson Welles and Katharine Hepburn, whose voice he described in one of his best lines as a cross between Donald Duck and a Stradivarius.

How did he persuade Hepburn to cooperate with him for *Kate: The Life of Katharine Hepburn,* when she had turned down other would-be biographers?

"She liked me and I liked her," he said, when I spoke with him.*

---

*Interview with Charles Higham, July 16, 1986.

"You don't think she met an author she liked until she met you?"

"Maybe she liked me more than the others. [He laughed.] But we hit it off incredibly. We sat there laughing hour after hour. It was the most happy experience I've had in my life of any sort. She was just wonderful." He also hit it off with Patricia Braham, protector of Rasputin's daughter, Maria. Braham told Higham—something that has escaped historians— how Prince Yussoupov had a homosexual crush on Rasputin and after the Russian "holy man" was murdered, the prince cut off his penis for a keepsake. Higham says he was offered a glimpse of the penis, kept in a box, and said to resemble "a black banana," as an inducement to collaborate on Braham's memoirs. Higham, surprisingly, declined.

Some of his most memorable encounters were with Rita Hayworth while researching an Orson Welles biography. "I met her several times," he said. "Offscreen she was extremely shy, subdued, and nervous. But underneath it all, she was very intelligent. And terrified of everyone. She didn't trust anyone and yet this mousey person, who was absolutely sweet, became completely changed on camera and became the opposite."

Higham, too, is not always what he seems. He told *Contemporary Authors*:

> I have found a way to blend my poetic and more commercial talents. I have discovered, rather in the middle of life, a gift for fiction. This has been the greatest joy of my life. Since the masses do not read poetry, I can bring a poetic sensibility to bear on writing for a mass market. I am overjoyed.[1]

Rather than as a poet or novelist, fellow author Alyn Brodsky sees Higham as "a literary ghoul who deals in sordid secrets of famous people now dead, who can neither disprove his seemingly dubious charges, haul him into court, nor spit in his eye."[2]

Another reviewer did the next best thing, calling him "a viper-like biographer," conceding that everything Higham says about his subject in *Cary Grant: The Lonely Heart* may be true, but convincing evidence is missing.[3] To say the least. A third reviewer dismissed it as a "lurid book" in which Higham cruelly defames a man who couldn't defend himself.[4]

Cary Grant, Jewish Gigolo?

Mae West's death was supposed to confirm the long-held rumor that she was really a man. It didn't. But her one-time leading man, Cary Grant, believed the rumor wasn't far off the mark. According to him, she was genetically a male in a female body. At least, that's what he told his mistress, Maureen Donaldson, adding, "Poor thing. I don't think she ever really knew who she was."[5]

How about Cary Grant? Did he ever really know who he was? Chances are he wouldn't have recognized himself in Charles Higham's biography.[6]

Grant's friend, David Niven, described him to me in an interview on October 3, 1975, as "will-o-the wisp; a mixture of enthusiasm and mysticism. He's a highly sensitive fellow, and a terrifically private person. I don't think people know the nice, generous, and kind side to him."[7]

The public knew Grant as a charming, affable, urbane WASP; a master of light, romantic comedy, who married five times and fathered a daughter whom he idolized. He experimented with LSD and had an uneasy relationship with his mother. But the overall picture was of what used to be called a gentleman, and in the theater, a class act.

Higham obliterated this public image as well as David Niven's view of Grant, suggesting that instead of a movie set Grant belonged in a lunatic asylum. Higham's Grant was a dangerously schizophrenic bisexual who, despite his WASP image, was the bastard son of his father's Jewish mistress.

When Cary Grant (originally Archibald Leach) was ten, his father committed his mother to a mental institution in their hometown of Bristol, England, saying she had gone away for a rest. When she never returned, Grant believed his mother had abandoned him. Higham speculates that the father's motive in committing his wife was in order to live with a mistress— either a Jewish seamstress or Jewish actress—who was Grant's "true" mother. Higham's "evidence" for Grant being a Jew is that he was circumcised, a rarity at that time (the early 1900s) and place among non-Jewish boys. Shortly after his father died in 1935, Grant learned from relatives that his mother's long "rest" was a cover story, that she had not abandoned him as he had always thought, and was still in the mental institution.

Grant had her released and took care of her until she died in 1975, at age ninety-five. Their relationship was strained. For example, she once pushed him away when he tried to kiss her, and they had few interests in common. Higham cites this as further "evidence" that she was not his real mother.

That he was a "dangerous schizophrenic" is the remark of an ex-wife and is backed up by no one else who knew him.

In his bachelor days, says Higham, Grant had been a gigolo servicing wealthy women, then graduated to homosexual affairs with, among others, fellow actor and roommate Randolph Scott, and eccentric billionaire Howard Hughes. According to Higham, Grant was even arrested during World War II for sexual activity with an unidentified male in a public restroom. Where did he get this information? From unnamed informants and gossip. Grant himself, Randolph Scott, and Howard Hughes couldn't rebut him: they were all conveniently dead.[8]

Charles Higham sees himself as a romantic poet who writes celebrity biographies for a living. He fervently defends gossip as a rich source of information, saying: "When Saint-Simon did his unforgettable diaries of the court of Louis XIV, these were the ultimate gossip, but without them we would not have a picture of Louis XIV's court."[9] True, but it's a distorted picture. Higham does not mention that Saint-Simon was a petty, bitter, and envious man who eagerly recorded rumors, gossip, and speculation and seldom had a good word to say about anyone. His account of the French court is seen through the narrowed eyes of a wildly partisan and disappointed courtier.

In the spirit of Saint-Simon, Higham writes: "In the 1970s, Cary Grant and [Randolph] Scott would turn up at the Beverly Hillcrest Hotel late at night, after the other diners had gone, and in the near darkness of their table, at the back of the restaurant, the maitre d' would see the two old men surreptitiously holding hands."[10]

Who says so? The maitre d', who wished to remain anonymous.

Maureen Donaldson, who gave her own account of a four-year affair with Grant from 1973 to 1977, disputes the hand-holding story and challenges the maitre d' to come out of hiding. So far, he hasn't.

Fred Astaire's widow, Robin, also disputes the Grant-Scott affair. She contacted gossip columnist Liz Smith to say that her late husband and Randolph Scott were friends for twenty-five years and that Higham's calling Scott a homosexual "was a dastardly lie. Fred knew him so well. I know it's not true."

Donaldson challenges the accuracy of much of Higham's material covering the time she knew Grant. For example, Higham reports that she unburdened herself to a tennis coach about her sometimes rocky romance with Grant. She claims that the most she ever said to the coach, Tim Barry, was, "How's my backhand?" And although she describes an LSD session when Grant defecated on the psychiatrist's carpet, her view of Grant is compassionate where Higham's is degrading.

When pressed by Scott Sublett of the *Washington Times*

to say if she believed Grant was bisexual, Donaldson replied, "You never know what your partner does before or after you. . . . I simply do not know. But I certainly don't believe (he was homosexual) in his later years at all."[11]

Donaldson once asked Grant why he hired mostly gay male secretaries and he replied, "Homosexuals, in my opinion, work more diligently than heterosexual men. It's like having a woman, but not having a woman, if you know what I mean. You get so much more value. So if somebody is going to fall in love with me and be my secretary, I'd rather it be a man than a woman. Besides, a man can carry suitcases and take care of things like that which you just can't get a woman to do."[12]

Grant sued Chevy Chase for ten million dollars in 1980 when, during an interview with Tom Snyder on NBC, Chase said of him, "He really is a great physical comic and I understand was a homo. . . . What a gal!" Grant said it seriously damaged his "masculine image." Chase apologized, saying he only meant to parody those who used the word "homo." The case was settled out of court.

A homosexual magazine, In Touch, named Grant "Heterosexual of the Month" and published a photo of him and Randolph Scott having breakfast together in the early days when they were roommates. The magazine facetiously remarked how important it was for an executive of a perfume company with four failed marriages to sustain a "masculine image," but did not mention that Grant was also a director of MGM, and connected with a museum and a racecourse.[13]

In April 1990 I wrote the following to actor Stewart Granger: "I am now writing a book about the art of biography, essentially trying to discover the accuracy of modern biographers. One of my chapters is about Charles Higham who with Roy Moseley published a biography of Cary Grant. In it you are quoted as saying: 'I was fitting clothes for King Solomon's Mines and was testing for the leading role in Quo Vadis, a part which later went to Robert Taylor. As I entered the MGM commissary, Cary Grant was paying his bill. He gave me a warm smile. He said, without any preamble, "Would you like to come and have lunch with me?" I knew he was sexually attracted to me. He never laid a hand on me. But I knew.' " Granger returned my letter with those last three sentences circled in ink and his comment: "Bullshit!"

My letter to Granger continued: "Higham and Moseley also wrote: 'Stewart Granger and Ray Austin confirmed from firsthand knowledge that Cary Grant was circumcised.' Could you tell me how you knew?" Granger wrote, "Because he used to swim in the nude when his wife wasn't there—I saw him one time—no big deal."

I concluded in the letter: "In the notes the writers say that Grant and Howard Hughes had a homosexual affair. Do you believe this to be likely? Their sources for this are the late Noah Dietrich and the late Johnny Meyer."

Granger replied, "I really don't know and I don't give a shit!"

Shortly before his death, Grant said, according to his biographer Geoffrey Wansell, "I guess anyone that's publicized is not allowed to be a fairly decent individual. Whether it's from envy or whatever, it perpetuates itself. At my age [81], though, it doesn't matter." And he told a *New York Times* reporter, "When I was a young and popular star, I'd meet a girl with a man and maybe she'd say something nice about me and then the guy would say, 'Yeah, but I hear he's a fag.' It's ridiculous, but they say it about all of us."[14]

In Higham's book, Grant, the mentally unbalanced bisexual, is also a stingy and self-absorbed wife beater. There is evidence that he was a pennypincher—a legacy perhaps of his poor childhood—but he was also at times extremely generous. In 1940 he gave more than any other American to British War Relief—$137,500.[15]

In the same Grant biography, Higham described Gary Cooper as a Nazi sympathizer who was entertained by Hitler in Berlin in 1938—just a year before the start of World War II. Asked by William Safire to name the source for this information, Higham said, "Anthony Slide." But Slide denied this, telling Safire the first he heard of any Cooper-Nazi connection was from Higham.

"It's a despicable, bald-faced lie," Gary Cooper's widow, Veronica Cooper Converse, told Safire. What really happened, she explained, was that after Charles Lindbergh reported that Germany had an invincible air force, President Roosevelt asked her stepfather, Paul Shields, a banker friend and supporter of FDR, to get information about Germany's finances. She and Gary Cooper then went with Shields and his wife to Germany, in the spring of 1939. They met Hermann Goering's half-brother there, and he showed Shields around some Siemens industrial plants. But none of them, she said, met Hitler.[16]

Jonathan Yardley, the *Washington Post*'s top reviewer, summed up the Cary Grant biography as "wading through the slime."[17]

Still, it was pretty tame compared with Higham's picture of Errol Flynn.

Errol Flynn—Bisexual Nazi Spy?

Before they pass through Higham's typewriter, the ribald stories about Errol Flynn are good for a laugh. He's Peter Pan with balls. After the Higham treatment, you begin to believe in diabolic possession. If not the personification of evil, Flynn emerges well in the running.

Has Higham discovered the truth about Flynn in *Errol Flynn: The Untold Story,* or did he scrape up all the dirt he could find and to hell with a balanced portrait?[18] Flynn hardly tried to whitewash his life, titling his ghostwritten autobiography *My Wicked, Wicked Ways*. Friends and fans saw him as a charming, devil-may-care rogue, irresistible to women, whose personality disintegrated under the influence of drugs and drink. But that would apply to many other stars, John Barrymore, for one.

In Higham's book Flynn out-evils them all. And this view is supported by director Raoul Walsh, who said of Flynn: "I was watching a man I loved like a son go straight to hell."

Few were closer to Flynn in his Hollywood heyday than David Niven, so I asked him about their life together.* Niven laughed at the memory and said, "In the mid-thirties I was an absolute monster. Couldn't wait to enjoy myself more and more and more. But that becomes a very depressing sight if you carry it on into middle age and after. Flynn, bless his heart, had a hack at the famous kif, another word for hash in those days. He went on to all sorts of things after that, and he never stopped boozing away. We drank an awful lot in those days. On that one blissful day we got off a week, that one night, Saturday night, all hell broke loose."

"Was Flynn a sadist?"

"Self-centered, you could certainly call him. I don't think he was a sadist."

Not even when he left you in the Pacific a mile from shore with a shark in close pursuit?

"He didn't know there was a shark around. He was just being mischievous. His plan was to let me swim while he got away with my girl. That was a bit naughty, I must say. That was a joke. It wasn't to get me trapped by sharks. Don't forget those wooden skis were hugely broad, about eighteen inches, so all I had to do was lie on the things and paddle myself ashore. Since then I've read *Jaws*—God, it scared the hell out of me. But in those days you didn't read about people being

*Interview with David Niven, October 13, 1975.

attacked by sharks. We used to catch them all the time. They still do. When I was going to write about Flynn in my book *Bring on the Empty Horses,* I didn't want to read his autobiography because I suspected it was ghostwritten. [It was.] Flynn came on a bit strong with some of his stories about painting pennies silver and giving them to the natives as half-crowns. He used to tell me that story all the time.

"He bit his nails, you know. My own private theory is that he had some kind of inferiority complex."[19]

Flynn, who played with cool conviction the name role in *The Perfect Specimen,* felt inferior?

Higham, who claims to have been one of his fans, reveals in his *Errol Flynn: The Untold Story* a far more complicated and sinister character. Higham says he even cried when his exhaustive research revealed his hero to have been a bigoted, bisexual drug addict who betrayed his country as a Nazi spy! This last revelation was met with almost universal disbelief, if not ridicule. I asked Higham about it.* He replied: "James Bacon [Hollywood correspondent for the Associated Press] gave me a hard time in his column for many years. He claimed to be a close friend of Errol Flynn, which is highly questionable, and he took great exception to my disclosures about Flynn's Nazi connections. Also he claimed he knew Flynn well enough to know he was a complete patriot. So I sent a letter which was published in the *Los Angeles Herald Tribune.* It gave very careful documentary sources for my findings, and he wrote back an absurd letter, which was published after mine, which had absolutely no substance in it. Then I challenged him to examine some of the several thousand documents on deposit at the University of Southern California library with public access. He declined to look at them, which I thought was not in the interest of investigative or objective journalism."

---

*Interview with Charles Higham, July 16, 1986.

"Didn't Errol Flynn's daughters sue you?"

"They did, represented by Melvin Belli, the prominent attorney in San Francisco."

"But you can't libel the dead."

"No. They said I had misstated the facts, and had contrived to create a completely invented involvement with the Nazis. Also, that he was no bisexual. Interestingly enough, in the pages of the *Los Angeles Times,* Mr. Belli gave an interview disclosing his personal knowledge of Errol Flynn's relationship with Tyrone Power, and that he knew Flynn had Nazi connections. It seems extraordinary, in view of that, that he would represent the plaintiffs in a lawsuit. The case was thrown out in the lower court because there was no legislation available for libel of the dead. Then it went to the [California] Supreme Court and in a rare unanimous decision under Justice Bird the case was rejected."

"David Niven told me he didn't believe Flynn was a pro-German traitor."

"I was very annoyed with David Niven because I sent him some crucial documents to the South of France, including Flynn's letters in praise of Hitler, and documents from the State Department showing his illegal conducting of Dr. Hermann Erben into Spain during the Spanish civil war. The entire record of Flynn's involvement is so closely documented, down to exact dates, times, and places, which you seldom get in any book of investigative journalism. He didn't even give me the courtesy of a response, which was disgraceful, because I challenged him—since he'd attacked me without even considering the evidence—to look at it and then give me his views on it. And he didn't."

"Wasn't he ill by then?" (Higham's book was published by Doubleday in 1980. Niven's fatal illness, motor-neuron disease, had already begun. He died in the summer of 1983.)

"I don't know. He wasn't ill enough not to say some very rude things about me on public media, which I took great exception to. It was stated by Hugh Downs on TV's '20/20' that Mr. Niven regarded me as 'a looney who should be put in the cooler.' But I was holding a royal flush. I had and have conclusive evidence—it's not a question of random FBI reports— I have documents from foreign embassies. I have absolutely irrefutable material from consuls and vice-consuls who are not in the business, like FBI agents, of concocting something to earn a living. This was the real thing. And when the furor broke, no one took the trouble to ask me where I'd found the material. When I volunteered the information, they chose not to have it examined until the *Washington Post*'s West Coast correspondent in San Francisco went to the trouble, instead of calling absurd people like Olivia de Havilland and David Niven. She spent six weeks with a team of researchers and the conclusions were absolutely and totally corroborative of my findings. When I was on a talk show in San Francisco, a lady called who had been with Sir Percy Sillitoe [Head of Britain's MI5, 1946–1953] in Curzon Street. This was the office in London of MI5. It's almost next door to the office of my father, Sir Charles Higham. I checked her out in London and found she had been on Sir Percy's staff, in charge of the 'Flynn Espionage File' at Curzon Street. She said she was restricted by the Official Secrets Act, but would give me a lead. It led me to find the file at the Ministry of Defense. Unfortunately, the Home Office took a dim view and the files were transferred there and have since been put into the further Security area, only available after seventy years or so. The information she gave me was quite extraordinary—the Flynn–IRA connection. I hadn't know when I wrote Flynn's biography of his IRA connections through Sean Russell [an IRA leader]. They are detailed in my later 1985 book *American Swastika*."

"Why did foreign embassies give you this controversial information?"

"It's not with them. Everything is filed with the State Department. They can declassify documents on request. I asked for all the documents on Errol Flynn and Dr. Hermann Erben. Since then I've taken core documents and had them bound for handy reading and put them in the vaults of the University of Southern California. The most interesting thing in the FBI files are the interrogative reports with Flynn where he protected Dr. Erben, pretending Erben was a helpless refugee from Hitler. There are also some very interesting documents in the Roosevelt Memorial Library. In 1943 Flynn tried to enlist with American Intelligence in Ireland, which is a fairly typical ploy for someone working for enemy intelligence. It's interesting that it went up through the lower reaches of the OSS and then got stopped. As far as I could tell, reading through interoffice memos, the president himself [FDR] personally stopped this. It's interesting, too, that Flynn, with his black sense of humor, said in his application that he had exposed the details of the Nazi head- quarters in Mexico and then gave a description of it, which he couldn't have known unless he had been there. Also, in his application to go to Ireland he said no one would suspect a movie star of being a spy. So this was obviously his idea of humor."

"Do you think his pro-Nazi, pro-IRA activities were because of his daredevil nature or did he genuinely support their causes?"

"It began from his deeply anti-Semitic letters. He wrote to Erben from the Finsbury Park Hotel, London, in September 1933—which I have in my collection in Flynn's handwriting— saying a filthy Jew had cheated him out of his claim and that he therefore felt Hitler should come to England and get rid of the Jews. So you have the basis of a fanatical anti-Semitism, as conclusively evidenced by a private letter to a secret agent of the Nazi government that was never supposed to have been read by anyone else. We have that plus the fact that he grew up in a society in Australia so deeply racist that it wiped out all except one or two blacks in the Black Wars of Tasmania. As I know very well, having spent years in Australia, it has a "White Australia" policy. The atmosphere, as many confirmed in letters to me from Tasmania, could not have been more racist. Flynn grew up as a complete classic WASP. There's no question that Dr. Erben met him and gave Flynn shelter as a distressed Irish seaman on the *Friderun* [so Flynn could sail to Hong Kong for free] even though he was neither distressed, Irish, or a seaman.

"He undoubtedly inculcated Flynn into the Nazi philosophy. Hitler had just taken over in the Reichstag in January 1933. When Flynn met Dr. Erben, who had an extraordinarily charismatic personality, a strange, not directly sexual, but powerful homoerotic relationship developed between them. So it was natural that Flynn would come under his influence and be a ready target. The roles were reversed eventually, because in 1937 Flynn became the more imposing figure.

"Then, when Dr. Erben had his passport taken away in Valparaiso, Flynn got him onto the *Queen Mary* without a passport, and into Britain by an ingenious device, without documents. He got him to meet the Duke of Alba, a friend of Lili Damita [Flynn's wife]. The Duke of Alba became ambassador to The Court of St. James. Alba was not just an agent but a full-fledged financial backer of Franco.

"Then Flynn got Dr. Erben into Spain on the ruse that Erben was his personal physician and photographer [during the Spanish civil war]. Their mission was espionage pure and simple. An Austrian journalist, Rudolf Stoiber, published an article in *Der Stern* magazine in which he gives his documentation of the Flynn-Erben situation and analyzes the details of their Nazi association.

"After I had interrogated Dr. Erben on tape, Stoiber got hold of him on the pretext he was going to do his life story as a whitewash. And he deceived Dr. Erben deliberately, interviewed him for hours, and examined his diaries. Under the pretext of being pro-Loyalist, Flynn enlisted in the International Brigade in Spain and took thirteen reels of film of the Brigade and of the Loyalist installations. Stoiber has a complete record of the film numbers, the lab that developed them, and what was in them. They were delivered to agents of Franco in Paris at a meeting at the Plaza Athenée. Erben was present and took another set of copies to Berlin, first to the headquarters of the Abwehr. Count Cassina [was the] nephew of the Duke of Alba and the protégé of Cary Grant. Cassina—[who] was himself a Gestapo agent—witnessed the handing over of the photographs. Now, Flynn's contact in Spain, Bradish Johnson, was the *Newsweek* correspondent and a Franco agent. Philby [the British traitor and Soviet agent] organized Johnson's death through an explosion in front of his armored car. It's an extraordinary story. Franco was so deeply moved by the death of this supposedly obscure journalist that he gave him a state funeral. And Stoiber has the complete documentation from the Erben diaries on the whole story.

"Flynn was a kind of Philby in reverse [Philby posed as an anti-Communist; Flynn, says Higham, posed as an anti-Fascist]."

"How did the Australians respond to your revelations about Flynn? Do they accept your account?"

"The British and Australian press took a completely different position from the Americans. Especially in Australia, idolatory is not known. It's not a national problem. In America, it is. So there's a natural skepticism, to some extent in England but very much so in Australia. So no one was hysterical or defensive on Flynn's behalf. They were interested and I didn't get anything like the response I got here. It was fury, an emotional reaction exemplified by the columnist Liz Smith, who later sent me a note of abject apology, saying she'd had 'a knee-jerk reaction,' when she said I was 'out on a limb with chainsaw'—a rather colorful turn of phrase. But she realized she'd been horribly wrong."

"Did she publish a retraction?"

"No, unfortunately, but she sent it to me. If you examine the paperback of my Flynn book, you'll see how one person after another started to come forward once the story broke, some threatened that if I revealed what they had to say they would see that my legs were broken—rather amusing."

"If the British authorities knew Flynn had been a traitor, why did they let him make movies in Britain after World War II?"

"He was on a very restricted passport: only allowed in for six months at a time. He was under a constant watch order. He was never off the watch list, according to my correspondent in London. [Rather a gentle way to treat a traitor!] What is probably more interesting is how he got into America in view of his background. It was because all the channels were open to Nazi sympathizers. First of all, the British consul in New York was Charles Howard Ellis, a self-confessed Nazi agent. He was in charge of the British passport division. Flynn originally came to the United States in 1934, but his last reentry was in 1940, when Britain was at war. Flynn had no difficulty, as you would expect. On the American end, the head of the Visa Division of the State Department, the former ambassador to Italy, was Breckinridge Long. He was a close friend of Mussolini and supporter of his invasion of Ethiopia, and the one who stopped the cables coming in from Switzerland about the plight of the Jews. As far as domestic relations are concerned, Major Lemuel Schofield was head of immigration. His mistress was Hitler's leading agent in the Americas, Princess Stefanie von Hohenlohe. Major Schofield was an outright Nazi collaborator and was asked for his resignation in 1943. All kinds of breaches of American security took place in those days. The channels were closed to the Jews and wide-open to the enemy."

"Wasn't Flynn's daughters' court case against you dismissed?"

"It was just a nuisance suit which was quickly got rid of:

thrown out in the lower courts. Not long after I came across a book called *The Deal,* by William Marshall, which describes Errol Flynn's involvement in a murder in France."

"What was his motive for murder?"

"I think it was his intense perversity. He hugely enjoyed getting involved with danger, terror, and you can see from the terrible book by his widow, Nora Eddington, *Errol and Me,* that he was capable of appalling violence. He almost killed his poor father on the deck of the *Sirocco.*"

"Most women saw only his charismatic side."

"Olivia de Havilland was a young and somewhat difficult woman who was giving Warner Brothers a very hard time, and of all their players she probably was one of the most temperamental and difficult to work with. She evidently saw Flynn's charm but didn't succumb to it, as she made a big point of telling us all. When this whole thing came up, it's only natural she would react with dismay and disbelief. Obviously, if you're working for an enemy government, you certainly don't go about telling people who are liable to chatter and gossip. Because you could wind up in prison. People kept saying to me, 'Why don't they [his friends and colleagues] know?' I said, 'They didn't know because he was what he was.' If you're working for the enemy, you don't tell someone like David Niven, who was a patriot, or Olivia de Havilland about it. The idea that people go around saying, 'I'm a spy,' is laughable."

"But David Niven knew him well. Shared a house with him."

"That isn't quite correct. I've been to that address. Niven lived in the garage apartment. He deliberately lied in his book to cover the fact that he was living off Merle Oberon as her gigolo and as a young up-and-coming actor, and she was paying all the bills. He was living with her at the beach. I pointed this out while he was still alive, in my book on Merle Oberon. And, in fact, she was working for our side during the war, with Alexander Korda, as a courier. David Niven never lived with Flynn at the beach; he lived in the garage apartment in Beverly Hills and when war broke out, left Hollywood to enlist."

"So Flynn was a good spy."

"Of course he was: that's why he went undetected. If he'd started blabbing to David Niven, he would have been imprisoned for the entire war. That's why it's so utterly dumb of people to rely on what David Niven says. If I had been a journalist faced with this controversy, the first thing I would do, instead of calling celebrities, which is a total waste of time, is to go to the government and say, 'What evidence does Higham have?' Then I'd look at it. There would never have been a controversy. It would have been settled from the beginning and I would instantly have been nominated for a Pulitzer Prize. Instead of which, I was practically burned at the stake."

"How long did you work on the Flynn book?"

"I started in 1978 and delivered it in 1979. Just after I delivered it I was tipped off to his Nazi connections and I immediately pulled the book back. I asked for another year. I had to delve into the money from my Katharine Hepburn biography to finance all this work. But I had to go on and on until I got to the bottom of it. It was horrible what it cost me to unearth all this information. The paperback sale was almost half a million and that picked up my losses and put me back in shape again."

"What was your evidence for Flynn's bisexuality?"

"Truman Capote came to the office of the *New Yorker* where he was working as a copy boy and discussed his night with Flynn the next morning. Of course, none of us was actually in the room, but the repetition of it later in his *Chameleon* book indicates he was still prepared to say it had taken place. And I saw no reason to differ with it. [Except that Capote was a notorious liar.]

"First of all, the pattern of all of Flynn's relationships was with very young and very delicate boys—Tyrone Power was an exception. It's quite typical of men like Flynn to experiment. I don't take it that Flynn was a homosexual. I think he was oversexed and inventive and interested in rare experiences. And Tyrone Power was witnessed by his secretary in Acapulco [with Flynn]. I interviewed her very extensively and was convinced she was telling the truth, or I wouldn't have published it. Melvin Belli, the attorney, was another source. He knew about it from Flynn himself, who quite openly discussed his sexual relations to some people."[20]

Pretty convincing, huh? All those declassified top secret documents! All those informants with inside information!

But when I questioned Melvin Belli, he denied knowing of Flynn's secret life, writing to me on September 22, 1986:

> I spent a couple of months with Flynn in France and he became a dear friend and client thereafter. I can only judge from my conversations with him and [in] my judgment he was absolutely a 100 percent American, he didn't like the Nazis, he didn't have anything to do with them, and that's a despicable lie that Higham puts out when he says either that Errol was a homosexual or a Nazi sympathizer. I can't prove the negative but my judgment, my conversation with him and his friends and everything else that you need to pass judgment on someone, is that he was neither a *homosexual* nor a *Nazi sympathizer,* and he was one hell of a guy—and friend!

Belli characterized Flynn in *Variety* on February 6, 1985, as "so much a pixie that in Hollywood he was caged. He belonged in the wild, or dangling in the bowsprit of the *Zaca*" (Flynn's yacht). To Belli, the Australian-born Flynn, who became American, was "one of the sweetest guys I've ever known, although he did get provoked at times when he thought his privacy was being invaded. Some seemingly flamboyant moving picture heroes and public figures do have great regard for their personal privacy right."[21]

The lawyer's last encounter with Flynn was when "Errol had invited Jack Rosenbaum, the columnist, to my penthouse for a drink. Leaning back in bed in his bathrobe, he smilingly said, 'Ah, old boy, who could have it so great? At fifty, alive, a beautiful lissome blonde, teenage mistress, and a fairy for a valet!' A week later the flame had been extinguished."[22]

Despite Higham's apparently strong evidence from official sources David Niven still ridiculed the suggestion that his old pal Flynn had been a Nazi spy. "Absolute nonsense," he told me.* "He was a lovely fellow. A London newspaper called me up when I went to India and asked me about Flynn being a spy. And I said, 'If he had been, he wouldn't have confided in me.' " (Higham's point, too. Niven served with distinction in the British army in World War II.)

Niven's final glimpse of Flynn was a far cry from Belli's: "He was incredibly calm the last time I saw him, not long before his death. I got the shock of my life when he told me he was reading the Bible and got solace from it."[23]

The Donati Counterattack

Were Niven and Belli right in denying Flynn was a traitor? The weight of Higham's evidence seemed heavily against them, until William Donati came on the scene. Donati was working on a piece called *The Flynn Controversy* when he met Buster Wiles, Flynn's stunt double and close friend. Out of that encounter came *My Days with Errol Flynn* by Wiles with Donati, which questioned Higham's research and his integrity.[24]

---

*Interview with David Niven, October 13, 1975.

Donati told me,* "I knew something about Flynn. I had obtained a book from Australia called *The Young Errol: Flynn Before Hollywood*. The author, John Hammond Moore, had investigated Flynn's early life in New Guinea and Australia. When the controversy broke out [over Higham's book] I wrote a letter to the *Los Angeles Times* saying we should hold off any judgment that Flynn was a Nazi agent. And they published my letter next to a three-page article called, 'A Cloud of Nazism Over Errol Flynn.' That afternoon, Mr. Higham phoned and told me how wrong I was about this, that he had spent a lot of time and effort in obtaining thousands of classified surveillance files that showed Flynn was a Nazi agent. I said, 'Okay, I'll suspend judgment on your book until I read it.' And when I read it I was very surprised that there was no professional documentation. My background is academic and if I've learned anything it's this: you use footnotes and an appendix and a bibliography, and you inform the reader where the source material comes from.

"I started making phone calls to determine the veracity of Mr. Higham's claims and I went to Vienna to interview Dr. Erben, who spoke fluent English. I spoke to as many of Flynn's friends as I could. I obtained thousands of documents Mr. Higham had.

"I proved conclusively that one of Mr. Higham's main points, that Flynn helped Dr. Erben escape from the United States to the Mexican border—which would have been an act of treason—did not occur, because that day Flynn was on a Burbank film set [where he was making *Footsteps in the Dark*].

"There's no doubt that Dr. Erben was a Nazi spy. The man was just fascinating: I was mesmerized by him. Higham could have written a damn good book, but he went for sensationalism rather than an objective biography. Any

---

*Interview with William Donati, March 11, 1990.

biographer would have had to have analyzed the relationship between Flynn and Erben.

"I think Flynn knew when they met that Dr. Erben was a Nazi sympathizer. Erben himself told me, 'Yes, I admired Hitler because he rebuilt the German economy. I also admired President Roosevelt because he rebuilt the American economy.' Erben was a man of many faces. I don't think Flynn knew Erben was a Nazi agent. Flynn told the FBI, 'Dr. Erben is the kind of man to do everything in his power to make it appear that he was indeed a German agent.' It was a strange statement. In other words, Flynn had heard some of Erben's tales: that he went to Berlin, that he did this or that. But Erben was a consummate liar."

"But, if Flynn was a patriotic Australian or American, why did he remain friends with a Nazi sympathizer?"

"That's a good point. Why did Flynn remain friends with David Niven who was one of the most patriotic [Brits] in Hollywood?"

"Do you go along with Higham's contention that Flynn was a bisexual?"

"Absolutely not. That was the easiest thing to disprove. Buster Wiles met Flynn on the set of *Captain Blood* in 1935 and he brought Flynn's body back from Hollywood in 1959. He scoffs at the bisexuality charge. He said to me, 'Bill, I lived at Mulholland Farm [Flynn's home] for three and a half years, and he had no secrets from me.' And all of Flynn's friends told me that. Jerry Courneya, the still photographer for Errol Flynn Productions, said: 'I was about seventeen and would have been very approachable if Flynn had any homosexual tendencies.' "

"Higham quotes several who confirm Flynn's bisexuality."

"Once again, the point comes down to credibility, doesn't it? When you purchase someone's book you presume the author's credible. I prove Higham played around with a government document and God knows what he did with conversations. I spoke with Irving Rapper, the director who's one of Higham's sources, and he told me, 'Higham twisted my words about Flynn.'

"Buster Wiles is the most credible source, and was the only friend to know Flynn was in touch with William Stephenson of British Intelligence in World War II. There's no doubt that when Flynn went to South America in 1940 for his goodwill tour, it was at the request of the British government.

"When Higham went on TV on 'Good Morning Los Angeles' [to tout his Flynn biography], and said the British Ministry of Defense had all the secret files [revealing Flynn had been a spy], that very day I got a letter in the mail from the Ministry of Defense [reproduced in this book] saying it was all nonsense."

"Surprising no one else has revealed these things."

"Higham intimidates reporters. He says, 'I've got these 30,000 documents in the Charles Higham Collection.' And the implication is that you haven't read them. And most journalists are too lazy to get off their asses and go read the papers.

"When the paperback came out I guess the publisher felt defensive, so they included documentary evidence. But the very first document is not what the report says. It's Mr. Higham's doctoring of the document to prove his thesis that Errol Flynn had been identified as a Nazi agent."[25]

The Smoking Gun

This was an extraordinary catch by Donati: Higham had misquoted three crucial sentences in an FBI document (reproduced in this chapter) to make it appear that Flynn was Erben's partner in crime. Higham introduces it as follows:

> The Vejarano report fit into everything that I had known about the Flynn-Erben mission in Spain. The attempt to obtain entry on the Franco side; the fact that Flynn instigated the

mission; Erben's accreditation as Flynn's cameraman; Flynn's presence at Erben's cover when the secret Loyalist installations were being photographed—it was all there. Here is the report, slightly condensed, and with the name of Vejarano's Spanish contact removed by the FBI.[26]

It is not only slightly condensed, it is completely distorted. The actual FBI report reads:

this German [Erben] had just completed a tour of the various Spanish fronts in company with ERROL FLYNN, the movie actor, and had taken numerous pictures of gun establishments and military objectives in "Red" Spain.[27]

The faked account by Higham reads "and they had taken numerous pictures." Higham added "they," implicating Flynn where the original document does not.

The FBI report continues:

One of the German military officials had called the Embassy advising that they were sending this man over in order that members of the Spanish Embassy in Berlin, who were at that time superiors of General Franco, could view the pictures that their agent [referring to Erben] had taken in Spain with a view that this might be some help to the Franco forces.[28]

The faked account by Higham reads "the pictures that their agents had taken," instead of the singular "agent," which referred only to Erben.

A later sentence of the FBI report reads as follows:

VEJARANO advised that he had looked through these pictures and noticed several pictures of the German in company with ERROL FLYNN and the various military objectives which the German had photographed.[29]

The faked account by Higham reads "the various military objectives which he [referring to Flynn] had photographed," while the original stipulates "the German."

Higham even had the gall to emphasize that altered sentence by putting it in italics!

And he might have gotten away with it, but for Donati, who concluded: "There is absolutely nothing in the FBI files, the CIA, or any of the files in which Flynn is suspected of being a German agent or being involved with Dr. Erben as a German sympathizer. Mr. Higham concocted the theory."[30]

The files are all about Dr. Erben. Flynn simply liked him and was his friend.

"I was at the American Booksellers Convention," Donati told me,* "when Higham launched his book about the Duchess of Windsor. And I sat down in the press room and sure enough it was the same sensationalism. But not one journalist stood up and said, 'Mr. Higham, before I do a story on this I'd like to see some documentation.' At that point I raised my hand and said, 'Mr. Higham, I've retraced your research on *Errol Flynn: The Untold Story,* and I've come to the conclusion that you've written an absolutely fraudulent book.' He looked a bit defensive and said, 'You haven't read the documents in the Charles Higham Collection in USC.' I was the first person to read those documents and had to bulldoze my way in. He claimed that he controlled access to the collection. I sent a letter to the president of USC where they'd been sleeping in an ivory tower for a while, and he said, 'Yes, we adhere to the principle of scholarly access.' Finally, they let me see the documents."[31]

---

*Interview with William Donati, March 11, 1990.

Flynn the Bigot?

Donati continued: "Higham wrote to the *Los Angeles Times* on August 7, 1988, quoting a letter from Flynn to Dr. Erben written in August 1933 after the two had met. Higham quotes one line from the letter because he knew I was coming after him. And the line was 'I do wish we could bring Hitler here to teach these Isaacs a lesson or two.' And Higham had been telling the *Los Angeles Times* that he had this letter saying Hitler should be brought to England to drive the Jews out. It's quite different when you read the whole letter. In it Flynn was writing about a dispute over money. Apparently he felt someone in London was cheating him. The letter reads: 'I do wish we could bring Hitler here to teach these Isaacs a lesson or two. The bastards have absolutely no business probity or honor whatsoever and I do believe would even accept a bribe were I so weak as to offer one.' "

"You could say that indicates he was anti-Semitic."

"A good point. But I asked Wiles, 'Did you ever hear Flynn make any anti-Semitic statement?' He said, 'No, I didn't, except that sometimes he'd get mad at Jack Warner.'

"Vincent Sherman, director of *The Adventures of Don Juan,* told me: 'I found him [Flynn] a perfectly delightful and charming human being, with a fantastic sense of humor. He certainly knew I was Jewish and he could not have been more pleasant and friendly to me.' "

And Earl Conrad, the ghostwriter of Flynn's autobiography, *My Wicked, Wicked Ways,* said to Donati, "Flynn knew I was Jewish on the day we started work together. We became good friends." He described Higham's biography as "shades of Joe McCarthy and guilt by association . . . literary ghoulism."

Donati continued: "There is no evidence that Flynn was ever a Nazi spy, but there is solid evidence that Higham fabricated information. And, of course, you can lie with authority when someone is dead. Cary Grant is another bullshit biography. We all know celebrities should be left to humiliate themselves rather than have us writers humiliate them. Unfortunately, it seems to be the genre of today's biographies. As I told the *Los Angeles Times,* 'The more humiliated the celebrity, the bigger the advance.'

"Higham uses pseudonyms in the book and invents quotes for Flynn. In the prologue to the biography he even has Flynn's ghost talking to him, which, in my opinion is very unprofessional."[32]

Flynn's ghost verifies Higham's conclusions and welcomes the exposure!

"Well, old sport," says the actor's spirit, "you've blown my cover, have you? Good luck. You know what? I don't give a God damn. Where I am, there are no politics, no sex, no death, no contraband, no theft, no greed—though I've got to admit there are one hell of a lot of Nazis."[33]

Higham is surely the first biographer to get his subject's ghost to give him a good advance review. But when Donati obtained responses from more reliable and substantial sources, Higham's thesis on Flynn the Nazi spy took a nosedive.

Sir William Stephenson, head of British Intelligence in the United States during World War II, wrote on May 5, 1980: "I am unaware of any connection Flynn had with any Nazi Dept., and doubtless the FBI would have had knowledge of it if he had. Appears nonsensical on the face of it."[34]

Lieutenant Colonel D. A. Betley of Britain's Ministry of Defense wrote on May 6, 1980: "We see no reason to question the reported statement of his friend and fellow actor David Niven that the suggestion that Errol Flynn was a spy was a 'lot of nonsense.' "[35]

And David Flanders, Chief of the FBI's Freedom of Information Branch, wrote on July 16, 1980: "In response to the claim of author Charles Higham that Errol Flynn was a Nazi spy, any conclusions reached by Mr. Higham were no doubt based on his review of records released to Mr. Higham by this Bureau as well as documents obtained from other Federal Government agencies. As you are aware, while Errol Flynn was either the victim or subject of several investigations conducted by the FBI none were based on alleged espionage activities and no information was developed to indicate that he had been a Nazi agent."[36]

When Donati phoned Flynn's friend Buster Wiles for his opinion of the Higham biography, Wiles said: "It's a terrible lie. Believe me, I knew Flynn, and he certainly did not admire the Nazis. You can get it from the horse's mouth, or you can get it from the other end." Wiles added: "I had provided information to Higham for the biography, but I was never informed of the Nazi angle. I felt as if I had been swindled. I spoke of Flynn as I had known him—a fine fellow who always treated me like a brother.

"Flynn was certainly no saint. He had his faults; yet to call him a Nazi was a vicious smear. Flynn would have been furious over such a rotten book. . . . I knew Errol Flynn for twenty-four years. Never did I hear him say the least sympathetic comment towards Hitler, Nazism, or Fascism. His opinion of the Nazis was one of detestation. He was a fervent admirer of President Roosevelt and democracy.

"According to the appallingly incorrect biography, Flynn was also a Jew hater and a racist. Lies. Flynn had no animosity against any creed or race. He simply accepted or rejected people for what they were.

"The vicious book about Flynn is filled with so many lies and inaccuracies, it's amazing it was ever published. Believe me, I knew Errol Flynn *very well.*"[37]

The OSS Files

But might the CIA have information that would confirm Higham's charges? In his Author's Note, Higham states: "At time of writing, the CIA has not yet released its OSS files on Flynn, which are understood to include his clandestine letters to Dr. Erben in World War II."[38]

Again Higham was proved wrong. After waiting over four years, Donati received the declassified OSS file. In it, he says, there were "no incriminating letters or otherwise between Flynn and Erben."

Biography with a Hell of a Twist

Charles Higham made a fatal mistake in the very first lines of his biography of Flynn. In the paperback edition, under "Author's Note," he writes:

> Because of their length and complexity, and the fact that they have to be read in juxtaposition, it has proved impossible to reproduce evidential documents in this edition. However, any member of the public may obtain them on application to the FBI, the State Department, Military and Naval Intelligence and the National Archives. Since the documents have been declassified by me, they may be obtained quickly.[39]

Seems like a generous offer, doesn't it? He both indicates he has nothing to hide and is willing to share the results of his massive research with anyone interested. It couldn't have seemed much of a risk. Who is going to wade through thousands of official documents when Higham has already done the work for them? Also, it's a good way of handling potential skeptics: challenging them to put up or shut up.

Certainly no reviewer took Higham up on his offer. Who had the time? The critics found the biography, "riveting,"[40] "a sensation,"[41] "sobering,"[42] and "revealing."[43] The *Houston Home Journal* praised him for delivering "on what he promised . . . page after page of information," and the *Dallas News,* because "Higham has done his homework." *Penthouse* gave it thumbs up for its "certain style and class that sets [it] above the common popular biography," and the *Denver Post* believed "Higham has succeeded in digging up some amazing dirt. . . . Bound to be a smash best seller." It was cheers all the way. The *Berkeley Independent Gazette* came closer to the truth with "the most controversial Hollywood biography yet!" But one relevant adjective was missing from the paeans of praise: "fraudulent." He had conned the lot of them—and almost got away with it.

What Was Flynn Up To in Spain?

Because Flynn wasn't a Nazi agent doesn't make him an admirable or heroic figure, especially in Spain during the civil war. When I was working on a biography of Ernest Hemingway, George Seldes, a former foreign correspondent for the *New York Post,* gave me a plausible firsthand account of what Flynn was really up to.

"We were in Paris waiting for them to process our passports when two of the most beautiful people I've ever seen, a handsome man and a beautiful woman, came over. It was Errol Flynn and his wife, Lili Damita. . . . She was helping him get a visa. As we sat there we introduced each other, and he said, 'I've got a million dollars which I've raised among the friends of Loyalist Spain in Hollywood. I'm going to Madrid and we're going to build a hospital and buy ambulances for the Loyalists.'

"This was my first meeting with Flynn. To go to Madrid

my wife and I had to go to Valencia or Barcelona and wait for vacant places in an automobile. Cars that went to Madrid usually carried only the highest officials or food or medicine. A pint of gasoline, they said, was worth a pint of blood. Although the whole country was starving, they raked up a banquet for Flynn in Barcelona and he accepted this. He told them all the wonders he was going to do, and believe it or not, they supplied him with a car. He got to Madrid by car and he told the same story in Madrid.

"We met frequently, usually at the entrance to the Hotel Victoria, before going out. Flynn kept talking and everybody bowed to him and said he was one of their great benefactors. He was a goddamned liar!

"I've met three sons-of-bitches in my life. One was Mussolini; the second was D'Annunzio, who betrayed Duse; and the third is Errol Flynn for his betrayal of the Spanish Republic to make publicity for himself for a Hollywood movie.

"Now this is what he did. He went out with Ernest Hemingway and Herbert Matthews of the *New York Times,* who were often together at the front in the same building. When they got close to the front, Flynn didn't mind the occasional boomings of the cannon—nobody minded that; but when he heard machine-gun rattles and rifle fire, he got scared. He said, and I'll give you his exact words: 'Do any of you gents know the address of a good, clean whorehouse?' At that time, April 1937, Flynn was already known as 'the grim raper.' But all of us seemed to forgive him because of the million dollars he was bringing from Hollywood to establish a hospital and to supply medicines and ambulances for the wounded.

"But the whole thing was a hoax. After Flynn asked Hemingway and Matthews the way to the nearest whorehouse, he disappeared. He did nothing for the Loyalist cause. As for the million dollars he promised, he didn't have a cent on him.

"When he got back to Barcelona, he had a scratch on his

arm or face and a little mercurochrome on it. Then he sent a very innocent cable: 'Everything is set,' or 'Everything is all right.' That was a tip to whomever he was working for to release a story that he was shot at the front. The *New York Daily News,* on the front page, came out with 'Errol Flynn Killed at the Spanish Front.' That was changed in a later edition to 'Wounded.'

"He spread the story that he was wounded, because he was about to make a movie [*They Died With Their Boots On,* directed by Raoul Walsh] in which the character is wounded in a cavalry charge. It was all a plot which he and the Hollywood people were engaged in. I think it was one of the dirtiest things in history."[44]

"Ernest not only despised Flynn," said his brother, Leicester Hemingway, "he felt the guy was a triple phony. Ernest never doublecrossed people. Ernest always kept his word. Flynn you could always count on to let you down."[45]

When I tried to contact Higham again, directly and through his agent, to question him about Donati's damning discoveries and Seldes's opinion, he was always unavailable, preoccupied, perhaps, with another shocker—the life of the Duchess of Windsor.

The Wicked Windsors?

The Duke and Duchess of Windsor were sitting ducks, dead ducks in fact, when Charles Higham took a shot at them. The duchess, he claims, faked her memoirs to hide an unsavory past; and his research in official files shows her to have been a drug peddler; sexual pervert; and lover of, among others, the Nazi ambassador to Britain, Joachim von Ribbentrop, and Count Ciano, Mussolini's son-in-law, whose child she aborted.[46]

Higham portrays Wallis Simpson as a ruthless and insatiably

ambitious American who craved the title "Her Royal Highness." The duke, who abdicated his throne to marry her, emerges as an effete wimp under her thumb. According to Higham, the future King Edward VIII blamed Roosevelt and the Jews for World War II, which he hoped Hitler would win and then restore him to the throne of a Nazi-controlled Britain, with the duchess as his queen. To that end, Higham concludes, the couple gave military secrets to the enemy.

After the war they settled in France, where the duke died in 1972 at age seventy-seven; his last words a poignant paraphrase of his life, "England . . . not away . . . the waste . . . the waste."[47] He and the duchesss had been married almost thirty-five years. Unlike the duke, she had no dying words. In 1984 the ninety-year-old woman lay in a darkened room, unable to speak or move. Her attorney, Suzanne Blum, described those already launched on a television series and biographies about the Windsors, as "vultures crowding around the garbage cans."[48] But few biographers are deterred by insults, deserved or not.

Two years after the duchess died, Charles Higham's *The Duchess of Windsor: The Secret Life* (McGraw-Hill) provided the ammunition that destroyed any view of the Windsors as star-crossed lovers, or misguided innocents trapped in a world at war. Higham's depiction of the duchess has a Grand Guignol quality. She seems a nasty piece of work: ruthless, predatory, greedy, and vengeful—a woman who mistreated her servants and bullied her pathetic husband. He was like a not-quite-house-trained puppy, according to Higham, overeager to satisfy her every whim. And both, says their biographer, were traitors, in cahoots with the enemy. If you find that hard to believe, Higham cites thousands of once-secret documents in his possession.

The Verdict

Was the Duke of Windsor, the one-time king, a traitor, as Higham says? Or just a silly ass? Or neither? If a traitor, why wasn't he hanged, like William Joyce (Lord Haw-Haw), or at least courtmartialed? And if, as seems likely, the French knew what he was, why, after the war, did they give him a mansion at Neuilly at a nominal rent of twenty-five pounds a year, and exempt him and the duchess from income tax? They had, after all, executed their own homegrown traitor and former premier, Pierre Laval.

If, as Higham maintains, the duke was anti-Semitic, why did he help several Austrian Jews to emigrate to England after the Nazis took over Austria in 1938? Among them were an Austrian official, Dr. Ernest Brunert; pianists Radicz and Landauer; and the chief engineer of Vienna's principal steam bath.[49]

Because Higham treats biography as a blood sport, his victims' friends and relatives rarely join the hunt. So he chases down, at best, secondhand gossip, throws in rumors from questionable or anonymous sources, and, in Errol Flynn's case, publishes fake documents and even conjures up his victim's ghost as witness to his muckraking prowess. His picture of the duke and duchess appears to be another distortion.

Helen Rich, a Palm Beach friend of the Windsors, told me,* "I understand Higham's book is very derogatory, but I knew them only as delightful people. They were always pleasant. If she humiliated him, or told him off in public, I never was on the scene, thank God. He obviously adored her."

"How about Higham's contention that the duke was henpecked; that Wallis was strong and he was weak?"

"I didn't get that impression."

---

*Interview with Helen Rich, November 30, 1988.

"You never saw her humiliate him in public?"

"She was too smart for that. She was not stupid, you know. She knew perfectly well that they were being observed every minute from all directions. All the people who knew them very well on Palm Beach, except for C. Z. Guest, are no longer on the planet."[50]

C. Z. Guest, a socialite and writer on gardening, and her son, Alexander, entertained the Windsors in their homes on Long Island and Palm Beach and frequently met them in Europe.

I asked Mrs. Guest* if she had been a friend of the couple.

"Oh, yes, very close."

"This," I told her, "is from a review of Higham's book about them: 'They were a strange pair, this intellectually deficient part-time royal drag queen, and his anorexic-looking trull whose plain face stopped just short of downright ugliness, roaming the world parasitically for decades in well-upholstered luxury, sponging off people and scattering their pretensions and idiocies as if they were papal benedictions.'[51]

"An accurate description?"

"It's disgusting. I think all those people [unauthorized biographers] do it because they make money."

"Here's something specific from the same source: 'He squandered literally millions of dollars on her, all the while subjecting himself willingly to her constant verbal abuse and frequent public humiliation.'

"Did you ever witness anything like that?"

"Absolutely not. First of all, he loved her very, very much. He adored her."

"Did the duchess criticize the duke in front of others?"

"No. Absolutely not. She was wonderful to him. She adored him. They were very, very happy."

---

*Interview with C. Z. Guest, December 21, 1988.

"How about the duke sponging off people?"

"That's not true. And for twenty-five years we were intimate friends."

"The picture is that they invited themselves to people's homes."

"That's not true at all. Everybody wanted to have them."

"And she did not, in your sight or hearing, ever humiliate him publicly?"

"Never."

"And never abused him verbally?"

"No. Did you ever hear anybody say that who knew them intimately? Of course you didn't. Somebody came to see me once about her, and told me how terrible she was to her servants. And I said, 'Well, that's pretty funny. Her butler's been with her for forty years, and her chef has been with her over forty years, and her personal maid is a great friend of my personal maid.' I mean, all these accusations are incredible."

"She still might have been tough with her servants."

"Well, then, they wouldn't have stayed with her for over forty years."

"Unless they were well paid."

"I never saw her rude to her butler, George, or to her personal maid, or the chef, or anybody. Of course not. You can't be intimate friends with anybody and not admire and like them. You don't see them for any other reason. They were just very good friends of ours. He was one of my late husband's best friends. They used to play golf together all the time when they stayed here."

"Was the duke weak compared with the duchess?"

"I never found him weak. I was very fond of him. He was another generation from me. I ignore all these people: if they want to do terrible things let them go ahead and do it."

"Higham gives a view of the duke as a henpecked little man whom the duchess humiliated in public. You don't think that's true?"

"I think it's outrageous."

"Did you get the impression he was unhappy?"

"No. He had a wonderful sense of humor, was absolutely charming, and great fun. He was a fascinating man for somebody my age: I first met him when I was twenty-five. My late husband knew him when he was presented at court years and years ago, and knew his father, George V. I knew him very, very well, for almost thirty years. I first met him here in Palm Beach at the home of Mr. and Mrs. Young, right after I got married [in Ernest Hemingway's home]."

"Do you think that characterizing the duke of Windsor as 'a pompous little twit' is off the mark? You never saw him pompous?"

"Of course not."

"Sir Dudley Forward, Windsor's longtime equerry, admitted that, 'whereas the duke, duchess, and I had no idea the Germans were or would be committing mass murder of the Jews, we were none of us averse to Hitler politically. We all felt that the Nazi regime was a more appropriate government than the Weimar Republic which had been extremely socialist and under which, we felt, Germany might have turned socialist. Instead of *National* Socialist, which we thought was the lesser of two evils.' Any comment?"

"Esmond Rothemere [owner of the *Daily Mail*] told me that he went to Germany for two days to be with Hitler, and when he first met him thought he was a very, very attractive and very, very powerful man. And a lot of people felt that way. This is before he started eliminating the Jews and marched into Austria and the Sudetenland and Poland."

"Despite what Higham says, you still dispute his description of the duchess henpecking the duke?"

"Absolutely. I never saw it, and I saw them a lot. He was godfather to both of my children. They stayed with us here in Palm Beach and on Long Island, and I saw them in Europe all the time."

"According to Higham, the Earl of Crawford called the Duke of Windsor, 'a chatterbox, eager to spill everything to his untrustworthy wife.' "

"I never heard him talk like that, for godssake. I don't think he was very interested in gossip. He was a very sophisticated man, and very, very well educated. He spoke Spanish, French, German, and, of course, English. He had an amazing memory, too."

"Higham says the duke wanted revenge on his family for withholding recognition of his wife as a "Royal Highness," and forbidding British subjects to curtsy to her. Did you get the impression he wanted revenge?"

"No and I never heard him talk against his family."

"Did you ever hear him say anything pro-Nazi?"

"Never. My late husband was in Intelligence in the Marines. He would have known all these things, if they were true. Of course not. And I never heard anyone talk like that about the duke, ever, ever, my god! Those are very serious accusations. I never heard anybody, for Christ's sake, say things like that. Was this book a big seller?"

"Yes. On the best-seller list for months."

"I personally found them a delight. So did my late husband."

"Kitty Kelley is at work on another book."

"She's doing it to make money, of course."

"If she calls will you tell her anything? She believes people talk about others because they want the truth to come out."

"Well, that's her business. I don't do it. I didn't do it about my very good friend Brenda Frazier or Barbara Hutton. They did one on Barbara Hutton and wrote a disgusting book about Brenda Frazier. All these poor tragic people."

"I remember you were offered a million dollars for a book on the Windsors and you turned it down."

"Absolutely. I wouldn't do it about any of my friends."

"Although your account could be a positive one."

Nancy Reagan seems especially happy on January 14, 1989, as she's about to leave the White House for good. The First Lady wanted to be remembered, she said, for her work against drug abuse. In an interview with the author, Fred Barnes of the *New Republic* described Mrs. Reagan as "a very smart woman. Brittle but very smart." (AP/Wide World Photos)

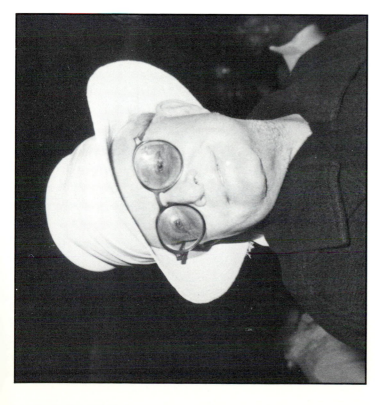

Truman Capote, aged 54, on June 22, 1978. He is about to watch the action at a trendy Manhattan disco, Studio 54. After contemplating suicide, he was now in an upbeat mood. Capote gave his biographer, Gerald Clarke, access to his personal letters and private diaries and encouraged him to speak with friends and enemies alike, as if anxious that the truth should, at last, be told. (AP/Wide World Photos)

Frank Sinatra and wife, Barbara, leaving a party in Los Angeles on July 31, 1982. His scare tactics did not stop Kitty Kelley from publishing her 1986 "tell-all" biography of him. Though Sinatra complained that she concentrated on sensational and scandalous events, Kelley said many of his fans liked the book. (AP/Wide World Photos)

Elizabeth Taylor with her friend, publishing tycoon Malcolm Forbes. Her biographer, Kitty Kelley, not only focused on Taylor's human companions but on her incontinent pets. (AP/Wide World Photos)

Jacqueline Kennedy Onassis with brother-in-law, Senator Edward Kennedy; daughter, Caroline; and son, John F. Kennedy, Jr., in Boston on May 25, 1989, where she announced the creation of an annual "John F. Kennedy Profile in Courage Award." A former reporter-photographer herself, once she became a celebrity Mrs. Onassis was reluctant to speak with reporters or would-be biographers. (AP/Wide World Photos)

"But I don't want to do it. I'd never do a book about my close friends. All the books people are writing I find appalling."

"But you work among newspaper people and know they're basically after the truth about others."

"It's very hard to find the truth."[52]

The Duke Takes a Bath

C. Z. Guest's son, Alexander Guest, a gemologist, also had only positive memories of the Windsors and was at odds with Higham's account of them. I spoke with him on December 28, 1988, when he said:

"I first met them when I was eight or ten, in the 1960s, when they came to our house in Glenhead, Long Island. They were very, very close friends of my parents, and I always thought them very pleasant people with no pretensions at all. My room wasn't far from his bathroom and I used to pretty much wander around the house at will and knock on the door and he'd say 'Come in.' I also used to visit my father in such a way. And my father would often be cleaning his shotgun in the bathroom. So I entered the duke's bathroom and wandered over. I think if I'd been twelve or fourteen I probably wouldn't have done this. [He laughed.] I was between being an infant and a child, when you get into the medicine closet without knowing what you're doing. The duke said he would never have done that with his father. [Talk to him while he was in the bath.] He didn't have such a warm relationship with his father. I was eighteen when he died in 1972. I think the last time I saw him was in 1970, when I went to Paris with my mother and father because we had a horse running, named Gyr, in the Grand Prix de Saint Cloud. I think a man called Sandy Bertram, the duke, and I played golf outside Paris and I had a hole in one that day. And I have the score card of that game signed by the duke. That was quite something: my first hole in one. The duke was a very accomplished golfer and he absolutely loved playing golf. At that stage in his life it was one of the major attractions for him."

"How did he compare with your parents other friends?"

"He was terribly kind and an excellent listener—with anybody. He was very unassuming, with a very good memory, and told wonderful stories. He had a distinct way about him, very English, very proper. My father, being born in England, had wonderful manners, too, and always said, 'manners maketh man.' I was taught that all my life."

"What was the relationship between the duke and duchess?"

"They always seemed very, very happy."

"He is portrayed as the one who was more loving, and she as being more mother than wife, dominating him, telling him what to do."

"They seemed to be one of the closest couples I've ever seen and they traveled everywhere together: I never saw them apart."

"Was she witty?"

"Yes. So was he. They were very 'with it.' "

"How did they treat your family's servants?"

"Very well. They had impeccable manners."

"In contrast to many of their biographers, you have nothing negative to say about them."

"I really don't. And I think that, having the innocence of a child and later an adolescent, one tends to remember things in a clear way, without the intellectual undercurrents. He was an erudite man and he knew history well. One year they brought with them a film of him in India shaking so many hands—people swarmed around him wherever he went. He also went to Wales and met with the coal miners. He was, above all, very sensitive and intelligent. My father, who was Winston Churchill's second cousin, found the duke wonderful company."

"Noel Coward knew them fairly well and called the duke 'stupid and ridiculous.'[53] Yet you and your father thought him very intelligent."

"Exactly. If anything, I think that perhaps being the ex-king there was a degree of exclusivity involved which always puts peoples' noses out of joint. It's somewhat like wanting to be invited to the White House. There are people climbing all over each other to have that honor. From what I read in the *New York Times* and other papers, it's obviously books with a lot of trashy material in them that seem to do very well. People always want to know the dirt about everyone else."[54]

Sweeping Up the Dirt

How does Higham authenticate the dirt he collects? He says, for example, that writer Leslie Field told him of a dossier compiled at the request of King George V, the duke's father, which substantiates the duchess's "exotic party tricks" learned during visits to whorehouses, such as "lesbianism and Fang Chung, an Eastern sexual practice that can purportedly arouse even a corpse."[55]

But Philip Ziegler Fang Chunged that fantasy when he authored *King Edward VIII: The Official Biography,* for which Queen Elizabeth gave him access to the royal archives. Zeigler concluded that there is no truth to allegations that the Duchess of Windsor learned exotic sexual techniques in Far Eastern bordellos, or had affairs with Count Ciano and von Ribbentrop.[56]

As for Higham's contention that the duchess helped the Nazis, he struck out again, according to Aline, Countess of Romanones. She reveals in a book, authenticated by CIA director William Casey, that she worked as an OSS agent during World War II and afterward for the CIA. The Duchess of Windsor, she says, helped her expose a mole who was stealing secret NATO documents.[57] And she called the charge that the Windsors were Nazi sympathizers, "preposterous," adding, "I know those stories backwards and forwards and they're absolutely untrue. The duchess was extremely American, and one of the most patriotic women I've ever known. I would only involve someone in a mission if I felt they were totally conscientious and trustworthy."[58]

Even more compelling is an account by Walter Schellenberg, head of the Nazi Secret Service, who was ordered by Hitler to kidnap the Windsors while they were staying in Portugal. According to Schellenberg, whose account is vouched for by Oxford historian and Hitler biographer Alan Bullock, there was no evidence that the couple approved of the Nazi regime or had leaked any secret information. In the summer of 1940 Schellenberg said to the Nazi ambassador to Portugal, Von Huene, "Help me, especially in securing information, so that I could get a clear picture of what the Duke of Windsor's attitude really was." Von Huene said that he had indeed heard that the Duke had expressed dissatisfaction about his situation, but thought the whole thing had been grossly exaggerated by gossipmongers. "Within six days I had a full picture," said Schellenberg, "the Duke of Windsor . . . was most annoyed by the close surveillance of the British Secret Service; he did not like his appointment to Bermuda [the Bahamas] and would have much preferred to remain in Europe. But he obviously had no intention whatever of going to live either in a neutral or an enemy country. According to my reports the furthest he ever went in this direction was once to have said in his circle of Portugese friends that he would rather live in any European country than go to Bermuda [the Bahamas]. . . . Since the Duke was so little in sympathy with our plans, an abduction would be madness."[59] The kidnapping was eventually called off and the Windsors sailed for the Bahamas.

Forgotten Tears

Charles Higham shamelessly mangles the truth as if it's play dough. His creed seems to be: If you can't say anything good about someone, stick it in a book. And if facts get in the way, ignore or twist them.[60] He even pulled this trick on himself, but didn't cover his tracks. It's on the record. In the Flynn biography, for example, he confides:

> The greatest shock came almost as a personal blow. Flynn had been an idol of my boyhood and young manhood. I could have forgiven him anything. . . . When I sat in the National Archives in Washington, with the evidence of Flynn's Fifth Column activities staring me in the face, I felt tears of grief and shock rolling down my cheeks.[61]

But when interviewed by Susan Brenna, he seemed to be suffering from amnesia or talking about somebody else: "I've never been a fan of anyone," he said. "I've never identified with stars in movies, as a child even."[62]

Let's hope the now dry-eyed Charles Higham devotes himself to his newfound delight—writing fiction. It is obviously his metier.

Notes

1. *Contemporary Authors,* vol. 33–36 (Detroit: Gale, 1978), p. 400.

2. Alyn Brodsky, "No More Secrets for the Duchess," *Miami Herald,* July 24, 1988, p. 7C.

3. *Variety,* May 24, 1989, p. 78.

4. *People,* May 8, 1989, p. 33.

5. Maureen Donaldson and William Royce, *An Affair to Re-*

member: My Life with Cary Grant (Boston: G. K. Hall, 1990), p. 325.

6. Charles Higham and Roy Moseley, *Cary Grant: The Lonely Heart* (New York: Harcourt Brace Jovanovich, 1989).

7. Interview with David Niven, October 3, 1975.

8. Grant died in 1986, aged 82.

9. Scott Sublett, "Bios Uncover the Warts that Grant Fans Never Saw," *Washington Times,* April 17, 1989, pp. E1, E2.

10. Higham and Moseley, *Cary Grant: The Lonely Heart,* p. 315.

11. Sublett, *Washington Times,* April 17, 1989, p. E3.

12. Donaldson and Royce, *An Affair to Remember,* pp. 270–73.

13. Warren G. Harris, *Cary Grant: A Touch of Elegance* (New York: Doubleday, 1987), p. 253.

14. Geoffrey Wansell, *Haunted Idol* (New York: Morrow, 1983), pp. 302, 306.

15. Phil Pearman, ed. and comp., *Dear Editor: Letters to Time Magazine, 1923–1984* (Salem House, 1985), p. 159.

16. William Safire, "Libeling the Dead," and "Was Gary Cooper Entertained by Hitler in 1938?" *New York Times,* April 13, 1989, p. A27.

17. Jonathan Yardley, "Graceless Cary Grant: Higham & Moseley's Poisonous Biography," *Washington Post,* April 5, 1989, p. D2.

18. Charles Higham, *Errol Flynn: The Untold Story* (New York: Dell, 1981).

19. Interview with David Niven, October 13, 1975.

20. Interview with Charles Higham, July 16, 1986.

21. Melvin M. Belli, "TV's 'Wicked Ways' Triggers Recall of a Trip with Flynn," *Variety,* February 6, 1985, pp. 2, 92.

22. Belli's investigative prowess was questioned in 1988. Judge Raymond Acosta in Puerto Rico fined Belli and an associate $5,000 each for filing suit in "The Dupont Plaza Hotel fire case on behalf of a man who was dead long before the 1986 blaze" (ten years, in fact). "Before filing," said the judge, "Messrs. Belli and Brown failed to conduct any type of inquiry as to a fundamental prerequisite for

Mr. Andino's claim—that he be alive," *Miami Herald,* December 30, 1988, p. 13A.

23. Interview with David Niven, October 13, 1975.

24. Buster Wiles with William Donati, *The Flynn Controversy* became the appendix to *My Days with Errol Flynn* (Santa Monica: Roundtable, 1988).

25. Interview with William Donati, March 11, 1990.

26. Higham, *Errol Flynn: The Untold Story,* pp. 498–500.

27. FBI report, January 29, 1944, p. 1.

28. Ibid., p. 2.

29. Ibid.

30. Interview with William Donati, March 11, 1990.

31. Ibid.

32. Ibid.

33. Higham, *Errol Flynn: The Untold Story,* pp. 15, 16.

34. Letter from William Stephenson to Trudy McVicker, May 5, 1980.

35. Letter to Donati from British Ministry of Defense, May 6, 1980.

36. Letter to Donati from FBI, July 16, 1980.

37. Wiles and Donati, *My Days with Errol Flynn,* p. 208.

38. Higham, *Errol Flynn: The Untold Story,* p. 11.

39. Ibid.

40. *Cosmopolitan.*

41. *New York Post.*

42. *Library Journal.*

43. *Gallery.*

44. Denis Brian, *The True Gen: An Intimate Portrait of Hemingway by Those Who Knew Him* (New York: Grove Press, 1988), pp. 112, 113.

45. Ibid., p. 114.

46. Judy Bass, "The Duchess and the Nazis," *Boston Herald,* July 17, 1988, p. S17.

47. Michael Thornton, *Royal Feud* (New York: Simon & Schuster, 1985), p. 517.

48. David Price-Jones, "TV Tale of Two Windsors," *New York*

Times Magazine, March 18, 1979, p. 112.

49. Michael Bloch, ed., *Wallis and Edward, Letters 1931–1937* (New York: Summit, 1986), p. 296n; and Michael Bloch, *The Secret File of the Duke of Windsor, The Private Papers 1937–1972* (New York: Harper & Row, 1988), p. 135.

50. Interview with Helen Rich, November 30, 1988.

51. Brodsky, "No More Secrets for the Duchess," p. 7C.

52. Interview with C. Z. Guest, December 21, 1988.

53. Perhaps Noel Coward's animosity sprang from when he entertained the duke and friends at a party and the next day the duke failed to recognize him. "How beastly," Coward wrote in his diary.

54. Interview with Alexander Guest, December 28, 1988.

55. From Brodsky's review of Higham's book, *Miami Herald,* July 24, 1988, p. 7C.

56. Walter Scott, *Parade,* December 9, 1990, p. 2.

57. Aline, Countess of Romanones, *The Spy Went Dancing* (New York: Putnam's, 1990), p. 309.

58. *People,* May 7, 1990, pp. 181–83.

59. Walter Schellenberg, *Hitler's Secret Service* (New York: Pyramid, 1971), pp. 127–30.

60. Wiles with Donati, *My Days with Errol Flynn,* pp. 102, 103. For instance, Higham does not mention that before Pearl Harbor, when the British were fighting the Nazis, columnist Jimmie Fidler criticized Hollywood producers for making "pro-British propaganda" movies. Soon after, Flynn saw Fidler in the Mocambo Club, and gave him a slap on the head, saying, "You're not worth a fist."

61. Higham, *Errol Flynn: The Untold Story,* p. 19.

62. Susan Brenna, "Hang-'Em Higham . . . Cary Grant's Latest Biographer Charles Higham Didn't Let the Dirty Work Get in the Way of His Dirty Work," *Newsday,* April 11, 1989, II, p. 8.

4

Bob Woodward, "Deep Throat," and CIA Chief Bill Casey

Bob Woodward took on two of the world's most powerful men, the president of the United States and the director of the Central Intelligence Agency. He won the fight against Nixon in a knockout and the more friendly tussle with William Casey on points. He demonstrated the power of the pen to bring down the government and to expose the nefarious activities of the CIA chief. By resigning, Nixon conceded defeat but disdained to name Woodward and coauthor Carl Bernstein as instruments of his fall. To him they were "some book authors . . . who write history as fiction on thirdhand knowledge, [for whom] I have nothing but utter contempt. And I will never forgive them. Never!"[1] Woodward apparently got much help from a mysterious source still unidentified and protected under the pseudonym "Deep Throat"—the title of a porno movie.

Casey was not alive to justify himself when "exposed" in Woodward's book *Veil,* though several former lieutenants were eager and willing to defend his reputation. To be fair to Woodward, he had often tackled the living Casey while reporting for the *Washington Post.*

To admirers, Woodward is the world's greatest investigative reporter, perhaps of all time, and his picture of Nixon in *All the President's Men* and *The Final Days* (helped by Carl Bernstein and others) is a triumph.[2] Fellow writers and reporters speak with awe of how he outwitted CIA Chief Casey into revealing secrets he had hoped to bury. To them Bob Woodward is Superman, able, if not to leap buildings in a single bound, to penetrate Casey's heavily guarded hospital room for what amounted to a "death-bed" confession.[3] Columnist Liz Smith calls him, "A prince among men," adding, "I have never known him to tell a lie."[4]

Hold it, say his critics, especially Nixon fans, and particularly Gordon Liddy, who told me, "I wouldn't believe a word Woodward says even under oath." He's lying about that last conversation with Casey, other skeptics charge, or if he did sneak in the room, the CIA chief was incoherent at best and Woodward's version of it is hogwash. Many of his so-called informants are unnamed, his detractors continue, especially the famous "Deep Throat," so readers can never judge their reliability, expertise, or prejudices, or ask them if they were correctly quoted—if they're not figments of Woodward's imagination. The man's a fraud, says this faction.

Is he a wizard of biography, able to wrest secrets from those sworn to keep them, or a charlatan who hides his mistakes as tenaciously as he protects his sources? To find out where the truth lies and to explore Woodward's skill and integrity as a biographer, I questioned, among others, his editors during the Watergate investigation, Ben Bradlee and Barry Sussman; rival reporters, Seymour Hersh and Jack Anderson; rival biographer, Joseph Persico; Woodward biographer, Adrian Havill; William Casey's widow, Sophia; Casey's surgeon, Dr. Alfred Luessenhop; CIA veterans Constantine Menges, Herb Meyer, William Colby, Bobby Ray Inman, and George Carver; and CIA spokesperson Gwen Cohen—and Woodward himself.

All the President's Men was called the most devastating detective story of the century. Much still remains unsolved, but the sleuth who came up with most clues and nailed the criminals was a young police reporter, Bob Woodward.

A product of the Midwest, Woodward was born in 1943 and raised in the Chicago suburb of Wheaton, Illinois, a Republican WASP stronghold. He attended the same high school as non-WASP and future subject John Belushi, and future coauthor Scott Armstrong. He had a younger sister, Anne, and a brother, David. His attorney father, Al, was a pillar of society, a staunch Republican, and an officer in both the Lions Club and the American Legion. But it was not a happy household. His parents divorced when he was twelve, and his mother moved out of town to marry a Sears executive, leaving Bob and his siblings in their father's care. Three years later, Al married a divorcee with three children. And they soon had a child of their own.

Bob was a curious youngster, in both senses. Ferreting through his father's legal papers, when occasionally working as office janitor, he got the idea that most people lived secret lives. He shared Wheaton's conventional wisdom that Richard Nixon would be their "savior," and was disturbed by glimpses of a John Fitzgerald Kennedy on television. Kennedy's odd accent and gestures made Bob uneasy: the guy was obviously "a homo."[5]

One Christmas, when he was sixteen, Bob discovered, not for the first time, that he was getting the short end of the stick: his stepbrothers and sisters had the expensive gifts. Twenty years later he recalled how he had confronted his father, and "showed him that the money he spent on them and on us was so dramatically out of balance . . . it was kind of sad, but the fact is that it's a very competitive world when two families are brought together that way."[6] This was a surprisingly frank disclosure to an interviewer who still found him "temperamentally secretive, loath to volunteer information about himself."[7]

Voted "most likely to succeed," Woodward headed for Yale University on a government grant as a dual history and English major. There he joined the Book and Snake Club, wrote an unpublished novel, its alternate chapters aping Faulkner and Hemingway and reflecting his somewhat troubled childhood, as did his usual worried expression—as if he'd just missed his train. According to one keen observer, he entered college a "crypto facist" and left a "crypto liberal."[8]

It was pay-back time: he owed the government for his education. So, in 1965, he joined the Navy as a communications officer on the USS *Wright,* which was loaded with state-of-the-art communication facilities, like a seagoing Pentagon. He hated most of his life for the next five years, and to kill time he took correspondence courses in English and literature, wrote a column for the ship's paper, and worked on a second novel. After a year at sea, he married his high school sweetheart, Kathleen Middlekauff. Woodward escaped Vietnam by volunteering for destroyer duty, completing his service career as a Pentagon courier in 1970. By then his brief marriage was over.

That same year, when voters elected Al Woodward a circuit court judge, his twenty-seven-year-old son quit the Navy, planning to follow in his footsteps or to become a news reporter. And, even though Harvard Law School had a place for him, journalism won out.

He failed his trial as a reporter for the *Washington Post,* being strong on enthusiasm, but weak on know-how. But they steered him to a job on a nearby small-town paper, the *Sentinel* in Montgomery County. He made his mark there over the next year as a dogged and productive workaholic, while persistently reapplying at the *Post,* often phoning Harry Rosenfeld, the *Post*'s assistant managing editor, at his home. Rosenfeld was up a ladder painting his house one weekend in September 1971 and, glancing down, saw Woodward with his foot on the bottom rung. Woodward "treed" his now-captive audience and kept him there until he agreed to give him a second chance. Bob Woodward was on his way.

His enormously effective interviewing style worked, believes rival biographer Joseph Persico because

> There was something trustworthy and sympathetic in his low-key manner. Bob Woodward spoke with the voice of a young priest in the confessional who had adopted a tolerance for the failings of his flock: just tell him—he would understand. It was only when he himself talked at length, surmising whirls and whorls of conspiracy, that the soft brown eyes began to narrow and harden; the lips curled in almost diabolic pleasure at the skulduggery he suspected. The smooth face started tightening when he heard objections to his views or sensed a hostile listener. But then the young priest quickly returned. The favorite expletive of this man, who in his books was prone to put four-letter words into the mouths of others, appeared to be "gee." The nodding, unthreatening, "I certainly understand" manner was capable of seducing the wariest of interviewees.[9]

Bob Gates, then deputy for intelligence and chairman of the National Intelligence Council, agreed: "His manner was so vulnerable and nonintimidating: 'Gee, I don't understand that. Could you please go over it again?' He would have made a great case officer."[10] Even master of intrigue Henry Kissinger admitted, after an exchange with Woodward: "In five years in Washington, I've never been trapped into talking like this."[11]

What chance was there of Woodward sharing the secrets of his triumphs and failures? He had already rebuffed his would-be biographer Adrian Havill. I would eventually discover why.

I phoned Woodward, and he agreed to several tape-recorded phone conversations. We started next morning.*

---

*Interview with Bob Woodward, February 14, 1994.

After a while he said, "There are a series of questions you're asking on multiple levels. What's my standard for truth in what I write? What are my techniques? And what are other people's comments about me and my work? I've said it before and I'll say it to you: I've made mistakes in my reporting. I've got things wrong. In *All the President's Men* we talk about it in greatest detail. There are things I don't know; there are missed perspectives, all kinds of things. Step back and say, 'What's the essential nature of what Watergate was?' The hundreds of stories that Bernstein and I wrote and the two books are confirmed by hundreds of tapes, documents, testimony, numerous memoirs."

Though I never expected Woodward to reveal the identity of Deep Throat, the mystery man who apparently played such a pivotal role in his phenomenal success, my aim was to discover if he told the truth in his book or if, as others suspected, Deep Throat was either imaginary or a composite, and Woodward hid behind the guise of an honorable reporter protecting his source to maintain a fiction.

With this in mind, I said, "When Mrs. Graham [*Washington Post* publisher] asked you to identify Deep Throat, you were shaken and then it passed over because she didn't insist. Why didn't you say to her, 'I'll check if he'd be comfortable with that.' It seems the reasonable thing to do, if you've got a secret source."

Sounding slightly aggrieved, Woodward replied, "Your style of interviewing is very kind of 'Why didn't you?' Because she made it clear she didn't need to know."

"But you were startled and worried when she asked. Why?"

"Again, look at exactly what it says in the book," said Woodward.

"This is what it says in the book *All the President's Men*: 'Howard Simons [managing editor] outlined the purpose of the lunch, a confidential discussion of the sources for Watergate sources. Woodward had finished two bites of his eggs benedict and now he was going to have to give a monologue. . . . Mrs. Graham said she was less interested in the names than in the positions they held. Woodward said he had told no one the name of Deep Throat. Mrs. Graham paused. "Tell *me*," she said. Woodward froze. He was praying she wouldn't press it. Mrs. Graham laughed, touched his arm and said she was only kidding, she didn't really want to carry that burden around with her.' "12

Woodward continued answering me: "In the context she kind of laughed it off. 'Oh, I don't need to know.' "

"But that was after you were very disturbed."

"What do you mean 'very disturbed'?"

"You froze."

"Again, look at it in context."

This was a poor answer. He was simply repeating himself. Why did he pray not to be pressed? Presumably the paper's publisher could keep the name confidential.

I tried another tack. "I heard Ben Bradlee say on TV that he knew who it was."

"I know who I've told and it's much broader than that. But I don't think it's relative to what you're doing who I have told."

"Okay," I said, meaning to come back to it, because if Deep Throat was merely a convenient fiction, it would reflect on his honesty as a biographer.

He explained his modus operandi. "What I tend to do is what I call saturation reporting. Talk to everyone, go back again and then again. And in the process, I attempt to focus on decision making, to how exactly important decisions were made. Say there are six people at a crucial meeting and twenty people know about it. I will try to interview all those people as often as possible, going back, seeing if any have contemporaneous notes, diaries, memos written before or after; getting from the participants and others what their strategy and motivations are.

The reinterviewing process tends to *cleanse out* what happened and what didn't. Not that everyone will agree on every word, but you can get general agreement about what happened if people are candid. Everything I've done is scrupulously reported. If you were to go into my archives and look, there is a specific source for everything that's in any of my books."

"Bill Gulley [former director of the White House Military Office] told me he wouldn't discuss Watergate with you and you said: 'We have some information about things that are going on in the military I'm sure you wouldn't want to come out. We could publish them if we wanted. We have enough to publish.' And he says he told you, 'Publish any goddamn thing you like, I'm not playing your game.' "[13]

"I read that in his book," said Woodward. "It's a total untruth. I don't talk to people like that. First of all I wouldn't dare. It's a form of extortion."[14]

Bill Gulley spoke to me from his Palm Springs home:* "In those days I was doing so many goddamned things that weren't legal, really directed by President Nixon, and I presumed that was what Woodward was speaking about. I had an unaudited four-million-dollar fund. That money was used for things it was never intended for, and I was administering the fund. I assumed Woodward may have picked up on that. Or someone told him we could switch tail numbers to make civilian planes or air force planes out of them, whichever we wanted. I'd read the *Post* almost every morning through Watergate and I knew Woodward was very much like Jack Anderson. He would get just a little bit of truth and build around it with a bunch of lies. And that's what he did with this Deep Throat thing. Hugh Sloan was one of their providers early on. He worked at the Republican National Committee although he one time had been in the White House in a minor job. He was one

---

*Interview with Bill Gulley, March 3, 1994.

of the people handling the money at the Republican National Committee. He had some knowledge of the expenditures out of those funds. I'm sure that's where the information came that Rose Woods [Nixon's private secretary] had $185,000 or $200,000 in her safe in the White House that was really CREEP [Committee for the Re-election of the President] funds directed by Haldeman. There's no doubt Scott Armstrong was Deep Throat. The only reason the *Post* hired him and Woodward wrote a book with him was because of the stuff he brought back from the Senate committee investigating Watergate." (Armstrong denied to me that he was Deep Throat.)[15]

When I told Woodward the gist of Gulley's remarks, he said, "You're entering into the realm of what I would call— this may be useful to you—contested territory. Somebody saying something didn't happen and somebody saying something did happen. Are you familiar with the famous Kissinger-Nixon praying scene?"[16]

Nixon and Kissinger Pray Together?

Woodward and Bernstein give a detailed account in *The Final Days* of a highly unlikely event: two men, not known for their religious fervor, praying on their knees together in the White House.

> The President broke down and sobbed. . . . Between sobs, Nixon was plaintive. What had he done to the country and its people? He needed some explanation. How had it come to this? How had a simple burglary, a breaking and entering, done all this? . . . He was hysterical. "Henry," he said, "you are not a very orthodox Jew, and I am not an orthodox Quaker, but we need to pray." Nixon got down on his knees. Kissinger felt he had no alternative but to kneel down, too.

The President prayed out loud, asking for help, rest, peace, and love. How could a President and a country be torn apart by such small things? Kissinger thought he had finished. But the President did not rise. He was weeping. And then, still sobbing, Nixon leaned over and struck his fist on the carpet, crying, "What have I done? What has happened?"[17]

Did Kissinger blab? Or was Deep Throat's eye at a keyhole?

Bill Gulley said to me,* "President Nixon and I had almost the identical conversation that you and I are having about certain people [Kissinger] meeting Nixon, and they decided to do this [pray]. And Nixon said to me, "Who the hell told them? Who could have told them? Look, I'm a Quaker and Quakers don't kneel."[18]

Gulley thought that was true and the Woodward-Bernstein account false, "until I read Nixon's memoirs in which he admits he had knelt and prayed."

I told Woodward that Gulley had confirmed the account, as had Nixon himself and Kissinger, in his memoirs, and Kissinger's biographer, Walter Isaacson. "Who the hell" told Woodward is still a mystery.

Gulley was especially intrigued with the identity of Deep Throat and checked if it could have been Haig, as many suspected. As a courier between the Pentagon and White House before he became a *Post* reporter, Woodward was rumored to have had close contacts with Haig.

"I looked to see who Woodward was with," Gulley explained,† "by checking the trip sheets that were damned accurate, showing all the trips White House cars made during the Watergate period, day and night. There were only one or two occasions when you could put Woodward and Haig together in the White

*Interview with Bill Gulley, February 22, 1994.
†Interview with Bill Gulley, February 22, 1994.

House Situation Room when nobody else was there. Rose Woods [Nixon's secretary] always thought Haig was Deep Throat, primarily because, the way they shaped their book, it looked like this guy was the source of information only a very, very few had. I have the record of times these people went on and off their beepers. The system was, when you were awakened by signals board at the White House, you went on your beeper. Then, when you reached a telephone, you'd take yourself off the beeper and notify the switchboard what number you could be reached at. Haig had some peculiar late night visits in Washington, and 95 percent of them were to the Pentagon. He was leaking stuff over there because he always thought he'd go back to the Army and be chairman of the Joint Chiefs someday at that time. But Haig was in a position to have quite a bit of knowledge about things they attributed to Deep Throat."[19]

Haig is taking a bum rap, according to former Secretary of Defense Melvin Laird:* "Haig came over to the Department of Defense every time the White House wanted some assistance. For Henry's trip to China they wanted an airplane and wanted it kept secret. I think we gave Haig briefings every two days on the targets I had had approved in Vietnam. I would only talk to the president or Henry Kissinger. I wouldn't allow any of the president's men over in the Department of Defense. Haig had to talk to my assistant, General Robert Pursley. Haig later tapped his phone."[20]

"What did you think of *The Final Days*?" I asked Gulley.†

"There's so much bullshit in it. [Though he excepted the prayer scene.] I was the liaison to former presidents, and was spending some time with Nixon after he resigned. Some of that stuff was outright lies and some was third- or fourthhand gossip. It's gutter journalism."

---

*Interview with Melvin Laird, March 2, 1994.
†Interview with Bill Gulley, February 22, 1994.

"Don't you think Nixon is a strange man?"

"Very strange. We were down in Biscayne Bay when the Watergate break-in occurred, just a little squib in the Sunday *Post* that was delivered there. He hardly paid any attention, other than to say, 'What dumb bastard would do something like that?' Then when he found out how deep Haldeman and Ehrlichman were in, he thought he was so big he could take care of it. And trying to protect them he got himself in more and more trouble. I mean, John Mitchell was no choirboy, but some of the people that worked for him were out-and-out gangsters. I don't think Nixon ever expected to find himself so deeply involved with some of the people involved in the break-in."

"Did you know Gordon Liddy?"

"That's who I'm talking about."[21]

Woodward versus Liddy

Woodward is not one of Liddy's heroes. After all, the reporter helped send him to prison. Yet, in reviewing Liddy's vivid account of his life in *Will*, Woodward gave it an unexpected positive review, praising it as "meticulous" and ending with "I believe that he has been as honest as he could be."

I asked Woodward,* "Is there any reservation in that 'as he could be'?"

"Of course. I think somebody like Liddy is professionally self-deceived in lots of ways. But I thought it was a good book. The review said it was kind of a portrait of a psychopath. He had some new things to tell which I thought were footnotes to the Watergate story. He is so passionate and involved and is such a true believer that you have to append that his capacity

---

*Interview with Bob Woodward, February 22, 1994.

for being a neutral watcher, or being able to look at what happened in his own life, is not very high."

"When I asked Liddy his opinion of you, he said: 'In the spring of 1973, when I was in prison, following my Watergate conviction, an article in the *Washington Post* by Woodward or Woodward and Berstein appeared. The gist of it was that I and possibly [E. Howard] Hunt had wiretapped a whole host of newsmen. The fact is that not only had I not wiretapped these newsmen, but Woodward knew who tapped them—Al Haig and Dr. Kissinger. I have no personal knowledge of Woodward's motive, but according to *Silent Coup,* it was to protect his source and very close friend, Al Haig, who was about to become chief of staff, replacing Haldeman.[22] And if it came out that Haig and Kissinger had wiretapped these newsmen, he would not have been appointed. A problem for Woodward, because Haig was such a good source. I was on a TV show with Woodward moderated by Bernard Shaw of CNN and had the article with me and Woodward strongly denied it and wouldn't look at the article.' "

When I repeated this to Woodward, he asked, "Have you got the article? You'd better get it, because he's misrepresented what the article said: that I knew something about what came to be called 'The Kissinger Wire Taps.' There's a slipperiness and imprecision in that."

"I will get that article."* I continued my conversation with

---

*When I got it, I found Liddy was at least half right. The page one *Washington Post* headline for May 3, 1973, reads, "Wiretaps Put on Phones of 2 Reporters." The bylines are Bob Woodward and Carl Bernstein, and the first three paragraphs are, "The Nixon administration tapped the telephones of at least two newspaper reporters in 1971 as part of the investigation reportedly ordered by President Nixon into the leaks of the Pentagon Papers to the press, according to two highly placed sources in the executive branch.

"The wiretapping was supervised by Watergate conspirators E. Howard Hunt and G. Gordon Liddy who were then working in the White House,

Woodward: "When I spoke with Seymour Hersh he said that although he was your rival on the Watergate story, he'd trust you implicitly to tell the truth. I told this to Liddy, who replied, 'I'd say the direct opposite. I wouldn't believe a word Woodward said, even under oath. I would not trust anything he wrote unless it was totally verifiable. If he told me it was noon I'd go outside and look to see where the sun was. The man, as far as I am concerned, is an inveterate liar in his work.' "

Woodward chuckled: "I mean that's comic."

"He said he wouldn't even send you to the corner store to buy a pound of coffee."

Woodward gasped with exasperation and asked, "What is he talking about? Again, did we get the Watergate story correct?"

"I think he's talking about what you wrote about him. He cites *Silent Coup*. Did you read 'The Golden Boy' part?"

"Yes."

"Well, Liddy says everything in it referring to him is absolutely true and presumes the rest of the book is equally researched and confirmed." [Among other things, that Haig was Deep Throat. Conspiracy theories depend largely on Haig being Woodward's secret informant.]

"It's just total horseshit. It's been established to be total horseshit."[23]

So I asked those most likely to know.

Admiral Bobby Inman,† former executive assistant to the

---

and it was authorized by John N. Mitchell while he was Attorney General, one of the sources said.

"In this electronic surveillance, according to the source, Hunt and Liddy supervised an independent team or so-called 'vigilante squad' of wiretappers not employed by the FBI—the agency that normally performs legal wiretapping."

However, I could find no evidence that Woodward knew that Haig and Kissinger, not Liddy and Hunt, were behind the wiretapping. Or that he had lied to protect Haig as a source.

†Interview with Bobby Inman, February 22, 1994.

Navy's vice chief (during Watergate) and later director of the NSA (1977–81), and deputy director of the CIA (1981–82), told me: "People have added my name to the list. If they'd done even the least bit of checking, they would know I was executive assistant to the Navy's vice chief from June 1972 to the end of November 1973, then I was in Hawaii from December 1973 until September 1974, as assistant chief staffer, Intelligence, of the Pacific Fleet."

When I pointed out that he was in Washington during the critical Watergate months, he said his job kept him in one spot from about six in the morning to often ten at night: "When you're executive assistant to one of the Service chiefs, you are chained to the office for all but your very few sleeping hours. Totally isolated from the White House. And no time to go wander off to meetings in parking garages or whatever."

Who is your candidate for Deep Throat?

"Fred Buzhardt, the DOD [Department of Defense] general counsel. He was sent over to the White House to work the problem [of Watergate]. He became an alcoholic and died of alcoholism. What you'll have to check is when he moved from the Pentagon over to the White House to actually begin handling things."

I checked. Buzhardt was appointed special counsel to the president for Watergate on May 10, 1973, a job he held until August 9, 1974, when Nixon resigned. According to Woodward, he was getting information from Deep Throat as early as June 9, 1972.

When I asked Inman his attitude toward Watergate, he said, "It remains a great mystery to me how someone who was so incredibly astute politically could let himself get involved and caught in something that was so amateurish."[24]

It's a mystery to Melvin Laird, Nixon's Secretary of Defense, why Inman thinks Buzhardt was Woodward's secret source:

"Fred Buzhardt was not Deep Throat," Laird said emphatically.*
"He was my general counsel when I went to the White House
to get Agnew's resignation. I was there during that very difficult
period. I guarantee it is not Buzhardt. And Bobby Inman is
absolutely incorrect and I've told him so. I've got all of Fred's
papers, all of those things were turned over to me. And he
was not Deep Throat."[25]

However, there is no question that Buzhardt was an important source for the subsequent Woodward-Bernstein book
The Final Days, cooperating with Al Haig's tacit approval.

Columnist Jack Anderson,† who also protected his anonymous sources, points to a possible Deep Throat in the FBI field
office, where "they had orders to try to get to the bottom of
Watergate. Their reports were falling on blind eyes and their
statements on deaf ears. So, people inside the field office were
leaking information to both Woodward and to my column. I
know that because I recognized some of the material. Woodward
got a figure wrong, which we all do in this business. It was
the number of dirty-trick specialist Don Segretti's associates. He
used the wrong number the FBI had in a classified report. I
had access to the same report. The Washington field office of
the FBI pulled together most of the facts on Watergate."[26]

Haldeman aide Steve Bull** is one of many who don't
believe "that Deep Throat existed. I suspect that they needed
a corroborating source and they manufactured one. It may have
been convenient and expedient for them to attribute the information, which may have been right, to a figure existing only
in their imagination."

"You think Woodward conned Ben Bradlee?" I asked.
"That's pretty gutsy."

---

*Interview with Melvin Laird, March 2, 1994.
†Interview with Jack Anderson, December 4, 1993.
**Interview with Steve Bull, March 2, 1994.

"He's a pretty gutsy guy. I think over the years he's continued to manufacture."[27]

Writers Bob Gettlin and Len Colodny, authors of *Silent Coup,* are convinced Alexander Haig was Deep Throat, and that Woodward had carefully cultivated him to be his eyes in the White House, even before Woodward had decided to become a reporter. They already had what seemed ironclad tape-recorded evidence from Melvin Laird and Admiral Thomas H. Moorer that during his last months in the Navy, while stationed in the Pentagon, Woodward had briefed Haig with classified information. At the time Haig was Kissinger's deputy on the National Security Council. Who would be better informed about any Haig-Woodward meetings than Laird, then secretary of defense, and Moorer, chief of naval operations? Hoping to get Woodward to admit to this early connection with Haig, the writers quizzed Woodward in his kitchen and taped their conversation. But "he absolutely denied it," said Gettlin,* "and was very defensive. What he said didn't jibe with what we found out from Laird and Moorer. I believe Woodward wanted to hide his sources because it would get into his cachet and relationships and change the whole picture developed over the years of how he uncovered Watergate."[28]

Adrian Havill also checked on this while researching for his biography of Woodward, and concluded that although

> Moorer attempted to back away from his recorded statement, making contradictory statements and sounding befuddled, Laird said he was "aware that Haig was briefed by Woodward." . . . Considering the evidence, Bob Woodward's denial more strongly suggests intelligence than it does uninvolvement in White House briefings.[29]

---

*Interview with Bob Gettlin, December 4, 1993.

But does it? Had Woodward the foresight and opportunity to develop ties with Haig—a Deep Throat in the making, or agent in place? And how solid was the evidence from Laird and Moorer?

In 1982, when questioned by Jim Hougan about Woodward, Moorer "seemed to levitate in his chair and then exploded. 'He should have been courtmartialed,' Moorer said. 'I gave him a tongue-lashing. The book of his is nothing but fiction—pure fiction. He should have been prosecuted.' "

"For writing *All the President's Men*?" Hougan asked.

"No, for the other stories. You don't just walk out of the Navy with classified information. There are debriefings, oaths. What he did is inexcusable. He should have been kicked out of the service!" Moorer confirmed that "the other stories" were those Woodward had written about Task Force 157 [an undercover U.S. Navy intelligence program that used CIA agents] and former CIA agent Edwin P. Wilson's relationship to it. In Moorer's view, their publication was a breach of national security, and a breach, also, of the oaths that Woodward had taken.

Informed of Moorer's apoplexy, Woodward asked rhetorically, "How could he courtmartial me, or kick me out of the service, if I was already a civilian? . . ." Woodward denied that he had violated his security oath, and said his articles were based on information that he acquired while a reporter.[30]

To clear the air, I first questioned Admiral Moorer.* When I called, the admiral had just cleared six inches of snow from his driveway and sounded anything but befuddled, though he had apparently mellowed after that explosive twelve-year-old exchange with Hougan. I asked how he could reconcile reliable reports that he first said Woodward was a briefer and then said he wasn't.

---

*Interview with Admiral Moorer, March 3, 1994.

"The point is," Moorer replied, not breathing heavily even after his struggle with the snow, "how you define the word 'brief.' He [Woodward] was in the White House back and forth as a courier [from the Pentagon]. I'm sure, as normally happens, people there asked him questions. But I do not recall any time he was sent over with a specific mission, to sit Haig down in a chair and brief him on something."

I understood now how Moorer might have confused previous interviewers, giving the impression that Woodward had been a briefer. There were too many of them for Moorer to identify individually. And, as Chairman of the Joint Chiefs he was preoccupied with some six hundred messages a day flooding his office. "There were a lot of briefers in the Pentagon," he explained. "Every morning at nine I had a meeting in the Intelligence Room with many people. Some talked about NATO, some about Vietnam, some about the Russian issues of the moment, et cetera, et cetera."

"Did Haig attend those Pentagon briefings?"

"Not to my knowledge. I've been into this a couple of times before. When you get a contentious individual like Woodward. . . . If you start getting into an argument about whether Woodward briefed Haig, I can only say Woodward was not given a set objective to go over to Haig's office and brief him. He was acting as a courier."

"Do you think he's a good reporter?"

"If a good reporter is one who can put together stories that sell, and tickle the curiosity of the passive reader, I guess he's pretty damn successful. I'm not one who admires Woodward. I think he would do almost anything to be the subject of some controversy."

"Has he ever written anything inaccurate about you?"

"No. I had a policy: when I had a press conference I had a tape recorder and I told them to bring their tape recorders. What they do, you see, is to ask you for an appointment. So you talk to them and next morning the *Washington Post* will say, 'A senior official from the Pentagon said so-and-so.' So then the secretary of defense or the president says, 'Find out who talked to Woodward yesterday.' And he's in your appointments book and they jump to the conclusion that you're the one. So I told them [reporters] if they were going to say anything that came up in my press conference, I wanted them to say, 'Tom Moorer told me so-and-so.' And I'd have the recording. But if I hadn't told them that, then I had 'em!"

"If Woodward had a serious question to ask, would you give him an interview?"

"Yes, but I'd record everything I said."[31]

When I told Woodward of my conversation with the admiral,* he laughed and said, "I took Moorer to lunch and explained that I had never been a briefer, just a courier. And he said, 'Well, you all looked alike.' I wish I had been a briefer: it was more interesting."[32]

Bobby Inman, former deputy director of the CIA, emphatically denied the early Woodward-Haig connection, saying,† "There's absolutely no truth to it. Woodward never had responsibilities like that. His was a very low-level staff job [as a courier]."[33]

Melvin Laird, Nixon's defense secretary, agreed with Inman, telling me he had been misquoted or misunderstood by those convinced Woodward had been a briefer. Laird had no personal knowledge of Woodward's work in the Pentagon, nor of any contacts between Woodward and Haig at that time.[34]

Still, Haig found it impossible to escape the stigma of being the most likely Deep Throat. On anyone's list of the usual suspects, he invariably topped the list. Incensed at the inference that he was a disloyal snitch, and coming across editor Ben

---

*Interview with Bob Woodward, March 8, 1994.
†Interview with Bobby Inman, February 28, 1994.

Bradlee in the dining room of the Madison Hotel, Haig asked if the *Post* was "still the champion of truth and justice?" "Sure it is, Al," said Bradlee. "That never changes." Haig then suggested that the newspaper tell readers the truth, that he wasn't Deep Throat. "I'm not suggesting that you reveal who it *is*. All I want is for you to nail the lie." Now Bradlee could have asked Woodward to confirm Haig's innocence. It would hardly risk exposing Deep Throat's real identity. It still left dozens of suspects. But Bradlee refused to let him off the hook.[35]

Adrian Havill, working on an unauthorized Woodward biography, meticulously followed in his subject's footsteps, going over the ground he had described to get to his clandestine meetings with Deep Throat, casing the various joints himself, and even checking if it had rained when Woodward said it did. And his verdict was that some scenarios were wildly unlikely. For instance,

> The walking fifteen blocks to find a cab at night or being "terrified" because Bob had to spend an hour in a parking garage or ducking into an alley to avoid being followed was manufactured hokum that added drama and suspense to the book. It also created empathy for the protagonists.[36]

Havill's suspicions were further aroused by an account of those heady times by Peter Schwed, former chairman of Simon & Schuster's editorial board. According to Schwed, Richard Snyder (head of the company), "assigned the editorial role [for *All the President's Men*] to Alice Mayhew and cut her loose to work night and day with Woodward and Bernstein. Alice was the one who told the authors that the peg was to build up the Deep Throat character and make him interesting."[37]

"Thus," concludes Havill, "with Mayhew goading the two on one side and Robert Redford standing in the wings on the other, with nearly half a million dollars and a piece of the profits waiting for the two reporters whose combined income was less than $30,000 a year, what Bob and Carl produced was a sort of Hardy Boys at the White House. Part of it—the impossible and lunatic Deep Throat cloak-and-dagger derring-do, and much of the literary effect—was dreamed up. Those parts were a hoax, a relatively harmless hoax designed to sell books and make a movie. The core of the book, the step-by-step rehash of the fall of Richard Nixon and the men around him, was written from their clips and reporters' notes. Those details were largely accurate. Bob and Carl certainly did have several important sources in the executive branch of government."[38]

Is Havill on to something? Did Woodward stray from the straight and narrow, with the prospect of fame and fortune nudging him, and a few ankle taps from editor Mayhew and movie mogul Redford? Alice Mayhew denies she was "cut loose" from other duties to work on *All the President's Men,* or that she told Woodward to build up Deep Throat to make him interesting. She told me she still believes in the existence of Deep Throat and has "an educated guess as to his identity." Much of the criticism of Bob Woodward, said Mayhew, is from jealousy.[39]

When I told Schwed of Mayhew's response, he said he would "take her word for it, because what I wrote was hearsay."[40]

But shouldn't hearsay—when it came directly from an insider, the publisher—be given weight? Snyder declined to speak with me but, through a representative, confirmed Mayhew's account. The verdict? As the Scots would say: Not proven.

"General, I Can Make You a Hero or a Bum"

In their follow-up book, *The Final Days* (of the Nixon presidency), Woodward and Bernstein gave an intimate account of Nixon's torment. In one scene, Haig was apparently the only witness.

As soon as he read it, he cabled the former president: "I want to reassure you that I have not contributed in any way to the book."[41]

He also informed a friend, on April 15, 1976: "With respect to the . . . book, I, too, am depressed and appalled. As you know, I have steadfastly declined to contribute to any post-mortems which in my view would never be objectively viewed in the current environment. This was all the more true in the case of Woodward and Bernstein. For this reason, you can imagine my disgust with the plethora of so-called direct quotes, sometimes the product of alleged one-on-one discussions with members of the President's team, who should have known better."[42]

He also wrote to journalist Victor Lasky, "I want to assure you personally that I did not contribute to the contents of the book despite repeated efforts by the author to get me to do so. Mr. Woodward even traveled to Europe where, in the presence of a note-taking witness [Bratton], I declined to comment in any way on the last days of the Nixon presidency. This past week in San Antonio, I reiterated this fact publicly and emphasized the imprecision of the book's revelations."[43]

Lasky concluded that, "Haig's meeting with Woodward was short and sweet. According to an unimpeachable source [Bratton presumably], Woodward walked into Haig's office and said, 'General, I can make you either a hero or a bum. Which is it to be?' Haig told the intrepid reporter to get lost."[44]

Haig dropped the "bum" in his 1992 memoir, *Inner Circles,* writing: "Woodward arrived on February 12, 1975. The meeting was short. After describing some of the topics covered in his book, Woodward earnestly told me, 'You can come off as a hero in our book—or not. It's up to you.' That ended the discussion. Brig. Gen. Joseph Bratton, who was serving as my executive officer at that time, was present during the encounter."[45]

Woodward denied using either remark when I spoke with

him on March 8, 1994: "It's absolutely not true," he said. "I don't talk like that."

Later that day I tried to check with Haig, but he chose not to talk. Instead, he left a message with his secretary: "Everything I want to say about Woodward is in my book."

Why did Haig see Woodward after the revelations in *All the President's Men,* which implied that he or Kissinger was leaking information? Pity, Haig implies, as he explained:

> After I became NATO commander, with headquarters at Mons, Belgium, Woodward called me from London, saying that he had spent his own money on an airline ticket to go there in the hope that I would agree to see him if he continued on to Belgium. I replied that I could not and would not discuss with him or anyone else what I knew about Nixon or Watergate or any other subject connected to my duties in the White House. He persisted. Something in his urgent tone of voice made me think that he might be going to all this trouble to discharge some professional obligation. I told him that I would see him in my office but warned him once again that he could expect to hear nothing of substance from me. "If you want to do it on a pro forma basis, come on over," I said. "But it will be a waste of time for both of us, because there is absolutely nothing I can tell you."[46]

That "urgent tone" of Woodward's seems to be one of the secrets of his success. He used it to good effect when he said, "I want to work here so bad I can taste it," which moved the *Sentinel* editor to hire him.

If Haig told Woodward "absolutely nothing," how did the following get into *The Final Days*? Haig is alone in the White House with a desperate Nixon, who says, " 'You fellows, in your business,' meaning the Army . . . 'you have a way of handling problems like this. Somebody leaves a pistol in a drawer.' Haig waited. 'I don't have a pistol,' the President said sadly, as if it were one more deprivation in a long history of underprivilege. As if he were half asking to be given one. It was the same tone he used when he talked about his parents not having any money. Afterward, Haig called the President's doctors. He ordered that all pills be denied the President, and that the sleeping pills and tranquilizers he already had be taken away. Haig also discusssed the matter with Buzhardt."[47]

Haig confirmed this incident in his subsequent memoir, but put the finger on Buzhardt:

> In compiling [their] book, Woodward and Bernstein benefited from the advice of the late J. Fred Buzhardt, President Nixon's Special Counsel for Watergate. Buzhardt . . . phoned me after Nixon had left the White House to inform me that he was trying to decide whether to talk to the two journalists, who had approached him to provide background for his book. . . . Buzhardt asked me whether I thought it would be wrong for him to cooperate with the writers. I told him this was a matter for his own judgment but that I could not imagine him saying or doing anything that would harm Nixon or distort the record, whereas many others could be counted upon to do both. He told me that he intended to go ahead with the arrangement, and, on the basis of the unusual level of truthfulness achieved in certain passages of the published work, I have assumed that he did so.[48]

By identifying Buzhardt as a source, had Haig cleared himself? I needed to check that with Woodward.

Cutting Deep Throat Down to Size

"Deep Throat is the only secret in the world!" boasted Carl Bernstein recently to a Florida audience.[49]

Many still believe that he was a fiction adopted by Woodward to cover himself, and protect a slew of anonymous insiders. Perhaps it began as a game.

Woodward "loves playing games," says Robert Fink, the researcher for *All the President's Men.* But insiders like Fink sustain the mystery of Deep Throat: he would neither name his favorite candidate nor say if he thought the man existed.[50]

Barry Sussman was more forthcoming.* As city editor of the *Washington Post,* he had worked closely with Woodward and Bernstein on Watergate, then wrote his own upfront view of it in *The Great Cover-Up.*[51] A great title, cynics might think, for Woodward's protection of Deep Throat.

I said to Sussman,[52] who was reluctant to discuss Woodward, "When Katharine Graham asked him 'Who is Deep Throat?' he acted nervously. My question is: Why would you, Bradlee, and Graham put the reputation of the *Washington Post* on the line with information from an anonymous source?"

He replied, "The contributions of Deep Throat to the Watergate story are almost total myth and very little reality."

"Did you all believe it was a myth at the time?"

"I'm telling you that Deep Throat was *irrelevant* to the Woodward-Watergate coverage."

"Why did Katharine Graham want to know who he was if he was irrelevant?"

"Why not?"

"Well, you're an editor. If it's a major source of tremendous help to you . . ."

He interrupted, like an impatient teacher. "You say major source. And I keep telling you he was *unimportant.*"

"But in your own Watergate book you say, 'Over the months Bob's friend became more and more important to us.' "

"At what point in the Watergate story does Deep Throat come into my book?"

---

*Interview with Barry Sussman, March 1, 1994.

"You wrote: 'In September and October, as we began to get deeply into the Watergate scandal, "my friend," as Woodward called him, or "Bob's friend," as the rest of us referred to him, came to play a mysterious and crucial role. . . . The first time Woodward came to me with something from his friend, he asked if it would be possible not to tell his friend's name. Woodward said he would tell me if I insisted, but that he would rather not. It was the only time he had made such a request. I didn't ask. Over the months, Bob's friend became more and more important to us, and Howard Simons gave him a new name: "Deep Throat." ' "53

Sussman responded: "The reason I didn't ask [his identity] was it was a very minor story."

"But then you go on to write, 'Deep Throat seemed to know everything about Watergate.' "

"I don't say no to that. I said he was an important source and his role is greatly exaggerated."

"So there was a Deep Throat."

"I'm not going to go into that with you. I think what I said is clear enough."

The next day, when I called Barry Sussman back, he decided to tape our conversation, too.

I began: "Could you settle what seems a contradiction between your book and what you said yesterday? Your book says, 'He seemed to know everything about Watergate.' But then you say he was an unimportant source."

"Let me be very clear about that. Deep Throat did not provide us with leads to stories. He confirmed things every now and then. He also pulled us off of things we should have written. For example, if my memory is right, around the end of 1972 we were working on a piece, 'John Mitchell is ruined.' This source said no, that's not the correct story. That kind of thing. It's not that Deep Throat was no use whatsoever, but his importance in our coverage has been totally exaggerated. It's a myth. The references to Deep Throat in the Woodward-Bernstein book are sometimes made up to throw readers off the trail—the authors say that. There's no way of the ordinary person knowing how valuable he was or wasn't. In terms of covering the story Deep Throat was never important at all."

"Are the secret meetings in underground garages, et cetera, also putting the reader off the scent?"

"I don't know if they're true or not."

"But at the time didn't he seem to be a tremendous source?"

"It was a little comforting to have somebody who could be helpful now and then. We did not rely on him for leads. To my knowledge we got no leads from him."

"And was there comfort when there was only one other source for the story?"

"That's another myth. We didn't have any two-source rule. If we had a story that rang true and we felt it was reported well enough, we ran it."

"What do you think of Woodward as a reporter?"

"You're going to try without ending, aren't you? I'm really not interested in discussing Bob Woodward."[54]

Ben Bradlee was two-thirds through writing his memoirs when I reached him.* At first he seemed doubtful that Sussman had spoken so frankly with me. However, he did not challenge Sussman's remarks about Deep Throat, adding, "Barry was very involved, is a very intelligent man, and wrote a good book about Watergate. But I would quibble about the one source. Perhaps in some circumstances, if you got the President of the United States, but normally we had at least two and normally more."[55]

Tantalizing questions about the Watergate era still cry out for answers. There's evidence that the Democrats were warned of plans to break into their headquarters well in advance of

---

*Interview with Ben Bradlee, March 2, 1994.

the deed and then let it happen, even though they knew the site held incriminating material about Democratic national chairman Larry O'Brien.[56] And what was the real reason for Liddy volunteering to assassinate columnist Jack Anderson? (See chapter 6.)

But what Woodward and Bernstein did uncover earned them such accolades as: "Close to the top in the history of journalism," "It is likely that our free press has saved freedom for all of us," and "This book is written about two people who made a difference."[57]

Few readers knew, as Havill points out, that the book was written with a movie in mind. Robert Redford had already shown interest in screening their exploits, focusing on the two young reporters against the establishment. So, in the interest of film excitement, who knows what edge-of-the seat incidents were invented or inflated to energize an otherwise less-than-thrilling account of phone calls, knocking on doors, and riffling through documents?

Editors Sussman and Bradlee, both credible and informed witnesses, imply that the literal truth was sacrificed to make the book a hot property. Though not a mythic creation like Superman or the Invisible Man, it's likely that Deep Throat got star billing when he only rated credit as an extra.

Nevertheless, Woodward insists that not only is Deep Throat a real person but also that their clandestine encounters occurred as he described them in the book. He admits that he makes mistakes and is not infallible.[58] He may have gotten the weather wrong, brought down rain on a dry day, walked nine blocks instead of ten, but essentially that is what happened. His detailed description of Deep Throat is also accurate, he says, which makes it astonishing that in a city of perpetual leaks and world-class investigators, after twenty years the man is still a mystery.

The Janet Cooke Fiasco

Woodward married his second wife, Francie Barnard, in 1974. She shared his interest in news-breaking stories as Washington correspondent for the *Fort Worth-Telegram*. They had a daughter, Taliesin, in 1976. The marriage lasted less than four years. Woodward blamed his workaholic habits.

As Watergate was the high spot of his career, the "Jimmy's World" feature story killed any chance he might have had to be the paper's editor.

He was assistant managing editor in 1981, encouraging the work of reporter Janet Cooke when she turned in a poignant, superbly written story about Jimmy, an eight-year-old heroin addict in the nation's capital. It won her the 1981 Pulitzer Prize, but then it was discovered that the piece was fiction. Jimmy did not exist. Cooke had conned Woodward and Ben Bradlee into accepting her assertion that, to protect them, everyone in her story had to remain anonymous. Only she would know their true identities.

She returned the prize and quit the paper, which then investigated the deception and in the spirit of full disclosure published a series spelling out what had happened.

I asked Woodward what he learned from it.*

"Oh, Jesus!" he said.

"Let me rephrase it. How concerned were you afterwards about using anonymous sources?"

"It wasn't an anonymous source issue. It was a total fabrication. The whole situation had to remain anonymous, which never should have been permitted. There wasn't a person [truly] named in the article."

"Everybody in charge goofed."

"I particularly blame myself for what I've said publicly many

---

*Interview with Bob Woodward, March 8, 1994.

times was a moral failure." (For pursuing the story, when he thought "Jimmy" really existed, instead of alerting the authorities to rescue a child addict.)

"Since then, how have you ensured the credibility of your stories?"

"When I write books about George Bush, Colin Powell, or William Casey, it's about them in situations when I say the following happened, the following was said."

"Janet Cooke said the following happened, the following was said."

"Yes, but there was no one around to have any [credibility]. No address, no place, no mother, no father, no kid. The whole situation was anonymous."

"Were you surprised you couldn't get Janet Cooke to confess to you personally? She said, 'I'm not going to tell Bob Woodward.' "

"Well, I was pretty mad at her. I spent hours that whole night talking to her. Pretty aggressive."

"She said you shouted. You realize now that's not the way to get someone to talk, right? Not to get you to talk, either."

"Right."[59]

Casey and the CIA: Off the Reservation?

If his portrait of Nixon caused a flurry of agitated denials and questions about Woodward's integrity, morality, and parentage, his insider's less-than-admiring picture in *Veil* of CIA Director William Casey brought cries of "liar!" from Casey's widow, and, "He's a fraud!" from almost every CIA veteran who knew Casey well and was willing to talk. Constantine Menges, for one, Casey's foreign affairs advisor, contested Woodward's accuracy.

After interviewing Menges about the 1983 U.S. invasion of Grenada, Woodward wrote in *Veil*: "Menges suggested that the captured Cuban prisoners not be released. He urged that the Cubans be made to suffer."[60]

On the contrary, Menges told me,* "Woodward was totally wrong about that. I was deeply concerned that all the captured persons be treated humanely. Where did Woodward get the false statement about me? And why didn't he ask me about it or about many of the things he wrote about me?"[61]

When I brought this up with Woodward,† he asked, "Did he deny that the basic portrait of him is correct?"

"No. Just some details that helped make the portrait."

Woodward read his words about Menges a couple of times, and said, "That's the slippery nature of this. What this says is they not be released. Not being released is suffering, being in jail. I'm not saying he's saying, 'Don't let's treat them humanely.' "

Isn't that exactly what Woodward was saying? Sentence one: Keep them in prison. Sentence two. Make them suffer.

He interrupted my unexpressed thoughts: "Look at it in context. It's very clear what Menges said. Have you asked him, did he want the Cuban prisoners released?"

"No. But he pointed out that he wanted them treated humanely."

"That's setting up a straw man," Woodward replied. "You need to be better at what you do. May I be candid with you? It's very clear what I say he says. It's well known among lots of people what his attitude was. [He reads his account again, this time aloud.] 'As an alternative he suggested that the prisoners not be released. He urged that the Cubans be made to suffer.' Being held in jail and not released is suffering."

"But, in ordinary military circumstances, when you capture the enemy, they're automatically put in prison. Then it's a question of whether they're treated harshly or not."

---

*Interview with Constantine Menges, October 19, 1990.
†Interview with Bob Woodward, February 22, 1994.

"*Veil* has got it so right," Woodward insisted. "When somebody doesn't like it, they take things out of context. Then you [should] hold their feet to the fire. Look at the instances where Menges is quoted and referred to and say to him, 'Is this true? Is this true? Is this true?'"

"What I did is to say to Menges, 'You were interviewed by Woodward. How accurate is he?' Another CIA veteran who complained to me was Herb Meyer, Casey's assistant. He said that in *Veil,* you got at least one account 180 degrees wrong, and your language for Casey wasn't the way he spoke. He also complained you didn't get him right, either. You quoted him saying, 'I think it stinks.' He says it's not the way he talks."

Woodward kept his cool, somewhat professorial tone: "You've got to understand there's a guerrilla political war that goes on, particularly about someone like Casey, in which the Herb Meyers and Constantine Mengeses, who have very extreme political views [are engaged]. You must acknowledge that."

"Absolutely."

"Don't you see what they're doing? They're both very passionate advocates. Fine, we need passionate advocates on the Left and the Right in this country. But, what are they trying to say?"

"You're inaccurate, so you can't be trusted in anything."

"Exactly. It's a kind of interior decorator's critique of it. Like somebody saying, 'I never talk like that.' But there's the whole question of biography or reporting. Do you have a credible reason for writing what you write? What I'm saying to you is, if you come over here and I was to decide I'm going to open up all my files to you and you were to pick ten cases or twenty or a thousand and say, 'I talked to X, Y, and Z, and they say something was different or didn't happen, let's go and see the basis on which you wrote what you wrote.' And you'd go into my archives and see in every single case that I had a substantial and powerful and credible basis for everything I wrote. Now, does it mean that if there were twenty people in the room, I talked to all twenty, twenty times? No. But you would be amazed at the precision and care, and that [the information] came from people who were authoritative. Everything I've done is scrupulously reported. There is a specific source for everything that's in my books."

"Will you let your future biographer see your files?"

"Sure. You need, may I suggest to you, to think about what's going on. What's the politics? There's a guy who wrote a review of *Veil,* staff director of the Senate Intelligence Committee, working for Goldwater, Rob Simmons. And he made a point I thought was very good. He said, 'Is *Veil* an engineer's drawing of what happened?' He said, 'No. Is it essentially correct? Absolutely, yes.' As a reporter, I don't go around with a video recorder or a tape recorder as things are happening. I try to get at them soon afterwards. In fact, biography is an engineer's drawing."[62]

But would a loyal American have provided some of those drawings? No, says Barry Goldwater: "Woodward's book covered very sensitive material. . . . It caused and will continue to cause this country real problems by compromising certain agents and activities, disclosing particular techniques in collecting intelligence, and harming our intelligence relations with other nations."[63] Goldwater did not blame Woodward, but those who "spilled their guts" to him.

Blood on Whose Hands?

Woodward and Casey were patriots who thought they were defending democracy, one by breaking the law and the other by blowing the whistle on him for doing it. Woodward was for the public's right to know, Casey for the nation's right to be secure. Because of Casey's actions and Woodward's reports, both believed the other had "blood on his hands." Maybe both were right.

Woodward's exposure of the 1983 Fadlallah disaster points out to me his biggest defect. In *Veil* he writes what seems a firsthand account of a secret conversation between Casey and Prince Faud of Saudi Arabia, a conversation both men denied occurred. As a result of that conversation, says Woodward, a bomb exploded in Beirut on March 8, 1985. It was meant for Sheikh Fadlallah, who was suspected of being a terrorist leader. Instead of killing him, it took the lives of some eighty bystanders.

For that, Woodward believed Casey had blood on his hands.

What Woodward does not tell is revealed by Casey's authorized biographer Joseph Persico: investigations absolved Casey and the CIA from any involvement in the Fadlallah affair. Furthermore, although Woodward mentions the hijacking of TWA Flight 847 three months later, he does not connect it with his exposure of American involvement in the Fadlallah incident. Yet, as Persico writes,

gunmen [aboard the hijacked plane] shot to death a twenty-three-year-old U.S. Navy diver named Robert Dean Stethem and threw his body on the tarmac. Over the radio circuit between the plane and the central tower, a voice rebuked the hijackers for the cold-blooded killing. One terrorist shouted back, "We have not forgotten the massacre of Bir al-Abed!" The hijackers were members of the militant band connected to Sheikh Fadlallah.

To Casey, what was happening was instantly clear. The March 8, 1985, car bombing that had killed eighty people in the Beirut suburb of Bir al-Abed had been aimed at Fadlallah. The *Washington Post* story of May 12 had revealed a link between the CIA and the Lebanese team involved in the attempt on Fadlallah's life. Fadlallah's people were taking

their revenge against America. Woodward had been warned
by George Lauder [CIA press officer] not to run the story
precisely because it would provoke vengeance. As Casey saw
it, there was blood on the reporter's hands.[64]

The Democratic-controlled House Select Committee on Intelligence investigated the bombing and concluded: "No U.S.
government complicity, direct or indirect, can be established."
Bernie McMahon, who ran the Senate Select Committee on
Intelligence, also absolved Casey, saying: "[We] could not trace
a line from Casey to the Fadlallah bombing, and we had a
hell of a lot more capability to look into it than Bob Woodward."[65]

It's unlikely Casey or Faud shared their "conspiratorial"
conversation with Woodward. So, accepting the conclusion of
the investigating committees, the misinformation or disinformation must have come from others. Woodward was reckless,
at the very least, in accepting the account of even several secondhand sources, especially with lives at stake. As Herb Meyer,
Casey's former assistant, said to me, "I can get ten people to
swear you had an affair with a pig last night. Doesn't mean
it's true!"

What seems to be closest to the truth was a later admission
by McMahon that although the CIA did not participate in the
bombing, "they created a mechanism which ultimately got out
of control and led to the bombing."[66] This, I think, leaves both
Casey and Woodward on shaky ground.

His critics claim that Woodward boasts of nearly fifty
interviews with Casey, when released CIA records show there
were only fourteen. Jack Anderson supports Woodward on this,
knowing that Casey often slipped away from his guards and
colleagues to meet reporters in safe houses, meetings for which
the CIA would have no record.

The "Death-Bed" Interview

Those bent on discrediting Woodward seize on the last four pages of *Veil* in which he describes an extraordinary last conversation with Casey, who had recently undergone brain surgery. During that terse conversation in Casey's Georgetown University Hospital room, he acknowledges his involvement in Iran-contra, because "I believed."

Absolute lies, say Woodward's critics: even if by some subterfuge he had gotten into Casey's heavily guarded room, brain surgery had left the CIA director incapable of speech.

An informed skeptic, Arnaud de Borchgrave, editor-at-large for the *Washington Times,* thinks,* "Woodward has one of the most overrated reputations in the business. And I happen to know that he lied about this so-called death-bed scene with Bill Casey. The doctor who operated on Bill Casey, Professor Luessenhop, also operated on my son who had a similar brain tumor. Sophia [Casey's widow], a dear friend of mine, called me the day Woodward tried to break into Casey's hospital room in various disguises and using his various subterfuges. Finally he was challenged and admitted his identity and was thrown out. As you may notice in *Veil,* he doesn't describe whether Bill Casey was sitting up or lying down; whether he was on a life-support system or not; didn't describe the hospital room; and when asked why he didn't do that, he said he would have been betraying the person who let him into the room. That's nonsense. You don't betray anyone by describing what the room looked like and what Casey looked like. When I confronted Bob Woodward at the one hundred fortieth anniversary of the *Chicago Tribune* reception, he challenged me and said, 'I know you wrote about it in your paper, but the incident you describe was on January 23. I got in after that.' I said, 'Bob, that is

---

*Interview with Arnaud de Borchgrave, April 20, 1990.

impossible. Even on January 23, the part of his brain that receives and sends messages was totally paralyzed. You could not have had any kind of conversation with him even if you had gotten in. And I happen to know from Sophia and CIA security that you'd gotten nowhere near him.' "

I asked de Borchgrave why he thought Woodward had lied.

"He had to hype his book. Like many people now have to find gimmicks to hype their books to get on talk shows."

"But with his reputation and record, why would he lie about something so important?"

"Why not? The Iran-contra thing occurred after he'd finished his book. He obviously had to include something sensational about Iran-contra. And it was made out of whole cloth."[67]

"Nobody could understand him [his speech]," confirmed Sophia Casey. "It was a very sad thing."[68]

Former CIA Director William Colby is among the few who assume Woodward might have sneaked into the room undetected for a few minutes despite all the security. Colby was also impressed with the accuracy of some details in *Veil*, "but," he added,* "that quote of Casey's is very ambiguous. 'I believed.' That could be the beginning of a sentence, 'I believed' something entirely different."

"Wasn't Casey difficult to understand normally?" I asked.

"There was a joke about him," said Colby, "that he never needed a scrambler."[69]

George Carver, another CIA veteran, agreed:† "Bill frequently mumbled, but I regarded that as one of his many excellent acts. Earlier when Woodward was detected trying to get in, they were hypersensitized to such an intrusion and took added precautions. All things are possible, of course, if, like

---

*Interview with William Colby, September 30, 1990.
†Interview with George Carver, October 4, 1990.

Woodward, you're hustling for a story and not squeamish about how you get it. The concept of that Irishman looking up into Woodward's eyes and saying 'I believed' is totally out of character. Of course, it's always much more convenient to quote dead people, because they can't take issue with you." (Casey was dead when *Veil* was published.)[70]

But columnist Jack Anderson couldn't believe that "Woodward would fabricate the interview. I know Bob, and he's a fine, enterprising reporter. I also knew Casey, an enormously secretive man. He loved to play cloak-and-dagger games. I sent my partner to arrange secret meetings with Casey, meetings no one else knew about. Nobody, not his public relations people nor his subordinates, would know he was conferring with us. It's the way he played the game. He loved mystery and intrigue."[71]

Woodward resisted all attempts to get him to explain how he entered Casey's hospital room. Television interviewers such as Ted Koppel failed to make him come clean. Sophia Casey called him a liar on "60 Minutes," as they sat side by side, and Casey's nephew suggested someone should turn the tables on Woodward and investigate him.

In preparing an authorized biography of Casey, Joseph Persico interviewed Woodward doggedly about the controversial hospital room conversation, but got nowhere. Persico told me* "Woodward says he can't reveal his sources. It's an honorable journalistic position; also a very handy device for supporting your version of events. I put the evidence on a scale. If I had an unanimous agreed reaction that Casey was incoherent, it would have been easy, but I had a jury in which eleven jurors said he made no sense and one, Bill Gates, said, 'I might have understood him at one point.' It came down to the weight of evidence. Those who told me they didn't understand a word he said were, on the whole, people who in terms of their intimacy

*Interview with Joseph Persico, February 26, 1994.

with the man and reputation for credibility, believable. His son-in-law, for example, had no reason to mislead me. He knew Casey very well and had worked for him for twenty years. And he couldn't understand him.

"Hustling my book, I was on a Washington TV station and had just come off and was getting ready to leave and was told I had a phone call. It was a young woman who identified herself as the Georgetown University Hospital speech therapist for Casey. She said, 'I just heard you discuss the controversy of the so-called death-bed confession Mr. Woodward supposedly extracted from Mr. Casey. Let me tell you something, sir. My job was to work with Mr. Casey on his speech. I can tell you, and my colleagues will confirm, that we could not make clear to him or he to us what he was having for breakfast, much less carry on any kind of substantive conversation about a highly sophisticated issue like Iran-contra.' "72

Persico admitted he hadn't checked up on the woman. After all, she might have been a CIA plant. But when I pressed him to say how he felt about the death-bed conversation, he replied, "Can I say it as clearly and finally as possible? He didn't prove it to me." Yet he conceded that "Woodward's capture of Casey's essence was very good. I knew Casey fairly well. Woodward read him very well. That's why I feel unhappy about my disagreement in the final pages of both our books [*Veil* and *Casey*]."

"What I don't understand," said Persico, "is why Woodward didn't go off the record and tell me, a journalistic colleague, not who helped him, but how he got into Casey's room. I'm sure he knew I would have kept it confidential. As it is the whole thing looks like a smokescreen."

We discussed Woodward's interviewing technique and I said: "There's almost a hypnotic quality in the way he talks, very slowly, controlled, and easy. I wonder if he hypnotizes people into telling the truth."

"He has this magnificent capacity," Persico added, "and

perhaps it explains 51 percent of his success—to lull people into frankness, a way of making them think, 'This guy wouldn't hurt me.' [We both laughed.] And then these people walk away and their heads fall off!" (We laughed harder.)[73]

Surprisingly, someone de Borchgrave thought would agree that Woodward was a complete liar would only go halfway. The chief surgeon who operated on Casey, Dr. Alfred Luessenhop, was among the few who believed Woodward might have entered the room. But he discounted any coherent conversation between the two.

To refresh his memory, the surgeon asked me to send him copies of the pages in Woodward's book describing the event, and then to call him back. When I did, he said,* "In recalling what happened, my reaction was that Casey's security was extraordinary. His wife was in all the time. There was always a guy sitting in front of the door and two or three in the hall. My opinion at the time was that he got in by extraordinary luck when no one happened to be in the room. That part could have happened. He could have done it, a sleazy character like that; but he could not have had any meaningful conversation with Casey or one that could be interpreted in any meaningful way."[74]

Speaking on behalf of the CIA, Gwen Cohen denied there could have been any kind of conversation, coherent or incoherent. She discussed the matter with the man in charge of Casey's security, who assured her, and she in turn assured me, there was no way Woodward could have entered that room.[75]

If it was a question of whose word to take, Seymour Hersh, Woodward's rival for top spot in the reporting field, favored Woodward: "I've no problem in just telling you that if Woodward said he saw Casey, he saw him. He's certainly not going to fantasize about it. I've just worked against him, never with him,

*Interview with Alfred Luessenhop, October 2, 1990.

but it's inconceivable to me that he didn't do everything he said he did do."[76]

I obviously had a way to go before I reached a reasonable conclusion. In *Veil* Woodward writes of his last conversation with Casey as follows:

I asked Casey how he was getting along. Hope and then realism flashed in his eyes. "Okay . . . better . . . no." I took his hand to shake it in greeting. He grabbed my hand and squeezed, peace and sunlight in the room for a moment. "You finished yet?" he asked, referring to the book. I said I'd never finish, never get it all, there were so many questions. I'd never find out everything he had done. The left side of his mouth hooked up in a smile, and he grunted. "Look at all the trouble you've caused," I said, "the whole Adminstration under investigation [Iran-contra]." He didn't seem to hear. So I repeated it and for a moment he looked proud, raising his head. "It hurts," he said, and I thought he was in physical pain. "What hurts, sir?" "Oh," he said, stopping. He seemed to be saying that it was being out of it, out of the action, I thought. But he suddenly spoke up, apparently on the same track about hurt. "What you don't know," he said. In the end, I realized, what was hidden was greater. The unknown had the power, he seemed to be saying, or at least that's what I thought. He was so frail, at life's edge, and he knew, making a comment about death. "I'm gone," he said. I said no. "You knew, didn't you?" I said. "The contra diversion had to be the first question: you knew all along." His head jerked up hard. He stared, and finally nodded yes. "Why?" I asked. "I believed." "What?" "I believed." Then he was asleep, and I didn't get to ask another question.[77]

That brief, awkward exchange, with all its uncertainties and Woodward's "I thoughts" and "it seemeds," is not unlike a verbal Rorschach test—everyone gets to guess what he meant—with echoes of *Waiting for Godot.* By "You finished yet?" Casey might have meant, "Have you finished asking me your annoying questions?" And so on.

I asked Woodward:* "What were your motives in getting that last interview in his hospital room? Someone suggested, 'Woodward has to see things for himself. It's an empirical approach. And he may have been checking rumors that Casey was in hiding to avoid testifying about Irangate, even rumors that he was dead after being poisoned to prevent him from testifying.' I thought you were just trying to get final answers from him."

"No," he said. "I think the first month I was a reporter at the *Washington Post* in 1971, I went to a hospital to talk. Three or four kids had been killed in a fire and I went to talk to the parents and get reactions. It's kind of Police Reporting 101. People in the Casey camp have conducted a campaign on this issue. Everyone tried to get into the debate [over] how well I knew him. It's all documented. It's in my records and in CIA records. I knew this man very well and I knew Sophia Casey. She and I had very nice conversations. If I had gone to the hospital and I'd talked to her, she'd probably have taken me in herself." (He chuckled.)

"It didn't concern you that your appearing there might have shocked him, harmed his recovery?"

"Why?"

"A man who's very ill after a brain operation being asked very serious questions about his work—challenging questions."

"My tone is not challenging. [He said very soothingly. But his questions to Casey sure were.] It's taken on a mystique that was certainly not intended. It's the most basic thing you do as a reporter. I knew this man very well. As it turned out it was not his deathbed, as you know. He went home from the

---

*Interview with Bob Woodward, March 8, 1994.

hospital and Sophia moved him to Long Island, and then he went into a hospital and that's where he died."

"When the guard first caught you in the hospital . . ."

"I went up to the door and the security guards turned me away."

"Weren't you disguised as a doctor or a CIA man?"

"I would urge upon you great care in talking to people about this."

"When I discussed it with Persico, he told me if you had leveled with him and said to him, 'We understand the rules of journalism. Let me go off the record and I'll tell you how I did this,' he would have respected that and you would have made a sale. 'But, instead,' said Persico, 'I had a great deal of smoke. And nothing Woodward said, I think, would have persuaded a reasonable person he did this.' "

Persico's disappointment did the trick. Woodward decided to go off the record and tell me how he got into Casey's hospital room, trusting me not to break a confidence. His explanation was surprisingly simple—and plausible. And, although I believe him, of course, it doesn't mean it's true. And it does not address the question of their conversation.

Woodward cited Bill Gates (later CIA director) as tending to support him. "He came to the *Post* after Casey had had his stroke, when he was in the hospital, and said Casey was 'lucid.' And there were only twenty people there who heard him say that. Now he kind of says, 'Well, I really didn't mean that.' These people have such . . . I'm trying to figure out the nicest way to say it. They kind of want to undermine or attempt to undermine what somebody does that's critical. But Gates has said privately, 'Casey was off the reservation from Day One. The CIA director was in contempt of Congress from Day One.' What time shows, frankly, is that I got it devastatingly correct who Casey was, the nature of his involvement, the nature of him being the intellectual godfather of the covert operations and the clandestine mindset that dominated the CIA and the Reagan administration in that period, which eventually led to Iran-contra."[78]

"Woodward is very agile," said Persico.* "You don't trap him easily and he's disarming. That's what he did with the people at the CIA. He disarmed them."

"But surely Casey was too wiley an old bird to fall for that?"

"Casey liked fencing, particularly with writers," Persico explained. "He was a reader and something of a writer himself. My conviction is he found it too irresistible not to fence with the country's preeminent investigative reporter, because he thought he could outdo him."[79]

I asked former CIA Chief William Colby,† "Do you believe Casey may have been feeding Woodward information or disinformation for the purposes of the CIA?"

"Well, for the purposes of Casey, not the CIA particularly," he said. "He might well have been engaged in the process I've been engaged in—to try to tell a full story so the partial story fits in as a very small proportion that it really is."[80]

Woodward had something of a love-hate relationship with Casey and much in common with his most challenging subject. Both were driven, daring, and controversial, and adopted similar tactics of evasion and omission, while being seemingly frank and even ingenuous. Some agree with Persico that Casey saw Woodward as a worthy "opponent." Woodward's job was to unearth secrets; Casey's, to keep them buried or leak them to his, or the country's, advantage. Who won is still debated.

Of those I questioned, I think that his admiring rival, Joseph Persico, had the best fix on Woodward. After his own book on Casey, Persico worked on one about the Nuremburg trials, and when we last spoke, he was collaborating with General

*Interview with Joseph Persico, March 2, 1994.
†Interview with William Colby, September 30, 1990,

Colin Powell on his autobiography. Powell had been a good source for Woodward when he wrote *The Commanders*.[81] "In that," said Persico,* "there are some parallels with *Veil*. People who were interviewed say, 'Yes, it's fascinating and some of it is incredible. How the hell does he get this stuff? He's got it all right.' And then they say, 'But this is shaded. That's not quite the way it was.' And I'm not saying who is right. I can't expect even the greatest investigative reporter on earth to get it right 100 hundred percent of the time.

"He's a very engaging writer and makes the stuff come to life. Writing in this area, with Powell piling lots of documents on me and having done research on similar subjects in the past, I'm aware how dull most official records read. And then you read it in Woodward: it's like being a fly on the ceiling. I think that is pretty high praise for the guy: I love to read his work. The reading of Casey's character that I saw in Bob's writing was not so much in capturing the accent. I may have a better ear for Casey's language because I come from that part of the world, New York, and have listened to the guy a long time. It was in Woodward's observations about Casey."[82]

Casey's good friend William Safire also recognized in Woodward's portrait "the William Casey I knew well . . . bluff, wideranging, impatient, daring, purposeful, enthusiastic, patriotic, secretive, cunning, deceptive."[83] Hardly the man of whom Senator Daniel Patrick Moynihan asked, "Is this man dangerously dangerous, or is he dangerously dumb?"[84]

Barry Goldwater acknowledged that Woodward had never lied to him but doubted he had entered Casey's hospital room, and so might have lied to others. Even if Woodward had achieved the seemingly impossible, Goldwater asked, "Was it right to put pressure on a dying man? And can the testimony of a man as sick as Casey be relied upon?"[85]

---

*Interview with Joseph Persico, March 2, 1994.

Former CIA Director Richard Helms also doubted that Woodward got in the room.[86]

Woodward failed to convince me that Casey's gasps and grunts were coherent responses. And when I pressed him, he conceded the replies were "ambiguous."[87] So much for the interview that aroused such a furor.

In the mid-1980s, Woodward tackled his next book, *Wired,* the life of actor and former Wheaton High School classmate John Belushi, who had died of a drug overdose.[88] The biography was greeted with raves, raspberries, and three lawsuits. It was "brilliant" to the *Chicago Tribune* reviewer; *Kirkus Reviews* knocked it as "pointless docudrama." Belushi's actor friend Dan Aykroyd said that the man's warmth and humor were missing from Woodward's biography, and called it "sleaze." Belushi's father threatened to use his shotgun on Woodward if he ever came back to Wheaton. One thing could be said for Woodward: he never wrote a book that didn't cause an uproar.

Woodward married for a third time, in 1989; his bride, Elsa Walsh (to whom he had dedicated *Veil*), a fellow *Post* reporter.

Woodward Taped

His most vehement critics ridicule Woodward as an interviewer of the dead and of secret sources who can never be questioned by others to check the accuracy of the information. To them, he's a liar and a fraud, and they quote CIA Chief William Casey: "Some of our sources have not been heard from after their information has been published in the U.S. press," to imply that Woodward has blood on his hands.[89]

I hoped that Woodward had good answers for these critics, and was curious to discover if he confirmed his reputation, when pressed, for being evasive and less than candid, like a man with much to hide. I put him to the test in a tape-recorded interview on March 8, 1994. He was still working on his latest book, about President Clinton, due to hit the bookstores in three months, so I was surprised he didn't cry off or cut the interview short.

In response to the query, "Alexander Haig denies he was an important source for your book about Nixon's last days in the White House. What's your evidence to refute him?" Woodward began searching for relevant passages in his books and in Alexander Haig's memoir *Inner Circles*. "Hang on just a second," he said, and then, after a minute or so, finding what he wanted, murmured, "You're a patient man. He who waits [a pause as he double-checked] is rewarded." A critic might call it soft-soaping, but I sensed he believed an investigation of biography and its practioners was worthwhile, as well as a chance to pan his critics.

Who's Telling the Truth—Haig or Woodward?

"And here's what Haig writes in his *Inner Circles*," Woodward said: " 'Returning home late at night, I found them [Woodward and Bernstein] sitting on my doorstep and invited them inside. They were looking for confirmation of a report that I had issued orders to the White House medical staff in the closing days of the resignation crisis to keep a close watch on the disheartened President in case he should try to harm himself by taking an overdose of prescription pills. I told them I could not [Woodward chuckled] provide information for their newspaper, but we chatted in a desultory way for an hour or so. It was a civil encounter. Woodward has recently assured me that this conversation was helpful to him and his partner in their effort to understand the Watergate affair. From what I remembered of what was said, I was surprised that this should be so.' "90

Woodward stopped reading, to give his version of events: "Now, what I did when I went to see Haig in Belgium [in 1974], I read the notes of the hour-long conversation Carl and I had with him, and he says in his book—and this is the classic Haig—'I told them I could not provide information for their newspaper but we chatted for an hour or so.' We did chat for an hour or so for the book *The Final Days*. And he told us all about the prescription thing. [How Haig had warned the White House staff to be on guard against Nixon taking an overdose of prescription pills.] We weren't seeking confirmation of that. We had never heard of it! [Until Haig revealed it.]

"Haig goes on to say in his footnote: 'On the basis of the unusual level of truthfulness achieved in certain passages of the published work I have always assumed that he did so.' [That Buzhardt cooperated.] Well, Haig says he talked to us for an hour. What he leaves out is—for the book *The Final Days*."

"Did he know he was giving you information for the book?"

"Absolutely. We told him. [Yet when the book came out, Haig vehemently denied he had been a source and until now has not been convincingly refuted.] So, when I went to see him in Belgium [still in 1974] I hoped to get more information. Then, he's right, he didn't budge [didn't give more information on that occasion], and he had his general note-taker there [Brig. General Joseph Bratton]. I then took out a copy of the notes Carl and I had typed that night and said to Haig, 'Just to make sure I have this right, let me read you these notes.' And I read out about the pills, and suicide fears, and lots of other stuff."

"And Haig's reaction?"

"To sit there and give me an if-looks-could-kill."

"I tried to check with General Bratton. Army records don't have his address or phone number. He's disappeared."

"Another thing to illustrate my point that as time goes by the truth emerges: all this business, which of course was roundly denied and scoffed at when *The Final Days* came out, about Nixon urging Buzhardt to manufacture a new Dictabelt.* Look at *Inner Circles,* page 426, third paragraph: ' "You know, Al," he [Nixon] said, "as far as the Dictabelt is concerned, all we have to do is create [fake] another one." It took me [Haig] a long moment to respond to this statement. Nixon's words shocked me, in the literal sense that I felt something like a tingle of an electrical current along my scalp.' That's Haig's reaction, and we got that account from Buzhardt. It was a major point of *The Final Days* that Nixon was so desperate that he would say, 'Let's manufacture new evidence,' when Dictabelts were missing. Compare Haig's account and ours. [Both cover the feared suicide and Dictabelt problem, though *The Final Days* is more detailed.] Of course when Haig wrote that 'Mr. Woodward even traveled to Europe where in the presence of a note-taking witness, I declined to comment in any way on the last days of the Nixon presidency,' that is technically correct. He had already given us the information."

Straightening Out Haig

"You know what Haig did in that meeting?" Woodward asked. "I might as well tell you. I've never told anybody, but Haig knows this. And that general, wherever he is, who sat there bug-eyed taking notes. I had come to try to get more information. I read the notes Carl and I had of the meeting Haig refers to in his memoir. Read Haig's memoir. Now go to *The Final Days* and look under Haig and the quote is there. In his own memoir he says, 'We talked for an hour. Woodward recently

*An IBM Dictabelt system was hooked into Nixon's telephone, which was activated whenever he picked up the receiver. It then recorded his phone conversations.

assured me that this conversation was helpful. I was surprised that it would be so.' In 1991 or so I went up [to see Haig], when I heard he was doing this book [*Inner Circles*], and again read him the notes, and said, 'Why don't you be straight and direct with this?' Well, if you read what he writes, he's saying 'unusual level of truthfulness,' and in substance he winds up confirming it all."

"I agree. This is why almost everyone reading between the lines thought Haig was also Deep Throat."

"Well he was not. And he's right in his book in saying he was not Deep Throat."

"So, Haig was not Deep Throat. But he was, despite his denials, a good source for inside information on Nixon and Watergate. Why didn't you say so? Haig once asked Ben Bradlee to announce that he, Haig, wasn't Deep Throat, and Bradlee refused. It wouldn't have exposed the real Deep Throat to let Haig off the hook."

"I've said for years that Haig was not Deep Throat. It's impossible to have been Haig. [Haig was, for example, in Paris, France, on a night Woodward met Deep Throat in Washington, D.C.]

"When Haig read your *The Final Days,* he assumed from the accuracy of the material that Fred Buzhardt had cooperated with you."

"Right. He did [cooperate with us]."

"Did you disguise your description of Deep Throat and your meetings with him to hide his identity?"

"No."

"Your description of him is accurate?"

"Correct."

"Why doesn't he appear as a character in *The Final Days*?"

"What do you mean?"

"You still needed inside information about how Nixon was behaving in the White House. Why wasn't that anonymous man who knew so much still an important source?"

"Because everyone was named in *The Final Days*."

"Deep Throat was named?"

"Everyone was named who was a character in *The Final Days*."

"Were you still going to Deep Throat for information?"

"I'm just not going to say." (Presumably Deep Throat is named in *The Final Days*, which narrows the field.)

William Casey and the "Death-Bed" Interview

"Would you mind me writing in my book that you told me, off the record, how you got into Casey's hospital room? Or shall I say I got it from an anonymous source?"

"You phrase it whatever way you want."

"You don't mind me saying you told me?"

"No. Don't say it's off the record. Then people are going to say. . . . It's not a mystery, not literally, and the time, and how . . ."

"I know that. You told me how, but no details such as the time you did it. But what puzzles me is that when you were asked to describe Casey's room by Mike Wallace and Ted Koppel, you said, 'No, I want to hide the identity of the person who helped get me in.' How would a description of the room have blown the guy's identity?"

"When this came out it became an issue. I was surprised, because it was so absurd. As I described to you, someone helped me, somebody in a position that they were not happy that this had become an issue, for either family or medical reasons. It was embarrassing and could be criticized. I wasn't going to add any more details. I don't know that they'd moved Casey. I don't know, when I saw him, whether they'd moved him to a different room. I don't know what was going on. I heard at the time people were trying to get affidavits from people and I didn't want to take any action to add to what seemed to me had become a witch hunt, and one where somebody had helped me with good intentions. But it was such a jolt to Mrs. Casey."

"How did you feel when she sat next to you in the TV studio and called you a liar?"

"I turned to her and in a nice, gentlemanly way called her a liar. She admitted she was. She said I'd never been in her house. And I said, 'D'you remember serving us breakfast?' She said, 'Oh well, etc.' Look, she's a nice widow. After that was over, Koppel said he'd never seen such a show where somebody came out of it smelling like a rose."

"Is David Halberstam's description of you as 'totally compulsive, a classic workaholic, wildly ambitious, obsessed by his work and career,' accurate?"[91]

"Yes, but he's talking about me in 1972 covering Watergate."

"You got out of Vietnam by volunteering for destroyer duty?"

"Yes."

"It's amazing you'd tell me that."

"Why?"

"Well, surely you're not proud of it?"

"But it's true. And I didn't run to Canada."

"Are you using anonymous sources for your Clinton book?"

"I don't like the term. Most of the interviews were done on background or deep background."

"Did you go into it liking him or neutral?"

"I go in as a neutral, as you know. What have you concluded, as you've thought this through now?"

"I first have to transcribe lots of tapes and do a lot of comparing. What strikes me, after all the reports that you're secretive and evasive, is how frank you've been."

"I'm frank with everyone."

"You weren't with Havill [his unauthorized biographer]."

"He wrote me one letter and then I got reports that he was asking stupid questions. The thing you have to look at, and the reason I urge you to make a serious study of it, is that I'm very careful, and there's a reason for everything I've written. I attempt to confirm, to reconfirm, triangulate everything."

"I have to tell you frankly I had an interview with Barry Sussman who gave a very different picture of Deep Throat from the one that appears in *All the President's Men,* and when I read the interview to Bradlee, he didn't challenge it."

"What is it that Sussman's different in?"

"That the excitement, adventure, and derring-do about the meetings with Deep Throat were a myth, and his importance overrated; he never gave you leads, merely confirmed and was sometimes wrong."

"He may have a different interpretation or look at it in a different way. What happened is in *All the President's Men.* What you're doing is interesting. Keep going to the record. Just look at Haig's 'I never cooperated,' and then in his book talking about our accuracy, confirming major points, not quarreling about one thing. Read the footnote with the mention of our one-hour conversation, and see there are a number of things in there exactly like in *The Final Days,* and draw your own conclusions. People aren't very precise. We interviewed Haig for that hour as he says in his book. I think it was a month after Nixon resigned. He said it wasn't for the newspaper, only for the book. He helped us a great deal."

"Memory is such a tricky thing. I remember Kissinger writing in his memoirs that he wasn't sure if he put his arm on Nixon's shoulder during those emotional moments. He believed he intended to, but wasn't sure if he had done."

"The question for your book is, how precise is the art? How good is it? How careful is it? The first hurdle is: Is there a good-faith effort? Is there a method of checking and double-checking? I'd be very disappointed in you if you go through this and don't say I have a very solid basis for everything I write. You can certainly quote me saying, 'But I am not perfect, and I too often make mistakes. It happens.' You have to ask yourself some very interesting questions about great historical biographies. How good are they? How good is Boswell on Johnson? Can he be checked? Is there a Denis Brian around, redoing it?"

"To out-Boswell Boswell?"

"Yes. And what might you find? You'll inevitably find some of it is contested territory. I try to resolve that as best I can. That's why people still talk to me, because they know I'm fair and that I will include and go back and go back and go back. That somebody didn't like something or looked at it a little differently is inevitable."

"You're talking of the ideal biographer. But there's another school described in [my use of the phrase] 'The Crafty Art of Biography.' "

"Yeh."

"That's not you."

"Of course it's not. I told you, people got mad at my portrait of Casey because it was too sympathetic. I let him have his say. You set up the parallelism on some of these things and find, 'Gee, Goldwater contradicted himself. Gee, Haig contradicted himself. Gee, So-and-So contradicted himself.' "

"What was your approach to the book on Clinton [*The Agenda,* Simon & Schuster, 1994]?"

"If you've done your work you'll know I'm a reporter, not an evaluator. Keep digging deeper. And good luck!"[92]

Digging deeper into Woodward's books, I found he had evaluated Nixon, Haig, Kissinger, Reagan, and Casey. In his recent *The Commanders,* a lively account of the leaders who planned and executed the Persian Gulf War, we learn that General Schwarzkopf is "a terror as a boss, often furious when unhappy or dissatisfied, infamous for shooting the messengers who brought bad news";[93] that Bush "liked to keep everyone around the table smiling [and] clear decisions rarely emerged";[94] and that Brent Scowcroft "had a priestlike dedication to his work. It was his one interest. . . . A model of the trustworthy, self-effacing staffer, [he] had been a low-profile presence in top national security circles for two decades."[95]

Woodward's special gift is the ability to get others to say more than they mean to. He approaches them with a reputation for never having betrayed a source he promised to protect, with Deep Throat as his talisman, an enduring witness to his word. He has the earnest, "please help me" look with the slightly baffled manner of a well-meaning younger brother. A great disguise, and more effective in unearthing hidden treasures than a stick of dynamite.

But where is he coming from? He remains a political enigma. When I suggested he was a hero to liberals because of Watergate, and a devil to conservatives, he denied it. He certainly surprised me by endorsing Quayle as presidential material. My guess is that it was empathy: Woodward is a lousy speller, too.

Bob Woodward is often attacked and even ridiculed by the *Washington Times,* which carries the skeptical anti-Woodward views of op-ed academics and think-tank ideologues. They're mostly firing blanks, a thick audience telling a magician it can't be done while he's picking their pockets.

But his fans overwhelm the opposition. To them he is "the most famous journalist of our time,"[96] who "not by gimmicks or cliff-hanging ends of chapters, but pure reporting"[97] "rewards his readers with the thrill of eavesdropping on the power elite. We meet here [in *The Commanders*] a president [George Bush] who is secretive even with his closest staff, dangerously vindictive and dazzlingly arbitary and impulsive."[98] It is "a compelling exhaustively researched study"[99] "filled with memorable anecdotes and quotes, ranging from the interservice rivalry inside the Pentagon to personalities who seemed to have stepped from the set of *Doctor Strangelove.*"[100] And a final accolade comes in the overawed question, "Does Woodward have the universe bugged?"[101]

If biography is a search for truth in the spirit of honest inquiry, Woodward rates near the top. If it is also an attention to scrupulous reporting of even minor details, he falls short. But who doesn't? That said, according to William Zinsser's recipe, he has what it takes for the task: "The insouciance of a psychiatrist or a priest . . . and the patience of a detective,"[102] especially the detective part.

Notes

1. In a 1977 interview with David Frost. Though Woodward says, "We were not after the president, we were after the story," the end result was Nixon's ignominious defeat.

2. *All the President's Men* (1974) and *The Final Days* (1976), both by Bob Woodward and Carl Bernstein, and published by Simon & Schuster.

3. Bob Woodward, *Veil: The Secret Wars of the CIA* (New York: Simon & Schuster, 1987), pp. 504–50.

4. Interview with Liz Smith, March 1, 1994.

5. David Halberstam, *The Powers That Be* (New York: Dell, 1979), p. 852.

6. J. Anthony Lucas, "A Candid Conversation . . . ," *Playboy,* February 1989, pp. 51–66.

7. Ibid.

8. Halberstam, *The Powers That Be,* pp. 851–52.

9. Joseph E. Persico, *Casey: From the OSS to the CIA* (New York: Viking, 1990), p. 423.

10. Ibid., p. 424.

11. Walter Isaacson, *Kissinger* (New York: Simon & Schuster, 1992), p. 498.

12. Carl Bernstein and Bob Woodward, *All the President's Men* (New York: Warner, 1976), pp. 262–63.

13. Bill Gulley with Mary Ellen Reese, *Breaking Cover* (New York: Simon & Schuster, 1980), p. 213.

14. Interview with Bob Woodward, March 8, 1994.

15. Interview with Bill Gulley, March 3, 1994.

16. Interview with Bob Woodward, March 8, 1994.

17. Bob Woodward and Carl Bernstein, *The Final Days* (New York: Avon, 1977), pp. 470–71.

18. Interview with Bill Gulley, February 22, 1994.

19. Ibid.

20. Interview with Melvin Laird, March 2, 1994.

21. Interview with Bill Gulley, February 22, 1994.

22. Len Colodny and Bob Gettlin, *Silent Coup* (New York: St. Martin's Press, 1991), pp. 280–82.

23. Interview with Bob Woodward, February 22, 1994.

24. Interview with Bobby Inman, February 22, 1994.

25. Interview with Melvin Laird, March 2, 1994.

26. Interview with Jack Anderson, December 4, 1993.

27. Interview with Steve Bull, March 2, 1994.

28. Interview with Bob Gettlin, December 4, 1993.

29. Adrian Havill, *Deep Truth: The Lives of Bob Woodward and Carl Bernstein* (New York: Carol, 1993), p. 55.

30. Jim Hougan, *Secret Agenda: Watergate, Deep Throat & the CIA* (New York: Random House, 1984), pp. 295–96.

31. Interview with Admiral Moorer, March 3, 1994.

32. Interview with Bob Woodward, March 8, 1994.

33. Interview with Bobby Inman, February 28, 1994.

34. Interview with Melvin Laird, March 2, 1994.

35. Alexander M. Haig with Charles McCarry, *Inner Circles* (New York: Warner, 1992), pp. 321–22.

36. Havill, *Deep Truth*, p. 87.

37. Peter Schwed, *Turning the Pages* (New York: Macmillan, 1984), pp. 280–81.

38. Havill, *Deep Truth*, p. 88.

39. Interview with Alice Mayhew, March 9, 1994.

40. Interview with Peter Schwed, March 9, 1994.

41. Victor Lasky, "The Woodstein Ripoff," *AIM Report* 5, no. 12 (October 1976): 11.

42. Ibid.

43. Ibid.

44. Ibid.

45. Haig, *Inner Circles,* p. 323.

46. Ibid.

47. Woodward and Bernstein, *The Final Days,* pp. 447–48.

48. Haig, *Inner Circles,* p. 323.

49. *Palm Beach Jewish World,* March 2–8, 1990, p. 22.

50. Interview with Robert Fink, February 28, 1994.

51. Barry Sussman, *The Great Cover-Up: Nixon and the Scandal of Watergate* (New York: Signet, 1974).

52. Interview with Barry Sussman, March 1, 1994.

53. Sussman, *The Great Cover-Up,* p. 110.

54. Interview with Barry Sussman, March 2, 1994.

55. Interview with Ben Bradlee, March 2, 1994.

56. Interview with Reed Irvine, March 2, 1994.

57. In order, *Houston Post,* Daniel Schorr, Dan Rather.

58. One example: Jeb Stuart Magruder, Haldeman's assistant, writes, "Woodward called and said—obviously on the basis of a leak from the Finance Committee—that he had information that I'd handled $50,000 in cash. The correct figure was $20,000. I therefore called Woodward and told him the $50,000 was wrong; nevertheless he went ahead and published it" (Jeb Stuart Magruder, *An American Life: One Man's Road to Watergate* [New York: Pocket Books, 1975], pp. 292–93).

59. Interview with Bob Woodward, March 8, 1994.

60. Woodward, *Veil,* p. 299. "Veil" was a top-secret code word, used during the Reagan administration, for covert operations to influence events abroad.

61. Interview with Constantine Menges, October 19, 1990.

62. Interview with Bob Woodward, February 22, 1994.

63. Barry Goldwater with Jack Casserly, *Goldwater* (New York: St. Martin's Press, 1988), p. 286.

64. Persico, *Casey,* p. 441.
65. Ibid., p. 443.
66. Ibid.
67. Interview with Arnaud de Borchgrave, April 20, 1990.
68. Interview with Sophia Casey, December 13, 1993.
69. Interview with William Colby, September 30, 1990.
70. Interview with George Carver, October 4, 1990.
71. Interview with Jack Anderson, March 10, 1994.
72. Interview with Joseph Persico, February 26, 1994.
73. Ibid.
74. Interview with Alfred Luessenhop, October 2, 1990.
75. Interview with Gwen Cohen, January 10, 1994.
76. Interview with Seymour Hersh, September 28, 1990.
77. Woodward, *Veil,* pp. 506–507.
78. Interview with Bob Woodward, March 8, 1994.
79. Interview with Joseph Persico, March 2, 1994.
80. Interview with William Colby, September 30, 1990.
81. Bob Woodward, *The Commanders* (New York: Pocket Books, 1991).
82. Interview with Joseph Persico, March 2, 1994.
83. *New York Times,* October 4, 1987, IV, p. 23.
84. Persico, *Casey,* p. 247.
85. Goldwater and Casserly, *Goldwater,* p. 303.
86. Interview with Richard Helms, March 12, 1994.
87. Interview with Bob Woodward, March 4, 1994.
88. Bob Woodward, *Wired* (New York: Simon & Schuster, 1984).
89. Casey in a speech made in New York, November 14, 1986.
90. Haig with McCarry, *Inner Circles,* p. 323.
91. Halberstam, *The Powers That Be,* p. 849.
92. Interview with Bob Woodward, March 8, 1994.
93. Woodward, *The Commanders,* p. 188.
94. Ibid., p. 286.
95. Ibid., p. 18.
96. Jeffrey Klein, *San Jose Mercury-News.*
97. Rick Tamble, *Nashville Banner.*
98. Robert Sherrill, *Miami Herald.*

99. Steve Neal, *Chicago Sun-Times.*

100. Curtis Wilkie, *Boston Sunday Globe.*

101. *Armed Forces Journal International.*

102. William Zinsser, ed., *Extraordinary Lives: The Art and Craft of American Biography* (New York: American Heritage, 1986), p. 10.

5

Joe McGinniss and His Enemies:
From Murderer MacDonald to
Ted Kennedy and William Manchester

The biographer at work, indeed, is like the professional burglar, breaking into a house, rifling through certain drawers that he has good reason to think contain the jewelry and the money, and triumphantly bearing his loot away.

—Janet Malcolm[1]

One of the things that makes this case . . . so fascinating, though horrible, and him [convicted murderer Jeffrey Mac-Donald] so intriguing is this very genuine ability he has to persuade people that they shouldn't look at facts A, B, and C, they should just look at him and he is so wonderful.

—Joe McGinniss[2]

Joe McGinniss has always been audacious. His first book, *The Selling of the President,* drove its subject, Richard Nixon, up the wall.[3] As a young *Philadelphia Inquirer* columnist, Mc-Ginniss persuaded Nixon's handlers to give him an inside look at their "packaging" of Nixon for TV appearances in his 1968 presidential campaign. They naively anticipated good publicity, but his book about it made them and Nixon look like idiots.

Enraged, Nixon ordered John Ehrlichman to get the "full story" on McGinniss. Ehrlichman put investigators on the writer's tail and they returned with the lowdown: he was "cunning, deceitful, and disarming."[4] An assessment that would be frequently echoed in the future.

His book, now considered a political classic, at least by Democrats, brought him instant success at twenty-six, and broke up his marriage. He left his pregnant wife and two children for a woman working for his publisher. But, says his friend John Katzenbach, "it was a troubled marriage. Joe has been a devoted father to all his children. He now has five. He really is a good guy."[5]

There followed one flop, *Heroes,* bemoaning the nonexistence of the same in America; and the successful *Going to Extremes,* a vivid account of his journey to Alaska. Next came the supersuccess *Fatal Vision,* touted with good cause as another *In Cold Blood,* except that Capote's work brought him only accolades. McGinniss's earned him the dubious distinction of being judged more harshly than the murderer he had portrayed, and that by fellow biographer Janet Malcolm. She puts him at the top of the heap "as a kind of confidence man, preying on people's vanity, ignorance, or loneliness, gaining their trust and betraying them without remorse."[6]

The man McGinniss "betrayed" was Army physician Jeffrey MacDonald. On trial for murdering his wife and two young daughters, MacDonald persuaded McGinniss to join the defense team with a writer-in-residence role. Whatever the verdict, McGinniss would produce a book about the case and MacDonald would get a third of the profits. The verdict was guilty.

When the book *Fatal Vision*[7] was published, its subject, MacDonald, was in a Texas prison serving three consecutive life sentences for murdering his wife and children. *Newsday* reporter Bob Keeler, who had covered the trial, went there to find out his reaction to the book's revelations.

Keeler found out that "Jeffrey MacDonald . . . spends much of [his] time worrying about a book that could make him a lot of money and lose him a lot of friends. [Lots of people] think that MacDonald, who will be forty next month, will be wearing prison khaki and sleeping in a cell in the year 2000 and beyond. . . . MacDonald has a financial interest in a book called *Fatal Vision,* the story of his case.

> His interest has already brought him more than $60,000 to pay defense costs . . . and if the book turns into a best seller, it could bring him thousands more. But *Fatal Vision* is not the vindication that he expected when he opened his life to the author, nor the story of a relentless government that chased him across a decade and convicted him unfairly because it was too incompetent to find the real killers.
>
> Instead, for 663 pages, it paints a picture of Jeffrey Mac-Donald—often in his own words—even worse than the picture that convinced a jury in 1979 that he was a murderer. It is the kind of book that could turn friends into enemies, could drive people away from his cause.[8]

Now he knows, wrote Keeler, "that McGinniss has painted him as a killer and a monstrously twisted human being, and he knows that his own words, given freely to McGinniss on tape and on paper have filled in that portrait. He is angry at McGinniss and fearful about what the book will do to his cause. 'All my friends are worried,' he says. 'Everyone feels a sense of betrayal. . . . I wish the book would burn.' "[9]

Far from turning to ash, it sold like hotcakes.

Reporter Keeler got to know both men when he covered the almost seven-week murder trial in Raleigh, North Carolina, and noted that they were "always together, eating together, sleeping in the same rented fraternity house, occasionally jogging together. But in the courtroom, the jury watched day after day as the government brought out its physical evidence to show what had happened in the MacDonald home at Fort Bragg. And McGinniss watched, too. Finally, the relentless accretion of evidence—the fibers found in the wrong places, the blood-stains, the bloody footprint, the holes that were in the wrong shape and the wrong place in MacDonald's bloody pajama top, the injuries that MacDonald didn't have—began to add up to one conclusion for McGinniss: His jogging partner, Jeffrey MacDonald, was a killer."[10]

But, although McGinniss now shared the jury's conviction that MacDonald was guilty of the hideous crime, he kept up the pretense of belief in his innocence, writing him supportive letters and encouraging him to supply intimate details for the book in progress.

In one such letter McGinniss wrote to MacDonald, "Total strangers can recognize within five minutes that you did not receive a fair trial." He ended with an encouraging, "It's a hell of a thing—spend the summer making a new friend and then the bastards come along and lock him up. But not for long, Jeffrey—not for long."[11]

Meanwhile, he was putting the finishing touches to the book *Fatal Vision*, portraying MacDonald as a womanizer and "pathological narcissist," who stabbed and beat to death his pregnant wife and their two young daughters in a drug-induced rage, then tried to make it look like the work of Manson-type hippies.

"Before the trial," said Bob Keeler,* "I had gone to Doubleday to get a book contract and they told me it was a good idea and to come back to them after the trial. But by then McGinniss had met Jeffrey MacDonald and had a contract from the same company and there was no way I was going to get one.

*Interview with Bob Keeler, August 30, 1993.

"We other reporters at the murder trial thought McGinniss was going to write a 'Jeffrey-the-Tortured-Innocent' book and didn't feel that was the truth. Later, from conversations I had with McGinniss, I got the sense that he had come to the conclusion that Jeffrey was not the tortured innocent, but had committed the murders. So I no longer saw his book as this terrible thing. I was having friendly chats with McGinniss and offering him what little bits of information I had.

"Much of the book is the grand jury minutes with a few transitional phrases he's thrown in. Another very large portion is these tapes he cajoled Jeffrey into sending him by writing letters saying, 'Oh, what a terrible tragedy it is for the nation and the world that you've been convicted. And don't talk to Keeler.'

"When MacDonald sent me copies of his letters I found out Joe had been actively persuading him not to talk to me. [Fearing Keeler would write a rival biography.] I was a little bit pissed off. I had been friendly to him. The whole process made me pretty angry at Joe.

"I thought he was very lazy in *Fatal Vision*. Instead of doing heavy reporting, he just sat and sucked his thumb until the teeth marks were showing and read some cockamamie Christopher Lasch* book about pathological narcissism and from his armchair decided the case on the basis of that.

"I don't quarrel with his approach, which was, 'What makes the mind of Jeffrey MacDonald tick?' But one way he did it was through the tapes, which is totally passive. Letting Jeffrey speak for himself, instead of going out and speaking to people who had witnessed his actions and behavior over the past years and finding out what he did, how he acted.

---

*Christopher Lasch, *The Culture of Narcissism* (New York: Norton, 1978). Two signs of narcissism, says Lasch, are calculating seductiveness and boundless repressed rage.

"I agree with him that MacDonald did this thing, but not with his theory that there was some pathological narcissism going on, because that seemed to me psychological mumbo jumbo. There certainly is a narcissistic element to his personality: Jeffrey has never met a person he considers smarter than he is."[12]

Keeler, the compulsive, hard-driving reporter, discovered that to get the "inside" story, McGinniss had lived for a week in MacDonald's condominium and had left the place with two suitcases crammed with thousands of documents. Afterward, MacDonald responded to McGinniss's questions, often about his sex life, by recording his feelings and experiences on tape. This happened when he was in and out of prison, when he was freed on appeal, and after the Supreme Court had reinstated his conviction.

MacDonald told Keeler he felt "uncomfortable making the tapes. Sometimes I would put them off for weeks . . . until he was really harassing me to get them."[13]

He was shocked, he said, when he saw them in the book, apparently verbatim, under the heading, "The Voice of Jeffrey MacDonald." MacDonald implied that he had been conned into giving these frank accounts of his sex life with his wife and other women, now published as "cheap paperback stuff. . . . I thought I had a man with integrity and honor who was going to edit, so I talked to him honestly."[14]

McGinniss countered that he had used the material as a key to MacDonald's character, explaining to Keeler, "The series of affairs, the callousness with which he treated Colette [his murdered wife], the absolute lack of shame or guilt is an integral part of his personality. I'm talking about him in his egomania, talking endlessly about how the women love him and his affairs with this one and with that one."[15]

MacDonald saw McGinniss as "intellectually arrogant. . . . I feel sorry for the guy, in a way, believe it or not, because he uses people. His whole life is spent using people. He doesn't ever seem to have a solid relationship with someone, other than one based on use."[16]

McGinniss responded, "If a man were to be judged by the enemies he makes, I could not be more proud than to have made an enemy of . . . a man who murdered his wife and children."[17]

Murderer Takes Biographer to Court

Incensed, MacDonald sued for breach of contract. He accused McGinniss of professing to be a friend and ally who was writing a "fair and open-minded" book, while stringing him along to gather material that would show him in a bad light.

He had expected the book to proclaim his innocence, but it clearly sided with the prosecution and had even provided additional evidence to explain what drove him to murder. It's "a novel masquerading as nonfiction," charged MacDonald.

> Joe and I had an agreement to do the book, but he has left my defense entirely out of it. [Not so. Much of it consists of trial transcripts, and MacDonald's own account of the murders is given fair play.] Any evidence that argues for my innocence, any character testimony that supports my decency and normalcy have been edited out. He has totally broken our agreement about "fair representation."[18]

Asked to respond, McGinniss said,

> I liked Jeff when I first met him, I thought he was very charming, almost seductive, sort of reminiscent of some politicians I've met, people who are very nice to you because you can help them. There's no doubt but that Jeff can be a great guy and he's saved lives and he's done wonderful things and a lot of

people like him very much. But he's not in prison because he took diet pills or is narcissistic. He's in prison because a jury convicted him of killing his family. After I sat through the trial in 1979, I was 100 percent convinced he was guilty. Still, I had been living with Jeff and his family and friends throughout the trial and I had become close to them and I wanted to believe that he was innocent. During the next four years I tried to reawaken some doubts about his guilt. I could not.[19]

At the 1987 trial for breach of contract, William F. Buckley, Jr., and Joseph Wambaugh testified for McGinniss, suggesting that, when the truth is at stake, a writer can't always be completely frank about his intentions or feelings. Tom Wolfe, Jimmy Breslin, and Bob Greene were also rooting for him.

Buckley got several laughs by citing Shirley Temple, Thomas Aquinas, and Senator Alan Cranston, in defense of an author's right to conceal his views from his subject. "If books were assigned," said Buckley, "in the same manner as medieval brick-layers were assigned to build a wall . . . all that is important about freedom of speech would evaporate." Outside the court, Buckley told reporters, "I'd be sued every day if book subjects could demand favorable treatment from writers."[20]

After a hung jury—all but one juror finding for the murderer—the case was settled out of court, with McGinniss handing over $325,000.

Agreeing with the majority on the jury who thought it unethical to deceive even a murderer, reporter Keeler asked McGinniss, "Is anybody ever going to trust you again?"

"They can trust me if they're innocent," he replied.

"You don't think," Keeler persisted, "that you in any sense betrayed Jeffrey or did him dirt or anything?"

"My only obligation is to the truth," said McGinniss.[21]

In an epilogue to the new 1989 paperback edition of *Fatal Vision*, Joe McGinniss tried to justify his modus operandi:

There was no committment, indication or even hint that my book would portray MacDonald as innocent. . . . I liked MacDonald when I was with him during his murder trial. I felt sorry for him for months afterward and wrote him letters genuinely expressing that sorrow, even after I'd formed my opinion as to his guilt.[22]

But critic Jonathan Yardley didn't buy it:

There is simply no getting around it: in order to protect his vested interest in Jeffrey MacDonald—he had a $300,000 advance on the book—McGinniss misrepresented his own feelings about MacDonald and his guilt in their private, intensely personal correspondence.[23]

Columnist Liz Smith is less critical: "When I read *Fatal Vision,*" she said,* "I was convinced the man was a killer. So, in a funny way, as far as I'm concerned, he loses his civil rights. He loses his right to have people be fair about him. But I think the author has to be judged. Was he unfair? Did he do the wrong thing? McGinniss is a really good writer, but he falls into the questionable category. Still, I don't know, if you've got a murderer, that you have to worry about whether you're misleading him. It's a real shadowy area."[24]

One thing was certain: the money was rolling in. The paperback sales had passed two million when MacDonald wrote another rebuttal:

People are buying Joe's trash. Nothing is being said about the decent things I did, the papers I wrote on emergency medicine, the lives I saved, the hundreds of hours of volunteer medical work I've done. . . . I didn't murder my family. This cheap, sleazy book has very carefully orchestrated an evil view

---

*Interview with Liz Smith, March 1, 1994.

of me. I am surprised that some investigative reporter has not globbed onto how shabby this book really is.[25]

MacDonald got the reporter he wanted in Janet Malcolm, although ironically, it was McGinniss who, seeking favorable publicity, invited her to cover the controversy. And she accepted.

Among those she interviewed was reporter Bob Keeler.

Experiencing Janet Malcolm

"Janet Malcolm visited me one day at *Newsday*," Keeler recalled.* "She was gathering material for what became *The Journalist and the Murderer*. She whipped out her little tape recorder and her little notebook, and I gave her some letters Jeffrey MacDonald had sent me, letters to him from Joe McGinniss, and some of my notebooks about the case.

"So we were chatting and she said something that alarmed me, to the effect that in these long pieces one had to condense them in order to get the essence.

"At that time I was not familiar with her relationship with Jeffrey Masson. [The psychonalyst who had sued Malcolm for libel, claiming she had fabricated quotes in writing about him, which she denied.] Nonetheless, I had this cold chill up my spine, and said, 'I don't think it's necessary to boil me down. I speak reasonably good English. You can quote me pretty well the way I talk.'

"And I said, 'By the way, I don't eschew violence against women.' Which, of course, was a total lie. I was just pulling her chain. Just being a little bit mischievous.

"So we went on and on and she would sit there and I would talk a lot, and she'd wait for questions to descend on her from

---

*Interview with Bob Keeler, August 30, 1993.

heaven, which I found rude. When I go to interview someone, I have a list of questions in advance. I don't necessarily refer to them, but I check them at the end to make sure I covered all the ground I wanted to. I guess she found my method too regimented, or anal, or compulsive. There's no question I'm compulsive.

"What she ultimately wrote in the book was that I got the same kind of information from my very compulsive methods as she got from her—obviously, she feels, much more superior, artistic, and Japanese—method, to sit and wait for the questions to descend from above.

"The conclusion she drew was that somehow subjects are waiting and ready to impale themselves on their own sword, no matter who is doing the interviewing. That's why she sees the journalist as an insidious character.

"When Janet Malcolm got up to leave, I gave her a copy of *Newsday*. We sell 800,000 papers a day in New York City and Long Island. It's not a small newspaper. So I handed her a copy of the Wednesday newspaper, which in those days was filled with supermarket ads. She was amazed by the size of the paper and said, 'Boy, this is a big paper. Tell me, how often do you come out?' I delivered myself into the hands of a total ding-a-ling. The woman lives in Manhattan, obviously she summers in the Hamptons, and anything in between is sort of an inconvenient interruption and she knows nothing whatsoever about it!' "26

Even if true, she had a telling way with words and her *The Journalist and the Murderer* made its mark. In it Malcolm deplored McGinniss's "betrayal" of the murderer, and spelled out his ingratiating tactics to get material for his book: Some forty friendly, at times effusive, letters to MacDonald, two prison visits, and several supportive phone calls. Meanwhile, he was assuring his editor that he was already convinced of MacDonald's guilt but would shape his book to prevent the killer from emerging as "too loathsome too soon."

Buoyed by Buckley's opinion that his research methods were legitimate, McGinniss insisted that he had approached the case with an open mind but eventually decided that MacDonald was guilty. He explained the misleading letters by saying, "There is a difference between what your head believes and what your heart wants to believe. . . . I was trying to reach out to him as one human being to another."[27]

The jury that voted against him five to one were persuaded, wrote Malcolm, that "a man who was serving three consecutive life sentences for the murder of his wife and two small children was deserving of more sympathy than the writer who had deceived him."[28] Malcolm's point was that McGinniss's first obligation was to tell MacDonald the truth. She was hardly an objective witness, having been impressed by MacDonald when visiting him in prison. Not only did she note his dexterity in handling a sugar doughnut without spilling the sugar, but thought he might be innocent, concluding her indictment with: "McGinniss betrayed him and devastated him and may have misjudged him."[29]

Moved by the murderer's plight, and charmed by him, Malcolm saw the journalist as a malevolent being, "a kind of confidence man, preying on people's vanity, ignorance, or loneliness, gaining their trust and betraying them without remorse."[30]

As a moralist, Malcolm was on shaky ground, having herself lost a libel suit over a 1983 *New Yorker* piece, published as a book titled *In the Freud Archives*. Ten years later, in June 1993, a jury found she had fabricated five quotes, two of them libelous. But they couldn't agree on damages, so the judge ordered a retrial.

Many writers were irked or outraged by Malcolm's sweeping indictment of their work, and McGinniss complained in the 1989 paperback edition of his book of her "numerous and egregious . . . omissions, distortions, and outright misstatements of fact" in writing about him. He particularly resented her views, because "the malice in her piece is so evident, the spitefulness, the hysteria."

McGinniss insisted that the supportive letters he wrote to MacDonald after he was convicted of the murders were sincere. So much so, that "when a letter came from MacDonald I would find myself shaken and moved, sometimes to the point of tears."[31]

He was no longer defensive when he attended an Amherst, Massachusetts, conference on nonfiction in April 1989. The writer, he said, is duty bound to tell "the unpleasant truth," rather than the "pleasant untruth" that his subject might prefer. He spoke, too, of the writer's obligation to his reader not to lie "by omission." (Malcolm, in writing about McGinniss, omitted to mention that she was being sued for libel.) Writer Tracy Kidder, at the conference, apparently understood McGinniss's dilemma, and admitted that if he were writing about Charles Manson, he would tell him he wasn't sure of his guilt or innocence.

McGinniss had no doubt of MacDonald's guilt, but, like Malcolm, he was sorry for him: "Such a tragic, terrible waste. . . . He is so different from what he appears to be that I feel very sad that he didn't turn out to be who he wanted me to think he was."[32]

"MacDonald does have a sort of crazy charm and a legion of followers," Keeler told me.* "He has some kind of weird magnetism you can't get away from. But it didn't work with me. Long before I met him, I'd met his in-laws, the Kassabs, and gone over all the evidence. It was overwhelmingly against him, so I was not swayed by his charm.

"McGinniss has a certain charm, too. The sort of Irish charm that pulls people in. His big mistake was teaming up with MacDonald. If you're covering the story of a man accused of and found guilty of three heinous murders, it's bad judgment

---

*Interview with Bob Keeler, August 30, 1993.

to put yourself in his company. I'm sure Joe would say, 'That's the only way the book was going to sell.' But he got himself into that mess. He put himself in the position of having to lie to preserve the relationship."[33]

One staunch McGinniss supporter is crime-reporter-turned-novelist John Katzenbach. "What Janet Malcolm never really acknowledged," he said to me,* "was the change that came over Joe in the process of coming to know Jeffrey MacDonald. The writing somehow brings out the way you feel in a sort of self-psychoanalysis, while your relationship with a person is clouded by situations, the events around you."[34]

I asked if he saw anything unethical in McGinniss taking away cases of documents from MacDonald's apartment, almost like a prosecuting attorney.

"It was in those documents," he replied, "that Joe came up with the genesis of the crime which made the most sense. Much greater than the prosecution ever came up with. The combination of drugs [diet pills], lack of sleep, mingled with the psychopathic personality."

"But MacDonald refuted the diet pill theory by saying McGinniss thought he'd taken them in a short period of time when, in fact, he'd taken them over several weeks, so that any ill effect would be unlikely."

"If you believe anything Jeffrey MacDonald says, you're a fool. He's a psychopath, a murdering psychopath, and he came close to persuading one jury to acquit him. He's had remarkable success persuading various news outlets to continue to give him space and time. An astonishing testimonial to what Hervey Cleckley called the 'Mask of Sanity.' "[35]

"What makes you believe MacDonald is a psychopath?"

"If you read Cleckley's book, which is probably the best thing about the psychopathic personality, you'll see that

*Interview with John Katzenbach, March 27, 1994.

MacDonald fits virtually every criterion. Similarly, if you look at every interview he's ever given, including to the BBC, and all the evidence produced at the trial, you'll see that Jeffrey MacDonald can explain everything except the fact that his wife and children are dead. It's all founded upon a simple empirical principle, which is, because he is white, middle class, educated at Princeton, and a physician, he could not have done these things. Because it's astonishing to us that someone like him could commit these murders; therefore, it must be these famous hippies."

"I don't disagree with your conclusions. But what do you think of McGinniss's ethics as a biographer?"

"I've known a lot of criminal psychopaths in my life as a reporter and writer," Katzenbach said, "and they're very persuasive individuals. In the McGinniss-MacDonald situation you must realize, MacDonald had been deceiving McGinniss all along in trying to persuade him of his innocence."[36]

"I admit that if we had a writer who produced a biography of Hitler using the same method as McGinniss, most of us would be delighted. Not many would question the ethics."

It was not all bad news for McGinniss. *Fatal Vision* sold in the millions and many more saw the television miniseries. NBC gave it a Rashomon-like treatment: the viewer sees the murders as MacDonald said they occurred, then through the eyes of the prosecuting attorney, and finally, the FBI version.

McGinniss followed up with *Blind Faith,* another murder book destined for television: it was the true story of a New Jersey insurance agent convicted of insuring his wife's life and then having her killed.[37] There was a rumble of criticism because he altered names and misrepresented some roles. He had warned readers that "certain scenes have been dramatically recreated in order to portray more effectively the personalities of those most intimately involved in this story," and that to protect their privacy the names of all except the main characters were pseudonyms.

Inside Ted Kennedy's Head

McGinniss seemed to reach next for the most provocative subject he could find: Senator Edward Kennedy. He called the biography *The Last Brother*.[38] To critics, it was the last straw. Not only did he invent dialogue, but assumed the gift of telepathic insight into Kennedy's mind. Less controversial writers might have gotten away with the blatant mix of fact and fancy, but McGinniss aroused an almost unanimous roar of disgust. This time his daring really did him in, daring to soar too high, as he might see it, or stoop too low, as scores of critics concluded. Sensing a Kennedy-led conspiracy in the attack, McGinniss complained, "I'm being blamed for everything but the fall of Western civilization."[39] He also suspected the Kennedys of hiring public relations people to discredit him:

> The Kennedys have long had two approaches to journalists: they either buy them or destroy them. They know they can't buy me. It's not just shooting the messenger, it's mutilating the body so badly that no other messenger is ever going to come down the pike.[40]

When William Manchester and Doris Kearns Goodwin joined his critics by accusing him of lifting material from their books, McGinniss admitted drawing "heavily on Manchester's account for the facts on which I have based my own interpretations of Teddy Kennedy's actions and reactions. . . . A restatement of fact already in the public domain is not plagiarism."[41] Stung by their attacks, he hit back, saying Manchester was an "awestruck" authorized biographer and Goodwin was in the lap of the Kennedys.

To a Kennedy spokesman the book was "the most cynical form of exploitation of the Kennedy family for profit. . . . When the author wasn't fantasizing, he was apparently plagiarizing."[42]

This was almost a pat on the back compared to the blows from critics. Christopher Lehmann-Haupt damned it as worse than bad, "it was awful." Jonathan Yardley's review, headlined "Invented Biography, Steeped in Slime," judged the embattled author to have written "the worst book I have reviewed in nearly three decades; quite simply, there is not an honest page in it."

Michiko Kakutani of the *New York Times* wanted to banish McGinniss from writing society, outraged by his putting imaginary thoughts into Joe Kennedy, Sr.'s head, thoughts that could never be confirmed or denied because the elder Kennedy was suffering from a stroke from which he never recovered.

Well, Capote got away with it in *In Cold Blood* because his two subjects were safely underground. Lacey Fosburgh got away with it in *Closing Time: The True Story of the "Goodbar" Murder* by calling it "interpretive biography," and explained that meant she "had created scenes or dialogue I think reasonable and fair to assume could have taken place, perhaps even did." Of course, many biographers have played around with the truth, or used literary license, as they prefer to call it.

Again, McGinniss found himself on the defensive and anxious to promote a book of which some 260,000 copies were languishing in bookstores, the sluggish sales surely due to the stunning barrage of brickbats.

Stymied by Kennedy, his family, and his friends, who refused to cooperate, McGinniss had explained in an author's note his way out of the dilemma:

> Different subjects call for different techniques. I would contend that when an individual is as encrusted with fable and lore as is Teddy Kennedy (and his brothers), a writer must attempt an approach that transcends that of traditional journalism or even perhaps, of conventional biography. . . . I have quite consciously written portions as if from inside his mind.[43]

Kennedy loyalist and biographer, Arthur Schlesinger, Jr., having read the result of McGinniss's unambiguous attitude to the truth, said to me,* "He hasn't written a biography. It's fiction. Low-grade fiction. Any other comment would not be printable."[44]

Columnist Liz Smith† "totally disapproved of McGinniss's Teddy Kennedy, though I felt he really got it. I've never seen a book get such a pasting for his rush-to-judgment conclusions. But in the end he emerges with a rounded portrait of Teddy Kennedy.

"It's just that his methods were so questionable, imagining things and making these big psychological judgments that reminded me of the way I used to write when I was young and didn't know any better, [when I] didn't know I was supposed to be fair to people. I remember writing psychological portraits of Mrs. Onassis after I was a freelancer: I just learned better as time went on. I learned I wasn't correct.

"As I said, I've never seen a writer take such a beating and I think some of it had to do with the fact that he told a lot of truths people don't want to hear anymore. They're exhausted with the attacks on Teddy Kennedy. At the same time he's voted the hardest working senator in the Senate. That was reported by an independent congressional newsletter.

"Not only did I enjoy the book and couldn't stop reading it, I disapproved of it completely at the same time.

"On the other hand, he has a very good point. The Kennedys were masters of myth and public relations and building their legend and never telling the truth about anything. But, of course, two wrongs don't make a right.

"One of the most distressing things about such books is how much in them is true. We're living in the shadow of Mr.

---

*Interview with Arthur Schlesinger, Jr., March 25, 1994.
†Interview with Liz Smith, March 1, 1994.

Gutenberg who, after inventing movable type, only printed things from the Bible. Everyone believed everything in the Bible to be true, except for a few enlightened people who kept their mouths shut. But there's still a tendency to believe what we see in print. It makes it particularly dangerous. The more I write my column, the more I feel convinced that it's criminal to write something you know isn't true.

"I don't think you're going to kill a rock star by saying he trashed a hotel room or maybe smoked marijuana, but it's a little different for other people.

"Think of such writers as Eleanor Roosevelt's biographer, Joseph Lash, and Bill Manchester, and people who really care. Not that they never make mistakes, but it's that they would never willingly lie."[45]

The Kennedys Take the Heat

To Janet Malcolm, biographers are no better than journalists. She should know; she's both. Malcolm scorns their "pose of fair-mindedness, the charade of evenhandedness, the striking of an attitude of detachment . . . [as] rhetorical ruses."[46] She would surely agree with the sour view of Edmund White, biographer of French playwright Jean Genet, that "biography has become the revenge of the little people on the big people, and that the biographer's real intent is to enact revenge.[47]

This last may be true of Joe McGinniss but, give him his due, he makes no pretense of detachment or of being evenhanded. After trashing Ted Kennedy he went after other family members: John and his father, Joe.

Let's begin with the lesser of two evils: John F. Kennedy. According to McGinniss, he accepted a Pulitzer Prize for *Profiles in Courage,* a book that he never wrote. In *The Last Brother,* McGinniss reveals that, "[Professor Jules] Davids wrote drafts of what would be the book's first four chapters (on political integrity!), after which Sorensen, working up to twelve hours a day for six months, did the rest of the writing. By midsummer (1955), Sorensen, a facile writer whose natural prose style enabled Jack to develop the sort of stirring, invigorating political rhetoric he so much admired in others, had finished the book."[48] And to make sure we don't forget, McGinniss writes, "Sorensen could not resist quoting from *Profiles in Courage,* the book he had ghostwritten for Jack."[49]

It's true that there have been persistent rumors that JFK had great help with the book, written while recovering from back surgery, and that influence got him the Pulitzer Prize. But let's check the facts with Sorensen, in print and in person. In his biography of Kennedy, Theodore Sorensen tells how,

> Convalescing from his back operation . . . the Senator dictated into a machine to local stenographers in Palm Beach and to stenographers I brought down on my two visits. He reshaped, rewrote, and coordinated historical memoranda prepared by Professor Jules Davids of Georgetown University, whom Jacqueline had recommended, by James Landis and by me. . . . The work was a tonic to his spirits and a distraction from his pain. . . . Of all the abuse he would receive throughout his life none would make him more angry than the charge . . . that he had not written his own book. The charge was long rumored in private. . . . Finally it was made public by columnist Drew Pearson on the ABC television "Mike Wallace Show" on Saturday night, December 7, 1957. When then asked by Wallace, "Who wrote the book for him?" Mr. Pearson replied, "I don't recall at the present moment."
>
> On Sunday morning the Senator called me in an unusual state of high agitation and anger. . . . He said, "This challenges my ability to write the book, my honesty in signing it and my integrity in accepting the Pulitzer Prize." . . . ABC executives, after privately cross-examining me at length, finally

agreed that the Senator was clearly the author of *Profiles in Courage* with sole responsibility for its concept and contents, and with such assistance, during his convalescence, as his Preface acknowledged. But they sought to avoid their own responsibility for publishing an untrue rumor by making a new and equally untrue charge—namely, that I had privately boasted of being the author. . . . It was agreed that I would furnish a sworn statement that I was not the author and had never claimed authorship of *Profiles in Courage,* and that ABC would make a complete statement of retraction and apology at the opening of the next "Mike Wallace Show." (Which they did.) Two months later, after a talk with the Senator and a review of the evidence, Drew Pearson . . . included in his column the small parenthetical note that the "author of *Profiles in Courage* is Senator Jack Kennedy of Massachusetts."[50]

Nevertheless, a skeptical note was struck by John H. Davis, a cousin of Jacqueline Onassis, who charged that a platoon of paid minions produced the book:

Instead of being written by Kennedy, it is now generally conceded that the drafts of *Profiles in Courage* were written, in part, by Prof. Jules Davids of Georgetown University, a teacher of Jackie's, and Theodore Sorensen, with major contributions from professors Arthur Schlesinger, Jr., James MacGregor Burns, Allan Nevins, and Arthur Holcombe. Sorensen then wrote the final, unified version, which, of course, Kennedy went over very carefully, making his corrections, deletions, insertions and additions. At least this is the opinion of Herbert Parmet, the Kennedy biographer who has done the most research on the subject.[51]

But, in a more recent JFK biography, Richard Reeves cut the platoon down to two. He also states that when Robert

McNamara asked Jack Kennedy if he'd written *Profiles in Courage* himself, he insisted he had. Reeves later comments that Kennedy's literary guide for the book was Churchill's *Great Contemporaries* and that he was helped by both Arthur Krock and Theodore Sorensen.[52]

If you believe Davis, then you believe Sorensen lied under oath and Kennedy lied to McNamara, and you discount Arthur Schlesinger, Jr.'s comment to me, "I was shown a couple of chapters and just made some comments about them. That was my contribution."[53]

But at least Sorensen and Davis name names, while McGinniss makes the bald and unattributed assertion that the book was ghostwritten by Sorensen, period.

I caught up with Theodore Sorensen as he was about to leave his Manhattan law office for lunch.* "Did you read the McGinniss book on Ted Kennedy?" I asked.

"I looked through it," he replied.

"What was your impression?"

"It's absurd."

"How about his statement that you were John Kennedy's ghostwriter?"

"The best answer to that is to get a copy of *Profiles in Courage* and see in the acknowledgments in front of the book a very generous and quite accurate description by JFK of what I did. There's no doubt about the fact I did a lot of research and preparation of the materials, but the final writing, indeed the final decision on every *word* of the book was made by JFK."

"Where are the drafts?"

"I've no idea."[54] (This is hardly cause for suspicion. I can't locate any drafts of my eight published books either.)

---

*Interview with Theodore Sorensen, March 28, 1994.

Joseph P. Kennedy

Even his good friend John Katzenbach thinks McGinniss went too far in suggesting that Joseph P. Kennedy may have sexually molested his mentally retarded daughter, Rosemary, then had her secretly lobotomized and shut away for life to prevent her from exposing him.

I asked Theodore Sorensen about it:* "What did you think of McGinniss's suggestion that Joseph Kennedy, Sr., may have sexually molested his daughter Rosemary and had her lobotomized to silence her?"

"I thought it was outrageous and obscene."

"There have been accounts of his making passes at his sons' and daughters' female friends. It was partly based on those stories, I believe, that McGinniss speculated."

"I've seen plenty of people go through [the home] and I have never seen any evidence of that."[55]

Looking for a word to explain his biographic technique, McGinniss chose "rumination. . . . This book is as much a 'rumination' as it is a biography, and a rumination not only on the life of Teddy Kennedy but on the nexus between myth and reality in our time."

Ruminating on Joe McGinniss's ruminations, I would place him as a graduate of the Capote-Kelley-Higham school for scandal, whose credo is: print even the ugliest rumors as if they're true. If you can't back them up, say the answer is in sealed documents.

But what did those who knew McGinniss think of him? I contacted three writers who were at an Amherst, Massachusetts, conference when he announced, obviously in jest, "I'm tired of trouble. I don't want any more trouble. So I think I'll write a book about Ted Kennedy."[56]

---

*Interview with Theodore Sorensen, March 28, 1994.

Anne Bernays remembers it well.* A novelist, teacher, and lecturer, she said, "My problem is I like Joe so much and I just wonder why he keeps getting into these literary scrapes. Trouble seems to have a fatal attraction for him, and in a funny way he doesn't seem to realize what he's doing. That goes against everything I know about him.

"He has a very warm, charming personality. And when I read his first book, *The Selling of the President,* I was dazzled by it. It was the first of its kind. It was absolutely wonderful. Brilliant.

"In that book the reader knew or guessed all along that he was out to get Nixon. He never told them [the Nixon campaign organizers] that he was going to be one way or the other. He said, 'I want to follow along with the campaign and I want to see how this is done.' Now they were the dumb ones. They were terribly stupid. When McGinniss did it, it was new. But I don't think he lied to them, nor do I think he said, 'I want to tell your side of the story,' or anything like that.

"Then I heard him read a part of his book *Going to Extremes,* about fishing in Alaska, and I thought it was absolutely wonderful.

"As for the thing about MacDonald, he [McGinniss] sincerely thought him to be innocent when he started. But during the trial he began to think he was guilty. He did admit—and at the time I remember nudging my husband and saying, 'He shouldn't have done that'—he had made a financial arrangement with MacDonald, which made it far more difficult in every which way. As a journalist you mustn't do that. It violates every understanding of what a good journalist is, and in that sense he didn't really betray MacDonald so much as betray his own calling. MacDonald did do it, didn't he [commit the three murders]?"

---

*Interview with Anne Bernays, March 26, 1994.

"I think so," I said.

"Then maybe they deserve each other. As for the Ted Kennedy book, I'm baffled. I can't understand what was going on. Justin [Kaplan, her husband], who is a biographer, and I, who am mainly a novelist, have had endless conversations about him.

"Justin is absolutely scrupulous in his work. If he ever tries to get inside a character's head, it's very tentative. 'He must have been feeling rather low after his daughter died.' That sort of thing. It's a 'must have. It would have been odd if he hadn't.' Something like that. But never, never, never, get inside a character's head unless there's a specific conversation recorded somewhere or it's written in a letter.

"I haven't seen Joe McGinniss in quite a few years so maybe he's changed. But he struck me as being a really straight arrow and a wonderful journalist.

"He doesn't seem to dig that the place is mined. The terrain is mined and it's going to blow off his foot or something."[57]

Pulitzer Prize winner Justin Kaplan has produced biographies of Mark Twain, Lincoln Steffens, and Walt Whitman, and his next subject may be William James. He coughed his way through our conversation and blamed the books he was moving from his shelves to have the room painted, after putting it off for twenty-five years. As he spoke, he gently remonstrated with his dog, which was trying to join our conversation.*

I brought up McGinniss's assertion that Sorensen was Jack Kennedy's ghostwriter, without quoting any rebuttal witnesses, and Kaplan remarked, "I guess whenever given the choice, Joe picks the more colorful story." He added, "Isn't there an old journalistic piece of advice: 'If you have a good story, don't check it'?"

"When I started out in Fleet Street I was told: 'When in doubt, leave it out.' "

---

*Interview with Justin Kaplan, March 27, 1994.

"That's the advice of lawyers," said Kaplan. "I was rather intrigued by the fact that after being pushed around by all sorts of deadlines, Joe McGinniss ended up characterizing his book as a rather innovative subgenre of biography called 'a rumination.' I thought that was amusing.

"I gave the keynote address last January at the annual Literary Seminar at Key West. Without claiming to have read the Kennedy biography, I did describe the whole McGinniss adventure, with the Kennedy family first going after Nigel Hamilton [for his negative portrait of John Kennedy[58]] and, as the *Times* said, they were now gearing up to go after McGinniss. My conclusion was that in the long run, McGinniss not only shot himself in the foot but drove off the bridge, too, like the Senator. It's a nasty comment."

"Why was that your conclusion?"

"Because it was an unsatisfactory answer to the problem of access and authenticity, and to call it 'a rumination' is fudging the whole issue."[59]

What does a loyal friend think?

"What ticks me off," said John Katzenbach,* "is the savagery with which the holier-than-thou people attacked him, people who have themselves written biographies in which they put thoughts in their characters' heads.

"Of all the successful writers I've know, Joe McGinniss has done more than anyone to help young writers, to find them publishers and get them started. As I said before, he's a really good guy. It makes me apoplectic that criticism of him has become a cottage industry for a lot of writers who haven't even read the Kennedy book."[60]

---

*Interview with John Katzenbach, March 27, 1994.

The Rise and Fall of Joe McGinniss

"Here's my analysis of what's happened with Joe McGinniss, said Bob Keeler.* "Take a look at the Nixon book, the Alaska book, the MacDonald book, and what they all seem to have in common is the technique of worming oneself into the confidence of those involved, living with them, and being involved and soaking up stuff at close distance.

"Now, MacDonald, afterwards, kicked himself for not picking this pattern up before it was too late. He thought Joe was going to do this very favorable book about him. But if he'd read the Nixon book he'd have known better.

"If you read the book *Heroes,* McGinnis relates how he visited William Styron's house and [got up early and] ate a can of crab meat Styron had been saving for a special occasion. So, McGinniss has a technique of using his charm, of which he has considerable measure, to get into people's confidences, get what he needs, then get out and write about it.

"There was no way on God's green earth Teddy Kennedy was going to let Joe McGinniss into his confidence. If I was Kennedy, I wouldn't touch McGinniss with a ten-foot pole. Here's a case where he couldn't get inside. So what does he do? He makes it up! *He makes it up!!* And tells people this is a noble effort to expand the envelope. It's such palpable bullshit. It's beyond belief.

"So that's my take on what happened to Joe. He found himself operating outside the normal environment he was used to, and when he couldn't get information, he made it up.

"For me, what Malcolm and McGinniss have in common and try to elevate to high principle—is laziness. They are both extraordinarily lazy reporters and they both talk about it as if they're pushing the envelope of the art form. It's crazy. It's bullshit.

---

*Interview with Bob Keeler, August 30, 1993.

"I taught for a while at Columbia [University], talking to a number of young journalists. We discussed Janet Malcolm's, 'Every journalist . . . is a kind of confidence man, preying on people's vanity, ignorance, or loneliness, gaining their trust and betraying them without remorse.' I said, 'There she fails to uphold one of the first rules of journalism: back up your lead. She makes a very sweeping assertion encompassing virtually all journalists, when really the kind of journalist she's talking about is herself and Joe McGinniss.' "[61]

Afterword: From McGinniss

Neither fax nor telephone calls to his publisher and agent persuaded Joe McGinniss to speak with me about his work. A close friend of his also chose not to answer my questions, saying, "I keep my friends by never talking about them." So I've gone to his Author's Note to *The Last Brother* to let him explain himself. In it he writes:

> Teddy Kennedy is a real person and the story I have told here is one I believe to be true. . . . I have tried to distill an essence. I have tried to convey to a reader what it might have been like to be Teddy Kennedy. . . . The events described herein took place as described, to the best of my knowledge. . . . My goal has been to make Teddy come alive for a reader as he never has in any of the previous published works I've read about him. . . . I never intended that it be viewed as a formal biography and, as the reader will have observed, it has not been constructed in a way that would encourage such a response. . . . In my effort to portray as richly and fully as possible, within the confines of historical fact (what life may have been like for Teddy), I have, as is apparent, written certain scenes and described certain events

from what I have inferred to be his point of view. . . . Towards this end, especially in the first section of the book, when I try to give the reader a sense of how truly awful the assassination of John F. Kennedy must have been, on a personal level, for Teddy, I have quite consciously written portions as if from inside his mind. . . . So immersed have I been in the lives and times of the Kennedy family . . . that I have not hesitated to present certain events as if from Teddy's viewpoint. . . . Unmistakably, it presents also a highly personal and subjective view.[62]

Notes

1. *Miami Herald,* August 19, 1993, p. 2A, quoting from Janet Malcolm's biography, *The Silent Woman: Sylvia Plath and Ted Hughes* (New York: Knopf, 1994).

2. Bob Keeler, "Convict and Writer: Two Men, Three Murders and a Book," *Newsday,* September 11, 1983, p. 29.

3. Joe McGinniss, *The Selling of the President* (New York: Pocket Books, 1972).

4. Stanley I. Kutler, *The Wars of Watergate* (New York: Knopf, 1990), p. 637.

5. Interview with John Katzenbach, March 27, 1994.

6. Janet Malcolm, *The Journalist and the Murderer* (New York: Knopf, 1990), p. 3.

7. Joe McGinniss, *Fatal Vision* (New York: Putnam's, 1983).

8. Keeler, "Convict and Writer," p. 11.

9. Interview with Bob Keeler, August 30, 1993.

10. Keeler, "Convict and Writer," p. 12.

11. Joel Achenbach, "Fatal Revision: A Story About a Story About a Book About a Murder," *Tropic Magazine, Miami Herald,* April 23, 1989, p. 14.

12. Interview with Bob Keeler, August 30, 1993.

13. Keeler, "Convict and Writer," p. 26.

14. Ibid.

15. Ibid.

16. Ibid., p. 29.

17. Ibid.

18. Dennis L. Breo, *Chicago Sun-Times* (adapted from *American Medical News*), January 13, 1985, p. 9.

19. Ibid., January 14, 1985, p. 31.

20. Paul Nussbaum, " 'Friends' Go to Court as Adversaries over Book about 1970 Murders," *Miami Herald,* July 26, 1987, p. 5B.

21. Malcolm, *The Journalist and the Murderer,* p. 25.

22. Jeremy Gerard, "McGinniss Adds Rebuttal to Book," *New York Times,* July 18, 1989.

23. Jonathan Yardley, "Of Nonfiction Writers and Bad Faith," *Washington Post,* March 27, 1989, C2.

24. Interview with Liz Smith, March 1, 1994.

25. Breo, *Chicago Sun-Times,* January 13, 1985, pp. 3, 9.

26. Interview with Bob Keeler, August 30, 1993.

27. Nussbaum, " 'Friends' Go to Court," p. 5B.

28. Fred W. Friendly, "Was Trust Betrayed?" *New York Times Book Review,* February 25, 1990, p. 41.

29. Achenbach, "Fatal Revision," p. 14.

30. Janet Malcolm, *In the Freud Archives* (New York: Knopf, 1984).

31. Nussbaum, " 'Friends' Go to Court," p. 5B.

32. Keeler, "Convict and Writer," p. 13.

33. Interview with Bob Keeler, August 30, 1993.

34. Interview with John Katzenbach, March 27, 1994.

35. Harvey Cleckley, *The Mask of Sanity* (St. Louis, Mo.: Mosby, 1976), pp. 337, 338.

36. Interview with John Katzenbach, March 27, 1994.

37. Joe McGinniss, *Blind Faith* (New York: Putnam's, 1989).

38. Joe McGinniss, *The Last Brother: The Rise and Fall of Ted Kennedy* (New York: Simon & Schuster, 1993).

39. Mike Capuzzo, "McGinniss Fights Back Against Barrage of Criticism," *Miami Herald,* August 18, 1993, p. 5E.

40. Ibid.

41. Sarah Lyall, "Manchester Enters Furor Over McGinniss Book," *New York Times,* July 21, 1993, p. B4.

42. Capuzzo, "McGinniss Fights Back," p. 5E.

43. McGinniss, *The Last Brother,* pp. 620, 621.

44. Interview with Arthur Schlesinger, Jr., March 25, 1994.

45. Interview with Liz Smith, March 1, 1994.

46. Malcolm, *The Silent Woman.*

47. James Atlas, "The Biographer and the Murderer," *New York Times Magazine,* December 12, 1993, p. 74.

48. McGinniss, *The Last Brother,* p. 207.

49. Ibid., p. 597.

50. Theodore C. Sorensen, *Kennedy* (New York: Bantam, 1966), pp. 75–77.

51. John H. Davis, *The Kennedys: Dynasty and Disaster* (New York: McGraw-Hill, 1985), p. 273.

52. Richard Reeves, *Kennedy* (New York: Simon & Schuster, 1993), pp. 24, 41.

53. Interview with Arthur Schlesinger, Jr., March 25, 1994.

54. Interview with Theodore Sorensen, March 28, 1994.

55. Ibid.

56. Interview with Anne Bernays, March 26, 1994. As she recalls McGinniss saying it.

57. Ibid.

58. Nigel Hamilton, *JFK: Reckless Youth* (New York: Random House, 1992).

59. Interview with Justin Kaplan, March 27, 1994.

60. Interview with John Katzenbach, March 27, 1994.

61. Interview with Bob Keeler, August 30, 1993.

62. McGinniss, *The Last Brother,* pp. 619–23.

6

Murder by Other Means: Leonardo da Vinci, Woodrow Wilson, Adolf Hitler, Winston Churchill, and Lawrence of Arabia

> A good biography must vividly recreate a character; it must present a full, careful, and unbiased record of his acts and experiences. . . . In presenting a personality, the ironic approach has its advantages—especially in depicting a villain.
> —Allan Nevins[1]

Motive, not method, predetermines the outcome of many biographies, notably the efforts of Sigmund Freud. An active member of the do-as-I-say-not-as-I-do school, he couldn't resist attempting what he warned others was an impossible pursuit, writing daringly speculative biographies of Leonardo da Vinci and Moses, cautiously labeling the latter a historical novel, and a hate-driven biography of U.S. President Woodrow Wilson.

Freud was attracted to Leonardo as a subject, not only because he was the most versatile genius ever, excelling at almost everything he touched, but, like Freud, da Vinci was torn between two passions, science and art. Leonardo's erotic life was also an intriguing mystery: though accused of homosexuality, this was never proved. He is not known to have had a love affair with anyone of either sex, and his twenty notebooks written backwards, to be read in a mirror, give few clues to his emotional interests.

Having pored over the meager record of Leonardo's life, Freud used as a guide a patient who had "the same constitution as Leonardo though without his genius."[2] Whatever he had learned of that patient's inner life, Freud applied to Leonardo.

His conclusion was that Leonardo's mother had smothered him with affection, "maturing too early his erotic life," which had sapped his virility as a man.[3] He then sublimated his diminished sex drive into his insatiable curiosity—searching for knowledge as intensely as a mystic seeks God—and into his inspired work.

As Freud thought his theory of dreams to be the core of psychoanalysis, he naturally focused on Leonardo's only recorded dream as the key to his character. In a rare personal revelation, Leonardo had described a dream or vision in which a bird—Freud wrote "vulture"—flew into his cradle and moved its tail in his open mouth. In his psychoanalytical biography of the man, Freud warned potential readers to control their moral indignation until they had read his complete analysis of the dream which, according to him, was a wish for fellatio. But, he added, the bird's tail could symbolize either the penis or nipple, fellatio merely being an elaboration of nursing, "another situation in which we all once felt comfort" as children.

Readers heard him out and were indignant anyway, even fellow psychoanalysts: L. Lowenfeld reported that otherwise sympathetic readers reacted in "horror," and Sandor Ferenczi called it shocking. But Freud was unruffled, remarking that it was one of his favorite works, and had convinced him that the biographical method was valid. He had even discovered why the child dreamed of a vulture. In his research, Freud had come across a belief popular in Leonardo's day that all vultures were female and gave birth after being impregnated by the wind. Leonardo was the illegitimate son of a peasant woman and a lawyer, and lived alone with his mother. Because there was no male around, Freud conjectured, the boy thought he had been conceived like the vulture.

Anticipating skeptics, Freud stressed that "nothing is too trifling as a manifestation of hidden processes."[4] It was marginally plausible, perhaps, until James, the psychoanalyst brother of flawed biographer Lytton Strachey, took a deadly potshot at the bird thesis. Freud, he pointed out, had mistranslated the Italian *nibbio* as "vulture," when, in fact, it means "kite." There was no mythology about wind as a male sex substitute among kites.

Freud died too soon to benefit from the cautious advice of Robert Todd Lincoln's biographer, John Goff, that, "Most of the time he [the biographer] can only describe what happened and to delve more deeply is to invite disaster."[5]

To be fair to Freud, his whole book did not hang on bird identification. He had warned his eventual biographer, Ernest Jones, not to expect too much—that it would reveal neither "the secret of the Vierge aux Rochers [a painting by da Vinci] nor the solution of the Mona Lisa puzzle."[6] Fifteen hundred copies were printed and only 573 had been sold in the first six months: it took nine years before these sold out and a second edition was in the works, in which Freud acceded to prudish protests and substituted the word "inversion" for "homosexuality."

Freud was not discouraged. Conceding that with Leonardo he had been handicapped by a lack of information, in 1930 he eagerly volunteered to coauthor a biography of a contemporary, U.S. President Woodrow Wilson, about whom there was plenty of material.

His collaborator, William Bullitt, a brilliant Yale graduate and later the first U.S. ambassador to the Soviet Union, inundated Freud with scores of books, fifteen hundred pages of notes, published interviews, and private diaries and letters, as well as details of his personal encounters with Wilson.

The result was fatally flawed and almost farcical, not only because of Freud's farfetched psychoanalytical input but also because of his motive. Freud undertook the project as a labor of hate, bitterly resenting Wilson for making political promises he hadn't kept, and both Bullitt and Freud blamed him for the inflation after World War I, which reduced Freud's thirty-thousand-dollar estate to nothing.

> The figure of the American President, as it rose above the horizon of Europeans, was from the beginning unsympathetic to me and this aversion increased the more severely we suffered from consequences of his intrusion into our destiny. . . . Wilson repeatedly declared that mere facts had no significance for him, that he esteemed highly nothing but human motives and opinions. As a result of this attitude it was natural for him in his thinking to ignore the facts of the real outer world, even to deny they existed if they conflicted with his hopes and wishes. He, therefore, lacked the motive to reduce his ignorance by learning the facts. Nothing mattered except noble intentions. As a result, when he crossed the ocean to bring to war-torn Europe a just and lasting peace, he put himself in the deplorable position of the benefactor who wishes to restore the eyesight of a patient but does not know the construction of the eye and has neglected to learn the necessary methods of operation.[7]

In ridiculing Wilson, Freud also took a swipe at Christian Science:

> Many bits of his [Wilson's] public activity almost produce the impression of the method of Christian Science applied to politics. God is good, illness is evil. Illness contradicts the

nature of God. Therefore, since God exists, illness does not exist. There is no illness. Who would expect a healer of this school to take an interest in symptomatology and diagnosis?[8]

Freud's image of Wilson was one of a promising candidate for a mental institution: an egomaniac who was convinced his father was God and that he was Jesus Christ, though a very ambivalent Christ who consciously adored his father, while unconsciously hating him. Ambivalent is hardly the word for it. According to Freud, Woodrow Wilson was split three ways: he also wanted to be his mother!

Freud concluded that Wilson had already achieved a sex change, albeit unconsciously, and was well on the way to being his own mother, based on two sentences written to a woman friend after the death of his first wife: "Even books have grown meaningless to me. I read detective stories to forget, as a man would get drunk!"[9]

"By a curious slip of the pen," Freud pointed out, "the words he used showed that in his unconscious he had withdrawn himself from the male sex. A woman, not a man, writes, 'I read detective stories to forget, as a man would get drunk.' "[10]

A more likely reading suggests that Wilson, a nondrinker, used the phrase "as a man would get drunk," as a variation of "as other men would get drunk."

In covering Wilson's nationwide campaign to boost the League of Nations, "One may be sure," Freud wrote, continuing the image of the president's godlike alter ego, that "when he boarded the train he was mounting an ass to ride to Jerusalem."

Recklessly ignoring his own warning about partisan biography, Freud plunged ahead, piling on the "evidence," without a flicker of doubt that Wilson was an effeminate, neurotic, egomaniac, multiple personality, teetering on the brink of madness.

Where was the Wilson of remarkable courage and resilience, the lifelong invalid, almost blind in one eye, who had difficulty breathing and endured fourteen nervous breakdowns, yet served as a dynamic president of Princeton University, governor of New Jersey, and president of the United States?

To sustain their vicious thesis, Bullitt and Freud all but ignored the off-duty president who entertained his two daughters by imitating drunks, pompous Englishmen, stage villains, and Teddy Roosevelt waving his fists and orating with flamboyant patriotic fervor, and the man who needed no encouragement to launch into

> There was a young monk from Siberia
> Whose existence grew drearier and drearier,
> Till he burst from his cell with a hell of a yell,
> And eloped with the Mother Superior.

The authors barely glanced at such lighthearted behavior, which at least would have given their subject another dimension.

What was Wilson's unconscious as a "woman" doing when, on his honeymoon with his second wife, he danced a jig down a train corridor, whistling jauntily, "Oh, you beautiful doll!" If Freud was right, his conscious and unconscious selves were badly out of tune.[11]

As biographers, Bullitt and Freud fall far short of the stiff standards set by John Garraty, who regards the role as godlike,

> for in his hands the dead can be brought to life and granted a measure of immortality. He should, at least, then, seek to emulate the more reliable divinities in his zeal for the truth, his tolerance of human frailty, and his love for mankind.[12]

Well aware that personality defies exact analysis, and that by selecting some facts and rejecting others they could damn, deride, and debunk—or deify—Freud and Bullitt chose to show Wilson as only his most rabid enemies would recognize him.

Because it was such a slanted portrait, the writers could hardly expect help from Wilson's widow. Not wanting to hurt her and perhaps fearing she might rebut or ridicule their efforts, they decided to delay publication until after her death. Meanwhile, to prevent the manuscript from being leaked, they locked it in a Washington, D.C., vault guarded by a U.S. Marine. It lay there for almost thirty years, and was published in December 1966 when both Wilson's widow and Freud were dead. Bullitt died two months later, his funeral attended by a friend and political ally Richard Nixon. But the book, with its vindictive picture of Wilson, lives after him.

Allen Dulles, former director of the CIA, hurried to the defense of Wilson's reputation. He had been a student at Princeton when Wilson was its president, and had served with the American peace delegation in 1919. "It does not describe the Wilson I knew," he wrote. "The authors have described Wilson as an ugly, unhealthy, 'intense' Presbyterian, with a neurotic constitution. . . . Yet during his Princeton days, the students considered him the most popular teacher there."[13]

Dulles also knew Bullitt. They had worked together at the Peace Conference. Dulles remembered him "as a man who espoused causes and individuals and then turned from them abruptly. . . . As I am charging others with prejudice, I must admit my own. The admiration I first gained for Wilson as an inspiring teacher during my Princeton days undoubtedly colors my own thought."[14]

Dulles failed to mention another reason for his possible bias against Bullitt, whose testimony before the Senate Foreign Relations Committee caused Robert Lansing to resign as secretary of state. Lansing was Dulles's uncle.

Bernard De Voto had expressed the virtually unanimous reaction to Freud's psychoanalytical biography of da Vinci, when he trashed it as "absolute bilge uncontaminated by the slightest possible filtration of reality." In his view, that applied to all psychoanalytical biography presented as fact.[15]

This did not discourage lesser lights from following the tricky trail blazed by Freud, prompting poet Stephen Vincent Benet to parody them: "As for the poor devil's really loving his wife—well I know that every authentic utterance of his on the subject said he did, and there are those dedications of his books that sound fairly sincere. But honestly, he simply hated her all the time. . . . Don't you realize that his unconscious portrait of her as the degenerate scrubwoman with leprosy in chapter four of 'Wedding and Wooed' represents his real feelings towards her?"[16]

In that line, and applying Freud's theory that "nothing is too trifling as a manifestation of hidden psychic processes," what about his choosing Bullitt as a partner, a man whose name— so close to "bullet"—suggests an urge to wound or destroy?

Even so, to expose Freud's fiasco is not to disparage the use of psychological insight in biography. Plutarch hit the right resonating note almost two thousand years ago:*

> The most glorious exploits do not always furnish us with the clearest discoveries of virtue or vice in men; sometimes a matter of less moment, an expression or jest, informs us better of their characters and inclinations.

During World War II, the psychoanalytical "treatment" of someone personally unknown to the author—Walter Langer— proved remarkably accurate, even prophetic. The subject was Adolf Hitler. The OSS and others in the American intelligence community were anxious to know what kind of man they were fighting. Previous biographies were obviously partisan for or against him. By knowing what Hitler was really like, the Allies might anticipate how he would conduct the war, and what

---

*In his *Parallel Lives,* Plutarch, a Greek biographer and philosopher, compared Greek and Roman notables.

methods to use against him, perhaps even outmatch him in a battle of wits.

The task went to Walter Langer, who had suggested the idea. As a psychoanalyst, it was his article of faith that a person couldn't be understood from a distance. But he did the best he could, almost exactly duplicating Freud's method in analyzing Woodrow Wilson. He read all the available printed material on Hitler, including diaries, letters, and interviews. He studied newsreels of the Nazi dictator and listened to his speeches. Langer also questioned a handful of refugees from Germany and some who had been interned as suspected Nazis. Meanwhile, he discussed Hitler with other psychoanalysts and psychiatrists, matching up the dictator with their patients whose behavior and personality traits most resembled his. Langer then used all that information to predict Hitler's probable actions in various circumstances.

Unlike Freud's work on Wilson, it was not animated by hate. Langer had no affection for Hitler, but his aim was to produce a faithful picture of the enemy leader. He spelled it out in six sections: Hitler (1) as he believes himself to be, (2) as the German people know him, (3) as his associates know him, (4) as he knows himself, (5) psychological analysis and reconstruction, and (6) his probable behavior in the future.

As Hitler's defeat became more likely, Langer dared to predict Hitler's future. Would he die of natural causes, escape to a neutral country, die in battle, be assassinated, go insane, be captured in a military coup, be captured by the Allies, or would he commit suicide? The last "is the most plausible outcome," Langer concluded. And, of course, his educated guess was right.

It was almost thirty years before Langer's secret wartime report, *The Mind of Adolf Hitler*, was made public.[17] Hailed as "probably the best attempt ever undertaken to find out why the evil genius of the Third Reich acted the way he did,"[18] it has stood the test of time.

I discussed his work with Langer* soon after it was published, first asking what obstacles he had faced and how he overcame them.

"Most of the written material about Hitler was propaganda: a lot by people who were against the Nazi party and tried to paint a very black picture of Hitler; a lot was contradictory; a lot couldn't be validated; a lot was merely personal impressions. We had to have something else to even weigh the evidence we had, and to judge its validity. This is where my psychoanalytical training came in handy: not only mine but my collaborators who had patients whose personalities were not dissimilar from Hitler's, even though they were not so extreme. This is not a scientific way of dealing with evidence, but when you haven't anything else and there's a war raging and they're clamoring for some understanding, you can't be fussy."

"What did you discover: do you believe he had an 'inner voice' telling him it was his destiny to be a great leader?"

"His voice was more intuition than revelation. Not the kind a saint would have that concrete pearls of wisdom are bestowed on an individual. When the time came to act, the 'voice' or intuition gave him the boost that this is the right time, right place, and right thing. So he had a very firm inner conviction. Often, he wouldn't act until he had this conviction."

"How did you work with your psychoanalytical collaborators?"

"We drew on our own clinical experience. I would say, 'I had a patient who had' this particular trait and 'his background was' such-and-such, 'and he had these problems.' And so on. One of my collaborators would say, 'Yes, I have a patient like that, too.' He'd discuss his patient's problems. We'd piece it together in this way. We sat around and gave free rein to our memories and the patients we'd treated: their problems,

---

*Interview with Walter Langer, August 21, 1973.

backgrounds, and what their outcome was—without naming names."

"And you judged Hitler to be a neurotic psychopath bordering on schizophrenia."

"Yes. The neurotic psychopath is bordering on the edge of reality, a dim zone where it isn't always clear whether he's reacting to an external or an internal reality. However, Hitler never lost contact with outer reality. Had he done so it would definitely have put him in the schizophrenic class. His ability to convince others that he was not saved him from insanity. He convinced them that he was a tough, ruthless leader. Whereas, underneath, on an unconscious level, he was soft and uncertain. Some of it was not too far buried in his unconscious and undoubtedly became conscious often, and troubled him. He had to suppress it."

"The Russian autopsy discovered Hitler had only one testicle. If you had known that, would that have been important?"

"It would have reinforced some things I suspected, particularly his adolescent years, and have explained his being overmasculine, overtough, and overcruel."

"Why was he so obsessed with his nickname, 'Wolf'?"

"Everywhere you look in Hitler's life, the name 'Wolf' keeps popping up. It must have had an unconscious influence, the inference being, of course, that the wolf is a wary predator."

"What did you make of reports that Hitler called himself 'shithead' and had three favorite riding whips, with which he used to strike himself on the hands? The whips were gifts from three female intimates his mother's age."

"It showed a great dependence on his own mother, probably from childhood. He was putty in the hands of some older women, particularly Frau Bechstein, the wife of the piano manufacturer who financed him and told him what to do. She used to lay him out in lavender [bawl him out]: we had that on good authority. Friedelinde Wagner witnessed this personally a number of times, and was amazed Hitler would sit still and take it."

"So Hitler kept his secret side well hidden, the soft man who could be intimidated by older women. Is it fair to say that the extremely ambitious—JFK, FDR, Nixon, for example— often have a secret side to them?"

"Definitely. I don't think any of us within the normal range would have the endurance, energy, persistence, or the feeling he was being guided and had a mission to perform for mankind. It takes this to be a leader, to convince people and get the necessary followers. I come from Massachusetts originally, and when he was running for senator, it was common knowledge that Kennedy had a couple of women tucked away in Beacon Hill, so I was not amazed at the revelations of the women in his life, except that he should pick a Mafia moll to fraternize with."

"Perhaps we should have our leaders psychoanalyzed before they run for president."

"It might help. But I think if you psychoanalyzed them, they wouldn't run for president. The mere fact that a man believes himself capable of being president of the United States makes him abnormal, in the ordinary sense of normal. Richard Helms (when director of the CIA) said they had psychiatrists in the CIA making psychological profiles of a great many people, without naming them. I wondered if these were foreign leaders in China, Israel, Egypt, and other countries."

"Why do most leaders keep secret the feeling that they have a special mission or are guided by some supernatural power?"

"Because it's unconscious. If it were revealed to them, in the course of analysis for example, it might lose its effect and they'd lose their drive. They might still believe some of the things they had believed in, but lose the energy to achieve their goals. This is true of religious leaders, too."

"Their secret might be that they unconsciously think they are God."

"Christ is a good example."

"But he expressed that belief. It wasn't a secret side of him."

"It must have had unconscious roots. Many of his teachings and precepts have stood the test of ages. They still guide us. So they might be very good or, in Hitler's case, very bad."

"So, if Christ had been psychoanalyzed he might have quit?"

"Yes. If he'd had a book written about him, people would have called him paranoid. I don't say that he was. I'm bringing up as an example of unconscious motivations that drive an individual through all kinds of dangerous and fatal situations in order to sustain an unconscious goal."

"What has been the response to your Hitler biography?"

"The response was amazing, mostly from the newer breed of historians, psychohistorians, at this almost pioneer attempt at psychohistory. They stress the method I used in the absence of concrete historical data to fill in the gaps in their knowledge. What also appealed to them was my going through Hitler's writings, particularly *Mein Kampf,* from a psychoanalytical point of view, and studying his similes and metaphors. From psychoanalytical work we notice how others very frequently give examples unconsciously that reflect their own childhood and their own problems. What also appealed to historians was that I stressed that Hitler did not make Nazism and did not make Germany what it was. He and the German people intermingled and reciprocated, one causing the other, and feeding the other, and leading them to extremes which neither one probably would have done if left to his own devices."

"Do you believe that given certain behavior and personality traits you can predict what an individual will do in many situations?"

"Only in terms of probabilities."

"Did you discover if accounts of his [Hitler's] perversions, wanting women to defecate on him, were true?"

"Probably. It came from two widely different sources

unknown to each other. It's an extreme form of masochism, and something probably only Hitler and Eva Braun would know for sure."

"It's remarkable the positive Jewish influence on Hitler in his early years, all of which seems to have been to his benefit. (Hitler sent the Jewish family physician, Dr. Bloch, a hand-painted postcard signed, 'Your eternally grateful patient, Adolf Hitler.'[19] Gestapo files revealed that Jewish art dealers befriended him, and paid him well for his unremarkable paintings.[20] The persistence of his Jewish regimental adjutant, Hugo Gutmann, got Hitler the Iron Cross in World War I.[21] His probably Jewish landlady in Vienna not only charged him a nominal rent, but moved out of her room to accommodate him.[22])"

"Very frequently you do someone a favor and they turn on you. Particularly people who are insecure. They can't bear the idea that they're obligated and they deny it to themselves as well as to the world."

"Why did Hitler trust (his physician) Morell who was poisoning him, when so many legitimate physicians warned him not to take Morell's advice?"

"A mystery to me. But you'll find some well-to-do patients prefer to take advice of a quack rather than an expert. It satisfies something in them. Hitler was tremendously drugged towards the end, and was probably an addict."[23]

Winston Churchill Bites the Dust

Winston Churchill, too, went for quacks and, like Hitler, attracted armies of biographers, among them foreigners and fellow countrymen, political supporters and opponents, a woman friend, his private and cabinet secretaries, his male nurse, and even his bodyguard. After protecting Churchill for almost twenty years, Walter Thompson lowered his guard to write what the

San Francisco Chronicle called "as intimate a portrait of Church-ill as has ever been committed to print." In it he told of a naked Churchill in his White House bedroom greeting Roose-velt with "You see, Mr. President, I have nothing to hide!"[24]

Churchill's doctor, Lord Moran, took him at his word and eventually published an account that far exceeded the body-guard's intimate revelations.

Sigmund Freud tried to destroy the reputation of a man he never knew. Churchill's nemesis, on the other hand, was a man who knew him more intimately than anyone, apart from his wife, and was surreptitiously recording details of his bodily functions, fears, and foibles. Moran had the instincts of a biographer and a direct way with words. He noted how Churchill responded to a heart attack in the White House caused by trying to raise a stuck window, and recorded his frequent physical and mental problems: a rupture and subsequent surgery, con-junctivitis, dyspepsia, diverticulitis, four bouts of pneumonia, three strokes, and frequent depression.

Moran told himself he was doing this as a conscientious doctor, hoping such information would help him treat his patient more effectively. He clearly had a tell-all book in mind. He pressed on with his doctor's-eye view of Churchill from his days of glory in World War II to his pathetic last years as a senile old man. Each time Moran left Churchill, he jotted down their conversation and his observations, often on the backs of envelopes, while fresh in his memory. So we learn:

> Attempts to pump the P.M. never get anywhere: if he is going to be indiscreet, he does not want anyone's help. (p. 23)

> I heard the P.M. singing in the bath this morning. (p. 73)

> He takes instinctively to a quack, gulping down his patter and his nostrums indiscriminately. During the twenty-five years he was in my care, I had to call a number of doctors for

various parts of his body and he took to them in inverse ratio to their scientific attainments. (p. 96)

"Some day, when I have time, I shall write a thriller," Winston said. "The villain, a doctor, will destroy his victims by breaking down their immunity." (p. 101)

Three "bloodys" bespattered his conversation, and twice, while I was with him, he lost his temper with his servant, shouting at him in a painful way. (p. 128)

It is one of Winston's engaging qualities that he will never say "I told you so." (p. 231)[25]

Moran frequently deflates the warrior-statesman conception of Churchill, as if wielding a needle rather than a pen, literally showing the emperor without his clothes. At times the doctor views his subject with derision, for example, giving a demeaning rear-view glimpse of the leader of the free world on hands and knees, dressed only in a skimpy undershirt, frantically trying to plug drafts in a cold, high-flying plane. He shows a petty, childish, and arrogant Churchill, although the overall impression is of an endearing character—if you weren't working for him—whose flaws are greatly outweighed by his good nature and superb achievements.

Nevertheless, when the book appeared, Churchill's widow accused Moran of betraying the doctor-patient relationship. The British medical journal *Lancet* agreed.

Moran countered that he had been urged by Churchill's friend Brendan Bracken to be "Winston's Boswell," and encouraged by the remark of historian G. M. Trevelyan that "it is inevitable that everything about this man will be known in time. Let us have the truth."

Unlike Freud, Moran was not motivated by hate, but it was hardly the act of a friend, and was, in a sense, a betrayal.

Yet future biographers will be grateful to Moran. Martin

Gilbert, Churchill's official biographer, has already made use of these unofficial disclosures. Without them much about Churchill would still be hearsay and myth.

The Enigma

> When I am dead they will rattle my bones with their curiosity.
> —T. E. Lawrence[26]

> One of the greatest beings alive in our time.
> —Winston Churchill[27]

> I am not . . . much of a hero-worshiper but I could have followed over the edge of the world.
> —John Buchan[28]

One of Winston Churchill's heroes who was also mauled by biographers was Thomas Edward Lawrence. Lawrence would be unknown and unsung today but for an American newspaperman, Lowell Thomas. Taking newsreel shots of the Arab revolt against Turkish domination in 1917, he featured a slight British colonel, T. E. Lawrence, who led a guerrilla group, often in brutal hand-to-hand combat. Thomas gave his illustrated lecture, "With Allenby in Palestine and Lawrence in Arabia," in London's huge Albert Hall to overflow audiences, among them Winston Churchill. Six million people had seen the show when Thomas took it to New York. There, the audience was put in the mood by a woman performing the "Dance of the Seven Veils," while offstage an Irishman sang the Moslem call to prayer. Then Thomas stepped into the spotlight onstage to narrate; his opening line, "Come with me to the lands of mystery and romance."

The five-foot-five-inch British colonel-turned-desert-warrior was soon internationally acclaimed as "Lawrence of Arabia."

He was ambivalent about his fame which brought reporters to his door urging him to tell all. He repeatedly declined.

After the war he worked for Churchill as a Middle East expert, until he had a nervous breakdown. When he recovered, he joined the Royal Air Force in the lowest rank. He was soon recognized and kicked out because of unwelcome publicity. He enlisted in the tank corps for a while, and when the publicity died down, he was transferred back to the air force.

Writing to poet friend Alfred Perceval Graves, Lawrence confessed: "Honestly I couldn't tell you exactly why I joined up. . . . Partly I came here to eat dirt, till the taste is normal to me."[29] And later to another friend, Mrs. George Bernard Shaw: "I long for people to look down on me and despise me, and I am too shy to take the filthy steps which would publicly shame me."[30]

The puzzling questions about the war hero who had gone into hiding brought biographers scurrying to join the hunt. In time they found some answers.

His Irish father, Sir Thomas Chapman, left wife and four daughters to elope with the children's nurse, and changed his name to Lawrence. The couple had five sons; all were illegitimate because Chapman's wife refused a divorce. Lawrence's discovery at ten that he was illegitimate had a lasting traumatic effect. His mother, having committed adultery, fiercely adhered to the other nine commandments, raising her sons to be Calvinists, highly moral high achievers, as if to compensate for her "sin." His eldest brother, Robert, became a missionary-doctor in China, and the youngest, William, an archeology professor of note.

Lawrence had an unusual mind, both playful and profound; an ascetic attitude; a love of books and music; and a distaste for pleasures of the flesh. After graduating from Jesus College, Oxford, he enlisted during World War I and became a lieutenant colonel in the British Army, during which he led a guerrilla band of Arabs in their bid for freedom from the Turks. Lawrence suffered physically and mentally from the bloodthirsty fighting and was briefly captured and brutally sodomized.

In 1935, at age forty-seven, Lawrence was killed when he crashed his motorcycle. Churchill wept at his funeral.

I twice wrote to his archeologist brother, William, asking if he could explain the mystery surrounding Lawrence. He replied that the horrors of war had caused the nervous breakdown and that there was no other mystery: it had simply been concocted by the press.[31]

Not until recent times when "the mystery" was solved could a comprehensive biography of Lawrence be written. When his brother knew this information had been made public, he allowed several biographers access to correspondence between Lawrence and Mrs. George Bernard Shaw, one of the few women in whom he confided. (Otherwise, this correspondence would have been withheld until the year 2000.)

Shortly before Lowell Thomas died in 1981, I had a conversation with him about Lawrence, the subject of many biographies, several films and plays, but still something of an enigma.*

"There have been over a hundred books on Lawrence of Arabia, all written by people who did not know him. In the world of journalism long ago we called this 'dope material.' That is, you would imagine what the man would be like or what he might do [shades of Joe McGinniss]. I have found that most of these books are largely inaccurate. Many said I was responsible for making Lawrence a legend, a demigod, et cetera. [Though Lawrence helped with his own *Seven Pillars of Wisdom* and his published correspondence.]"

"Do you think he was a masochist?"

"I never saw anything in my association with Lawrence that even suggested that might be possible. So it puzzled me very much."

---

*Interview with Lowell Thomas, September 9, 1979.

"Was Lawrence truthful?"

"I would say so, although books about him indicate he would tell one person one thing and another, another about the same situation."

"Didn't he toy with the truth?"

"I once asked him to verify an account of one incident and he laughed and said, 'Use it if it fits your needs. What difference does it make if it's true—history is seldom true.' He had a self-deprecating sense of humor and loved to play pranks on people. There's no doubt about that."

"Churchill attended your newsreel extravaganza on Lawrence, I recall."

"Yes, when he was Home Secretary, he came to hear me speak one night in London. He came with Lloyd George, then prime minister."

"Was Lawrence homosexual?"

"The Prince of Wales [later the Duke of Windsor] called me up one day and asked if I thought Lawrence was a queer. I told him that definitely I didn't think so, because had he been that way, there were so few Europeans with him in the campaign that they would have known about it. There would have been no avoiding it. His closest associate was a Scottish doctor, a Major Marshall, who was a very high-class fellow. They were sort of tent mates. Not all the time, because Lawrence was gone so much. There was nothing strange about Lawrence that I could see. He was a brilliant conversationalist, a most charming man. A scholar and a man of action. He was the kind of man that you don't find too often and I think you find them more among your countrymen [the British] than you do almost anywhere else in the world."

"You once wrote, 'I admired the man beyond any other human being I have ever met in a lifetime of travel around the Seven Seas.' "

"He was a phenomenon, an extraordinary man."

"Yet so many biographers tried to put him down."

"I know. The Richard Aldington book [*Lawrence of Arabia: A Biographical Enquiry* (London: Collins, 1955)] was very bad: sheer nonsense." (One blurb on the book reads: "The most violent attack ever made on Lawrence. Richard Aldington, outstanding poet and writer, exposes the legend of the English officer who found fame with the desert tribesmen. Aldington condemns Lawrence as a poseur, liar, homosexual. Is Aldington just? The reader must decide for himself.")

"The *Guardian* said, 'There is a passion behind this book which strangely puts one in mind of a personal vendetta.' "

"And you know the reason for that? Aldington was really a Frenchman. A Francophile. He lived in France a large part of his life and he had the French point of view on the outcome of the First World War and on the Near East. The French thought they were entitled to Syria and Lebanon and so on. Aldington had the French slant on the whole thing. He wanted France to triumph from the World War I peace treaty, and to emerge as the dominant European power in the Near East. Lawrence worked for British supremacy, and Aldington resented Lawrence's successful influence."

"Aldington wrote critically of Lawrence backing into the limelight all the time."

"I told Aldington that."

"Was that a quirk in Lawrence's character?"

"Yes and no. He was a perfectly normal human being in most ways. Most people don't mind being in the limelight, getting fame. But he didn't want to do it by pushing himself out in front. I don't think he minded backing into it."[32]

Eventually, Boston psychiatrist John E. Mack routed all the skeptics who claimed Lawrence was a fraud whose trivial deeds had been grossly inflated by Lowell Thomas. In the 1970s, Mack questioned many people who knew Lawrence during his desert days, including sheiks who fought in his guerrilla band. They established that Lawrence's account of his role in the fighting was essentially correct. If anything, "he would customarily leave out information that was to his credit."[33]

According to Mack, Lawrence was not just another burnt-out case. After the war, he had become obsessed by erotic feelings he had experienced under torture. This obsession brought on his nervous breakdown and self-disgust. As he wrote to Mrs. Shaw: "For fear of being hurt or rather to earn five minutes respite from the pain which drove me mad, I gave away the only possession we are born in the world with—our bodily integrity." He also admitted that during the torture, "a delicious warmth, probably sexual, was swelling through me." So he sought both sexual gratification along with agony and humiliation, a reliving of the trauma of torture. To that end, he persuaded a fellow soldier to whip him. Either his masochism had been inherent since birth or aroused by the sadistic sexual attack during the war. His brother William saw it as self-induced punishment for failing to live up to impossibly high standards, and ever protective of his memory, compared it with the flagellation of saints.[34]

One fact is still missing from Lawrence's biographies. Though a champion of the Arabs, his great hero was a Jew: Chaim Weizmann, the Zionist leader and first president of Israel.

It took a hundred or so biographers producing slanted or superficial books before one approached the truth about Lawrence: writer/psychiatrist John E. Mack, who treated his subject with enlightened empathy and went to the desert to see for himself. Once again, the motive made the difference.

Watergate Revisited

Although Bob Woodward and Carl Bernstein, Jack Anderson, Seymour Hersh, and others covered Watergate, and almost all who testified at the Senate hearings wrote their memoirs, loose ends still remain. I tried to hunt one down. As an example of the difficulties a biographer intent on culling a nugget of truth will face—even in such a well-documented area—I'm reproducing my attempts to resolve the questions: Was G. Gordon Liddy's offer to kill Jack Anderson justified? Were Liddy and Anderson as malevolent as they were painted by their critics?

While asking Liddy and Anderson their opinions of Bob Woodward, I strayed to Liddy's much publicized offer, as a patriotic duty, to kill Anderson.*

"Do you still admire President Nixon?" I asked Liddy

"Absolutely."

"Do you regret offering to kill Jack Anderson?"

"No. Remember what the circumstances were. Mr. Hunt came to me and said his principals, as he put it, which is intelligence jargon, had said that Mr. Anderson had gone too far. As you will recall, the history was we had been listening in as Brezhnev and other Russian leaders had been driving about the streets of Moscow in their limousines speaking, they believed, confidentially to the Kremlin and sometimes to one another. The CIA was intercepting all of that and reading it. Now, Anderson found that out. It was so important we not lose that tremendous source of intelligence that the matter was not delegated. Mr. Helms, who was the director of the CIA then, went to Mr. Anderson and explained how important it was and Anderson promised he would not publish it. Whereupon he did and we lost it. With that history behind us of Anderson's promises not to do things and to do it anyway, that's the background. Mr. Hunt said, 'Our principal says he's gone too far. He has already caused the death under torture, or the imminent death under torture, of one of our human assets posted abroad. We are tasked with coming up with a plan to see to

---

*Interview with G. Gordon Liddy, March 10, 1994.

it that Mr. Anderson is guaranteed not to do that.' The key operative word there is 'guarantee.' The only way you can guarantee that someone will not do something is to kill him. So we discussed whether or not that sanction was warranted. We said, given the fact that he had previously been asked to cease and desist doing something and had not complied after promising, and as he now had killed and could be presumed to kill again by revealing our human assets posted abroad, the sanction of death was warranted. That being the case the discussion then progressed to 'How shall it be done?' We decided to give it to a Cuban asset. Bear in mind we had with us at the time a CIA assassination expert, and the fact that we had been asked to meet with him is what someone might call a clue as to what was wanted. In any event, Hunt said, 'If our superiors believe it's too sensitive to give to the Cuban asset, then who shall do it?' And I said, 'All right, then I'll do it.' And Hunt proceeded and came back and they had said, 'Too severe a sanction.' And, of course, it wasn't done. That's the whole story and I don't regret it at all."

"'Has Anderson ever responded?"

"Oh yes. He regularly goes into a midlife crisis and snits at me when he can remember his name."

"No, I mean did he explain why he revealed that information after promising not to?"

"If he did, he did not to me."

"Someone wrote an article about you describing Nazi insignia in your home. Was that a cheap shot, making you out to be an extreme rightwinger?"

"I'll tell you what it was. They looked through the back window of my home on Ivanhoe Road in Oxon Hill that looked directly into my bookcase. My bookcase contained a copy of William L. Shirer's book *The Rise and Fall of the Third Reich*. The dust jacket was all black and the spine had a great big white circle on it in which was a swastika. That's what he saw."

"Can you laugh about it now?"

"Of course. Shows you how ridiculous they are."[35]

I called Jack Anderson the following evening.*

"Did Liddy ever explain his offer to kill you?"

"I appeared on 'Prime Time ABC' and 'Good Morning America' with him."

I told Anderson the explanation Liddy had given me.

"I hadn't heard that explanation. That's revisionist. It's absolutely true that Helms called on me and asked me not to use the story because I knew the CIA had intercepted the conversations of Russian officials traveling in limousines. I pointed out that those conversations indicated strongly that the Russians knew they were being intercepted so I didn't see how reporting the story would change what they knew already. He argued yes, but sometimes they get careless and forget it, and we don't want to remind them. I decided to cooperate. I said, 'The story isn't all that important. If you think it's a matter of national security I won't use it.' I did not, repeat, did not publish the story after talking to him, until the *Washington Post* published it on the front page. Then I reported that I'd been sitting on the story at the request of Helms."

"Did you ever give that account when Liddy was on those shows with you?"

"No, because he never raised it. That's why I say it's revisionist. He also never raised the question about somebody being tortured. But he apparently raised that on a radio show recently and I was called by the host of the show, down south somewhere, and he repeated what you said about some CIA asset being tortured or killed because of something I had written. And I said, 'Tell Mr. Liddy I don't know a better way of settling it: Let him put up any amount up to $100,000, because I can

---

*Interview with Jack Anderson, March 11, 1994.

afford that, and you can hold it. If he can name the person I killed and provide evidence I was responsible, he gets to keep the $200,000, and if he can't, I get to keep it.' "

"What happened?"

"He didn't take me up on it."

"Do you know who broke the story in the *Washington Post?*"

"I don't recall. But it was on the front page. I had probably used some radio report on 'Good Morning America,' or was preparing a piece and that's what precipitated Helms on it with me. So I broke the story before Helms called. He apparently heard me on the radio or was alerted that I intended to, and he asked to see me at the Madison Hotel."

On March 17, 1972, CIA officers closely observed the luncheon meeting in an attempt to discover if Anderson was secretly taping his conversation with Helms.[36]

"With all your experience, how would you resolve the two accounts? Liddy says one thing. You say it's revisionist."

"You can do it the same way. I've just given you my version, okay? I'll put up $100,000 if he will. If my version is wrong he gets to keep two hundred grand."

"As a reporter?"

"If I can't resolve it, I print the two versions. If I can resolve it, my obligation as a reporter is to print the truth."

"I suppose you'd check with Helms."

"Certainly. I have to warn you, he's extremely unfriendly. I caught him in a lie, some very serious breach on Capitol Hill, and that led to a reprimand. I think he even faced trial. So he has a strong resentment against me. But as far as I know, he'll tell the truth about that conversation. I've no objection to your contacting him."[37]

I called Richard Helms next day and told him what Anderson had said.*

"The only thing I can vouch for is I did indeed have lunch with him; I did indeed tell him that I thought it would injure the national security if he wrote anything about it and he agreed not to do so. The rest of it I don't know anything about."

"Liddy said he had been willing to kill Anderson because a CIA agent had been tortured and killed as a result of Anderson's leaks and that he'd broken promises not to publish things, so they thought the only way to stop him was to kill him. Have you ever heard of an agent being tortured and killed as a result of Anderson's columns?"

"No. Nor do I know anything about any threats against Anderson. This business about somebody being tortured, I never heard this story and know nothing to support it."[38]

I got back to Liddy.†

"Anderson said that in your previous encounters with him you never brought up your belief that he was responsible for the death of a CIA asset."

"That's ridiculous. I doubt if the old man can even remember his name."

"And he said you didn't accept his $100,000 bet."

"How in the world could I, at this remove, show the evidence? The evidence is held by the CIA. Do you think I kept it in my basement?"

"Helms said he didn't know of any CIA asset who had been tortured and executed because of anything Anderson had revealed."

"Well, that's his story now. That's fine. All I can tell you is what I was told by Mr. Hunt, that he got from, as he put it, his principal."

---

*Interview with Richard Helms, March 12, 1994.
†Interview with G. Gordon Liddy, March 12, 1994.

"Would you believe Hunt over Helms?"

"Yes."

"It almost seems to me one could ask questions endlessly of people like you, Anderson, and Helms and never get at the truth, don't you agree?"

"No."

"What would you do in my position?"

"I would accept my word. Bear in mind that rather than lie I did years in prison."

"I know your history, but don't you think Helms is a man of integrity?"

"Helms is a man of the agency. He will do or say what is necessary."

"People might say that you're a man of the Nixon White House."

"If I were being loyal to the White House, why would I have discussed the incident of Hunt coming with the tasking from the White House?"

"But that was after Nixon had resigned."

"But he's still resigned, is he not?"

"But what you revealed [about offering to kill Anderson] wouldn't damage Nixon, or do you think it would?"

"No. That's why I don't know what relevance your suggestion is that I'm being loyal to the Nixon White House. You're arguing circularly and you're arguing against yourself."

"I'm just trying to find the truth. In my position, I take it, you'd believe your account?"

"Yes."

"You brought up prison. Lots of men have gone to prison for their beliefs."

"You either believe it or you don't. You asked me who you should believe and I gave you an answer."[39]

The right answer I leave to future biographers.

A biographer's motive is almost all-important in judging

the work. The hatchet job is a clear giveway, when every mistake is magnified and the subject is rarely given an even break. The whitewash, too, is easy to spot. The more subtle propagandists are, of course, harder to detect. But the vital clues are the motives and character of the biographer, and his/her propensities and prejudices. As in every line of work, we have our SOBs, too, of both sexes.

Wait for the Green Flash or Eagles Mating in Mid-Air

The field is overcrowded, says Justin Kaplan. No biographer who aspires to excellence should attempt to add to it unless there is a passionate interest in the subject and "a profoundly intimate and intricate link, not invariably of admiration but certainly of empathy."

"If you need to have empathy with your subject," I asked,* "does that mean none of us can write a worthwhile biography of Hitler?"

"Absolutely not. Empathy and passionate interest have nothing to do with supporting that person. I could see myself absolutely fascinated by Hitler as a subject. Empathy has to do with the ability to feel with someone, to put yourself in his place and say, 'What would it feel like to be Adolf Hitler? [Exactly what Walter Langer did so effectively.] The guy is crazy, he's paranoid, he feels himself oppressed by everyone, he wants power,' and so on. If you could do that mental exercise to a sufficient degree you might be able to write a very good biography of Hitler."

"By assuming the qualities of a good actor?"

"Yes. It's an existential improvisation, basically, that you're doing."

---

*Interview with Justin Kaplan, March 29, 1994.

"How often do you think a writer and subject have that intimate, empathic, intricate connection?"

"It's as rare an occurrence as seeing the green flash at sunset or eagles mating in mid-air."

"This is new to me."

"I've been looking for the green flash for years, but I've never seen it. But people I know who live on Cape Cod have seen it. When the sun goes down over the water, people sometimes observe a quick green flash. It's described in the Chekhov story, 'The Duel,' when the protagonist of the duel sees the green flash in the evening and knows he is not going to be killed.

"It's a genuine phenomenon, not an hallucination. But very rare. And the mating of eagles in mid-air is in reference to a poem by Walt Whitman. It happens."[40]

Chekov has the last word. In "The Duel" he writes,

In the search for truth men take two steps forward and one back. Suffering, errors, and the tedium of life push them back, but a thirst for truth and a stubborn will drives them on. And who knows? Perhaps they will arrive at the real truth.

He could be describing the ideal biographer.[41]

Notes

1. Allan Nevins, *The Gateway to History* (New York: Double-day, 1962), p. 364.

2. Ernest Jones, M.D., *The Life and Works of Sigmund Freud*, vol. 2 (New York: Basic Books, 1955), p. 346.

3. Sigmund Freud, "Leonardo da Vinci and a Memory of Childhood," 1910, Heft 7, Schriften zur angewandten Seelenkunde, Gesammelte Werke VIII, pp. 121–28.

4. John A. Garraty, *The Nature of Biography* (New York: Knopf, 1957), p. 114.

5. John S. Goff, *Robert Todd Lincoln* (University of Oklahoma Press, 1969).

6. Jones, *The Life and Works of Sigmund Freud,* p. 64.

7. William Bullitt and Sigmund Freud, *Thomas Woodrow Wilson: A Psychological Study* (Boston: Houghton Mifflin, 1967), p. xi.

8. Ibid., p. xiii.

9. Ibid., p. 156.

10. Ibid.

11. August Heckscher, *Woodrow Wilson* (New York: Scribner's, 1991), pp. 117, 282. Also, Marianne Means, *The Woman in the White House* (New York: Signet, 1962), p. 150.

12. Garraty, *The Nature of Biography,* p. 28.

13. Will Brownell and Richard N. Billings, *So Close to Greatness: A Biography of William C. Bullitt* (New York: Macmillan, 1987), p. 328.

14. Ibid., p. 329.

15. Garraty, *The Nature of Biography,* p. 144.

16. Ibid., p. 143.

17. Walter C. Langer, *The Mind of Adolf Hitler: The Secret Wartime Report* (New York: Signet, 1973).

18. *Chicago Tribune.*

19. Langer, *The Mind of Adolf Hitler,* p. 236.

20. Ibid., p. 237.

21. Ibid.

22. Ibid., p. 236.

23. Interview with Walter Langer, August 21, 1973.

24. Walter Thompson, *Assignment: Churchill* (New York: Popular Library, 1961), p. 240.

25. Lord Moran, *Churchill: Taken from the Diaries of Lord Moran* (Boston: Houghton Mifflin, 1966).

26. Interview with Lowell Thomas, September 9, 1979.

27. A. W. Lawrence, ed., *T. E. Lawrence by His Friends* (McGraw-Hill, 1963), p. 161.

28. Stanley Weintraub, *Private Shaw and Public Shaw* (George Braziller, 1963), p. 51.

29. Phillip Knightley and Colin Simpson, *The Secret Lives of Lawrence of Arabia* (New York: McGraw-Hill, 1970), p. 187.

30. Ibid., p. 292.

31. A. W. Lawrence wrote to me on July 11, 1965: "I do not agree that my brother mystified his close friends and the reason why he wished to live in obscurity has been clear to anybody who thought about it; Churchill, who of all people he knew was avid for the opposite, understood it and sympathized. I refer to Churchill's *Great Contemporaries*. The idea that there was a mystery was promoted and is kept going by journalistic vested interest; where there is no mystery there's no subject. Since I think there should be a moratorium in writing on my bother, I refuse all applications for the Mrs. Shaw material."

32. Interview with Lowell Thomas, September 9, 1979.

33. John E. Mack, *A Prince of Our Disorder: The Life of T. E. Lawrence* (Boston: Little, Brown, 1976), p. 459.

34. A. W. Lawrence wrote: "I am the only writer who met my brother at regular intervals from his boyhood to his last few months. It was this horror of the physical intimacies that he never experienced with anyone—we have his word for it—which inspired his abstinent habits. 'A one-man monastery' he has been called by a philosopher who did not know him, and his subjection of the body was achieved by methods advocated by the saints whose lives he read. In my opinion he neglected the body's claims unfairly at a cost so terrible in waste and suffering, that its author would himself, I believe, have agreed that it was a failure" (A. W. Lawrence, ed., *T. E. Lawrence by His Friends* [New York: McGraw-Hill, 1963], pp. 387, 394).

35. Interview with G. Gordon Liddy, March 10, 1994.

36. Thomas Powers, *The Man Who Kept the Secrets: Richard Helms and the CIA* (New York: Knopf, 1979), p. 207.

37. Interview with Jack Anderson, March 11, 1994.

38. Interview with Richard Helms, March 12, 1994.

39. Interview with G. Gordon Liddy, March 12, 1994.

40. Interview with Justin Kaplan, March 29, 1994.

41. Chekov was indifferent to the truth being told about himself. He had the same attitude as T. E. Lawrence, responding to a would-be biographer in a letter dated February 22, 1892: "Write whatever you like. If you haven't the facts, substitute lyricism." This might explain why Lillian Hellman could write of him, "Much of his life is still not known to us and much of what is known is not understood." Anton Chekhov, *The Selected Letters of Anton Chekov,* ed. Lillian Hellman, trans. Sidonie K. Lederer (New York: McGraw-Hill, 1965), p. xxvi.

Index

ABC (American Broadcasting Company) television, 312, 313, 349

Achenbach, Joel, 321n, 322n

Adventures of Don Juan, 210

Agenda, The, 285

Agnew, Spiro, 246

Alba, Duke of, 198, 199

Aldington, Richard, 28, 345

Algren, Nelson, 29, 30

All the President's Men, 232–33, 236, 248, 252, 254, 256, 284, 287n

Allegro, John, 65

Allenby, General, 341

American Swastika, 196

Anderson, Jack, 13–14, 232, 246, 259, 266, 269, 288n, 290n, 346–52, 356n

Andrews, Julie, 118

Answered Prayers, 13, 46, 66, 68–

72, 77, 85, 92, 100–101, 107, 114n

Aristoxenus, 21

Armstrong, Scott, 139, 233, 239

Artful Partners, 21

Astaire, Fred, 189

Astaire, Robin, 189

Atlas, James, 323n

Austin, Ray, 191

Autobiography of Henry Adams, 49

Aykroyd, Dan, 277

Babe (Sinatra's uncle), 157, 164

Bacon, James, 144, 194

Bair, Deidre, 40n

Baker, Carlos, 23

Baltimore Sun, 139, 159, 181

Bankhead, Tallulah, 14

Bantam Books, 140

Barbarto, Nancy, 152

Barker, Ma, 164
Barnard, Francie, 260
Barnes, Fred, 15, 173, 182
Barry, Philip, 56
Barry, Tim, 189
Barrymore, John, 193
Barthelmes, Wes, 122
Bass, Judy, 229n
Baumgold, Julie, 113n
BBC (British Broadcasting Corporation), 307
Beaton, Cecil, 50, 56
Beauvoir, Simone de, 29
Bechstein, Frau, 335
Beck, Martha, 88
Belli, Melvin, 15, 195, 203–204, 228n
Belushi, John, 233, 277
Benet, Stephen Vincent, 332
Bennetts, Leslie, 112n
Berenson, Bernard, 21
Berkeley Independent Gazette, 214
Bernays, Anne, 15, 316, 323n
Bernstein, Burton, 24
Bernstein, Carl, 231–32, 236, 239–40, 243, 246, 251–53, 255–56, 258–59, 278–80, 287n, 288n, 289n, 346
Bernstein, Leonard, 24
Betley, Lieut.-Col., 211
Beveridge, Albert, 33, 34
Biden, Sen. Joe, 122
Billings, Lem, 59
Billings, Richard, 355n
Birmingham, Stephen, 176

Bishop, Joey, 141, 150
Blind Faith, 307
Bloch, Dr., 338
Bloch, Michael, 230n
Blum, Suzanne, 217
Bonanno, Joseph, 138
Borchgrave, Arnaud de, 15, 17, 267–68, 271, 290n
Boswell, James, 25, 55, 285
Bouvier, Jacqueline, 123–24. *See also* Kennedy, Jacqueline, and Onassis, Jacqueline.
Bouviers, The, 130
Bracken, Brendan, 340
Bradlee, Ben, 14, 118–19, 128, 132–34, 181, 232, 237, 246, 251, 256, 258–60, 281, 284, 289n
Braham, Patricia, 186
Brando, Marlon, 13, 43, 45–48, 53, 66, 107, 109
Bratton, Brig.-Gen. Joseph, 253, 279
Braun, Eva, 338
Brenna, Susan, 227, 230n
Brentano's Bookstore, 110
Breo, Dennis, 322n
Breslin, Jimmy, 300
Brezhnev, Leonid, 347
Bring on the Empty Horses, 194
Brinnin, John Malcom, 112n
Brodsky, Alyn, 21, 186, 227n, 230n
Brogan, Lewis, 29
Brooks-Baker, Harold, 178, 183
Brown, John Mason, 15n

Brown, Tina, 73–74, 112n
Brownell, Will, 355n
Brunert, Dr. Ernest, 218
Buchan, John, 341
Bull, Steve, 246, 288n
Bullitt, William, 327–32, 355n
Bullock, Alan, 226
Burns, James MacGregor, 313
Burstein, Patricia, 112n, 113n
Burton, Richard, 36
Bush, George, 12, 171, 261, 286
Buzhardt, Fred, 245–46, 255, 279–81

Cakes and Ale, 27–28
Campbell, Sandy, 52
Capiello, Steve, 158, 182
Capote, Joe, 79, 87, 90
Capote, Truman, 11–14, 16n, 17, 43–113, 170, 202, 309
Capuzzo, Mike, 322n, 323n
Caro, Robert A., 25–26
Carpozi, George, Jr., 14, 117, 123, 164–67, 170, 177, 179, 181–83
Carson, Joanne, 72, 75, 83–84
Carson, Johnny, 147
Carter, Mary Ida, 85, 93
Carver, George, 15, 232, 268, 290n
Cary Grant: The Loney Heart, 187
Casey, 270
Casey, Sophia, 15, 172, 232, 261, 267–69, 273–74, 283, 290n
Casey, William, 13, 15, 17, 162, 172, 225, 232, 261, 263–77, 282, 285, 290n

Casserly, Jack, 289n, 290n
Cassina, Count, 199
Cather, Willa, 83, 231
CBS (Columbia Broadcasting System), 67, 72, 98
Cerf, Bennett, 68
Chaille-Long, Colonel, 20
Chameleon, 202
Chaplin, Charlie, 141
Chapman, Sir Thomas, 342
Chase, Chevy, 190
Chekhov, Anton, 354, 356n
Chicago Tribune, 18, 267, 277, 35n
Church, Roy, 103
Churchill, Winston, 12, 14, 33, 224, 314, 325, 338–44
CIA (Central Intelligence Agency), 13, 15, 17, 20, 35, 161–62, 172, 209, 213, 225, 231–32, 245, 248, 250, 261, 263, 265–68, 270–71, 273–75, 331, 336, 347–51
Ciano, Count, 216, 225
Cincotti, Joseph A., 41n
Clarke, Gerald, 14, 75–79, 84–85, 87–88, 90–94, 96, 100, 102, 105–106, 109, 111n, 112n, 113n, 114n
Cleckley, Hervey, 306, 322n
Clemons, Walter, 81, 113n
Clinton, Bill and Hillary Rodham, 177, 278, 283, 285
Clutter family, 47, 54, 73, 104
CNN (Cable News Network), 243
Cohen, Gwen, 232, 271, 290n

Cohen, Richard, 15
Cohen, Roger, 183
Colby, William, 15, 232, 268, 275, 290n
Collier, Peter, 176
Colodny, Len, 247, 288n
Commanders, The, 276, 285–86
Connelly, Mary, 111n
Conrad, Earl, 210
Conversations with Kennedy, 133
Converse, Veronica Cooper, 192
Cooke, Janet, 260–61
Coolidge, Calvin, 15n, 26
Cooper, Arthur, 24, 40n
Cooper, Gary, 192
Cope, Newton, 62
Cote Basque, 101
Courneya, Jerry, 206
Coward, Noel, 225, 230n
Cowley, Malcolm, 48, 111n
Crawford, Earl of, 222
Crispen, Elaine, 177
Crown, David, 161, 182
Crowley, Brian E., 183
Cushing, Harvey, 67

Dallas News, 214
Damita, Lili, 198, 214
D'Annunzio, Gabriele, 215
Dark Victory: Ronald Reagan, MCA and the Mob, 163
Davids, Jules, 311, 313
Davis, John H., 130, 313–14, 323n
Death of a Hero, 28
"Deep Throat," 13, 231–32, 236–41, 244–48, 250–52, 255–59,

281–82, 284, 286
Delfino, Josephine, 126
Demaris, Ovid, 115
Denver Post, 214
Der Stern, 198
De Voto, Bernard, 331
Dewey, Alvin, 47, 79, 102–103
Dietrich, Noah, 191
Donahue, Phil, 141, 150
Donaldson, Maureen, 187, 189–90, 227n, 228n
Donati, William, 15, 204–205, 207, 209–13, 216, 229n, 230n
Dowd, Maureen, 176, 183
Dr. Strangelove, 287
Duchess of Windsor: The Secret Life, 217
Duchin, Peter and Cheray, 133
Duke, Doris, 66
Duke in His Domain, The, 45
Dulles, Allen, 331
Dunphy, Jack, 79
Duntz, Clarence, 103
Durrell, Lawrence, 27
Duveen, Joseph, 21

Eagleton, Sen. Thomas, 122, 125
Eddington, Nora, 201
Edgley, Mike, 135, 168
Ehrlichman, John, 242, 294
Elizabeth Taylor: The Last Star, 135, 170
Ellis, Charles Howard, 200
Erben, Dr. Hermann, 195, 197–98, 205–10, 213
Errol and Me, 201

Errol Flynn: The Untold Story, 192, 194, 209
Esquire, 66, 101, 107
Exner, Judith, 148, 163, 165, 179

Fadlallah disaster, 265–66
Fadlallah, Sheik, 265
Farrow, Mia, 149–50, 159
Fatal Vision, 294–97, 300–301, 307
Faud, Prince, 265–66
Faulk, Sook, 84, 86
FBI (Federal Bureau of Investigation), 17, 35, 65, 104, 116, 140–41, 145, 159, 196–97, 206–209, 211–13, 229n, 246, 307
Feibelman, Peter, 36
Ferenczi, Sandor, 326
Field, Leslie, 225
Final Days, The, 232, 239, 241, 246, 254, 279–82, 284, 287
Fink, Robert, 256, 289n
Fisher, Bobby, 67
Fisher, Eddie, 169
Fitzgerald, F. Scott, 23
Fitzgerald, Scottie, 23
Flanders, David, 211
Flynn Controversy, The, 204
Flynn, Errol, 13, 17, 96–97, 185, 192–216, 227
Fort-Worth Telegram, 260
Forward, Sir Dudley, 221
Fosburgh, Lacey, 309
Franco, Francisco, 199
Frankel, Haskell, 101

Frazier, Brenda, 222
Freeman, Edward, 18
Freud, Sigmund, 13, 30, 40n, 325–32, 339, 354n, 355n
Friendly, Fred W., 322n
Frost, David, 287n
Froude, James Anthony, 18

Galbraith, J. K., 14, 59–60
Galileo, 33
Garavante, Babe, 157
Garbo, Greta, 56
Gardner, Ava, 148, 159, 168–69
Garraty, John A., 39, 40n, 41n, 330, 355n
Garrick, Frank, 142–43, 151, 155
Garrick, Mrs. Frank, 151–54, 182
Gates, Bob, 235, 269, 274
Genet, Jean, 311
George V, King, 221, 225
Gestapo, 199
Gettlin, Bob, 247, 288n
Geyelin, Philip, 14, 118, 181
Giancana, Sam, 165
Gibbon, Edward, 25
Gibson, Ian, 37
Gilbert, Martin, 341
Gill, Brendan, 24
Gin and Bitters, 27
Glamour Spas, 116
Goering, Hermann, 192
Goff, John S., 41n, 327, 355n
Going to Extremes, 294, 316
Goldman, Albert, 36
Goldwater, Barry, 264, 276, 285, 289n, 290n

Goldwyn, Sam, 32

Golightly, Bonnie, 67–68, 112n

Golightly, Holly, 67–68

"Good Morning America," 349–50

Goodwin, Doris Kearns, 308

Gordon, General, 20

Gosse, Edmund, 26

Grable, Betty, 144

Graham, Katherine, 118–19, 236–37, 256

Granger, Stewart, 15, 190–91

Grant, Cary, 13, 185, 187–92, 199, 211, 228n

Graves, Alfred Perceval, 342

Great Contemporaries, 314

Great Cover-Up, The, 256

Great Gatsby, The, 150

Greene, Bob, 300

Greene, Graham, 28

Grobel, Larry, 70, 98

Guardian, 345

Guest, Alexander, 15, 219, 223, 230n

Guest, C. Z., 15, 72, 80, 219–20, 230n

Guest, Winston, 80

Gulley, Bill, 238–41, 288n

Gutmann, Hugo, 338

Haber, Joyce, 115, 144

Hackett, Pat, 112n

Haig, Alexander, 240–41, 243–44, 246–55, 278–81, 284–285, 288n, 289n, 290n

Halberstam, David, 283, 287n, 290n

Halderman, Bob, 239, 242–43, 246, 289n

Halston, 62

Hamill, Pete, 167

Hamilton, Nigel, 318, 323n

Hammond, Sally, 112n

Handcarved Coffins, 13, 80, 82, 105

Hardwick, Elizabeth, 34, 41n

Harmetz, Aljean, 32, 40n

Harris, Warren G., 228n

Harrison, Barbara Grizzuti, 147–48, 182

Haskell, Molly, 73, 84–85, 112n, 114n

Havill, Adrian, 232, 235, 247, 251–52, 259, 283, 288n

Havilland, Olivia de, 196, 201

Hay, John, 33–34

Hayworth, Rita, 185–86

Heckscher, August, 355n

Hellman, Lillian, 36

Helms, Richard, 13, 277, 290n, 336, 347, 349–52, 356n

Hemingway, Ernest, 14, 22–24, 43, 130, 214–16, 221

Hemingway, Leicester, 15, 216

Hemingway, Mary, 22–23

Hepburn, Katharine, 185, 202

Herndon, William, 34, 41n

Heroes, 294, 319

Hersh, Seymour, 15, 139, 232, 244, 271, 290n, 346

Heymann, David, 15, 123, 129–130, 136, 140, 181n, 182n

Hickock, Richard, 47–49, 54, 63, 73, 101, 103–104
Higham, Charles, 12–13, 15, 17, 36, 185–227, 227n, 228n, 229n, 230n
Higham, Sir Charles, 196
Hirshey, Gerri, 14, 117, 160–61, 181
His Way: The Unauthorized Biography of Frank Sinatra, 136, 139
Hitler, Adolf, 12, 14, 32, 120, 192, 195, 197, 200, 206, 210, 212, 217, 221, 226, 307, 325, 332–39, 353
Hohenlohe, Princess Stefanie, 200
Holcombe, Arthur, 313
Holroyd, Michael, 37
Hoover, J. Edgar, 55, 104
Hotchner, A. E., 22–24
Hougan, Jim, 248, 288n
Houston Home Journal, 214
Houston Post, 289n
Howar, Barbara, 14, 115, 120–22, 167, 170, 181
Huffington, Arianna Stassinoulos, 36
Hughes, Howard, 30–31, 164, 188, 191
Hunt, E. Howard, 243, 347–48, 351–52
Hurle, Leverson, 27
Hussein, King, 119
Hussein, Saddam, 12
Huston, John, 43
Hutton, Barbara, 129, 222
Huxley, Aldous, 28

In Cold Blood, 13–14, 17, 49, 51–52, 54, 62–64, 71, 79, 102, 105, 108–10, 112n, 294, 309
In the Freud Archives, 304
Inman, Bobby Ray, 15, 232, 244–46, 250, 288n
Inner Circles, 253, 278, 280–81
Interview Magazine, 82
IRA (Irish Republican Army), 196–97
Iran-contra, 267–68, 270, 275
Irvine, Reed, 289n
Irving, Clifford, 31, 40n
Isaacson, Walter, 240, 287n

Jackie Oh!, 11, 124, 128, 163, 170, 181
Jackson, Michael, 147
Jacobson, Dr. Max (Dr. Feelgood), 136, 181
James, Henry, 55, 71
James, Robert, 106
James, William, 317
Janeway, Elizabeth, 15n
Jersey Observer, 155
Jesus Christ, 52, 64–65, 329, 337
"Jimmy's World," 260–61
Johnson, Bradish, 199
Johnson, Dr., 101
Johnson, Lady Bird, 25
Johnson, Lyndon, 26, 34
Jones, Ernest, 327, 354n, 355n
Jong, Erica, 21–22
Journalist and the Murderer, The, 13, 16n, 302–303

Kahn, E. J., Jr., 14, 24–25, 41n, 137, 181

Kakutani, Michiko, 309

Kaplan, Justin, 14–15, 40n, 41n, 141, 182, 317–18, 323n, 353, 356n

Kantor, Dr. Edward, 129

Kassabs (Jeffrey MacDonald's in-laws), 305

Katzenbach, John, 15, 294, 306–307, 315, 318, 321n, 323n

Keeler, Bob, 295–98, 300, 302, 305, 319, 321n, 323n

Keith, Slim, 72, 100

Kelley, Kitty, 11–14, 17, 115–80, 181n, 182n, 183n

Kempton, Beverly Gary, 102, 114n

Kennedy, Jacqueline, 44, 55, 57–60, 67, 99–100, 118, 125–26, 128–30, 132–33, 313. *See also* Bouvier, Jacqueline, and Onassis, Jacqueline.

Kennedy, Joan, 116

Kennedy, John F., 11, 15n, 33–34, 36, 38, 41n, 55, 71, 116, 123–25, 128–29, 132, 134, 140, 148, 163, 165–66, 171, 179, 233, 311–15, 317, 321, 336

Kennedy, Joseph, Sr., 71, 100, 309, 311, 315

Kennedy, Robert, 15, 38, 57–60

Kennedy, Rosemary, 315

Kennedy, Ted, 13, 17, 293, 308–11, 315, 317–21

Kennedy family, 163, 179, 308, 310, 321

Kennedys: Dynasty and Disaster, The, 130

Kidder, Tracy, 305

Kidwell, Nancy, 102

Kirkus Reviews, 277

Kissinger, Henry, 120, 139, 235, 239–41, 243, 247, 254, 284–85

Klein, Jeffrey, 290n

Knightley, Phillip, 355n

Koch, Mayor Ed, 177

Koppel, Ted, 269, 282–83

Korda, Alexander, 202

Krauthammer, Charles, 21, 40n

Kutler, Stanley, 321n

Laird, Melvin, 15, 241, 245–48, 250, 288n

Landis, James, 312

Langer, Walter, 332–34, 353, 355n

Lansing, Robert, 331

Lansky, Meyer, 163

"Larry King," 165, 170

Lasch, Christopher, 297

Lash, Joseph, 311

Lasky, Victor, 253, 289n

Last Brother, The, 13, 17, 308, 311, 320, 323n

Lauder, George, 266

Lawford, Patricia Seaton, 140, 166, 182

Lawford, Peter, 36, 129, 141, 161–62, 165–67

Lawrence, A. W., 16n, 342–43, 346, 356n

Lawrence, D. H., 28

Lawrence, Robert, 342
Lawrence, T. E., 12, 14, 28, 325, 341, 343–46
Lawrence of Arabia: A Biographical Enquiry, 345
Lazar, Irving, 138
Lazlo, Dr., 66
Leach, Archibald, 188
Lee, Alice, 14, 53, 88, 90–92, 111n, 113n, 114n
Lee, Harper, 14, 51, 53, 76, 87–88, 90–91, 93, 103, 111n, 114n
Lehman-Haupt, Christopher, 309
Lennon, John, 36
Leonardo da Vinci, 325–27, 331
Lerner, Max, 136, 167
Lewis, Sinclair, 25
Library Journal, 229n
Liddy, G. Gordon, 13, 232, 242–44, 259, 347, 349–51, 356n
Lincoln, Abraham, 33–34, 41n
Lincoln, Mary Todd, 41n
Lincoln, Robert Todd, 33–34, 41n, 327
Lindbergh, Charles, 192
Logan, Joshua, 43–47, 71, 110n
Logan, Nedda, 71–72
Logan, Sanford, 103
Long, Breckinridge, 200
Lorca, Federico Garcia, 37
Los Angeles Examiner, 141
Los Angeles Herald Tribune, 194
Los Angeles Times, 15, 173, 195, 205, 210–11
Lowell family, 129
Lowenfeld, L., 326

Lucas, Anthony J., 287n
Luessenhop, Dr. Alfred, 15, 232, 267, 271, 290n
Lyall, Sarah, 322

McCarry, Charles, 288n, 290n
McCarthy, Eugene, 118
McCarthy, Joe, 210
MacDonald, Colette, 298
MacDonald, Jeffrey, 293–319
McGinniss, Joe, 12–13, 15, 17, 26, 70, 293–323, 343
McGovern, George, 125
Mack, John E., 345–46, 356n
McMahon, Bernie, 266
McNamara, Robert, 314
"Mad Bomber," 164
Mafia, 137–38, 141, 145, 148, 161–63, 165, 168–69, 179–80, 336
Maggie (Capote's pet bulldog), 77
Magruder, Jeb Stuart, 289n
Mailer, Norman, 74, 112n
Malcolm, Janet, 8, 12–13, 16n, 293–94, 302–306, 311, 319–20, 321n, 322n, 323n
Manchester, William, 17, 139, 293, 308, 311
Mandarins, The, 29
Manning, Henry Edward, 20
Manson murders, 63, 305
Marshall, Major, 344
Marshall, William, 201
Marx, Arthur, 31–32
Marx, Groucho, 31
Masson, Jeffrey, 302
Matthews, Herbert, 215

Maupassant, 55
Mayhew, Alice, 251–52, 288n
Meier, Josephine, 104–105
Meier, Wendel, 104–105, 114n
Mein Kampf, 337
Menges, Constantine, 15, 232, 261–63, 289n
Meyer, Herb, 232, 263, 266
Meyer, Johnny, 191
MGM (Metro-Goldwyn-Mayer), 149, 190–91
Miami Herald, 227n, 321n
Michener, James, 14, 44, 66–69, 112n
Middlekauff, Kathleen, 324
Mind of Adolf Hitler, The, 333
Minnelli, Liza, 116
Mitchell, John, 242, 257
Mitchell, Margaret, 29, 40n
Moldea, Dan, 161, 182
Monroe, Marilyn, 67, 80, 129
Moore, John Hammond, 205
Moorer, Admiral Thomas H., 15, 247–50, 288n
Moran, Lord, 14, 339–40, 355n
Mordaunt, Elinor, 28
Morell, Dr. Theodor, 338
Morrell, Lady Ottoline, 28
Morris, Edmund, 14, 171, 174–76, 182
Mosely, Roy, 190–91, 228n
Moses, 325
Moynihan, Daniel Patrick, 276
Murphy, Ryan P., 36, 41n
Muses Are Heard, The, 109
Music for Chameleons, 82, 113n

Mussolini, Benito, 200, 215
My Days with Errol Flynn, 204

Nancy Reagan: The Unauthorized Biography, 170, 175, 182
NBC (National Broadcasting Company), 190, 307
Neal, Steve, 291n
Nelson, Jack, 15, 173, 182
Nevins, Allan, 313, 325, 354n
Newquist, Roy, 114n
New Republic, 15, 173, 183
Newsday, 15, 294, 302–303
Newsweek, 81, 199
New York Daily News, 216
New York Herald Tribune, 111n
New York Journal American, 111n
New York Post, 83, 214, 229n
New York Review of Books, 52
New Yorker, 13, 43, 45, 51, 107, 137, 202, 304
Nicolay, John, 33
Nicolson, Harold, 20
Niven, David, 15, 187, 193, 195–96, 201–202, 204, 206, 211, 228n, 229n
Nixon, Richard, 22, 231–33, 238–42, 245, 250, 252–55, 261, 278–81, 284–85, 293–94, 316, 319, 331, 338, 347, 352
Nussbaum, Paul, 322n
Nutting, Anthony, 40n
Nye, Harold, 103

Oates, Stephen B., 41n

Oberon, Merle, 201
O'Brien, Larry, 250
O'Connor, Carroll, 30–32, 40n
O'Hara, John, 18
O'Hara, Scarlett, 29
Onassis, Aristotle, 123
Onassis, Jackie, 11–12, 55, 61, 71, 95, 116, 123, 129, 131–32, 134, 145, 147, 151, 163–64, 176, 179, 310, 313. *See also* Bouvier, Jacqueline, and Kennedy, Jacqueline.
Ono, Yoko, 36
O'Shea, John, 75–77, 80, 83, 98–99
OSS (Office of Strategic Services), 14, 197, 213, 225, 332
Oswald, Harvey, 63
Other Voices, Other Rooms, 85
O'Toole, Peter, 14

Paley, Barbara, 67, 92, 94–95, 98, 101
Paley, William, 67, 72, 98, 100
Palm Beach Jewish World, 289n
Palm Beach Post, 183
Papa Hemingway, 22–23
Parmet, Herbert, 313
Pearlman, Phil, 228n
Pearson, Drew, 312–13
Penthouse, 214
People, 94, 163, 165, 179, 227n, 230n
Pepper, Jake, 80–81
Persico, Joseph, 15, 232, 235, 265, 269, 274–76, 287n, 290n

Persons, Arch, 52, 85–86, 106
Philadelphia Inquirer, 293
Philby, Kim, 199
Picasso, Pablo, 36, 144
Playboy, 68, 98
Playgirl, 57
Plimpton, George, 59, 102, 114n
Plomer, William, 19
Poison Pen, 165, 181
Porgy and Bess, 109
Porter, Cole, 71
Porter, Katherine Anne, 71
Pound, Ezra, 129
Powell, Colin, 261, 276
Power, Tyrone, 96, 195, 203
Powers, Thomas, 356n
Presley, Elvis, 36
Price-Jones, David, 229n
"Prime Time ABC," 349
Profiles in Courage, 311–14
Proust, Marcel, 55, 69, 71, 95, 100
Pugh, Sinclair, 146
Pursley, General Robert, 241

Quayle, Dan, 286
Queenan, Joe, 174, 182
Quinn, Sally, 133

Radicz and Landauer (pianists), 218
Radziwill, Lee, 56–57, 59–62, 67, 71, 95, 99–100, 111n
Random House, 66, 68, 82, 129
Rapper, Irving, 207
Rasputin, Maria, 186
Rather, Dan, 289n

Reagan, Patti, 176
Reagan, Nancy, 12, 72, 116, 160, 170–80
Reagan, Ronald, 14, 146, 173, 175–76, 285
Redford, Robert, 150, 251–52, 259
Reed, Rex, 185
Reese, Mary Ellen, 288n
Reeves, Richard, 171, 182, 313–14, 323n
Regan, Don, 172, 174
Republican National Committee, 238–39
Ribbentrop, Joachim von, 216, 225
Rich, Helen, 15, 218, 230n
Rise and Fall of the Third Reich, The, 348
Rivers, Joan, 138, 147
Romanones, Aline Countess of, 225, 230n
Romine, Dannye, 113n
Roosevelt, Eleanor, 311
Roosevelt, Franklin D., 192, 197, 206, 212, 217, 336, 339
Roosevelt, Theodore, 175, 330
Rorem, Ned, 71
Rosenbaum, Jack, 204
Rosenfeld, Harry, 234
Ross, Harold, 43
Ross, Lillian, 43
Rosten, Leo, 11, 15n
Rothemere, Esmond, 221
Royce, William, 227n, 228n
Royko, Mike, 139

Ruas, Charles, 71, 102, 113n, 114n
Rudisill, Marie, 14, 84–90, 113n
Russell, Bertrand, 20, 40n

Safire, William, 140, 146, 192, 228n, 276
St. Aubyn, Giles, 21
Saint-Simon, 188–89
Salinger, J. D., 71
Sandburg, Carl, 33
San Francisco Chronicle, 339
Sansing, John, 128, 181
Schellenberg, Walter, 226, 230n
Schine, Cathleen, 136
Schlesinger, Arthur, Jr., 14–15, 33, 36, 38, 41n, 59–60, 111n, 310, 313–14, 323n
Schofield, Lemuel, 200
Schorer, Mark, 25, 40n
Schorr, Daniel, 289n
Schrieber, Marion Brush, 155, 182
Schwartz, Ted, 36
Schwarzkopf, General, 285
Schwed, Peter, 251–52, 288n, 289n
Scott, Randolph, 188–90
Scott, Walter, 230n
Scowcroft, Brent, 286
Seaton, George, 166
Segretti, Don, 246
Seldes, George, 214, 216
Selling of the President, The, 293, 316
Selznick, David O., 98
Sentinel, 234, 254
Seven Pillars of Wisdom, The, 343

Shaw, Bernard, 73, 243
Shaw, George Bernard, 342
Shaw, Mrs. George Bernard, 343, 346
Shawn, William, 43, 46
Sherman, Vincent, 210
Sherrill, Robert, 290n
Shields, Paul, 192
Shirer, William L., 348
Shor, Toots, 137
Sidey, Hugh, 170–72, 182
Silent Coup, 243–44, 247
Sillitoe, Sir Percy, 196
Simmons, Rob, 264
Simon & Schuster, 25, 94, 180, 251, 285
Simon, Neil, 75
Simons, Howard, 236, 257
Simpson, Colin, 21, 355n
Simpson, Wallis, 216. *See also* Windsor, Duchess of.
Sinatra, Barbara, 159
Sinatra, Dolly, 152–53, 155–58, 164
Sinatra, Frank, 12, 17, 116, 136–55, 157–60, 162–64, 166–71, 175, 178–80
Sinatra, Frank, Jr., 159
Sinatra, Marty, 152, 156–58, 164
Sinatra, Nancy, 115, 129, 150
Sinatra, Nancy (ex-wife), 159
Sinatra: Is This Man Mafia?, 169
"60 Minutes," 269
Slide, Anthony, 192
Sloan, Hugh, 238
Smathers, Sen. George, 116, 124, 163

Smith College, 178, 180
Smith, Liz, 15, 61, 95, 111n, 114n, 123, 146, 159, 178–79, 183, 189, 199, 232, 287n, 301, 310, 322n, 323n
Smith, Perry, 47, 49–51, 53, 63, 73, 101, 103–104
Snyder, Richard, 251–52
Snyder, Tom, 190
Sorensen, Theodore, 15, 38, 41n, 312–13, 315, 317, 323n
Stalin, Joseph, 33, 174
Star magazine, 166
Steffens, Lincoln, 25, 317
Stein, Gertrude, 66, 71
Steinbach, Alice, 159, 182
Stephenson, Sir William, 207, 211, 229n
Stethem, Robert Dean, 265
Stilwell, General George, 41n
Stoiber, Rudolf, 198–99
Strachey, Lytton, 19–21, 37, 40n, 41n, 327
Streisand, Barbra, 116
Stuart, Lyle, 123, 165
Styron, William, 319
Sublett, Scott, 189, 228n
Surtees, Robert, 159
Suskind, Richard, 31, 40n
Susskind, David, 57, 95, 149
Sussman, Barry, 232, 256–59, 284, 289n
Swerdlow, Joel, 82

Talese, Gay, 137–38
Tamble, Rick, 290n

Taylor, Elizabeth, 12, 116, 129, 135–36, 145–47, 151, 159–60, 167, 169

Taylor, Robert, 191

T. E. Lawrence by His Friends, 11n

Teller, Edward, 121

Thomas, Lowell, 341, 343, 345, 356n

Thompson, Walter, 338, 355n

Thornton, Michael, 229n

Thurber, Helen, 24–25

Thurber, James 24–25

Time, 57, 170, 173

Times (London), 29

To Kill a Mockingbird, 111n

Toklas, Alice, 66

Tretick, Stanley, 140, 142, 166, 180

True Detective, 40, 106

Trueheart, Charles, 70, 112n

Truman Capote: The Story of His Bizarre and Exotic Boyhood, 84

Truman, Margaret, 118

Tuchman, Barbara, 41n

Tuckerman, Nancy, 131–32, 135, 181

Tufo, Peter, 62

Tynan, Kathleen, 22

Tynan, Kenneth, 22, 49–51, 54, 65, 73, 104, 111n

Uffinger, Don, 126–27, 130, 141, 181

Updike, John, 21

Valleyhead, 125–27

Vanderbilt, Gloria, 71–72

Vanity Fair, 73

Variety, 203, 227n

Vaughn, Rose, 155

Veil, 241, 261, 263–65, 267–70, 272, 276–77, 287, 289n, 290n

Vidal, Gore, 14, 57–62, 95, 105, 107, 109, 111n, 114n

Vogue, 73

Von Huene, 226

Wagner, Friedelinde, 335

Wallace, Mike, 282, 312–13

Waller, John, 20, 40n

Walpole, Hugh, 27–28

Walsh, Elsa, 277

Walsh, Raoul, 193, 216

Walters, Barbara, 179

Walton, William, 131, 135, 181

Wambaugh, Joseph, 300

Wansell, Geoffrey, 191, 228n

Warhol, Andy, 60–63, 80, 82–83, 113n

Warner, Jack, 210

Warner, Sen. John, 135

Warren Commission, 34

Washingtonian, 120–22, 126, 128, 132, 167, 181

Washington Post, 15, 70, 118, 128, 133, 160–62, 171, 181, 192, 196, 231, 234, 236, 238–40, 242–43, 250–51, 256, 265, 273–74, 277, 349–50

Washington Star-News, 116

Washington Times, 15, 17, 189, 228n, 267, 286

Washington Times Herald, 124

Watergate, 13, 177, 232, 236, 238, 240, 242–47, 254, 256–58, 260, 278, 281, 283, 286, 346

Waugh, Evelyn, 29

Weatherby, W. J., 30

Weizmann, Chaim, 346

Welles, Orson, 185–86

Wells, Floyd, 103–104

West, Duane, 14, 102–105, 114n

West, Mae, 187

White, Edmund, 311

White, Theodore, 134

White, William Allen, 26

White House, 55–63, 120, 132, 171, 176–77, 225, 238–41, 243, 245–47, 249, 252, 254–55, 270–79, 281, 339, 352

Wilde, Oscar, 32, 37, 95

Wiles, Buster, 204, 206–207, 210, 212, 229n, 230n

Wilkie, Curtis, 290n

Will, 242

Will, George, 172, 182

Williams, Tennessee, 67, 71–72

Wilson, Allan, 165

Wilson, Earl, 136, 169

Wilson, Edwin P., 248

Wilson, Woodrow, 12–13, 26, 325, 328–31, 333

Windham, Donald, 54

Windsor, Duchess of, 13, 15, 36, 137, 185, 206, 216–27. *See also* Simpson, Wallis.

Windsor, Duke of, 13, 15, 36, 137, 217–27, 344

Winters, Ella, 25

Wired, 277

Wodehouse, P. G., 27–28

Wolfe, Tom, 300

Woman Named Jackie, A, 129, 140

Woods, Rose, 239, 241

Woodward, Ann, 100

Woodward, Bob, 12–15, 17, 139, 162, 231–90, 346–47

Writers Bloc, 82

Writer's World, The, 15n

Yale, 15n, 234

Yardley, Jonathan, 128, 160, 192, 228n, 301, 309, 322n

Yussoupov, Prince, 186

Ziegler, Philip, 225

Zinsser, William, 287, 291n

Zweig, Arnold, 30